**Praise for Valerie Bowman and *Secrets of a Wedding Night***

"Clever, fun, and fantastic!"

— *New York Times* bestselling author Suzanne Enoch

"*Secrets of a Wedding Night* is the most charming and clever debut I've read in years! With her sparkling dialogue, vivid characters, and self-assured writing style, Valerie Bowman has instantly established herself as a romance author with widespread appeal. This engaging and sweetly romantic story is just too delightful to miss."

—*New York Times* bestselling author Lisa Kleypas

"Ms. Bowman is quite the tease. How I love a good society scandal. The hero is absolutely yummy!"

—Donna MacMeans

# Secrets of a Wedding Night



VALERIE BOWMAN

St. Martin's Paperbacks

SECRETS OF A WEDDING NIGHT



For information address St. Martin's Press, 175 Fifth Avenue, New York, NY 10010.

ISBN: 978-1-250-00895-4

Printed in the United States of America

St. Martin's Paperbacks edition / October 2012

St. Martin's Paperbacks are published by St. Martin's Press, 175 Fifth Avenue, New York, NY 10010.

10 9 8 7 6 5 4 3 2 1

*For my sister, Melanie Minot Bowman Pikor, who said to me one day, "You should write a romance novel."*

*And I did.*

*Good idea.*

*I love you, Moosey.*

# ACKNOWLEDGMENTS

First, thanks to my fabulous editor, Holly Blanck. If you hadn't been digging my little story, it never would have seen the light o' day. You made my dreams come true.

To my wonderful agent, Kevan Lyon, who saw something in my writing she liked and stuck with me till we hit the mark. The day you first called me remains in my memory forever.

To my amazing critique partners past and present: Mary Behre, Lena Diaz, Sheila Athens, and Erica Barton. Your help and support have meant more to me than I can say.

To my mother, Judy Bowman-Rhodes, for the gift of storytelling (cough, cough, hyperbole); to my six actual sisters Janet, Laura, Leslie, Sandra, Sarah, and Melanie for your influence and support; and to my BFF Danielle Aguirre for being sister #7.

To the First Coast Romance Writers in Jacksonville, Florida, and the Beau Monde online chapter of Romance

Writers of America. I wouldn't be where I am today without the RWA and my chapter's support.

To marvelous Regency author, Gail Ranstrom, for giving me a kind and supportive critique at a time when I had no idea what I was doing.

To my Lalalas. I don't know what I'd do without you every day. I feel like this little book is a tribute to all of us. Keep the faith! La, la, la.

To Cheri Radliff for being my very first fan.

To my cousin, Kate Buckley, for being my fan, my friend, and my secret Carson. Much obliged. And to my aunts, Susan Spitz and Gale Bowman, for being so proud of their romance novelist niece.

To my father, Minot Bowman, who is not here to read my stories and to my stepfather, Stan Rhodes, who is.

To Jenni McQ, Rom, and Ash for your wise and honest beta reads. And to Candice for looking out for my commas.

To Dr. Janell Hart for your wise insight into the human condition. I'll get you reading romance novels yet!

Curtsy to my Secret Curtsy Society and 2011 Golden Heart nominee sisters, Ashlyn, Anne, Erin, and Sara. I'm so happy to be on this journey with you.

To the Dashing Duchesses for being such generally fabulous blog partners. Historical romance rocks! Your graces, I adore you.

To the incomparable Lisa Kleypas for saving me from a boring night stuck in a snowed-in airport in 2007, inspiring me to write, and for reading my story and providing the most beautiful cover quote a romance novelist could ask for. I am forever your fan!

To amazing historical romance authors Suzanne Enoch and Donna MacMeans for their generous praise. I owe you both a large and expensive drink.

To everyone at St. Martin's Press for publishing my story so well. I appreciate everything you do and I cannot stop staring at the gorgeous cover.

And finally, thank you to my tall, dark, handsome, and supportive fiancé, Marcus. You totally have a historical romance hero name (sigh) but you're better than any fictional character I could conjure.

# CHAPTER 1

***London, April 1816***

*Boom. Boom. Boom.*

The blows on the door echoed through the foyer. Lily heard them all the way in the study where she was poring over the dismal household accounts for the hundredth time.

"I demand to see the countess," a deep male voice thundered.

Lily stopped scribbling. She glanced at Leopold, the scruffy brown terrier who sat curled on a worn cushion at her feet. "Demand? Good heavens." She shook her head. "Which one of my so-called admirers is at it today?"

Returning her attention to the ledger, she mumbled, "Who knew? Apparently, twenty-two-year-old widows are all the rage this Season. That is, twenty-two-year-old widows *reportedly* worth a small fortune."

Leopold cocked his head and barked. Lily bit her lip. "Or it could be a debt collector."

Evans appeared in the doorway. Lily regarded her old friend with a weary sigh. "So, which is it? A fortune hunter or a creditor?"

"My lady, Lord Colton is in the white salon. He insists upon seeing you."

Lily sat up straight. "Colton?"

"The Marquis of Colton," Evans clarified, clearing his throat.

Leopold yipped as if he recognized the name. Evans gave the dog a dubious glance indicative of the strained relationship the two had shared over the last several years.

Lily rubbed the feathered tip of her quill against her nose, her brows knitting together. "Hmm. This *is* an interesting development."

She was grateful Evans had been awake to answer the door. Her butler had an unfortunate penchant for falling asleep at the most unexpected times. Though she suspected the racket had roused him.

Plopping the quill back into the well, she stood and smoothed her palms down her worn, gray skirts.

"Tell Lord Colton I'll be in momentarily, Evans." She nodded, enjoying the jolt of anticipation that leaped to life in her belly.

Devon Morgan, Marquis of Colton, in her house. Well. Of course she'd relish a distraction from the depressing house accounts, but there was something else. She'd relish the distraction from the simpering fops who'd been appearing on her doorstep smelling of too much sweet cologne and desperation. Lord Colton might be trouble, but there was nothing desperate about him.

She clapped her hands and her canine companion fell into line behind her. She and Leo whisked up the back staircase. Lily squelched the little smile that popped to her lips. Oh, yes. She knew exactly why Lord Colton was sitting in her salon. Though she hadn't expected to see him quite so soon.

A quarter hour later, Lily made her way down the main hallway, past the tattered carpets she couldn't afford to replace. She'd changed from the threadbare dove-gray gown into the darker morning dress she saved for company.

She drew in one last deep breath and pushed open the double doors to the white salon with both hands. She let the doors close behind her while her gaze scanned the room. It was beautifully decorated with delicate rosewood chairs, sterling silver candlesticks, and lovely antique vases filled with fresh flowers. The only room in the house so well appointed. Another concession to appearances.

Lily squared her shoulders. The confident smile she had pasted on her face belied the nervous knot of anticipation that roiled through her belly. She folded her hands serenely—a trick her mother taught her long ago—and made her way into the room.

Lord Colton sat in an embroidered chair, facing the window, his profile to her. He'd turned his head at the sound of her entrance. His countenance was a study in barely controlled anger. But years of breeding could not be denied. He rose to greet her.

Lily sucked in her breath. My, my, she hadn't seen the Marquis of Colton up close in an age. He'd always been handsome—how could she forget?—but she had failed to remember him being quite *this* good-looking.

He stood easily two inches over six feet tall, with slightly curly, raven-black hair. He had chiseled cheekbones and a perfectly sculpted mouth that could linger in one's memory, if one were interested in such things, which Lily decidedly was *not*. But most intriguing of all were his eyes. Deep, dark, and coffee brown, they shone with an off-putting intelligence and were framed by thick, long lashes that held an appeal all their own.

Lily pressed her lips together. Oh, yes, the Marquis of Colton was tall, dark, and handsome. Too much of all three for Lily's peace of mind.

She swept toward him, meeting his eyes, and his anger seemed to diffuse a bit. His shoulders settled and his stance became less rigid.

"Lord Colton." She curtsied and her dark skirts pooled around her ankles. "To what do I owe the pleasure of your visit? I haven't seen you in—what's it been—three years? Four?"

Leopold trotted past—affording Lord Colton with a distinctive growl indicative of the strained relationship *they* had shared in the past—before taking up residence on his favorite cushion in the corner.

Lily hid her smile and offered her hand to the marquis.

When he touched her small, cold fingers with his strong, warm ones, a frisson of awareness skittered up Lily's spine. He bowed. There was that breeding again.

"Four years, perhaps," he answered. "And whether or not this visit is pleasurable remains to be seen, my lady."

His voice seemed to seek out some sensitive place along her nerves and thrum a thrilling tune. Deep, masculine, and oh-so-powerful was Lord Colton's voice. And confident. She mustn't forget confident.

Pulling her hand away from his unsettling touch, Lily crossed her arms over her chest and drummed her fingertips along her elbows. Four years? It had been nearly five and he knew it.

They both knew it.

"How did you find me, my lord? Seems the last time you were expected to pay me a visit, you lost your way."

A muscle ticked in his jaw. "It was quite simple, really. I merely followed the trail of men to your door. Rumor has it your butler has had to beat away your suitors with a stick. When he can stay awake, that is."

Lily gritted her teeth. "It's indelicate of you to mention Evans's unfortunate condition, but I suppose I should expect no more of you. I also employ a maid who cannot remember her name from one moment to the next. Not all households can be as *illustrious* as yours, now can they?"

His only reply was a smirk. So much for that good breeding.

"But now that I think upon it, it is a fine idea," Lily continued. "I shall have to ask Evans to fetch a stick. It's unfortunate he didn't have one before *you* arrived."

Leopold's ears perked and Lily shook her head, assuring the dog there was, in fact, no stick to be had. He slumped back onto his cushion and closed his eyes.

Lord Colton's smile was tight. "I am not a suitor, and I assure you, your butler would need more than a stick to keep me from my mission today."

"Mission? My, it sounds dire. But please, be quick about it. I'm quite busy of late, planning Annie's debut." *And keeping the creditors at bay,* she thought with a grimace.

His face registered only mild surprise. "Annie? That little imp is eighteen already?"

Lily nodded. No doubt he recalled how a thirteen-year-old Annie used to hide behind the banister at the top of the staircase in their parents' house and giggle when Colton would come to pay a call on Lily.

She shook her head. That was all a long time ago. A very long time ago.

Colton's voice held a note of sarcasm. "No doubt your sister will be as sought after as you are."

Lily shrugged. "Annie doesn't know the dangers that await her in the marriage mart, but her heart remains set upon a debut and I would do anything to make her happy." Lily waved a hand in the air, dismissing the subject. She rang for Evans. "Would you care for some tea, my lord?" she asked in a deceptively sweet voice.

"No, thank you."

Lily sighed. Lord Colton's dark eyes tracked her every move. They seemed omniscient, as if he knew her secrets.

Could he tell how relieved she was that he'd refused the tea? Cream and sugar were as precious as gold.

"I'd prefer a brandy," he quickly added.

"It's half two," she replied with a disapproving stare. *And brandy isn't cheap either.*

His hooded eyes showed no emotion. "Your point?"

The muscles in Lily's cheeks ached from keeping the fake smile plastered to her face. She let the smile fade and turned to the sideboard where she splashed only a bit of brandy into a glass for Lord Colton. The man was exactly like her father, a drinker and a gambler.

And she'd known no one as useless as her father.

"I see in addition to your renowned gambling and your rakishness, you've also turned to the bottle. Are you trying for all seven of the deadly sins?"

His voice was calm. "And I see in addition to your renowned flirtations and your fickleness, your skills as a hostess leave much to be desired."

*Hmm. Well-played.*

Smile firmly in place, she turned back to begrudgingly hand Lord Colton his drink. His gaze flicked to Leopold. "I see you've still got your mongrel."

Leopold lifted a floppy ear and growled again.

Lily stiffened her spine. "I would never part with my Leo."

Lord Colton smiled a smile that made Lily wonder why it was so hot in the salon of a sudden. Some dark emotion kindled in his eyes. "You never could resist a stray."

Lily gave Colton a blatant once-over. Oh, no, they weren't talking about Leo anymore. She delicately cleared her throat. "Do tell me, what brings you here this afternoon?"

He waited for her to sit first, of course, before taking his place in the chair across from her. His size made the piece look like doll furniture. Her gaze traveled from the tip of his black Hessians up his long legs stretched in front of him, encased in biscuit-colored trousers. Her eyes lingered on his narrow hips and broad shoulders, before moving up to the decidedly irritated look on his perfect face.

*Confound it.* The man looked even better than he had five years ago. Five *long* years ago.

Lily shook her head to clear it of such thoughts. She folded her hands in her lap. "Tell me why you're here," she repeated. "And I shall attempt to seem as if I care what you have to say." She smiled prettily.

Colton's eyes narrowed. "I'd be surprised, *Countess,* if you did not already know the reason for my call."

She bristled at his not-so-subtle emphasis on her title. If he hoped for a reaction to his veiled barb, he was about to be disappointed. The title was hers. She'd paid for it dearly.

She refused to let him see it bothered her. "Is that so? Should I guess then? Stop me as soon as I am correct." She took a deep breath, prepared to rattle off a list of innocuous motives.

He thrust up a palm, stopping her. "That is unnecessary. I'm here to discuss a certain pamphlet that has been circulating in the company of young, unmarried females. A pamphlet entitled *Secrets of a Wedding Night.*"

Lily kept her face blank. As if on cue, the butler carried in a tea tray and set it on the table in front of her. "Thank you, Evans."

Lily busied herself with pouring the tea. "Hmm. *Secrets of a Wedding Night.* Yes, I've heard rumors of that scandalous bit of writing."

Colton crossed his long legs at the ankles. Casual. Perhaps too casual. She could be that casual if she chose.

"I assume you have also heard, then, my lady, that *you* are widely rumored to be the author of that particular piece."

She kept her eyes downcast and dropped only one costly lump of sugar into her teacup. She stirred slowly, set the tiny silver spoon aside, and raised her chin to stare him in the eye.

"Me?" she asked in a falsely shocked voice.

"Yes, everyone knows you and Viscount Medford are thick as thieves. He's been known to publish that sort of drivel."

"Keeping track of my friendships, are you, my lord?"

"Only when it affects me, my lady."

She clucked her tongue. "Ghastly thing, gossip."

"Well?" His voice held an edge.

This called for an innocent look, and Lily just so happened to have *perfected* an innocent look. "What are you asking, my lord?" *Positively saintly.*

His black eyebrow arched, his gaze pinning her in a way that made her teacup shake a bit on the saucer. *Drat!* She hastily set the cup on the table and snatched her hands away.

"Did you write it?" He drew out the words slowly. His deep voice echoed off the salon's aging wallpaper.

"My, my, my, Lord Colton." Thank heavens she'd also perfected tinkling laughter. "I must say you're the very first person to come out and ask me." Disconcerting. *Most* disconcerting.

"Did. You. Write. It?" he repeated, sounding like a man who was used to having his questions answered the first time.

Lily retrieved her teacup and took a tiny sip. Ah, yes. This was one of the reasons it hadn't worked between the two of them—one of the many reasons. "I'd forgotten you were this direct. Direct, domineering, and completely used to getting your way. Tiresome qualities in a man."

He set his glass aside and snapped the leather riding gloves he still held in his hand. "I won't ask a third time," he replied with his own type of smile—a decidedly angry one—that Lily was sure *he* had perfected.

She stirred her tea with the spoon and spoke slowly. "I assume you're here, asking these questions, because . . ."

His new smile was tight. "Because my affianced bride, Miss Templeton, just cried off, and according to her distraught mother, it was a direct result of her reading your pamphlet."

Lily averted her eyes. A strange sensation tugged at her. Guilt? No. Not possible. She tapped the spoon on the side of the porcelain cup. *Ping. Ping. Ping.*

Hmm. This little episode had the potential to become quite messy.

"I'm very sorry to hear that," she lied. "Though I cannot say I blame Miss Templeton. Marriage is not all it's purported to be. Awful business, really." She shuddered.

Colton did not look amused. "Did you write that blasted pamphlet or not?"

Lily raised her cup to her lips, hiding her expression behind it, watching him. Why, the cad was nearly shouting at her. Not to mention the swearing. Did she write the pamphlet? Of course she wrote it, and she happened to be exceedingly proud of it. But she couldn't very well admit it and still maintain her place in Polite Society. And she needed her place in Society, for Annie's sake.

"Tsk, tsk. Such language, Lord Colton." Another sip of tea. "If I wrote it—and I am not saying I did—I would stand behind its contents. Young ladies should know exactly what they're getting into, after all. That pamphlet provides a much-needed service to the uninformed."

She dropped her gaze. No use trying to make him understand. He could never know the fright of a wedding night, married to a man old enough to be your grandfather, someone you didn't know, didn't love. All with no choice in the matter. It was enough to shatter a girl's dreams. Just as Lord Colton had helped to shatter hers, though she'd die before she'd admit it to him.

He clenched his jaw and leaned toward her, bracing his forearms on his knees. His maddeningly masculine scent found her nostrils, a mixture of horse leather, the barest hint of expensive cologne, and something indefinable. Probably that blasted confidence.

His voice was silky, yet menacing, and held a promising tone that made it seem hot in the room again. "That pamphlet is a pack of lies told by a woman who hasn't been bedded properly."

She gasped. Good heavens. She should slap him and order him from her house for saying such an indelicate thing. Instead, his words caused a rush of heat to singe her nerves. But she refused to be shocked by him. She would give him back as good as he gave.

Lily kept her eyes hooded and leaned toward him. "Surely you're not implying that *you* are the authority on bedding women properly? Even *you* couldn't possibly be that arrogant, my lord. Or do I give you too much credit?"

The growl that followed was meant to intimidate. Lily was sure of it. Instead, it served to delight. *Finally*. She'd scored a hit in their war of words.

"I imply nothing," he ground out, mirroring her action by leaning toward her, his mouth merely inches from hers. Their eyes met. "I know *exactly* how to bed a woman properly." Lily sucked in her breath sharply, but she refused to look away. He stared her down. "Furthermore, I *accuse* you of writing that libelous bit of rubbish, and I *demand* you retract it."

Lily snapped her head to the side and bit her lip. Another flash of guilt—she was now quite convinced it was guilt—swept through her. He wanted a retraction? That's what he was after? He couldn't possibly be in love with the girl. Could he? She pressed a hand against her sinking stomach.

Giving her head a shake, she turned back to face him. "The fact that your fiancée allowed some silly pamphlet to scare her off may tell you something you don't want to know, Colton. Or have you never considered that?" She swept her hands across her lap and squared her shoulders. "At any rate, this conversation is entirely inappropriate, my lord. I think it would be best if you take your leave now."

Leopold's furry head shot up and he growled softly, watching his mistress as if ready to defend her if necessary.

Lord Colton gave the dog a distasteful glance and made no move to go. Instead, he stared Lily down again, a muscle ticking in his jaw once more. "Oh, no you don't. You cannot go about destroying people's lives without answering for it."

Lily stared right back. "Resorting to intimidation now, are you, my lord?" Time to put an end to this ridiculous conversation. And she knew just how to do it. "I realize you need to marry an heiress. Everyone knows your father left your estates completely penniless, and your own heedless gambling hasn't helped the situation, but it seems you'll just have to find another young woman to lure with empty promises." She smiled a fake-sweet smile. "Perhaps one who is less well read?"

Colton slapped the black gloves against his thigh, his dark eyes blazing. Leopold propped himself up on his two front paws, poised for action.

Colton's deep voice came through clenched teeth. "I want you to write a retraction. I want you to tell Miss Templeton what you wrote is only one young lady's experience."

"Souls in Hades want a drink of water." Lily gripped the arm of her rosewood chair until her fingers ached.

"You may be used to ordering about your servants and your timid little Miss Templeton, but you certainly shall not order *me* about. I am quite through with being ordered about by men." She leaped from her chair. Leopold sprang up and bared his teeth at the marquis.

Colton surged to his feet. He squeezed his gloves so hard, the whites of his knuckles showed.

*Good.*

Lily stretched to her full height. Though her own diminutive size of three inches over five feet was no match for him, she would not allow him to intimidate her. She had to strain her neck to stare up at him. "By the by, this is what it looks like, *my lord,* when someone fails to kowtow to you. No doubt it's a foreign concept, but one that exists, I assure you."

The muscle continued to tic in his jaw. "You *will* write a retraction."

"Will I?" she asked, nonchalant, struggling not to let him see how deeply he'd affected her. Her hands trembled. "And how exactly do you intend to force me to do that?" She crossed her arms over her chest and tapped her black slipper on the carpet, awaiting his answer.

Lord Colton pulled on one glove and then the other. He bowed to her, though anger still emanated from every pore. "I intend to prove to you that your bloody pamphlet is wrong. I intend to show you how a real man pleasures a woman." He stared her straight in the eye.

Sparks leaped between them. Lily's heart thumped in her throat.

"I *intend* to seduce you, Countess."

Lily's jaw dropped, and one second later, he spun her into his arms. She tried to push away, but his mouth swooped down to capture hers. Her hands struggled against his broad shoulders. The brush of his bold lips made her dizzy. Her head fell back. She stopped thinking. His hot, insistent tongue invaded her mouth, and Lily's stomach dropped in a way it hadn't in . . . five years. *Blast it.* She whimpered. Her hands crept up to wrap around his neck. She melted against him.

Lord Colton pulled his mouth from hers and took a step back. His breath came in heavy pants. His perfect hair was slightly mussed. Something akin to bewilderment flashed through his dark eyes. If Lily hadn't been intently watching, she might have missed it. She touched her fingertips to her burning lips.

Colton turned abruptly and strode toward the door. "Consider that an opening shot across your bow, my dear. You have been warned."

# CHAPTER 2

Devon Morgan descended the stone steps of Lily's town house with ground-devouring strides. He mounted Sampson, his chestnut gelding, and tugged on the reins to head toward the park.

Who did that woman think she was? Lily, the dowager Countess of Merrill. Bah. She'd gained that title after a month-long marriage. She had nerve. She'd baited him—acting as if she didn't write that blasted pamphlet—and in the end, had mocked him.

Infuriating.

And to make matters worse, since he'd last seen her, he'd somehow managed to forget what a striking beauty she was. When she'd finally deigned to grace him with her presence, he'd been taken aback . . . very well, *captivated,* by her walnut-brown hair, violet-blue eyes that slanted up slightly at the corners, her dark fringes of lashes, alabaster skin with a hint of pink at the cheeks, and lips that practically begged to be kissed. A blasted incomparable beauty.

Clearly, he'd also forgotten she was such a shrew.

No wonder. Beauties often proved more trouble than they were worth.

Devon made his way into the park, nudging Sampson

into a gallop. He passed the Serpentine and a field replete with daisies, before coming to a halt in a clearing that contained a mix of servants and his best friend, Jordan Holloway, the Earl of Ashbourne.

Feet braced, Jordan stood about twenty yards from a large canvas bull's-eye and held a bow and arrow in his grasp. With sure hands, he released the bow. The arrow shot through the air, hitting the canvas with a thud. It shivered perfectly in the center of the mark. A footman rushed to retrieve it.

"Well done," Devon called.

Jordan glanced up. "There you are, Colton," he replied. "I thought you were lost." Jordan took his time adjusting the leather straps of his gloves.

Devon dismounted and tossed Sampson's reins to a nearby groom. He tugged on his own gloves. "Hardly. I merely spent too much time on a fool's errand this afternoon."

The corner of Jordan's lip curved up in a mocking grin. "Ah, yes. So, was the poor little widow as charming as you expected?"

Devon snorted. "Poor little widow . . . More like a well-dressed viper. That woman is utterly mad."

The footman returned with the arrow, and with the canvas clear, Jordan took another shot. His aim was nearly perfect again. "You cannot entirely blame her, Colton. After all, Merrill had to have been thirty years older than she."

Devon pulled an arrow from a quiver propped against a nearby tree and took up his own bow. "Frankly, I would have thought more like forty years older." He squinted at the target.

"And she was what? Seventeen? It's no wonder she wrote so eloquently on the ills of the modern marriage." Jordan laughed and shook his head.

Devon released the bow. The arrow zipped to tremble unfailingly just left of the center of the bull's-eye. "She *chose* Merrill," he ground out. "It's difficult enough convincing a young woman she won't be pounced upon and attacked, without that mad countess filling her head with a lot of nonsense."

"Nice shot." Jordan whistled. "Now that I think on it, didn't you court the girl back when she made her debut?"

Devon scoffed. "There was no *courting* Lily. She was after one thing and one thing only. Money. Any interest she showed in anyone else was merely a form of amusement to her. The earl had the deepest pockets."

Devon's eyes remained on the target, but for a moment he was catapulted back through time to a ballroom and the sight of a remarkable beauty standing across from him, beckoning like some siren from the sea. He'd fallen for her. Hard. And she'd led him on a merry chase. A fruitless chase. All the while, she'd been planning to accept Merrill's suit. His hands tightened on the bow.

Lily's words from earlier echoed in Devon's brain. *"You'll just have to find another young woman to lure with empty promises."* What the hell had she meant by that? She was the one who had lured him with empty promises, damn it. She'd twisted everything. Just like a woman.

Gone was the girl with the sparkling eyes, the lilting laughter, and sweet tenderness he'd once thought could save him. Gone was the young lady who had appeared to look beyond the callous assumptions of Society. And in her place was a jaded she-devil. A mocking widow with a rapier for a tongue. But he'd be damned before he let her affect him.

Jordan hefted his bow in his hands and took aim again. "She's always been a beauty. It's no wonder you were interested."

His words shook Devon from his reverie. He was no

longer the twenty-six-year-old who had followed Lily around as though he were just out of the schoolroom. No, he was a man now and when he'd considered marriage this time, he'd made the decision with his head, not his idiotic heart. He eyed his friend carefully. "Interested? Yes. Serious? No. All I want from that woman now is for her to dine upon her words."

Jordan's shout of laughter echoed through the nearby trees. "So, the merry widow didn't agree to write a retraction, did she? Why does that not surprise me? Take heart. It's not as if she can stop marriage for all time, though God knows I wouldn't object if she did. A hideous matter, marriage, nothing good can come of it."

Devon grunted. "Yes. Well. I'm not as fortunate as you, Ashbourne. I have no siblings. You're the closest thing to a brother I'll ever have. I must produce a legitimate heir."

The truth was, the two of them had often been mistaken for brothers. Both were tall with similar muscular builds. Jordan's hair was more of a dark brown, not Devon's black, and Jordan's eyes were gray, but they'd been told on more than one occasion what striking figures they cut together.

Jordan clapped him on the back. "I do thank my brothers for being born every time I see them. But as to your predicament, why you insist upon letting everyone in town think you're destitute when you have more money than I do, for God's sake, eludes me. You've been gambling in the back alleys for years and won a bloody indecent fortune doing it, yet you act as if you've never played a game of cards in your life when you're in the clubs of St. James."

Jordan motioned to a second footman to pour him a drink and the servant hurried to a small table perched on the grass between two trees. He poured two glasses of brandy and returned to hand them to the two men.

Devon took his first sip and tried not to think about the

brandy he'd had earlier, or who had served it to him. "I'll give no one the satisfaction of judging me based on how much money they think I have. I'll never forget how my father was treated when he was penniless. Everyone is pleased to assume I live on an indecent amount of credit, and I've no intention of disabusing them of that notion."

Jordan took a sip of his own drink. "Have it your way. Surely Miss Templeton's mother will convince the girl to come to her senses. Though I'm sure she'd do so much more quickly if she knew her intended fiancé was as rich as Croesus in addition to holding one of the most esteemed titles in the country."

"That's just it, Ashbourne." Devon's voice was tight. "I don't want a wife who is obsessed with the size of my pockets. I want a wife who wants to marry *me.* I cannot hide my title, but I can damn well hide my fortune."

Jordan sipped his drink. "Fine. What's your next move, then, now that Lady Merrill has refused to write a retraction?"

"She will write a retraction all right," Devon promised. He scrubbed a hand through his hair. Damn it. His frustration wasn't even about Miss Templeton, or the retraction. He'd known that from the moment he'd seen Lily again. In truth, he'd been nothing but relieved when his fiancée had cried off. Miss Templeton's family was rich, but he'd never been entirely sure she hadn't wanted him for his title alone. And blast it all, Lily was right. The fact that Miss Templeton had allowed some silly pamphlet to scare her off just proved she was unsuitable.

No, it wasn't about Miss Templeton at all. It was Lily he couldn't take. She'd nearly destroyed him once. He refused to allow her to do it again.

Jordan propped his bow against the nearest tree. "What do you intend to do? Write the retraction for her and sign her name?" He paused, quirking a brow. "You know? That's not a half bad idea." He took another drink.

Devon shook his head. "No, damn it. I intend to bed her."

Jordan spit the brandy. "The devil you say!"

"I was angry. I couldn't think of anything else to threaten her with."

Slapping his open palm against his chest, Jordan wheezed. "You mean you *told* her you intend to bed her?"

A single nod this time.

"Well, well, well. This just went from interesting to fascinating. What, pray tell, did she reply?" Jordan leaned back against the tree, still cradling the drink in his hand.

Devon shrugged. "I didn't give her a chance to say anything."

"I daresay, this shall be the most diverting sport in all of London this Season," Jordan replied.

Devon raked a hand through his hair again. "This is not about sport. This is about proving that woman wrong and keeping her from interfering in my personal life."

"I'd say it's more than personal if you intend to bed her." Jordan chuckled.

Devon rolled his eyes.

"And it won't be easy," Jordan continued. "Seems you've made a contest out of bedding a woman who's being courted by nearly every eligible bachelor in town. They say she's spurned them all."

Devon snorted. "Oh, I know all too well how she can lead a man on. I was duped by her once. I will not make the same mistake again."

But another thought occurred to him. The threat of seduction may have been impetuous, but it would give Devon the perfect opportunity to finally seek his revenge against Lily Andrews. He would shame her. Make her want him and then toss her aside. She rejected him cruelly five years ago. This time, *he* would be the one to reject *her.*

"It's absolutely perfect," Jordan said. "These days, you're known for your rakishness while Lady Merrill is known for her disdain of men. The game is under way, and two more perfectly matched opponents there could not be."

Devon finished his drink in one hefty swallow. "It's not a contest." He handed his glass to the timid footman, grabbed up his bow, and hefted it to his shoulder. "But if it were . . . make no mistake as to who the victor would be."

"Not to worry. My money's on you, Colton." Jordan's eyebrow shot up. "Speaking of contests, when is your next appointment in the Rookery?"

*The Rookery.* Devon released the bow and the arrow zinged through the air. It missed the target entirely and landed in the soft grass behind the trees. "The day after tomorrow," he answered under his breath, lowering his arm. "Thank God I'm almost finished. Once that damned promise has been fulfilled, I'll never set foot in that detestable part of town again."

# CHAPTER 3

Sweets from Viscount Barton, a poem from Sir Berry, and more vases full of lilies than one could easily count, but not so much as a bud or a sweet from the Marquis of Colton. Lily made her way past the gifts crowded together on the table by her front door. Leo trotted near her feet. She paused to sort through the silver tray full of calling cards one more time.

She wrinkled her nose. No doubt that rogue wouldn't bother with flowers or calling cards. Why, she wouldn't be surprised if he showed up shirtless on her front stoop. She smiled. Despite the fact that she might actually enjoy that, perhaps it was a bit too bold, even for the despicable Colton. But it still rankled that he'd announced his intent to seduce her and hadn't so much as sent one trinket.

She'd acted like a complete and utter shrew to him, she knew. But something about his cold confidence brought out the worst in her. That and the fact that she refused to show weakness in front of the man who had decimated her heart.

"He's not doing a very good job," a young female voice piped from behind the vases near the end of the hallway.

Lily jumped. Clutching her chest, she slowed her breathing again and gave her younger sister her most formidable stare. "Annie! You gave me such a fright. Get out here this minute."

Annie emerged from behind the table, a proud smile on her pretty, eighteen-year-old face. Her dark brown curls bobbed about her cheeks. "Well, he isn't," Annie insisted with a firm nod. She bent down to scratch Leo behind the ears. If there was anyone besides Lily the dog was devoted to, it was Annie. Just like Lily, the girl had a way about her with animals, always helping them and rescuing them. Over the years the house had turned into a sort of menagerie of Annie's pets.

Lily dropped the cards to the tray and yanked her hand away. "Who is not doing a very good job at what?"

"Why, Lord Colton isn't doing a very good job at seducing you. That is the word, isn't it?" Annie whispered the last sentence, her dark eyes growing huge.

"Shh! Don't let anyone hear you say such a thing." Lily glanced over her shoulder to see if either of the servants was about. Thankfully, Evans was asleep in the chair next to the front door and Mary was nowhere to be seen.

"Oh, Evans and Mary have heard worse, I'm sure," Annie retorted. "Besides, they would never repeat it."

Annie was right. The two loyal servants had been with the sisters since they were children. When their parents had died without a shilling to their name, the sisters' third cousin, Percy, had tossed out both servants with no references. Lily, already a widow at the time, had taken them in. She might not have had much money herself, but she couldn't allow her friends to suffer.

Now, Evans proudly served as butler of Lily's dubious household, despite his penchant to nod off, and Mary was a lady's maid with an unfortunate and pronounced memory problem. Despite their faults, both servants would do anything to help their mistresses. Their loyalty was unfailing.

Annie kicked at the parquet flooring with her slippered foot. "I don't even know what 'seduce' means. And how many times must I ask you to call me Anne? I'm not Annie any longer. I'm all grown-up, about to have my come-out. Old enough for you to tell me what 'seduce' means." She batted her eyelashes at Lily.

Lily couldn't help but smile as she watched her sister. Annie was a bit taller than Lily. She had the same dark hair, but her eyes were dark, too, the color their mother's had been. Lily had inherited their father's violet ones. Annie was lovely and seemed to be growing lovelier by the day.

It was true that their parents had always fawned over Lily's beauty, but Lily had always made it a point to tell Annie how pretty she was. And she was very pretty. Pretty and sweet. No doubt she'd be in high demand when she made her debut in a matter of days. Lily sighed. Then she would be busy keeping men away from her little sister. Hmm. Perhaps Evans should employ that stick Colton had mentioned after all.

"You're still too young for that particular word," Lily insisted. "And I'm in no hurry to teach you anything of the sort."

Annie frowned before lowering her voice to a whisper. "You must admit Lord Colton isn't doing a very good job of attracting your attention, however. These gentlemen have been sending you flowers, and sweets, and poems for years and you've shown absolutely no interest in any of them. Lord Colton is not even trying."

Lily's fingertips caressed the cards on the silver tray momentarily before she snatched her hand behind her back again. "I could not care any less if the Marquis of Colton ever gives me so much as a calling card."

Annie picked up the nearest vase of lilies and spun around in a circle, her white skirts swirling around her bare ankles.

"Well, I should very much like the marquis to give me a calling card. Or even better, a bouquet." Annie buried her nose in the vase and inhaled deeply. "That man is positively beautiful."

Lily snatched the vase from her sister's arms and slid it back on the table. "Good heavens. Of all men, you do not want the Marquis of Colton paying you any attention."

Annie cocked her head to the side as if considering. "You're right. The marquis is much too old for me."

Lily expelled her breath. Finally, Annie was making some sense. Thinking logically as she should.

"I cannot wait to have a nice, young beau sending me flowers," Annie said. She twirled about again and paused to curtsy to an imaginary suitor.

So much for high hopes. Shaking her head, Lily pulled her sister into the nearby salon. "Think what you're saying, Annie. And please remember, you do not *have* to marry. I will find a way to take care of you. A come-out is not all you imagine it to be."

"But I *want* my debut. I'm greatly looking forward to it." Annie's pace slowed as she entered the room. Her shoulders slumped. "Lily, you've been exceedingly kind to me, taking me in after Mother and Father died four years ago, but I've been trying to tell you, I want my Season, I want a beau, I want flowers and sweets, and poems. I want to fall in love."

Annie said the last word with such reverence in her voice Lily couldn't bring herself to tell her there was no such thing. Annie's happiness was the most important thing to her. And she would never knowingly shatter her sister's dreams. Lily remembered the excitement of her own debut . . . vaguely. Annie had been looking forward to the questionable event for as long as she could remember, and Lily intended to provide it for her.

She had only to stave off the bill collectors long enough.

But she would be remiss if she didn't at least attempt to educate Annie. Lily steered her sister toward the settee. "Flowers, and sweets, and beaux are one thing, but husbands are quite another matter altogether."

Annie sighed and twirled around in another circle, her eyes sparkling. "I cannot wait to attend my first ball. Mr. Eggleston has already requested a dance."

Lily jerked up her head. "Mr. Eggleston? Who is Mr. Eggleston?"

Annie plopped down on the settee, one leg tucked beneath her, an enchanting smile on her face. "He's our neighbor, next door. I met him on Wednesday afternoon when Mary and I were coming back from the market."

Lily pulled out her sewing and arranged the perfectly ordered basket to her satisfaction. She glanced up at her sister and frowned. "You should not be meeting bachelors until after your debut and you know it."

Annie shrugged. "I couldn't be rude. We nearly ran into each other. I dropped one of my parcels and he retrieved it for me. He's so charming."

Lily scowled. "Who are his parents?"

"He's the second son of Baron Eggleston."

Lily narrowed her eyes. "How old is he?"

Annie shrugged. "Twenty-one, perhaps."

"And obviously impertinent. Mr. Eggleston should not be addressing you or asking for dances."

Annie set her jaw in a pout. "I know. You'd be happy if I had never spoken to any man. But, Lily, don't you remember? You were my age when you had your debut. You were my age when you were married."

Lily closed her eyes. "Yes, of course I remember. Which is precisely why—"

Annie turned her head away, refusing to look at Lily. "Mr. Eggleston is quite smitten with me, and I have every intention of dancing with him."

Lily expelled her breath in a rush, and then swallowed hard. She threaded a needle and began mending the handkerchief Leo had chewed a hole through the week before. "Lord knows I've been dreading it, but perhaps it's time you read my pamphlet."

Annie's head snapped back around. Her eyes wide, she pulled at her curls. "No! I do not want to read it. I'm sure to have nightmares for weeks afterward."

Lily bit her lip, considering the matter for a moment. "And that is precisely why I have not given it to you yet, but with all of your talk of beaux, I wonder . . ." She yanked the needle through the white linen square.

Annie slumped against the pillows and put the back of her hand to her forehead. "Oh, please, no more talk about the pamphlet. Let's talk of something else, like my chaperone. Who will accompany me to the events of the Season?"

"A chaperone is entirely unnecessary. I intend to escort you myself. But I'm trying to tell you . . . You've romanticized all of it. It's far less wonderful than you understand."

Annie groaned. "I'd die an old spinster if it were left to you."

Lily sighed. "Annie, listen to me—"

Annie sat up and faced Lily with accusing eyes. "That's your trouble, Lily. You're too calm. You show no emotion. You're heartless." Annie's voice shook. "When was the last time you let yourself feel? When was the last time you cried?"

Lily pushed her sewing aside and reached for her sister, but Annie flung off her hands. "No. No. I'm going to my bedchamber." Annie fled from the room, her handkerchief pressed to her mouth.

Lily watched her sister leave in a swirl of white. She closed her eyes. *That* was Annie's trouble. The girl was too emotional, too easily hurt. Her sister would fare so much better in the world if only she would be less trusting, less quick to believe in myths and fairy tales like true love.

Lily slumped back in her chair and Leo trotted out of the corner to cuddle at her feet. "I don't remember the last time I cried," she murmured softly. But it was a lie. She remembered the exact time. And place. A morning, nearly five years ago when she had waited for Devon Morgan to come for her, to take her to Gretna Green and marry her. It was a trip that never took place. And all Lily had received was a note. But, yes, that was the last time she had cried.

And after she'd wiped her tears away, she'd promised herself she would never be so weak again.

Mary wandered into the room then, a feather duster in her hands, whistling softly to herself. Lily sighed and shook her head. Clearly, the maid had been eavesdropping.

Lily pulled her sewing back into her lap. "You might as well say what's on your mind, Mary. I know you overheard my exchange with Annie."

Mary turned to her, a fake-innocent look on her face. "I may 'ave 'eard a bit o' it."

Lily clenched the fabric in her hands. "Annie doesn't understand. I can barely afford the cloth for the new gowns I've been sewing for her. I'm doing my best to provide her with a debut, but marriage . . . marriage is not what she thinks."

"She's young, me lady. Young and impetuous," Mary replied with a knowing smile.

Lily sighed. "But I'm protecting her. Why can't she see that? I was at the mercy of our dissolute father and my careless husband, but Annie . . . Annie doesn't have to live with the threat of a man controlling her."

Mary nodded. "She doesn't 'ave yer worries."

Lily laughed a humorless laugh. "You mean the fact that we're nearly destitute? And I sit in this house, day after day, struggling to pay bills while the *ton* assumes I'm living off a sizable dower?"

"If I could take yer troubles for ye, I would, me lady. But I've never known ye to not 'ave a plan."

Lily straightened her shoulders. "Yes. I will find a way to take care of all of us, and Annie will have her debut. Impetuous though she may be."

Mary squeezed Lily's hand. "I seem to recall another young woman who was young and impetuous once."

Lily scrunched up her nose. Mary's *long-term* memory was spot on . . . unfortunately. Lily sighed. "Was I ever *that* young? Or *that* impetuous?"

Mary didn't answer. Instead, she nodded solemnly. "I know ye're in a terrible state right now, me lady. But I 'ave every confidence in ye. Ye've lived through quite a lot, already. Yer 'usband died, then yer parents, and then ye took in Miss Annie and us. But ye've been stubborn since ye were a small girl, and I've never known a problem ye couldn't 'andle."

Lily smiled at that. Yes, she was stubborn. She'd had to be. And true, she'd handled every problem she'd come across. To date. But this particular problem was becoming more and more difficult to master.

"Money. Money. Money. It's all I can think about. I need money, not flowers and sweets and poems. Those I have in spades. Though not," Lily noted, brooding, "from the Marquis of Colton. Intending to seduce me indeed. So much for his promises. Just like a man."

"Doesn't Lord Medford say the pamphlet is selling well? Ye're sure ta make a fine penny off o' it."

Lily nodded. "Yes. That pamphlet may just save us. And not a moment too soon; the new earl may toss us onto the streets at any moment. We're only fortunate he hasn't done so before now."

Mary cleared her throat. "May I ask ye a question, me lady?"

"Of course."

Mary's eyes darted back and forth and her voice was a rough whisper. A nervous smile played about the maid's lips. "I've yet ta read yer pamphlet. What *was* the secret of yer wedding night?"

Lily clapped her hand to her forehead. "Oh, Mary. If I told you, you wouldn't believe me."

The maid picked up her skirts and moved over to the settee, hovering close. "Oh, ye must tell me," she whispered.

Lily bit her lip. The look of childlike curiosity on Mary's face tugged at Lily's heart. She chewed on the end of her fingernail. It would be such a relief to tell someone. To finally unload the burden. Besides, Mary would forget the entire conversation in a matter of minutes. What would be the harm?

Lily gave the maid a sidelong glance. "Very well. Sit down, if you will hear it."

Mary scrambled into the closest chair, her eyes wide, her knuckles turning white from clutching the arms of the chair. "Ye're going ta give me a copy o' the pamphlet?"

Lily laughed. "Oh, no, no, no. That pamphlet doesn't contain the secret. Not the *real* one at any rate. The real secret is . . ." She cleared her throat and leaned forward to whisper. "That is to say . . . Lord Merrill and I never . . . well, we never . . . quite . . . consummated our marriage."

# CHAPTER 4

"The countess is looking especially fine this evening, Colton." Jordan twisted his brandy glass in his hand and eyed Devon over its rim.

"Which countess?" Devon barely glanced up, but damn it, he knew exactly which countess, and the woman looked absolutely stunning. He'd seen her from across the ballroom, her dark hair pulled back in a chignon, her light gray gown accentuating her perfect figure, her violet-blue eyes sparkling. Blast it. He was already being plagued with indecent thoughts. This entire seduction plot would be that much easier if he weren't driven half mad just looking at her.

Seduction was much less complicated when one had the upper hand, after all. And that's exactly how he intended to proceed, with the upper hand firmly in place. His inconvenient attraction be damned.

"And Miss Templeton is here, too, I see. No doubt, her mama forced her to attend," Jordan continued.

Devon's gaze scanned the ballroom. Miss Templeton was a beauty, if one preferred tall, willowy blondes. And until recently, Devon had. But of late, a certain diminutive brunette had captured his interest again.

Devon pulled down his sleeve with a sharp movement. "No doubt Miss Templeton is scared senseless, and from what I've heard of that damned pamphlet, she has every right to be. It's a wonder Lady Merrill is allowed in Polite Society."

Jordan laughed. "Are you joking? No one knows for sure she wrote it. Not to mention the fact that she's a Society favorite due to her wit and beauty. I daresay the Prince Regent himself is smitten with her. Besides, other than scaring off a few silly misses who will eventually come to their senses, the pamphlet is more shocking and interesting than damaging, really."

"Not," Devon replied, "if you're trying to marry one of the silly misses."

Jordan's smile was wide. "All anyone can talk about is that pamphlet. I've heard it's gaining in popularity now that Miss Templeton has cried off because of it."

Devon expelled his breath. "Perfect. That's exactly what I needed to hear. Now I'm actually helping her to sell copies of the bloody thing."

Jordan's crack of laughter followed. "You know the *ton*, Colton. Where scandal goes, interest follows."

"You're not helping, Ashbourne," Devon bit back.

Jordan shrugged. "Why don't you dance with Miss Templeton?"

Devon squared his shoulders. "I'm dancing with someone this evening, but it won't be Miss Templeton." He tossed back his drink, shoved his empty glass into the hand of a passing footman, and stalked away.

Jordan's mocking voice followed him. "Give Lady Merrill my very best."

Devon found Lily in the arms of one of her many admirers. Dancing. And laughing. Irritation niggled at him. He narrowed his eyes and strode toward the couple. He wasn't about to let Lily enjoy herself while he was forced to endure the stares of half the *ton* attempting to gauge his reaction to his fiancée crying off.

He poked Lord Cox on the shoulder. "Make yourself scarce, Cox. I'm cutting in." Devon gave the shorter man a tight smile.

Cox gulped, excused himself hastily to Lily, and scurried off.

Devon easily spun Lily into his arms, taking the lead, and trying to ignore his body's instant reaction to her soft nearness. She smelled like . . . lilies. Of course she did. That smell had affected him for five years now. Did a witch invent her perfume? It drove him insane.

Lily only watched him, a decidedly disgruntled look on her face. "Why did you do that?" She nodded toward Lord Cox's hastily retreating figure. "You know perfectly well the entire ballroom will be abuzz with the news that you cut in."

Devon glanced down at her. He'd surprised her. Good. And he was not yet through surprising her. An important tactic when retaining the upper hand. "You've no idea how little I care what the ballroom buzzes about."

Lily pursed her lips. "You may not care, but my sister is about to make her debut. The less gossip the better."

His smile was tight. "Come now. If you cared about gossip, you wouldn't have written your precious pamphlet, now would you?"

Lily narrowed her eyes at him. "Who says I wrote that pamphlet?"

"Really? Denial? Still? I do, for one. And half of this ballroom does too."

She glanced around, aware of the whispers that had already started. "Whatever gossip exists about myself and my sister, Lord Colton, you are hardly helping with your behavior tonight."

He shook his head. "Why do you insist upon wearing mourning colors? Your husband died of a weak heart years ago."

The surprise on Lily's face quickly turned to scorn. "Why do you insist upon being so rude?"

He spun her around again, deliberately keeping her off balance. "Cox is a sniveling dandy. It's not a wonder you wrote that pamphlet if that's the kind of male company you keep."

Her eyes simmered. "How dare you—"

"Really?" he replied coolly. " 'How dare you'? Hardly original. I expected more charming repartee from you, *Countess.*"

She snapped her perfect pink mouth closed. Her eyes gleamed like amethysts. Oh, she was preparing to come back at him all right, and this time it would be neither unoriginal, nor charming.

She attempted to wrench herself from his arms. "I do not dance with men who do not *ask* me," she bit off through clenched teeth.

He did not relent, kept her pinned to his body. "How unfortunate for you," he bit back, "because I rarely ask women to dance."

This time, she pulled with all her might, nearly tugging him off balance. Not bad for such a small woman. But hardly a match for him. He kept his most falsely charming smile plastered on his face and she remained easily ensnared in his arms.

She finally gave in, relaxing her arms and dancing with him as if she hadn't a care in the world. "I'd have thought you'd have more skill with women, Colton. Be able to keep them by your side with cunning words and finesse instead of brute strength. Especially after all of your bragging."

Ah, now *there* was the barb he'd expected. *Not bad.* He barely managed to keep a grin from showing.

"You won't be questioning my skill for long," he promised, twirling her around again.

Lily sucked in another deep breath. No doubt she was calling upon her considerable resources and years of drilled-in manners for maintaining decorum in the face of his outlandish rudeness. Expelling her breath, she pasted a smile on her face and pretended to enjoy the dance. But she watched him carefully, and Devon knew without a doubt he was being evaluated for any sign of weakness. Then she would strike.

She focused her gaze on his shoulders, refusing to look him in the eye. "I forgot. You like to pretend you're interested in a woman and then disappear. I'll wait. If I remember correctly, it shouldn't take long."

He pressed his lips together. The woman was maddeningly unpredictable. And he'd always prided himself on being able to predict. Cards. Horses. People. Besides, what nonsense was that? She'd made it quite clear in her note that fateful morning years ago that her father would only accept a man with plenty of money. She'd thrown it in his face. She'd chosen that old man over him. Damn, it still rankled. And now she was mocking him for refusing to simper and scrape while he'd known he had no chance at winning her. He wasn't about to let her get away with it.

"And I forgot," he replied, "that *you* like to gather as many fawning admirers as you possibly can around your skirts, toy with their emotions, and send them on their way."

Lily fought the urge to grind her teeth. There was that confidence again. Tonight it was especially irritating. Maddening, even. She clenched her jaw and gave Colton a tight smile. How dare he hurl accusations at her when he was the one who abandoned her? She hadn't been nearly rich enough for him.

And the fact that he'd actually planned on marrying that twit Amelia Templeton just proved how obsessed he was with money. Why, the girl's family was nearly as rich as the king. No wonder Colton had waited five long years to marry. He'd been holding out for the largest dowry he could find. And now he had the nerve to imply that *she* was the one who toyed with people's emotions? It made her blood boil. She wasn't about to let him get away with it.

"It seems your fiancée has already jilted you, Colton. You might try looking for a young woman who has no fawning admirers. Of course the number of ladies who are rich enough for you isn't particularly large, but I'm sure you'll make do."

If she'd hit her mark, she couldn't tell by the look on his face. His grin did not waver.

"This is the second time you've mentioned my destitute financial state," he replied. "You seem a bit preoccupied with the matter. But then again, money has always been of great importance to you, has it not?"

Lily's nostrils flared. Preoccupied? With his financial state? Ridiculous. Everyone knew he had no financial state to speak of. And now he was being a hypocrite. He'd been the one obsessed with money. So much so he'd been willing to lie to her, pretend he was in love, to secure his finances.

She chose her words carefully. "Hardly preoccupied, Colton. I merely find it interesting to see you're still so desperate to wed a wealthy young woman about to make her debut. Seems little has changed in the last five years."

This time, *his* nostrils flared. "It should hardly be of interest to you, *Countess*, as you've had practice marrying someone for his wealth. You sold your hand to acquire Merrill's fortune, after all. And now I hear all of your suitors are wealthy."

That stung. Money had nothing to do with her marriage,

and he of all people should know it. She bit her lip to distract herself. She shook her head, and a wayward dark curl fell partially over her eyes. She'd had enough. It was time to finish this little game.

"At least the men who court me know how to treat a lady. It's been days since you threatened to seduce me and I've seen nary a flower, sweet, or poem from you. You are entirely out of your depth."

His sharp crack of laughter caught the attention of some of the nearby dancers. "You don't truly expect me to send you those baubles like all the fops who worship at your tiny feet, do you?"

Her cheeks flushed hot. She glanced around. "Lower your voice."

He leaned down and his warm breath caressed her temple. "It's not working for them, is it? Why would you assume I would follow suit? The first rule of winning at gaming, don't follow your opponent's lead."

Despite his reminder of his love of gambling, Lily couldn't control her shiver. "Very well. How exactly do you intend to seduce me then, Colton? Manhandling me in a ballroom certainly is not working."

He gave her his most lazy, charming smile. "Not, I assure you, by fawning over you. I know women well enough to know what folly that is."

She had to concentrate to keep the shadow of a smile from playing about her lips. Damn that Colton. One minute he made her angry and the next he made her laugh. He'd always done that to her. Kept her on edge. "How then?" she prodded.

A raised brow. "Do you think I am daft? I'm not about to give away my secrets to the opposition."

Lily briefly fantasized about tripping him. "If I thought for a moment you actually had a secret, I might be more willing to pursue this line of questioning. As it stands, I am growing quite bored with the entire conversation." She did her best to fake a yawn.

"You never answered me. Why do you insist on wearing mourning colors?"

Blast it. Her attempt to anger him had failed. She set her jaw. Why was he so curious? "I remain in mourning for my husband."

"Mourning? Really? For a man you barely knew? You were married, what, one month, two?"

She kept her gaze cast downward. "He may not have been with me long, but he was my husband." *God curse his sorry soul.* She only wore the blasted mourning clothes because she couldn't afford to replace them, but Colton surely didn't need to know it.

"That's unfortunate," Colton said. "Rumor has it you use your widow's robes as an excuse to fend off your many suitors. I suppose there is no truth to that?"

Lily squeezed his hand, wishing she could slap his face instead. "Not that it is any of your business, but I'm at a ball, aren't I? I'm dancing. I receive callers. I'm about to present my sister in a few days. What more does Society ask of me?"

Colton lowered his voice. He swept her past the other dancers. "I wonder. Would your late husband approve of your writing?"

A gasp escaped her throat. This time, she considered stepping on his foot. Hard.

He didn't give her time to reply. Instead, he leaned in closer and whispered. "One wouldn't think so, would one? I mean, your pamphlet does cast him in considerable doubt, doesn't it? As one is to assume Lord Merrill and his lack of skill is the reason for your antipathy toward the bedchamber."

"How dare you!" That was it. Lily trod on his foot. *Accidentally,* of course.

Colton winced, but managed not to miss a step. "How dare I? It seems to me, the more appropriate question is how dare *you,* Countess? I am not the one who wrote *Secrets of a Wedding Night,* after all. Besides, have a care. You are the one interested in protecting your reputation, are you not? You're causing a scene."

The music ended then, and when Colton released her, Lily breathed in deeply, inhaling lungfuls of air. She did what she could to quiet her body's visceral reaction to his monumental rudeness. She glanced around. He was right. Several of the other dancers were blatantly staring at the two of them. A handful of people along the sidelines were whispering and pointing. She must remain calm and extricate herself from his company. She would not, would *not,* let him get to her. She curtsied as if thanking him for the dance and counted to ten, preparing herself for the final round.

Lily's smile was tight. "This is how you go about seducing a woman, Colton? By insulting her and angering her? I often found it curious that you hadn't snapped up some fawning heiress by now, but it's not really a wonder you remain a bachelor, is it?"

The skin near his eye twitched a bit. Her comment had hit its mark. *Finally.*

His next words fell nonchalantly from his firmly molded lips. He bowed to her. "Who says I am still trying to seduce you? Given your viper's tongue and shrewish behavior, it's entirely possible I may have changed my mind."

A twinge of disappointment shot through her belly. Lily didn't stop to examine it. Instead, she lifted her chin. "That would explain your lack of skill, I suppose. Or perhaps it's nothing more than a convenient excuse." She swept her skirts aside and stalked away from him, intending to leave him alone in the middle of the dance floor.

Colton's hand shot out and grabbed her wrist. He spun

her around, back into his arms. Lily gasped, her gaze shot up to meet his dark eyes. A knowing smile rested on his perfect face. "Let me assure you, my lady, it will be soon, quite soon, and when I'm seducing you, you'll know."

He bent down and pressed his lips against hers in a quick, hard kiss. Amid the shocked gasps surrounding them, he released her, and strode away, leaving *her* standing alone in the middle of the dance floor.

# CHAPTER 5

The small boy sat at a writing table, his dark head bent over a piece of paper. His little dimpled fingers grasped a quill, diligently working on his letters. His tutor sat at the front of the room, repeating the Greek alphabet in a scholarly drone.

Devon stood with his arms crossed, his shoulder propped against the door frame, watching them both.

He was at Colton House. His ancestral estate. The vast acreage he now commanded. The place where he'd spent his childhood. It always made Devon feel younger to come to this place. Younger and also . . . melancholy.

He knocked lightly on the door with one knuckle. "May I interrupt?"

The boy's head popped up. Not for the first time, Devon was startled by the lad's resemblance to him, even at his young age. The dark eyes, the square jaw, the ruffle of black, slightly curly hair. A smile spread across the boy's face. He jumped up from the desk, tossed his quill aside, and ran to Devon. Devon held out his arms and snatched him into a tight embrace.

The tutor scrambled out of his seat and bowed. "My lord."

"Mr. Halifax." Devon nodded and the man hastily sat down again and went back to perusing the book opened on the desk in front of him.

"You're getting tall, lad," Devon said, hugging the boy close.

"I didn't know when I'd see you next," the boy replied, still grinning.

"I know." Devon mussed his hair. "I had a day away from Parliament, and I thought I would come out and visit."

"May we go fishing?" the boy asked, his dark eyes sparkling.

"Yes, but I must speak with Mr. Halifax for a few minutes first. Excuse us, won't you?"

The boy nodded happily and scampered from the room.

"I'll meet you in the foyer in a few minutes," Devon called after him, closing the door. He approached Mr. Halifax. The tutor rose to greet him.

"My lord," Mr. Halifax said, bowing to Devon.

"Please have a seat," Devon replied, gesturing to a nearby bench. He grabbed a wooden chair, turned it around, and straddled it. Folding his arms over the top, he regarded Mr. Halifax.

Mr. Halifax sat uneasily on the edge of his seat and pushed his silver spectacles up his narrow nose.

"How is he progressing?" Devon asked.

Halifax took a thin, shaky breath. "Master Justin is a pleasure to teach, my lord. He is intelligent, quick-witted, and humorous. His Greek and Latin are coming along quite nicely, and I needn't tell you his gift for arithmetic continues to be the most impressive I've ever seen."

Devon smiled wistfully. "Yes, it seems that trait runs in our family."

Halifax nodded. "He can be a bit rambunctious, defiant at times, but overall his penchant for learning astounds me. I've been forced to speed up my lessons on more than one occasion to keep pace with him. He's quite an intelligent lad. You should be exceedingly proud of him."

Devon nodded. His eyes scanned the room. The dark wooden walls, the small chairs, the table, the bench, even the smell of lemon juice used to clean the place. And the books, the sweet smell of books. It catapulted him back through space and time. He'd sat in the same spot Justin had been moments earlier, reciting numbers, numbers that seemed like words to him, numbers that came more easily to him than anything else in his world. When they clicked into place in his brain, everything made sense.

Devon stood and paced the room, his hands folded behind his back. He stopped in front of a bookshelf and eyed a tome of arithmetic. He ran his fingers along the worn leather binding. Pulling the book from the shelf, he thumbed open the first page. There they were. DMSM. His initials. Devon Marcus Sandridge Morgan. The Fifth Marquis of Colton. He rubbed his index finger back and forth across the letters, the shadow of a smile on his lips. He remembered the day he'd written them. His father had given him the book, delighted that his son was such a gifted student.

"He is fit to teach me, my lord," Devon's tutor had informed his father. "The best I have ever encountered."

His father had beamed. "My son is impressive," he would say, telling anyone who would listen. It had been Devon's greatest achievement, making his father proud of him.

And Devon had been proud too . . . until his father had started taking him to gaming hells, using his son's gift for numbers to help him win at the tables.

Devon shook his head, dispelling the bad memories. He slipped the book back into place on the shelf. Shoving his hands in his pockets, he turned back around to face Mr. Halifax.

"I'll return Justin in a couple of hours."

Mr. Halifax's voice shook. "Master Justin is very busy and I—"

"Two hours," Devon said in a voice that brooked no further discussion.

Halifax swallowed and nodded. "Will you be staying for dinner, my lord? Perhaps I might join you, and we can discuss Master Justin's studies at greater length."

"No," Devon replied, with true regret. "I cannot stay. I must return to London. I have an appointment tonight." Then, under his breath, "There is something I must do."

"Very well, my lord. I'll assist Master Justin in preparing everything for your fishing excursion. It will just be a few minutes." Halifax hurried from the room, shutting the door behind him.

Devon turned to face the classroom again. He expelled his breath. God, if only he didn't have to return to London tonight. The Rookery made his stomach turn. But he'd made his promises, and unlike his father, he would keep them.

His appointment in that unsavory part of town was at midnight, and he would be there. But since he must return to town, he might as well take the next step in his seduction of the countess. No sense in wasting an opportunity. He could fulfill his obligations and teach that shrew a lesson at the same time. He'd already ordered one thing to set his plan in motion.

He smiled to himself. Yes. He'd made her wait long enough. Long enough to make her wonder if he was serious. It was time to make the next move.

Devon stepped over to the windows. His hands folded behind his back again, he looked out across the vast expanse of grass and gardens behind the estate. His eyes immediately rested on a spot many yards away, nestled under a copse of trees. It had been there, over twenty years ago, that his father had first shown Devon the Morgan signet ring. Passed down, his father had said, through generations. Given to his great-great-grandfather by the king who had bestowed the title upon the family.

Devon recalled the pride that had welled up in his ten-year-old chest that day when his father had allowed him to hold the ring, slip it onto his too-small finger. "This shall be yours one day," his father had informed him. "And with it comes a great deal of responsibility."

Devon clenched his jaw at the memory. If only his father had taken his own responsibilities as seriously.

Devon had been so lost in his thoughts, he'd failed to hear the door open behind him.

"I was told you were here, my lord," the older woman said quietly, snapping Devon from his reverie. He turned to her, and a smile broke across his face.

"Mrs. Appleby," he called. "Good to see you." He looked at the woman who'd been more like a mother to him than a servant. It still seemed awkward to hear her call him "my lord," even after all these years.

The plump woman shuffled forth with a bright smile on her face and Devon ushered her into the room.

"I came to see Justin," he told her.

"I thought so. You know he loves you very much. He's sure the world revolves around you."

Devon's lips turned up at the corners. "Not quite."

"Shh," she laughed. "Don't tell him that. You're his hero."

Devon swallowed against the lump in his throat. "How is he, Mrs. Appleby?"

"Didn't Mr. Halifax tell you? He's learning like a true scholar. Just like you."

"But how *is* he? Is he happy here?"

Mrs. Appleby's aged hand slid over Devon's and she gave it a squeeze. "He's fine, my lord. Truly, he is."

"And still no word . . . from his mother?"

The housekeeper cast her eyes downward and shook her head solemnly. "No, my lord. As usual. Nothing."

Devon nodded. "And the rest of the household, Mrs. Appleby? I trust all of the servants are doing well."

"Absolutely, my lord."

Devon turned toward the door. "I should get out there. I believe the last time I left Justin alone for too long, he decided to go fishing by himself."

Mrs. Appleby laughed. "That he did. Just like you, he's not one to wait long for anything."

Devon's hand was on the cool brass doorknob when Mrs. Appleby's voice stopped him. "When might we expect to see you again, my lord?"

Devon turned the knob and yanked open the door. "I'll be back next month, in time for Justin's fifth birthday."

# CHAPTER 6

Lily was holed up in the study again, a quill clutched in her fist. This time, she was writing a list. A list of alternatives if the pamphlet did not earn her enough money to stay in town. Her cousin Althea in Northumberland might take them in. Althea had seven children, surely she could use help taking care of them. Lily and Annie were both adept at sewing. Perhaps they could find work as seamstresses. But would a seamstress hire them? Two former ladies forced to the streets?

Lily dunked her quill in the inkpot again. If she couldn't find a way to earn money, she would have to take more drastic measures. She snatched up the list of household accounts. No more buying meat at market. She slashed a line through the list. No more sugar. Or cream. Two more swift lines. No more tea. She sighed. Perhaps she'd ask Evans to reuse the leaves, first.

She tapped the tip of the quill against the parchment, fighting the panic that always rose in her throat when she examined her finances. Annie, Evans, and Mary knew their little household was in dire financial circumstances, but only Lily knew just how desperate a situation it truly was.

She eyed little Leopold asleep in the corner. Finding money to feed him was no small feat either, even when table scraps were his dinner. But she refused to let her beloved dog go. No, Leopold was family too, and he would no more be turned out on the streets than Annie would. But Annie would just have to stop bringing strays home, that was all. Lily sighed. She'd be powerless to deny her sister when she came home with a little, helpless animal. Very well. Now that she thought on it, tea wasn't *really* necessary.

A soft knock drew Lily's attention to the doorway. She glanced up to see Mary curtsy. Lily smiled at her old friend. "Yes, Mary? What is it?"

"I beg yer pardon, me lady, but ye'll be wantin' ta see this." The older woman bobbed another quick curtsy. "Wait. I 'aven't already announced this, 'ave I?" she asked sheepishly.

Lily shook her head.

"Come on and see then. 'Tis an impressive sight, ta be sure." Mary pulled her mobcap down over her ears and made her way back down the hall.

Cocking her head to the side, Lily tossed the quill onto the sad list of figures and stood to investigate. Leo leaped up from his corner to follow.

Before Lily passed the doorway, the scent found her nostrils. *Flowers.* That lovely, sweet smell. But there was something different about it this time. Normally, the scent of lilies drifted through the house, but this time it was roses. Roses, lilacs, and something else.

She quickened her step, rounding past the turn in the hallway. When she made it to the foyer—at least, she *thought* it had once been the foyer—she stopped, clutching at the wall.

The space had been transformed into a virtual hothouse. Flowers lined every available nook, every conceivable cranny. An unusually alert Evans, looking both inordinately pleased and mildly annoyed at the same time, scurried back and forth from the front door, ushering in the delivery.

Annie came rushing down the staircase, a bright smile on her face. "Oh, I know who these are from. Now, *this* is what I expected. Frances said her sister received a disconcerting amount of flowers from Lord Sitton, but I've no doubt they were a pittance compared to these."

Lily snapped her mouth shut, still busily scanning the colorful scene. There were roses. Gardenias. Petunias. Pretty little daffodils, tulips, bluebells, hyacinth, and lilacs.

"It looks as if he uprooted an entire garden," Annie said, spinning around. "What do you think, Lily? Are you sufficiently impressed by Lord Colton now?"

Lily bit the inside of her cheek to keep from smiling. "It's utterly ridiculous, that's what I think. Why, the cost of these flowers would be enough to run this entire household for a good period of time, and I cannot condone—"

"Good heavens." Annie slapped her open palm against her forehead. "It's a *romantic* gesture. Only you would think about money at a time like this."

Evans, who'd apparently finished his organization of the chaos, stepped forward. Clearing his throat, he handed Lily a card that was tied to a single flower stem. A lily. Just one lily in the entire ostentatious display.

She took the card from Evan's outstretched fingers. The words on it were written in a strong, bold hand, the black letters slashed across the parchment.

*Now you know.—D*

Lily pressed the card to her lips, hiding her slight smile.

"What does it say?" Annie asked in a singsong voice.

Lily's only answer was a raised brow.

"Ah, they are lovely, me lady. They must 'ave cost 'im a small fortune." Mary's nose was stuck in a vase full of roses. "If only we could sell 'em." She sighed.

Lily whirled around to face her, her gray skirts swishing around her ankles. "Sell them?"

Mary shook her head. "'Twas only a jest, me lady."

Lily snapped her fingers. "No, no. It's brilliant actually. Perfect!" She swung around again. "Annie, gather up the flowers. Mary, get the sweets from the cupboard. Evans, wave down a hack."

Evans straightened his shoulders and nodded. He marched off to do his lady's bidding while Mary shuffled off toward the pantry, shaking her head and mumbling under her breath.

Annie plunked her hands on her hips. "Lily, what exactly do you plan to do?" Her voice held a warning note.

"I plan to fetch my bonnet. Mary and I are going to Vauxhall and we're selling the lot of it."

Annie clapped a hand over her mouth and then slowly let it drop. "You cannot be serious! You cannot sell the flowers. They were gifts!"

"No? Watch me." Lily rushed toward the front door and snatched her bonnet from the brass hat stand in the corner. She pulled the hat over her head, pushed wayward tendrils of hair inside, and hastily tied the ribbons in a bow under her chin. Then she grabbed up two of the nearest vases. "Annie, help me with these, please."

Shaking her head, Annie reluctantly scooped up a vase.

It took the better part of a quarter hour for the four of them to pack everything into the rented hack that Evans had managed to secure. Mary and Lily sat in the middle of the garden of flowers, and Annie called through the window. "Be sure to pay Lord Colton a visit to thank him while you're out."

Lily rolled her eyes. "I will do no such thing."

The coach pulled away from the town house and clattered down the street. Lily sat snuggled in the flowers, a wide smile on her face. She expelled her breath, long and slow, enjoying the feeling of intense relief that poured through her veins. Her shoulders relaxed for the first time in months. With the money from the flowers, she would be able to feed her family for another sennight or more.

She adjusted her position within the flowers. Everyone in the *ton* knew the rumors about Colton's finances. Like his father, Devon Morgan enjoyed gambling. Too much. It had cost him his fortune and his prospects. The flowers, no doubt, were purchased on credit he could ill afford.

Colton might be a spendthrift, but Lily was not. If flowers were all she had to sell, then flowers she would sell. Fortune tended to help those who helped themselves.

*Now you know.* Indeed. The flowers were Colton's next volley. Well played. But the man obviously didn't know with whom he was dealing. She would show him.

Colton was sure to be at the Foxdowns' soiree tonight. She would attend too. She couldn't help but feel oddly grateful to him for being her savior in this particular instance. Worse, she couldn't tamp down the inexplicable urge to see him. She was appreciative, true. But if she thanked him, no doubt the blackguard would take it as a sign of weakness. He'd assume he was wearing her down. She hated to be rude, but there was no help for it.

She laid her head against the seat and closed her eyes. Hmm. Or, perhaps gratitude was just what this situation called for. Perhaps allowing him to *think* he was wearing her down was exactly what was needed. She smiled to herself.

She popped open her eyes. "Mary, as soon as we return home we must prepare my hair and clothing for the party tonight. I plan to wear my lavender ball gown." Lily readjusted a vase on her lap.

Mary glanced across the mounds of flowers and nodded.

"Very well, Lord Colton," Lily whispered into the petals. "I shall see your bet and raise you."

# CHAPTER 7

"I heard the pamphlet made Lady Underhill swoon. Swoon dead away in her own dressing room." Lady Foxdown's eyes sparkled with a hint of salaciousness as she spoke to her husband, not two paces away from Lily at the end of the ballroom.

Lily whipped out her fan. This particular conversation was not one she relished being a part of. "Is it insufferably hot in here?" she whispered to Viscount Medford who stood stalwart by her side.

"No warmer than usual," Medford replied in his own whisper, his grin barely discernible.

"And what did Lord Underhill do?" Lord Foxdown asked his wife.

"Why, called for the maid to bring the smelling salts, and then promptly removed that scandalous text from his wife's person."

Lily gave the couple a pained smile. "I do hope Lady Underhill recovered," she managed to say, fluttering the fan more quickly. Oh, but it was hot. And discussion of the pamphlet did nothing to improve her mood. She glanced longingly at the nearby double doors that led out onto the Foxdowns' veranda. If only she could escape.

To make matters worse, Colton had been watching her all evening. He'd made no move to approach her, but she could feel his dark eyes on her like heavy weights. She didn't know whether to be relieved or angry. The man had sent her a hothouse full of flowers this afternoon, and now he was staring her down. Obviously all part of his plot to drive her mad.

And why did he have to be so handsome? It would make the entire thing much simpler if he were not. Instead, he stood across the ballroom, with a bevy of beauties swirling about him like so many butterflies in a garden. His dark, superfine evening attire perfectly molded to his exquisite body, his height placed him head and shoulders above all other men in the room except Medford. His white teeth flashed when he laughed, his dark hair was slightly ruffled, and his unsettling gaze came back again and again to rest on Lily. And haunt her.

Her thoughts kept returning to the goodly sum of money she'd earned at Vauxhall that afternoon. Confound it, she had *him* to thank for it.

"And I heard another pamphlet is being written. One that promises to be even more scandalous," Lady Foxdown whispered to their little group as she cut another glance at Lily.

Lily kept her face carefully blank. She didn't dare look at Medford again. Lady Foxdown might interpret it as a sign of guilt. And oh, but she did so enjoy being guilty with Medford. The viscount, her very good friend, was the pinnacle of a Society gentleman. Respected, revered, a beacon of propriety. Only such a man could be a part of the *haut ton* and remain affiliated with a printing press. And only Medford could get away with printing that blasted pamphlet, without anyone disparaging him for it. No, the scandal was reserved for the anonymous author, not the gentleman who'd put the pamphlet into circulation.

Medford had a talent for having fun at the *ton*'s expense, without them realizing it. That was only one of his many endearing qualities. Another one was his deep sense of honor. He could always be counted upon, and had none of the airs one would expect from a man with his wealth, from an unimpeachable family. And he had the same wicked sense of humor that Lily did.

As Lady Foxdown droned on about the pamphlet, Lily's mind traveled back to the night she'd met Medford.

They'd been seated next to each other at a musicale one evening four years ago. When their host's daughter had begun singing in a voice that sounded much too much as if someone were slaughtering a sow, the two of them had been unable to contain their laughter.

Shaking, with tears threatening, they'd both bolted for the door at nearly the exact same moment. Medford had bowed politely to her, allowed her to precede him from the room, and managed to keep a straight face as he escorted her outside. They'd spent the remainder of that evening on the balcony, glad for the fresh air and the even more refreshing company.

Yes. Lord Medford was perfect in every particular, but those who knew him well, as Lily had come to, knew just how irreverent he could be. He was handsome, intelligent, and wealthy, but to Lily, Medford was just her stalwart companion. The only man she'd ever been able to trust. One upon whom she could always count. Her dear friend.

Lily sighed. It was beyond unfair that she felt no romantic attraction to Medford. He was like the brother she'd never had. Everything would have been so much easier if that were not the case. Why, if she could love the viscount, and he could love her back, all her money problems would be quite conveniently resolved.

But she didn't love him. And she would never even consider entering into a marriage without love. Not again.

Lily eyed the verbose Lady Foxdown. Apparently, she and her husband hadn't heard the rumors that Lily and Medford were responsible for the first pamphlet. Or perhaps the lady was merely fishing for information. Either way, Lady Foxdown would be disappointed. Besides, the gossip was false. Lily had no intention of writing another pamphlet. She'd taken an enormous risk to her reputation by writing the first one.

Lily rapidly fanned herself. The heat hadn't been relieved one bit. Oh, why wasn't she the kind of simpering twit who could fake an attack of the vapors? It would be the perfect excuse to remove herself from Lady Foxdown's insipid company. But Lily just couldn't bring herself to do it.

A flutter by her arm caught her attention, just before a large, warm, masculine hand slid across the small of her back. Gooseflesh sprinkled along her spine. She instinctively knew. Colton was there.

"Countess, you look as if you need some air. Allow me to escort you onto the veranda." Colton's voice. Deep, masculine, and tinged with arrogance as if he couldn't conceive of her refusing him.

Medford stepped forward, his eyes narrowing at Colton. "If Lady Merrill is in need of some air, I would be happy to—"

"Three's a crowd, Medford, or haven't you heard?" Devon flashed a wicked grin, taking Lily by the arm. "You were always such a scholar at Cambridge, Medford, but it seems you missed a social lesson."

Medford's teeth clenched and he gave Colton a dark look. He leaned down next to Lily's ear. "Don't go off with that blackguard," he whispered fiercely.

Lily pressed her lips together. She'd never heard such disapproval in Lord Medford's voice before. " 'Blackguard' is a bit harsh, don't you think?" she whispered back.

Medford straightened and gave her a stiff nod. "I await your decision, Lady Merrill."

Eager to avoid a scene, Lily hastened to reassure him. "Thank you, Lord Medford. I'll be fine." She gave him a pleading look and excused herself from the group.

Devon smirked at Medford and whisked Lily across the ballroom toward a set of double doors. His palm on the small of her back made Lily's breathing hitch, and thoughts of Medford quickly faded.

Colton's hand dropped away as they passed the refreshment table from which he plucked two glasses of champagne. Lily expelled her breath. Without him touching her she could breathe normally again. He nodded, ushering her through the open French doors.

Lily moved to a spot on the balcony far away from the other couples outside, and spread both hands on the railing.

It was truly a work of art, how Colton had so smoothly extricated her from the Foxdowns' company, not to mention a disapproving Medford. Oh, yes, Devon Morgan plied his social skills like a master painter with a brush.

Lily reveled in the cool night air. Ah, it was lovely to be free from the stifling ballroom. She sucked in a deep breath and turned to face Colton. He stood in the moonlight, his shoulder propped against the stone wall of the house, his booted feet crossed at the ankles. How did that man manage to make debonair look so effortless?

She straightened her shoulders. "I suppose I should thank you for rescuing me from the awful heat in there."

"No need," he replied with his roguish grin, moving away from the wall, making his way slowly toward her. "I consider it a public service to rescue beautiful ladies from exceedingly dull conversation. Having suffered through countless awful conversations myself, I know what a chore it can be."

Lily couldn't help her answering smile. She tamped down the twinge of pleasure that shot through her belly at his mention of the word "beautiful." "The conversation was worse than dull," she admitted.

Colton moved closer. He offered her one of the champagne glasses. "You look as if you could use this."

She didn't take the flute from his long fingers. "No, thank you."

He raised a brow. "You still don't drink?"

"No."

"Pity."

He set her glass on the balcony railing next to her and slid his free hand into his pocket. Then he tipped his own glass to his lips and leaned back against the railing, his elbow braced against the stone balustrade.

He crossed his legs at the ankles again and gave Lily a sideways glance. "Tell me. What was the subject of the worse-than-dull conversation? Retainers? Land management? The ungodly cost of tea? Medford isn't known for his stellar wit and repartee. I've no idea why you insist upon spending so much time in his company."

Lily arched a brow. "I didn't realize you were acquainted with Lord Medford, nor that you were aware of how much time I spend in his company."

Colton barely shrugged. "Unfortunately, we're more than acquainted. We were schoolmates at university."

Lily nodded. "Ah, I see. And something tells me you didn't like him back then either."

Colton rolled his eyes. "Suffice it to say, Ashbourne and I were interested in more . . . social pursuits, and Medford was all about his studies and his marks."

Lily laughed. "That sounds like Medford."

"Tell the truth. He hasn't gotten a bit more interesting, has he? What *were* you discussing back there?" Colton nodded toward the ballroom.

"We were discussing a certain pamphlet actually," she admitted with a wry smile.

"Ah, *Secrets of a Wedding Night*, the subject on everyone's lips these days. I must confess. I find it surprising you think it dull, considering you wrote the thing. Did you and Medford admit to your conspiracy to publish the piece?"

Lily traced a gloved finger around the edge of her reticule that hung from her wrist. She shook her head. "Absolutely not."

He flashed her a knee-weakening smile. "Still keeping up the pretense that you had nothing to do with it, I see. I may not be there to rescue you next time. You might try to fake a swoon."

She gave him a conspiratorial grin. "I did consider it."

His crack of laughter echoed against the stonework. "I should have known you'd take matters into your own hands." He winked at her.

"I always do." She winked back. Ooh, where had that bit of sauciness come from?

His eyes grew warm like melted chocolate. He pulled his hand from his pocket and pushed a wayward curl behind her ear. "I'm pleased to see you're no longer wearing those ridiculous mourning colors. You look absolutely stunning in that color."

She glanced away and shrugged. "I decided you had a point. Perhaps it is time I stop wearing mourning colors." It was a good thing that he liked the lavender. He'd certainly be seeing it more often. It was one of the few gowns she still possessed that hadn't been dyed black or gray.

He rubbed his thumb against her cheek. Sparks ignited along Lily's nerves at the touch of his hand. She clutched at the balustrade as if it were a lifeline and swallowed convulsively. "Thank you," she whispered softly. "For the compliment . . . and the flowers."

"You're welcome," he whispered back.

Lily fought her shiver and glanced away. They stood that way, comfortably silent, for several minutes. Finally, Lily sighed. "I suppose I had better return. No doubt Lord Medford will be looking for me soon."

"I'm sure of it," Colton replied. "But you cannot blame Medford. You are the most beautiful lady here, after all."

Lily's head snapped around to face him. That was twice he'd said she was beautiful. Was it possible he really meant it? "You . . . you think I'm beautiful?" Her voice cracked and she immediately regretted the question.

His coffee-colored eyes caught and held hers. "I've always thought you were beautiful, Lily."

Her chest constricted. She couldn't breathe. She was suspended in time. It was as if five years had never happened. She was back on the balcony with him at another ball, another night. And then, like now, she'd looked up into his eyes, and parted her lips, hoping he would kiss her.

Colton's breath hitched and his face tightened. He set his empty glass on the balustrade, took her hand, and pulled her down the stone steps and out into the night. Before she could turn to face him, he'd pulled her into a shallow, shadowed cove where the other guests could not see them. His lips swooped down to capture hers.

The hot brush of his tongue coaxed her lips apart. The slide of his mouth against hers made heat well in Lily's belly. Yes, finally. Colton was kissing her, just like she'd always wanted. She sank against him and moaned deep in her throat.

Wait, no. What was she doing? This was not how this was supposed to happen. She shouldn't be enjoying this, shouldn't be wanting this, but her traitorous body was fighting with her bossy mind and somehow her body was winning.

Desperate to regain control, she raised her hand to push him away. He grabbed her wrist in his fist and pulled it back to her side, pinioning her to him. He hoisted her against his rock-hard body.

Her demand for him to stop never passed between her lips. Instead, she groaned and squeezed Devon's fist. As if sensing her surrender, he let go of her hand. She feathered her fingers up his chest, into his hair, clasping him to her.

He broke the kiss and slid his lips down the sensitive skin of her neck. Heat dashed down Lily's spine. Oh, God, she already knew . . . she loved it when he did that. A firestorm ignited in her belly, and every nerve in her body tingled. She breathed him in. An intoxicating smell. The barest hint of horse leather mixed with a light cologne. It teased her senses.

This was unlike any of the innocent kisses Colton had given her years ago. Back then, she'd been young, had foolishly believed in love. Their kisses had been considerate pecks, respectable and chaste. But there was nothing either respectable or chaste about this kiss. It promised more than Lily had ever imagined.

He was a drug. That's what he was. Like opium. A maddening, unhealthy pleasure that left her senses reeling. She hated herself for not pushing him away. His mouth moved to her earlobe and tugged on the sensitive skin there. Ooh, if she'd missed that, she would've hated herself more for pushing him away.

His hot, wet mouth was on her neck, her collarbone, raining little kisses that burned her skin like tiny flames. She tilted her head back, lost in a world of incomprehensible yearning.

Devon's lips moved to the tip of her chin, returned to her mouth. He kissed her cheeks, her nose, and finally, her closed eyes, before pulling her arms from around his neck.

She shuddered and let her eyes flutter open. Scared. Terrified of the feelings he'd evoked in her. No one knew what this man meant to her—*had* meant to her—and no one ever would, but it didn't excuse the fact that she'd just behaved like a shameless wanton.

Lily looked up at him. She was undone. She'd expected to see that cocky self-assurance that made her want to shake him. Instead, she saw the same uncertainty she felt. Devon Morgan shuddered also, and in his eyes, she recognized . . . she was dangerous to him too.

She drew a shaky breath.

"My compliments on your finesse," she whispered.

He eyed her carefully. His voice was soft. "What do you mean by that?"

She pressed a palm to her hot cheek. "You, trying to seduce me. A very good start, actually. Wh . . . what do you intend to do next?"

Devon raised an eyebrow slightly, and the quirk of his firm lips made Lily press her legs together tightly. "Well, that's an interesting question, isn't it? But I never give away my hand."

And just like that, his arrogant demeanor was back. The wall between them erected again.

Disappointment surged through her. Had it really been a game to him? Had he felt nothing when he'd kissed her?

She pasted a smile on her lips, steeling herself against showing how deeply he'd affected her. She was trembling again. "Come now, Colton, you must be ready to spill your secrets."

"Spill my secrets? Hmm. Perhaps *I* should write a pamphlet."

There went his brow again. And just as easily, she was wanting him all over again. Even knowing it was all a game to him, she couldn't help but wonder just what it would be like to be with him.

He walked around her then, in a circle, giving Lily the impression he was a panther stalking his prey. He towered over her, examining her. Confusion warred with desire in her chest. Only Colton could make her feel like this. God knew, her husband never had. She'd never felt this quickening of her pulse, this increase in her breathing, this tingle in her midsection.

Colton finished his perusal, and Lily expelled her breath.

"Hmmm. If I were seducing you, I would encourage you to drink," Colton said at last, stopping behind her, leaning down and whispering into her ear. The tiny hairs on her neck stood up as his warm breath murmured past. She squeezed her reticule, hoping he wouldn't notice her shaking hands.

"I don't drink," she informed him, swallowing convulsively.

"Yes, we've established that. I'm sorry to hear it. You really should try it. It calms the mind. Takes the edge off." He leaned in close and whispered right next to her ear. "Lowers inhibitions."

Lily closed her eyes. Suddenly, lowered inhibitions sounded oh, so tempting.

"What would you do next?" she asked, breathless.

Colton stepped in front of her and pushed a curl away from her cheek with his finger, which he allowed to linger near her mouth. He lifted the finger and traced it along her cheekbone. His rough thumb dragged along her bottom lip while his eyes captured and held hers.

She squeezed her eyes shut this time. Could he see the gooseflesh that had popped out on her neck and shoulders? Oh, she hoped not.

"And then?" she asked through parted, wet lips.

"I would offer you a seat." He pulled her hand, taking her along with him toward a nearby stone bench. Colton sat first and pulled Lily onto his lap. Pretty, whisper-pink April flowers cascaded out of a box behind them and nodded on Lily's shoulders. The moonlit garden with its shadowy nooks and twinkling candles suddenly seemed nothing if not exceedingly romantic. And full of promise.

Wrapped in his warm embrace, Lily wanted to melt. "Then what?" she asked, her heart pounding a heady rhythm in her chest. "What's your secret?"

She could *hear* his smile. That lazy, sensuous smile. His head was behind her, his voice sliding huskily into her ear. His fingers moved boldly over her scalp. Another wayward curl came loose from her chignon and he wrapped it around his finger. Lily closed her eyes, reveling in the feel of his hardness beneath her.

His voice surrounded her. "Then I would tell you"—his mouth brushed against her ear—"it's high time we return to the house."

Lily shivered as if a cold breeze swept by. "What?" she asked, unable to keep the disappointment from her voice. "Why?"

He leaned in close again. The delicious tickle of his warm breath against her neck sent hot flashes zinging to her most private place. "Because," he whispered, "the secret to seducing a woman, dear countess, is to make her think she's chasing *you*."

The hazy cloud of lust that had been obscuring Lily's mind evaporated in a flash. She leaped from his lap and swung around to face him. Straightening her skirts, she gave both kid gloves a vicious tug. Her reticule bobbed dizzily from her wrist.

"Nothing could be further from the truth. I am *not* chasing you." She pushed the traitorous curl behind her ear and squeezed her eyes shut, hating herself for getting caught up in his game. And that's all this was to him. A game. She needed money, security, and Colton offered neither. She could not allow herself to fall for a man who had promised to seduce her and wanted to punish her.

For a moment, Devon looked as if he might reach for her again, but he didn't.

Lily spun around and stalked back toward the house, not giving him a backward glance.

Colton's confident voice followed her through the darkness. "Not yet, Countess. You're not chasing me. Yet."

# CHAPTER 8

Devon eyed the shifty man who sat across the table. Gilbert Winfrey. An inveterate gambler. An inveterate scoundrel. And a more arrogant bastard Devon had never met.

"What's the matter, Colton? Too rich fer yer blue blood?"

Devon pushed back his coat and consulted his silver timepiece. Quarter past midnight. He'd been right on time. He'd left the Foxdowns' affair after his stimulating interlude with Lily, and made it here in plenty of time to lose to Winfrey.

Devon shook his head, trying to clear his mind of thoughts of Lily. What had that business in the garden been? He'd begun with his goal of seducing her and had allowed himself to get too caught up, almost forgetting what she was, nearly falling for that false look of innocence in her eyes.

She'd been the one to remind him, actually. *"My compliments on your finesse,"* she'd said. And thank God for it. Just like that, he'd remembered that nothing between them was real anyway. It never had been and it never would be.

She was part of a game he was playing. Just like a card game. Nothing more. She was no different than a jack or a queen or any of the cards that sat in a pack, waiting to be played at the precise moment. And just like when he was playing cards, he must remember to keep his wits about him while he sought his revenge against Lily.

Slipping the watch back into his pocket, Devon scanned the dingy room. His gaze returned to his opponent's swarthy face. "It's you I'm worried about, Winfrey. Do you have the money to back up that voucher?"

A hush fell over the crowd. Devon eyed the slip of paper Winfrey had tossed onto the gaming table. The beady eyes of the other men were fastened on him. They were not in the gentlemanly quarters of St. James, but the seedy backwater of the Rookery, that squalid part of London where only the vermin of society dwelled. True gentlemen rarely came here, and when they did, it was for a purpose. For the sort of gaming they couldn't play in Polite Society.

Devon had been here many times. Too many times. And the stink of the place, the unwashed bodies, the rotting food, the refuse in the streets, the smell of the poor and the hopeless, never seemed to leave his nostrils.

At least he'd put his time here to good use. Employing his skill with numbers, he'd parlayed the money he'd earned gambling over the years into investments that had brought him more wealth than he could spend in several lifetimes. He owned a fleet of ships and a hefty interest in the canal system. He'd rehabilitated the Colton estates and purchased additional properties. But, still, that wealth and security wasn't enough. There was something else he wanted.

"I've got the money, yer high-and-mighty lordship," Winfrey sneered. "Besides, yer memory's short, t'seems. I've heard ye're the one what usually walks away wit' ye pockets empty of late. Seems yer luck has run out. Can ye match it or not?"

Devon smiled, a completely humorless smile. A smile

intended to project confidence, a smile intended to scare that bastard Winfrey into shutting the hell up for a moment. Devon reached into his pocket and withdrew his own voucher.

One thousand pounds.

A fortune. Five times as much as Winfrey had bet.

Devon tossed the voucher on the table. "Not only match it. I'll raise it."

A sharp gasp and a murmur rippled through the motley crowd.

Devon kept his eyes trained on Winfrey. The man was dangerous. When confronted like this, he might make a scene to avoid the bet, he might accuse Devon of cheating, might even pull a knife. All of these things and worse had happened before in this place. Devon's booted leg bobbed up and down on the grimy floor. He waited. Carefully, watching.

Winfrey's soulless eyes narrowed on him. He sniffed repeatedly and wiped a hand devoid of a handkerchief across his bulbous nose. "I'll match ye," he ground out, nodding once.

A little, round man stood next to him. Winfrey grabbed the man by the coat and pulled him down to whisper in his ear. The little man wore filthy clothing including a dark gray cravat Devon could only guess had once been white. The smaller man's grin revealed a hodgepodge of black, rotting teeth. Devon fought his shudder. The man scampered away with an odd, helter-skelter limp.

"Me man is off ta fetch me voucher," Winfrey announced with a sour look on his face.

"My pleasure to wait," Devon replied, relaxing a bit. "Though you could forfeit and end this whole thing now." He eyed Winfrey's left hand where the man wore a large gold and garnet ring.

Devon's father's signet ring.

Winfrey's sharp crack of laughter bounced off the dirty, wooden walls. "Oh, ye'd like that very much, wouldn't ye, Colton?"

Devon narrowed his eyes. Yes, gentlemen only came to this part of town with a purpose. And Devon's purpose had always been to win. But he was biding his time. He normally played against cutthroats and gamers. The type of men who gambled with money they'd got from begging, stealing, or worse. And he always won. But Winfrey was different. Winfrey was the man who'd stolen his father's fortune. Winfrey was worse than a thief or a ringer. The man was truly dangerous, and Devon wasn't about to show his hand to Winfrey. Not yet.

Devon wasn't here for himself. Or even his blasted dead father who'd left all the Colton estates barren and the coffers completely empty, tarnishing the family name. No, he wasn't here for either of them. He was here for one reason and one reason only. Justin. He would do anything for Justin. Even this.

The small man soon returned with a voucher and Devon nodded once as Winfrey tossed it onto the table.

Two hours later, Devon snapped orders to his coachman to get him the deuce out of the Rookery. He relaxed back into his seat. Yes, that fool Winfrey was an inveterate scoundrel. And only too willing to tout his luck and skill at a game of chance.

Devon shook his head. He'd lost one thousand pounds today, but that was part of his plan. He was that much closer to being done with the entire detestable business. Almost. But not quite. There was one more game he had to play. One in which the stakes were much higher. It would be a game involving every thief and rook in town. Every cheat and sharp would crawl from his hole for this particular game, and Devon would be there with them.

The prize was five thousand pounds. A fortune to those scoundrels. The money meant little to Devon. He wanted only one thing.

The Colton signet ring.

And Devon would be at a disadvantage. He wasn't a cheat or a liar. He wouldn't kill a man for winning his money, or for looking at him the wrong way. But he did have one thing in his favor. The numbers. They flowed through his brain and translated into decision-making in card games as quickly as the murky water flowing through the gutters. Yes, he was gifted, but if only he wasn't. He might not have been forced into this detestable pursuit in the dank belly of the Rookery in the first place.

Devon expelled his breath hard, trying to rid his nose of the awful stench. A sweet memory assaulted him. Lilies. His wayward thoughts turned to the countess.

A spark of excitement flickered in his chest. A challenge. One that compelled him more than any game of cards ever would. If Miss Templeton had been a simple game of spades, Lily was the most challenging game of faro. Kissing her tonight had been unholy torture. One he hadn't expected. It rattled him. Revenge was his game, not lovemaking. And he'd do well to remember that.

Devon's coach pulled to a stop in front of his town house. The coachman let out the stairs, and Devon bounded down them and jogged up to the house. Tonight, he needed sleep, but he would be going out again tomorrow evening. He must tell his valet to prepare his evening clothes. He was feeling quite lucky of a sudden. It was time to play the next card in his game against Lily.

# CHAPTER 9

"I heard she wrote the pamphlet to scare away the young ladies from the most eligible bachelors. To give her sister a better chance on the marriage mart," Lady Hathaway whispered behind her fan.

"I heard she's set her sights on Lord Medford. It's not a wonder she spends her time with him. The man positively drips with money," Lady Montebank replied with a twittering laugh.

"I have utterly failed in my many attempts to procure a copy of the pamphlet. Do you have one?" Lady Hathaway replied.

Lady Mountebank shook her head. "Perhaps we should ask Lady Merrill for a copy."

They both erupted into gales of laughter.

Lily backed away from the corner where she'd been standing. Thankfully, the other ladies hadn't noticed her. She'd been overhearing such unpleasantness more and more lately. And what nonsense! She'd written the pamphlet for the civic good, the public education of young, unwitting females. Nothing more or less. She'd been trying to *help*, for heavens' sake. And of course, the money was a definite boon.

She cut a wide path around them, giving both ladies a tight smile. They eyed her with knowing looks. Devon was right. The entire *ton* did suspect she was the author of that pamphlet. But as long as they didn't know for sure, she and Annie were quite safe.

Lily wandered into Lady Hathaway's dining room and took her seat at the long table. She eyed the occupants of the room warily. Everywhere she went, someone was talking about that pamphlet. Who would be the next to broach the subject? It was merely a matter of time. It plagued her as though she were the fox and it, the hound.

She'd come to the Hathaways' tonight for the free meal, to get out of the house, and, ah . . . very well, to see Devon Morgan. There. She could admit it to herself. It wasn't so bad. The truth was, she couldn't stop replaying that kiss in her mind. Over and over again, it haunted her. Had it been a figment of her imagination? Had her memories of him combined to make her think she was falling for him all over again? Surely, it was a blight in an otherwise orderly game of cat and mouse. And tonight she intended to prove it.

She wanted another kiss. She needed another kiss, to prove to herself the first one had been nothing more than an aberration. But this time, *she* would be doing the kissing.

Her gaze scanned the dinner table. Directly across from her sat one empty seat. Meant—so her hostess had informed her—for the Marquis of Colton. Lily couldn't take her eyes from the vacant chair. She glared at it, as if by sheer force of will, she could make the absent marquis appear.

"Lovely weather we've been having this year," Lord Tinsdale said from her right.

Lily turned toward the elderly man and allowed the ghost of a smile to play across her lips. She let out a sigh of relief. At least Lord Tinsdale wasn't discussing the blasted pamphlet. "Yes, lovely," she murmured.

Lord Tinsdale shook his head. "It's a wonder it doesn't rain fire and brimstone all over the city what with this hideous pamphlet being bandied about as if it's acceptable reading material."

Lily smiled at him wanly and stabbed her fork into her fish. If one more person made a remark about that pamphlet, she would hurtle her stuffed kippers at his head. And she was a fine shot, actually.

"My apologies for both my tardiness and arriving in such a condition."

Lily snapped up her head. She glanced toward the entrance to the dining room to see Colton bowing over Lady Hathaway's hand. That lady giggled and murmured something sweet and accommodating. When he straightened to his full height, Colton's brown eyes captured Lily's. What was that dark shadow on his chin?

In a few long strides, he was at his place, escorted by Lady Hathaway. And Lily struggled to pull her gaze from him.

"Pardon?" she stumbled over her reply to Lord Tinsdale. "Oh, yes, no doubt it has been even more unseasonably cool in Bath this year."

Colton slid into his seat and Lily's skin crackled, every nerve in her body aware of him. She dared a glance and did a double take. "What's happened to your face?"

She cringed. It was insufferably rude of her to say such a thing, especially since the man had barely taken his seat. No greetings had been exchanged. But she couldn't help it. Colton was sitting there, looking unbearably handsome as usual, with a dark bruise on his jaw. Come to think on it, his hair looked mussed and there were what appeared to be flecks of blood and streaks of dirt on his shirtfront.

"My apologies." He bowed his head toward her. "I'll spare you the details, but suffice it to say I was involved in an unfortunate altercation on my way here. I would have returned home to change my clothing, but I was loath to miss your company for even one more moment, Lady Hathaway." He turned his attention back to their hostess who giggled and blushed.

Lily rolled her eyes. Ah, now she understood. The man could not stop gambling for even one evening. "Unfortunate altercation? I suppose that's one way to put it. But gaming hells are hardly the safest institutions, are they, Colton?" She smirked at him from behind her water glass.

Devon's eyes bored into her. A footman rushed to fill Devon's wine glass and he took a sip. "Indeed they are not, Lady Merrill, but I'm at a loss as to understand how *you* would know such a thing."

Lily sucked in her breath between clenched teeth. The cad. How dare he imply she had ever been to a gaming hell?

Lady Hathaway looked as if she might wring off her hands. Lord Tinsdale looked as if he might choke on his kippers.

Lily narrowed her eyes on Colton over a plate filled with watercress sandwiches. "You appear to be the worse for wear, my lord. You weren't accused of cheating, were you?"

All chatter at the dinner table stopped. All eyes turned to watch. Lady Hathaway looked as if she might swoon.

"Cheating?" Colton replied, his voice smooth and calm. "No. Personally I've found cheating to be the stronghold of perfidious females and men who are much worse card players than I."

The occupants of the dinner table let out a collective sigh and resumed their chatter. Lily took another sip of water. Perfidious females? What the blast did he mean by that? And everyone knew he was a hideous card player. Just like his father, the man had lost every shilling he'd ever gambled in St. James.

Lord Tinsdale cleared his throat uncomfortably. "Yes, well, deuced glad to see you're not hurt worse, Colton."

Lady Hathaway seized upon the segue in the conversation to return to her own seat, looking relieved to escape her two quibbling guests.

Devon made himself comfortable, exchanging pleasantries with the other occupants of the table, while Lily did her best to ignore him. And to think she had actually been contemplating kissing him tonight. There was no need. The man was nothing but a money-obsessed gambler. His revered title might continue to afford him entrée to the best houses in London, but he was no more than a common rook as far as she was concerned.

As the night wore on, Lily spoke merrily with Lord Tinsdale and the other guests all the while studiously avoiding Colton's gaze. She could feel his dark eyes on her, evaluating her, watching her, but she did not return his interest. And she would not.

After the meal was cleared, she quickly excused herself to join the other ladies in the salon. She tossed her napkin on her chair and didn't so much as glance back at Colton, but she knew he watched her leave.

Lily drifted into the salon feeling vaguely dissatisfied with the entire evening. She'd expected things to go so differently, and then Colton had to arrive with a pummeled jaw, reminding her what a blackguard he was. She took a seat in a chair in the corner and only halfheartedly listened to the conversation floating around her. That is, until the talk turned to the Marquis of Colton.

"Did you hear?" Lady Cropton asked. "The marquis saved a man's life tonight."

"What's that?" Lady Hathaway descended upon the settee and Lily scooted her own chair a bit closer.

"Yes. McAllister just arrived and said Lord Colton stopped a robbery in progress on the way here tonight. Sent the crooks running and saved the poor man they'd nearly bludgeoned to death."

"Oh, my. Colton was alone?" Lady Hathaway asked, her hand gripping her chest.

"Yes," Lady Cropton replied. "Quite alone. And there were three of them. Apparently, he intervened at great risk to his personal safety."

Lily's face fell. She felt vaguely nauseated. Colton hadn't been gambling tonight after all. And she'd all but accused him of cheating. In public. She'd been unspeakably rude. Her face heated with shame. Apparently, he'd got into a fight trying to save someone. He could have been killed. Why did that man have such a death wish?

The women were all atwitter over Colton's bravery and good looks, giggling and laughing. The matrons had turned into schoolgirls. No matter his faults, Colton was a Society favorite.

"He may be penniless," giggled Lady Mountebank, "but I'd certainly overlook it if I were twenty years younger and unmarried."

"Oh, Louisa, you are *bad*," Lady Hathaway said, slapping at Lady Mountebank's arm.

That was it. The talk of Colton set Lily's nerves on edge. She had to get away and think clearly. She jerked herself out of her chair, wrapped her arms around her middle, and rushed from the room. She may have seemed inexcusably rude, but at the moment, she didn't care.

Colton. Colton. Colton. She had to escape that name.

She hurried down the corridor and turned the corner. When she came upon a small salon, she glanced inside. Dark and empty, thank heavens. Moving silently into the quiet room, she pushed the door shut behind her, leaned back against it, and closed her eyes. Thankful for the solitude and silence.

Moments later, the aroma of a fine cigar hit her nostrils. Lily's eyes shot open.

"Good evening, my lady. Dare I hope you were looking for me?"

# CHAPTER 10

Lily blinked, not quite believing it. Once her eyes adjusted to the darkness, she saw him. The Marquis of Colton was lounging on the settee. A cheroot hung from his lips and its smoke swirled in the air above him, forming a ghostlike pattern in the darkness. From the light of the sole flickering candle in the corner, Lily could see he had one long leg encased in black superfine trousers draped across the settee and the other was bent at the knee. One hand rested beneath his dark head and the other lay still at his side.

"Get out of here," she snapped.

He plucked the cheroot from his lips. "Did it escape your notice that I was here first?"

Lily pushed herself away from the door. He was right. She was being rude, yet again. "I'll leave then." She cracked the door, intending to flee, when his deep voice penetrated the darkness again.

"If privacy is what you are after, there is nowhere else. The men are in the study, the women in the salon, and you and I are here. Unless you intend to sit on the back stoop with the cook, you are trapped with me."

Lily bit her lip. The choices did seem grim. She couldn't face the laughing, chattering women any longer, and of course she could not join the men in the study. "I'll go home, then."

She wasn't one step out the door when his mocking laughter reached her ears. "Scared of me, are you?"

Scared? Scared? She wasn't *scared* of anyone. She was a grown woman, not a silly little girl afraid of the dark.

Without saying a word, she moved back into the room and shut the door behind her. She made her way to the large leather chair next to the settee.

"You don't frighten me, Colton. I'll stay. But do not speak to me. I'd like some peace and quiet."

Her only answer was a puff of smoke and then, "It was both peaceful and quiet here before you arrived."

She snorted and collapsed onto the seat. She leaned back and closed her eyes. Several seconds passed in which neither said a word. A comfortable silence, really.

"It's insufferably rude of you to continue to smoke that thing in my presence without asking if I object."

A short laugh. "You told me to remain silent, did you not?"

A delicate grunt. For heaven's sake, she needed to stop being so mean. "How have we managed it, Colton? Five years in the same town without seeing each other?"

The smoke puffs stopped. "I've seen you. I just haven't spoken to you."

Lily smiled in the darkness. "The same for me," she admitted with a sigh. "I have seen you at various events. I managed to successfully avoid you. However, it seems my streak of luck is decidedly at an end."

Devon sat up, the cheroot still dangling from his perfect mouth. "I admire your honesty. I thought for a moment you would pretend as if you hadn't seen me."

She shrugged. "Why pretend? I nearly broke my foot at the Wentworths' fete last spring fleeing from you and Lord Ashbourne when you entered the ballroom."

His crack of laughter echoed off the wood walls. "I thought I saw a flash of gray streak past."

Her eyes widened. "You did not!"

His white teeth flashed in the darkness. "No, I'm only jesting. But I do admit, I've done my best to avoid you."

Lily propped her elbow on the arm of the chair and rested her chin in her palm. "You were always with a bevy of beautiful women."

He pulled the cheroot from his lips. "Why, Countess, is that wistfulness I hear in your voice?"

"Absolutely not!" She hid her smile behind her fingertips.

Devon turned his head to face her. "You were always wearing mourning clothes and looked so unapproachable."

"I suppose that's true." Lifting her chin, she fluttered her hand in the air between them to dispel the smoke.

He sat up and crushed out his cheroot in a nearby tray. "Not to mention you've always got that sop Medford at your heels."

Lily raised a brow. "What exactly is your quarrel with the viscount?"

"He *irritates* me."

"He's a very good friend."

Devon turned to her, an intent look in his eye. "They say his fortune is the reason for your friendship. Is there any truth to that?"

Lily pressed her lips together. "Now who is being rude? They *say* a great many things. Medford and I have been friends for years. Besides, if money were the main factor in determining with whom I spend my time, how would *they* explain my being here with you?"

Devon inclined his head. "Well played."

"Gossip concerns me very little, Colton. As long as my sister isn't maligned, I couldn't care less what is said about me."

"Obviously, or no doubt you never would have written your infamous pamphlet. It's all anyone can talk about, or so I'm told. Is that why you left the company of the other ladies tonight?"

Lily rolled her eyes. "No. Tonight I was running away from something else entirely."

"What?" He moved forward on the settee, closer to her.

Lily cracked half a smile. "You wouldn't believe me if I told you."

"Try me."

She folded her arms across her chest and eyed him with a raised brow. "I was running away from you."

"The devil you say." His white smile flashed in the darkness again.

"Well, talk of you, at least. You and your heroics were the topic of conversation and I could not take it any longer."

He laughed. "My apologies. And here you've run smack into my arms."

She swallowed, and the silence spoke volumes.

Devon stood and moved over to the sideboard and poured a drink. When he returned to the settee he held out a glass to her. "My lady?"

She shook her head. "Did you forget that I do not drink?"

He dangled the glass in front of her. "I'd hoped you'd changed your mind."

Lily shrugged. "I have not."

Devon cracked a smile. "Are you sure? It's guaranteed to make the discussion of me more tolerable. Let alone being in my actual company. Take it."

Lily politely took the drink, but carefully set it on the side table next to her. "As to that, I apologize for assuming you were gambling. And for being so rude."

"Apology accepted." He sat back down on the end of the settee facing her, so close his knees nearly brushed hers.

She cleared her throat but didn't move away. "But you really shouldn't gamble so much."

"Really? How much is that?"

She couldn't quite decipher the look on his face. "At all, frankly. It's a detestable habit."

"Agreed. I lost a thousand pounds last night."

Lily's chest constricted. A thousand pounds? Lost? Here she'd been praising him for his selfless act to a stranger, but she hadn't missed the mark after all. He had been gambling, as recently as last night, and losing exorbitant sums of money. Oh, what she couldn't do with one thousand pounds! Thank God, Colton had just reminded her what a blackguard he was. She'd do well to remember it the next time she forgot the kind of man he really was.

"You think it humorous? To lose that amount of money on a game of chance?"

"No, I think it's a damn shame." He grinned. "But I hope to do better next time."

Lily clenched her fist and counted ten. There was no sense in arguing with a gambler. She'd pleaded with her father often enough to have learned that lesson well. "It will be such a shame when they throw you in debtor's prison."

Colton snorted. "No doubt you'll be beside yourself with worry."

"You could always just stop, you know."

"I shall certainly take your words under advisement, Countess."

"No you won't. You'll do exactly as you wish. But will you please stop calling me 'Countess'?"

"That is your title, is it not? And a hard-won one, I imagine."

Lily rubbed her temples. A headache had begun to form behind her eyes. "You've no idea how hard-won it really was, but I cannot stand to hear you say it."

Devon took another sip of his drink. "Very well, Lily, I daresay we were on a first-name basis once. Call me 'Devon.' "

She smiled in the darkness. She'd expected mockery. Perhaps she'd expected him to double his use of the title, but he'd surprised her. Devon. Yes. She had called him "Devon" once and it seemed wonderfully familiar to her. Very well. She would call him that again.

"Devon, what exactly happened to you tonight? To give you that bruise?"

He braced his arms on the settee behind him and pushed a long leg out in front of himself. His leg moved through the two of hers and she squirmed. Oh, the man was improper. But she refused to let him see it bothered her.

"The details are unimportant," he replied. "I simply saw an injustice being done and decided to right the matter."

"With no concern for your own safety?"

"On the contrary, I always have a great concern for my own safety."

"That bruise on your jaw begs to differ."

Devon put two fingers to his chin. "Oy. Seems it hasn't quite stopped bleeding."

Lily's gaze snapped to his face. "Oh, no." She fumbled in her reticule for her handkerchief and moved quickly over to the settee, pressing the white cotton square against his chin, studying him closely. "Does your head hurt? Do you feel dizzy? Nauseated?"

Devon chuckled softly. "Who knew you were such a devoted nurse? And the look of concern on your face might lead me to believe you actually—dare I say—care?"

Lily let her hand fall away from his face. "Don't flatter yourself. I simply cannot stand to see anyone or anything hurt." She dropped her head to hide her blush. "I suppose that's why I'm known to take in a stray dog. Annie's the same way."

Devon slid his warm fingers under hers and lifted her hand, pressing the cotton to his chin once again. "By all means, continue your ministrations. It's been an age since anyone cared whether I was bleeding."

Lily kept her eyes focused on his chin, refusing to look him in the eye. She dabbed at the blood and peered at the bruise in the shadowy darkness, trying to ignore how good he smelled.

"It appears to have stopped bleeding," she reported after a few moments of careful study. "Of course, I cannot tell exactly due to the lack of light in this room. Let me light a lamp." She attempted to stand, but Devon's warm hand slid up her arm, pulling her back to the settee.

He studied her lips. "Don't do that."

"Why"—she swallowed, trying to moisten her suddenly dry mouth—"not?"

"I'm fine," he whispered.

"Are you quite . . ." Her voice caught and she closed her eyes, a tremor running through her body. "Sure?"

"Mmm-hmmm."

Lily sucked in her breath. She turned to move back to the chair, but it was too late. Devon's hand came up to stroke her cheek. His fingertips' rough slide along her soft skin was her undoing. That and the intoxicating smell of his light cologne and whatever else made him such a *man*. Her lips fell open of their own accord and Devon wasted no time. He tipped her head back and lowered his mouth, teasing her with his slowness. When his tongue met hers, a surge of lust shot straight through her body.

His hands moved up to cup her cheeks. His rough thumbs brushed across her cheekbones. Her lips tentatively touched his and the hot, wet warmth of his mouth made her shudder. One of his arms reached around her back, and in one swift maneuver, he pulled her atop him and lay back against the arm of the settee. She covered him, her light blue skirts fanned out across his legs, her chest heaving against his shirtfront, her mouth pinned to his.

She knew it was wrong and indecent and a hundred other things, but she didn't care. True, Lady Hathaway and God-knew-who-else might venture in at any moment and catch them in such an embrace. Nothing good could come of it, but at the moment all that mattered was his insistent mouth, his rock-hard body, and the promise of more. Oh, God, what he did to her when he kissed her neck.

Now that Lily was firmly situated atop him, Devon let his hands roam. Her shoulders, her back, her hips. He pulled her tight against him and reveled in the little moan that escaped her petal-pink lips. His mouth traced her temple, her forehead, her cheek, her neck. Finally his lips came back to tangle with hers. Their tongues intertwined, and Devon whispered against her ear, "Lily, I want you."

Lily's answer was to grab his shirtfront and pull him closer, her mouth never leaving his. Devon wasn't sure who exactly had taught her to kiss like that, but it couldn't have been her aging fop of a husband. Medford? He'd have to kill Medford.

The woman needed to write a pamphlet about how to leave a man half mad with one kiss. Her mouth was on his cheek, his temple, his ear.

Good God, she had his earlobe in her mouth and she was slowly driving him insane. He couldn't remember the last time he was so mad with wanting a woman. So half out of his mind and wanting to rip every shred of clothing from her body and take her to bed to prove to her what a pleasure it could be.

Lily moaned against his mouth and Devon knew he had to stop it, before he took her. Here. Right here on the settee in the middle of the Hathaways' dinner party. Not that he didn't want to, damn it, and not that she might not actually enjoy herself. But he couldn't do it. She didn't deserve it. He must remember his plan. To make her want him, make her ache with wanting him. Want to die with wanting him. He had her right where he wanted her. And he could make her want him even more. No, now was neither the time nor the place to exact his revenge.

With supreme effort, Devon dragged his mouth away and rested his forehead against hers. Their breath commingled. "Come to my house for dinner tomorrow night, Lily," he breathed.

Lily's eyes remained closed. Obviously, she was still wrapped in a web of lust. Her eyes slowly blinked open. "Wha . . . what?"

"Dinner. My house. Tomorrow night."

She pushed herself away from him a little, shaking her head as if to clear it from the fog of desire. "I cannot."

His finger traced her cheekbone. "Why not?"

Lily pushed against his chest with all her might this time and scrambled away from him. Once she was an arm's length away, she slowed her breathing and eyed him cautiously. "It's out of the question. Completely inappropriate."

He scrubbed a hand through his hair. "Inappropriate how? No one need know. My servants are discreet, I assure you. Besides, it's not as if you're still an innocent."

She cleared her throat, stood up, and moved toward the door. "No, no, no. I give you credit for a very valiant attempt at seducing me tonight, my lord. But you've failed, nonetheless." She straightened her shoulders and ran her hands down her gown, smoothing her clothing back into place. "I must be getting back to Lady Hathaway and the other ladies now. I'm sure they are looking for me. Good evening, Lord Colton." Without giving him a chance to say a word, she made her way toward the door.

"Lily, wait. There's something I must tell you—"

She didn't stop. "No," she murmured. She slipped through the door and pulled it shut behind her with a resounding thud.

Devon expelled his breath. Lily was frightened. Frightened by him. And rattled, no doubt, by that kiss. And she didn't like it one bit. He leaned back against the settee again, his hands beneath his head, and willed his overheated body to cool down.

Yes. She was rattled.

Good.

Lily desperately needed to be rattled. And he wasn't through rattling her.

Not yet.

# CHAPTER 11

Lily hopped into the rented coach and hastily pulled the creaky door shut behind her. She pressed her palm to her chest as if the sheer force of it could set her breathing to rights again.

That kiss.

It had been unforgettable. It replayed again and again in her head.

And to make matters worse, she couldn't stop thinking about Devon's dinner invitation. She was tempted. Oh, yes, she was tempted to accept. But it was all an act. He might seem friendly and approachable, but he was just trying to seduce her. Every moment she'd spent with him tonight had been calculated.

He'd admitted it himself. He'd just lost *one thousand pounds.* A fortune. The man was completely irresponsible. He was a destitute gambler. No wonder he was so desperate to marry for money. He wanted his wealthy fiancée back. That was all. If he was interested in Lily, it was because she was rumored to be wealthy. Or because he truly believed his seduction scheme would force her to write a retraction. Both thoughts were equally maddening.

She shook her head. It was lunacy, all of it. Nothing

good could come from spending more time with him. Consorting with that man was like playing with fire. She needed to find a way to secure a future for herself and Annie without succumbing to the charms of a penniless scoundrel like Devon Morgan.

When the coach pulled to a stop in front of her town house, Lily scrambled into the street and turned to hurry up the stairs. She'd barely gone two steps when she stopped short.

Annie was there, standing near the bottom of the stairs. She was leaning over the railing, giggling at a handsome young man. A young man who could not have been more than twenty-one years old.

Lily cleared her throat.

Annie straightened up and pushed a dark curl back into the bun atop her head. Her eyes darted back and forth and she bit her lip. "Oh, Lily, there you are. I didn't think you'd be home from the Hathaway affair until later."

"Yes." Lily hurried forth and pulled Annie up the steps by her arm. "I am home and you shouldn't be out alone at this time of night. What are you thinking?"

Annie continued to worry her lower lip, her gaze flitting to the young man. "Allow me to introduce Mr. Eggleston. Mr. Arthur Eggleston. Arthur, this is my sister, Lady Merrill."

Lily glanced at the young man and gave him a once-over. He was tall, handsome, and seemed to possess a modicum of charm as evidenced by the jaunty smile on his face. All quite dangerous for Annie. And for Lily's peace of mind. He'd straightened to his full height and cleared his throat. "My pleasure, Lady Merrill."

Lily's eyes shot daggers at her sister. "Annie, please go inside. I'll be in in a moment."

Annie gave her a desperate look, but she obeyed, glancing back longingly at Arthur, who wished her a good evening, bowed, and stared after her. Annie gave Arthur a last longing glance before she marched up the steps and into the town house.

Lily waited for the door to close behind her sister before she turned to the young man.

"Mr. Eggleston," she said with as much pleasantness as she could muster.

"Lady Merrill," Arthur replied with a nod.

Lily crossed her arms over her chest and stared Mr. Eggleston down. "You must know it's completely inappropriate for you to be speaking to my sister alone in the middle of the night."

"Well, I—"

She gave him a tight smile. "If you do it again, you'll live to regret it. Do I make myself clear?"

Mr. Eggleston went pale. "Oh, yes, yes. I'm very sorry, Lady Merr—"

Arms still crossed, Lily drummed her fingertips along her elbows. "My sister tells me you've already asked for a dance at her debut."

His nod was much too enthusiastic. "I do hope you don't mind, Lady Merrill."

"Yes, well, I do. Very much. Annie has a very different idea about her debut than I do and I find it exceedingly inappropriate for you to be addressing her and asking for dances before you both are even formally introduced."

Arthur tugged at his cravat. "I understand, Lady Merrill. It's just that—"

"I shall trust that you'll see to it that you behave with more discretion in the future. Good evening, Mr. Eggleston." Giving him a dismissive nod, Lily stomped up the stairs, slipped inside the house, and shut the door behind her with a reverberating crack.

Annie was hovering in the foyer. "What did you say to him?" she asked in a high-pitched voice.

Lily's heart sank at Annie's lovesick expression. "That young man is lucky I don't sic Leopold on him."

Hearing his name, Leopold bounded up to greet them. Evans, sitting on his usual perch, shook himself awake, nodded briefly to the foyer's other occupants, and took himself to bed.

After bidding the butler good night, Lily glared at Annie and opened her mouth to speak.

Annie put up a hand. "Before you lecture me, I know something you'll want to hear."

Lily pulled her gloves from her fingers and gave her sister a dubious glare. "I highly doubt that. Now, listen—"

"Mr. Eggleston told me Miss Templeton's mama is positively beside herself since she cried off from the marquis."

Lily shut her mouth abruptly. For the first time, the spark of jealousy hit her. Devon was trying to seduce her, but was he also still courting Miss Templeton? Attempting to woo her back? And what did he see in Miss Templeton, anyway? Other than her ostentatiously large dowry, of course.

Lily blinked. "Beside herself? What else did he say?"

A sly smile lit Annie's face. "Mrs. Templeton has been pleading with Miss Templeton to reconsider."

Lily leaned in closer. "And did she convince her?"

"No, but she's said to be at her wits' end. It's expected to be just a matter of time before she persuades Miss Templeton to see reason."

Lily shook her head, dismissing the subject. Mrs. Templeton might be beside herself over her birdlike blond daughter, but Lily had a determined, curly-haired brunette to deal with. She couldn't allow Annie to change the subject.

"What do you think you were doing? You have absolutely no reason to be out on the front stairs, especially not in the middle of the night. What sort of a reputation do you think you'll get with behavior like that? And your debut two nights away!"

Annie shrugged. "It was nothing more than a harmless chat. Mr. Eggleston was on the other side of the balustrade from me the entire time."

Lily sighed. "Annie, that hardly matters and you know it. Well-reared young ladies are not out at all hours of the night speaking alone with strange gentlemen."

"He's not a strange gentleman. And I was only outside for a few moments." Annie gave her an exasperated glare and promptly turned away.

"I am your guardian, your sister. I am supposed to look out for you, ensure you don't ruin your reputation and—"

Annie whirled to face her. "My reputation? Your concern for reputation is quite ironic coming from the author of the most scandalous pamphlet of the decade."

Lily pinched the bridge of her nose. "That's a different matter altogether and you well know it. I did what I had to do in writing that pamphlet, but your reputation is of the utmost concern to me. Mr. Eggleston is not bchaving appropriately and I don't like it."

Annie threw up her hands. "Oh, you never made such a mistake as talking to a man late at night, did you, Lily? You're so perfect. You'd never do anything so unexpected as fall in love."

"Love?" Lily scoffed. "You don't know what you're talking about. You barely even know Mr. Eggleston and—"

Annie folded her arms across her chest and tapped her foot against the marble floor. "I knew you would say this when you met Mr. Eggleston. I knew it. You are so . . . so . . . *predictable,* Lily!" Annie turned and fled up the staircase.

Lily's shoulders slumped. She dropped her gloves, fan, and reticule on the table near the door and walked into the darkened salon. She collapsed on the edge of the settee and hung her head. How had this evening gone so wrong? When had everything become so complicated?

*Predictable.* Is that what she had become? Someone who held no surprise? No mystery? Well, what was wrong with that? Responsible people were predictable. Accountable people were predictable. And who wasn't predictable? Drunks and gamblers and silly young girls who believed in love. Being predictable wasn't half bad.

Lily propped her chin in one hand and with the other petted Leopold who'd jumped up to snuggle next to her.

What was she to do? She'd already sold off everything that belonged to her including her mother's jewels and her father's prized cigar box. The only other items of value at her disposal were part of Merrill's town house and they belonged to the new earl now. She'd rather live on the streets than disgrace herself by turning into a thief. Yes, things were very complicated lately. But there was no help for it. Annie's debut was her highest priority at the moment. For now, she had to find a way to make it through the next two days with what little money she had left from the sale of the flowers, and without succumbing to Devon Morgan's legendary charm.

# CHAPTER 12

"I've come, my lady, bearing the fruits of your labor." Viscount Medford strolled around the white salon where Lily sat in the center of the settee.

"What do you mean?" Lily was barely paying attention to her friend. She'd been mentally calculating how much money it would take to live out the rest of the Season in London.

Medford smiled at her, his bright hazel eyes sparkling. "Remember when you told me you wished you'd never written the pamphlet to begin with? If I recall correctly, 'confounded' was the word you used."

"How could I forget?" Lily answered, sipping her sugarless, creamless tea. She eyed her friend warily. What was he up to this morning?

Medford pulled a paper from his coat pocket and presented it to Lily with a flourish. "Ah, but I wonder if you will change your mind once you see this."

She snatched it from his hands and held it up to the light to inspect it.

"The last time we spoke, I believe you told me the pamphlet had brought you nothing but trouble," Medford said, still grinning.

Lily whispered. "A voucher for the sum of fifty pounds."

"Precisely."

"Made out to me," Lily continued, sucking in her breath.

"Exactly. Your share of the sales of *Secrets of a Wedding Night* to date."

Lily's hands trembled. She clutched the voucher to her chest. "This cannot be real."

"I assure you, it's very real. Koenig and Bensley tell me we've had every lady's maid in the city come to the printing shop asking for a copy of your pamphlet for their mistress. They come wearing draped hats and they don't allow their carriages to linger in the street too long. It's clandestine, my dear, make no mistake. Clandestine, but immensely popular."

Lily pressed the voucher to her chest more tightly. "I didn't write it to earn money."

"No, but you might as well reap the rewards."

She glanced away, biting her lip. Lily well remembered that day a few months ago. Medford had arrived at her house to pay a call and he'd brought a copy of the *Times*.

He'd had an inscrutable look on his face.

"What is it?" Lily had asked, beginning to be a bit concerned.

Medford cleared his throat. "You might want to look at page five."

Lily had taken the paper from him with cold, trembling hands. She knew page five. Page five contained engagement announcements. Her stomach dropped and she turned away from Medford, quickly shuffling open the pages until she found what she was looking for.

Her eyes scanned the parchment frantically until she saw it.

*Devon's engagement announcement.*

She turned back to face Medford, her smile probably

too bright. "Well, good luck to Miss Templeton, poor thing."

Medford had stepped toward her, but Lily stepped back. "Lily, I know how much he meant—"

Lily shook her head and turned away, swallowing past the lump in her throat and the unshed tears she refused to allow. "The girl has no idea what she's in for."

Medford, perhaps sensing she needed to make light of it, had shrugged. "Money meets title. It's a perfect *ton* match."

Lily tossed the paper onto the table, resisting the urge to scrunch the thing into a ball and fling it into the rubbish heap. "I'm quite serious. Miss Templeton has no idea. She's giving her life away to a man. Giving her *control* away to a man. And the poor girl doesn't even know it. Any more than any of those unwitting young women do."

Medford furrowed his brow. "What exactly do you mean?"

She tossed a hand in the air. "The young ladies making their debuts. All of them. They are at the beck and call of their fathers, men who are looking out for the best interests of other *men*. Who is there to warn these poor young women?"

Medford shrugged. "Their mothers?"

Lily rolled her eyes. "Hardly. Their mothers are part of the problem. They're on the men's side. Someone else needs to champion the young ladies. Or at least provide them with the facts. I spent my wedding night frightened half to death. I wish I could tell them. I wish I could shout it from the rooftops."

Medford narrowed his eyes, appearing to contemplate the matter for a few moments. "The rooftops might not be ready for such information, my lady, but there may be another way to get your message out. I just happen to know a certain nobleman who has recently invested heavily in a new form of printing press." He grinned. "My partners and I have published a few essays and the odd pamphlet to date, but just think how popular *this* subject would be."

Lily gave him a suspicious look. "What exactly do *you* mean?"

Medford snapped his fingers. "Think of it. *Secrets of a Wedding Night,* you could call it. There won't be an unmarried female in town who wouldn't give her eyeteeth for a copy. Why, I'll start the rumor of its existence at a finishing school and we'll be sold out by week's end."

Lily's eyes widened. "No. No, I couldn't possibly."

Medford gave her a wicked grin, one very few people knew he was capable of. "Why not?"

Lily bit her lip. "It would cause a scandal."

"Wouldn't be the first scandal this town's witnessed."

Lily contemplated him from the corners of her eyes. "I suppose that's true."

"C'mon, Lily. You said yourself, you'd be doing a public service."

A thrill shot through her. She tapped a fingernail against her cheek. "It would have to be anonymous, of course."

Medford nodded. "Goes without saying."

"And I mean for it to be informative, mind you, *not* indecent." Of course she hadn't mentioned to Medford that she hadn't anything indecent to write.

"Decency shall be our highest priority."

Lily winced. "Oh, I suppose it *will* cause an awful scandal."

Medford cracked a smile. "Oh, no doubt. But it cannot be as scandalous as Mr. Paine's pamphlet in America was many years ago."

Lily allowed a broad smile to sweep across her face. "Ah, yes, *Common Sense.* And may ours sell just as well!"

"Is that a yes?"

Lily held out her hand to him. "Lord Medford, I believe we have a bargain."

And the rest had been history.

Now, she glanced up at Medford who was staring at the voucher she held pressed to her chest.

His eyes searched her face. "If you need money, Lily, you know you have only to ask me."

Lily shook her head. She tried to laugh. "What makes you think—?"

Medford's voice was solemn. "I've seen the threadbare rugs. I've noticed you're no longer taking sugar in your tea. You adore sugar in your tea."

Lily swallowed and glanced away. "I'm fine. Truly. Besides, you're already doing me a large favor by hosting Annie's come-out ball. You're a true friend, Medford. I could ask no more from you."

"I've asked you a dozen times to call me 'James.' We're friends, Lily." Medford's probing hazel eyes did not leave her face. "I'm worried about you."

"Worried? About me? Whatever for?" She fluttered a hand in the air.

"You've been telling me for months you're fine, yet you've just welcomed fifty pounds as if it were the only thing keeping you from debtor's prison, and you've been spending far too much time lately with that good-for-naught Colton."

Lily laughed. "Now, there I shall agree with you, my friend. Any time I spend in Colton's company is too much. But I am quite capable of handling Lord Colton. Don't worry about me."

Medford looked suspicious. He crossed his arms over his chest and nodded toward the voucher still clutched to her chest. "And the money?"

Lily allowed a slow smile to spread across her face. Fifty pounds was a virtual fortune. But it would only last so long. A lesson she'd learned well enough over the last five years.

Yes, it might be indecent, what she was contemplating, and no doubt it was risky. But Lily no longer cared. For one thing, it was anonymous, even if people did suspect her, and for another, as a woman, Society had left her little choice.

"My lord, I have only one question."

"Ask it, my lady." Medford bowed to her formally. "Your wish is my command."

"What shall I write next?"

Medford threw back his head and shouted with laughter. "That's the spirit!"

# CHAPTER 13

*Boom. Boom. Boom.*

This time Lily recognized the blows on the door. The sheer volume of the knocks left her little doubt as to the identity of her caller. What did Colton want with her now? He'd already proved he could steal her breath with his kisses. What else was there? She needed to stay far away from him. She had begun to think he might actually have a chance at making good his threat to seduce her, were he allowed full rein.

And there was another complication. At present, she was sitting in the study with a bill collector. She'd just finished handing over a goodly amount of the money she'd received from Medford, and she was doing her best to rid herself of her visitor without parting with the remainder. Not to mention she would sink through the floor with embarrassment if Devon were to see the man and begin asking questions.

She stared at Mr. Hogsmeade's balding pate as he informed her she owed him another five pounds.

"We've provided you with a great deal of credit, Lady Merrill, in the name of your late husband," the round man said, "but now that you have failed to repay—"

"I understand perfectly, Mr. Hogsmeade," she replied, barely attending to his uncomfortable, practiced speech, a speech she'd heard so often she could recite it herself. "There is no need to worry. I have recently acquired an income and will get you the rest of what I owe by the end of the month."

She escorted the short man to the side door and breathed a sigh of relief when Evans indicated Lord Colton was already ensconced in the salon. That was close!

Lily kept Devon waiting for the requisite quarter hour. She sauntered into the salon as if she hadn't a care in the world, Leopold running around her heels. "My lord, I thought that was you trying to break down my door."

*Confound it.* Why did he have to look so dashing? Buckskin breeches, a white lawn shirt, chocolate polished Hessians, and windswept hair. Clearly, no good could come of him looking that way.

He bowed over the hand she presented him. "Ah, but you're mistaken, my lady. Had I intended to break down the door, it would not still be standing." His smile was downright challenging. "Where are the flowers I sent you?"

Lily nearly choked. "I . . . ah . . . I . . . we took them to the sick house."

He gave her a suspicious look. "The sick house?"

"Yes. I saw no need to let them wilt in the foyer when sick people could enjoy them." She cleared her throat. "Please. Sit."

He waited for her to sit first, of course, but instead of taking a seat in the chair she'd indicated, he slid next to her on the settee. She tried not to let him see it flustered her.

"To what do I owe the pleasure of your visit?" she asked in what she hoped was a nonchalant voice. To her chagrin, her voice cracked a bit at the end, but otherwise, good form.

"I've come, my lady, to ask if you would allow me to escort you on a ride through the park this afternoon."

Lily blinked. "A ride?"

"Yes."

"Through the park?"

"That is the customary location, is it not? Now, of course it's predictable that you'll say no, but hear me out—"

Lily heard one word, and one word only. "Predictable." She shot off the settee. "Very well, let's go."

She quickly moved toward the door, intent on gathering her cloak, bonnet, and gloves. Of course a ride in the park with Lord Colton was a bad idea. A very bad idea indeed. But she'd already declined his offer of dinner, and she refused to be *predictable.* Besides, if they remained here, another creditor might come to call.

Devon blinked a few times, obviously surprised by the ease with which she had capitulated, but he got himself together quickly and followed her out the door.

A new phaeton waited outside, a groom stood nearby, and two lovely sorrels pulled the thing. Lily nearly whistled as she marched down the steps toward it.

"Not bad, Colton," she whispered under her breath.

"What was that?" he asked, taking the steps two at a time to catch up to her.

"A fine bit of luxury for someone deeply in debt," she said. "The creditors won't take it from you while we're in the park, will they? I'd hate to have to walk all the way back home."

"Ah, Lily, so nice of you to be so preoccupied with my finances, as usual. I do appreciate your concern. I expect you have no such concerns for Lord Medford."

"You and Lord Medford are two *very* different men."

"Thank God," Devon spat out.

Lily raised a brow. "Why do you dislike Lord Medford so?" she asked as Devon helped her into the conveyance.

Devon rolled his eyes. "Let's just say we weren't exactly friends at school."

"Did something happen between the two of you?"

Devon grunted. "Nothing specific. He's just the kind of bloke whom everyone adores. He's too blasted perfect for my taste. Perfect breeding, perfect fortune, perfect manners, perfect . . . everything."

Lily hid her smile. "You mean he's the opposite of you."

Devon narrowed his eyes at her but the smile that lingered around his lips told her he wasn't truly angry.

She settled into the seat and arranged her skirts. Something squirmed near her ankles and she pulled up her feet sharply, stifling a yelp. "What's that?" She tentatively leaned down to have a look. A puppy jumped into her lap.

Lily squealed with delight. "Oh, good heavens. Devon, she is adorable!" She lifted the puppy, her thumbs under the dog's top paws, and examined her. An abundance of dark gray curls, with white patches around both eyes and at the tips of all four paws. "The spots make her look like a bandit," she said, still laughing.

Devon's face wore a bright smile. "Do you like her?"

Lily kissed the wriggly little animal on the top of her head. "Like her? Of course I do."

"I think she looks like an animal the Americans call a raccoon. Only her tail is much shorter."

Lily turned the puppy around to inspect her stubby tail, which was wagging so fast Lily thought it might fly off. "Yes, definitely not a raccoon tail, but otherwise, I'm quite certain she has raccoon in her lineage." The puppy spun around and licked Lily's face. She laughed. "Where did you get her?"

Devon nodded to the groom and told him to stay behind. Then he climbed up next to Lily, took a seat, and shook out the reins. "I found her, actually. That's what I was trying to tell you last night. The men I . . . dispatched, had this little ball of fur with them. I'm not sure what their plans were, to sell her no doubt, but I couldn't allow such blackguards to take her."

Lily squeezed the puppy close and tucked the dog's little head under her chin. "No, no, of course not."

Devon gave her an almost shy look that made Lily feel things she didn't want to examine.

"I thought you might take better care of her." He cleared his throat.

Lily gulped. "Me? You're giving her to me?"

"Do you want her?"

Lily smiled. "God knows if Annie ever discovered I turned down an animal in need, I'd never hear the end of it. But I'd no idea you have a soft spot for animals, Devon." She scratched the puppy's ears and the dog snuggled up happily into her lap. Ah, she'd just have to find the money to feed this little one somewhere.

Devon clucked to the horses and soon they were on their way into the park. "Like I said, I couldn't leave such an innocent with those scoundrels."

Lily smiled at that too. "You're nicer than you want anyone to think you are."

Devon gave her a mock-aghast look. "Please. Do not tell anyone. It would ruin my black reputation."

Once they passed through the gates of Hyde Park, Devon maneuvered along the foothills and valleys. Then he took the phaeton down a secluded little dirt path that ended underneath a bridge. Most secluded.

"Ah, so, this is more of your plot," Lily said. "Though I must admit this is quite the picturesque scene."

"My plot? I don't know what you're talking about. I merely thought you might enjoy the scenery. I thought we might take Bandit, here, for a walk."

Lily watched him warily from the corner of her eye. "It's lovely," she conceded. "And no doubt Bandit will love it." With one arm, she scooped up the puppy and allowed Devon to help her from the phaeton with the other. They walked along the bank and Lily let Bandit down onto the ground. The tiny dog hopped around and rolled in the grass, causing Lily to laugh and Devon to smile.

Lily slowed her pace and Bandit kept up beside them, stopping every few paces to roll around or sniff out some interesting smell.

"Where is Miss Templeton this afternoon while her fiancé is off with me?" Lily asked, unable to stop herself.

Devon's eyebrows shot up. "You know very well I am no longer affianced to Miss Templeton because of that pamphlet of yours."

Lily crossed her arms over her chest. "If you've asked me to go riding today in an effort to convince me to write a retraction, you're wasting your time. *If* I had authored the pamphlet, I would have no intention of writing a retraction. Your time would be much better spent looking for another wealthy young woman to marry. After all, you need to pay for that impressive phaeton of yours."

Devon turned to face her, his eyes so intent that she thought for the span of an instant he was going to take her face in his hands and kiss her. And God help her, she wanted him to. She closed her eyes. She leaned forward.

"Got you!"

Lily's eyes flew open just as Devon's hand closed around something on her shoulder. He jogged away a bit to the nearest tree, knelt down, and opened his hand.

"What was it?" Lily asked, brushing off her shoulders.

"Just a spider."

"A spider!" Lily twirled around in a frenzy, swatting at her skirts. Bandit barked and hopped around her ankles, clearly convinced her new mistress was playing some sort of fun game. In an effort to avoid hitting Bandit, Lily knocked herself off balance, tripped over a tree limb, and would have gone flying if Devon's arm hadn't snaked around her middle and stopped her fall.

His warm, strong hands set her upright and lingered on her hips.

"You're safe. I've got it," Devon said, his mouth hovering barely above hers.

Lily trembled at his touch. She stepped away and continued to swipe at her shoulders. "If one spider found me, his friends and family might not be far behind." She ran her hands across her arms and face and swooshed away the invisible spider, squirming the entire time.

"Settle down," Devon commanded with another chuckle. "I told you I got the thing. Don't worry."

"Don't worry?" she repeated, still brushing off her arms and her dress. "Do you know how much I *detest* spiders?"

"I thought you told me you couldn't stand to see anything hurt."

Lily shuddered. "Ugh. I make one exception and that is for spiders."

"They eat bugs."

"They have eight legs. Eight! It's unnatural."

"Their webs are quite amazing, actually."

"Death traps! Not to mention, they *jump*!" She didn't stop running her hands up and down her arms.

"Here now." Devon plucked her hands away. He brushed off her bonnet, her arms, and her back and led her over to a stone bench where they sat, somehow calming her and making her feel safe at the same time. Bandit hopped over, curled up beneath the bench, and soon was exhaling little puppy snores.

Lily took a deep breath and gave a self-conscious laugh. "I suppose you think I'm a complete ninny now, but you haven't any idea how much I detest those creatures."

"Yes. I do." Devon smiled. "I remember your reaction at the Medleys' picnic five years ago. I've never seen such a sight. One would have thought a wild boar was after you."

Lily stopped squirming. "You remember that?"

"I daresay all company present remembers that. You carried on as if you were being chased by a pack of wild hounds."

Lily winced. "Ah, well, yes. It's always rather been a flaw of mine, being frightened of spiders, that is. I believe I am quite brave when it comes to many things, but spiders scare me senseless."

"So I've gathered," he said with another knee-weakening smile.

Lily straightened her shoulders and cleared her throat. She patted the top of her bonnet self-consciously. "Yes. Well. Thank you very much for dispatching the blackguard."

He nodded. Once. His lips twitched suspiciously. "You're most welcome."

"That was awfully nice of you," she conceded. "To remove it without alerting me to its presence, that is."

"No more thanks necessary."

They sat in silence for several minutes and Lily once again had the thought that it was a comfortable silence. Not one that seemed awkward, needing to be filled like it was with so many of her suitors or other acquaintances.

Lily leaned over to watch Bandit sleep. Then she shut her own eyes and let the spring wind blow across her cheeks. She breathed in the air that was always so much better in the park and she opened her eyes to watch water flow beneath the bridge. Devon seemed perfectly content to take in his surroundings too.

The water trickled beneath the bridge. The air floated by smelling of spring flowers. The green grass waved in the wind. Lily watched the outline of the phaeton in the distance. She sighed. Ah, how wonderful it felt to be sitting in the warm sun next to a handsome man. If only love really did exist. If only she didn't have to care about money or responsibilities. If only the world was . . . perfect. In such a world, perhaps she could be his.

She shook her head. But it did no good to think such useless thoughts. Instead, she broke the silence. "So, you just stopped by today to give me Bandit and take me riding in the park, is that it?"

Devon cracked a smile. "Why, Lily, what are you implying?"

She shrugged. "I'm a bit wary of you, I suppose. What with your promise to seduce me."

Devon slid his warm hand over her cold one that lay in her lap. He covered her fingers with his and squeezed. "Don't worry. I'm hardly trying to pounce on you now, am I? What sort of finesse would that exhibit?"

She stared into the depths of his dark eyes. She swallowed. "What if I told you I would be disappointed if you didn't try something this afternoon?"

Good heavens. Why had she said that? Clearly, sauciness was her new style.

The hint of a smile played around Devon's lips and he lifted his hand and pushed a curl under her bonnet. The brush of his thumb against her cool skin sent a shudder down her spine. He must have noticed.

"Disappointed, eh?"

She nodded. Her mouth fell open and she wet her bottom lip with her tongue. Devon's eyes were riveted to the spot.

"We can't have that now, can we?"

She shook her head, knowing she shouldn't encourage him. But right now she wanted to kiss him more than anything else in the world. Consequences be damned.

His mouth descended toward hers so slowly Lily wanted to sob. She nearly moaned when his warm lips finally touched hers. The contact was almost unbearable. It was the softest, smoothest, least aggressive kiss he'd ever given her. It demanded nothing from her and made her feel more than all the other kisses combined.

His tongue barely brushed into her mouth, his lips plied hers without any force, but they were still strong and wonderful. He kept his hands at her hips but didn't try to pull her toward him or make any other movement. And it drove Lily insane like she'd never imagined possible. She wanted to grab him, kiss him, lie atop him like she did in the library last night. She wanted . . . more.

And then it struck her. Devon was challenging her with this kiss. Showing her he had no intention of forcing himself upon her. If they continued this, it was a choice both of them were making.

Seduction, she thought wistfully, was an art form after all. And she was kissing the master artist.

When Devon's lips left hers, Lily was shaking. The kiss hadn't been enough. It promised everything but gave little. She exhaled deeply.

Devon rested his forehead against hers. "Come to dinner. My house. Tonight," he whispered.

Lily didn't open her eyes, but she continued to rest her forehead against his. "No."

"Why not?" He kissed the side of her lip. Her cheek. Her closed eyes. Her forehead.

Her will weakened with each touch. "You really think it is such a good idea?"

"It's only dinner." Another kiss.

"Oh, it's much more than dinner, and you know it."

He ran his roughened thumb over her bottom lip and Lily shuddered. "I have every confidence you can resist my charms." He smiled. "Don't you?"

Lily exhaled a shaky breath. She nodded a nod she didn't believe.

He kissed her lips again. So softly. "Is that a yes?"

Lily sighed. Devon had given her an adorable puppy and he'd saved her from a murderous spider. Both things were exceedingly kind of him.

Very well. She was going to say yes, for two reasons. First, if she refused his offer, there was every chance he would call her "predictable" again. And second, despite herself, she was charmed by the gentler side of Devon. The kinder side. And she wanted to see more.

Apparently even dissolute, drinking gamblers could have a compassionate side.

Her voice shook when she answered him. "I'll come." She kissed him this time. "But only because you weren't expecting it. I take great pleasure in surprising you."

He smiled against her cheek and rested his lips on her temple. "I'll expect you around nine o'clock. By all means, surprise me."

# CHAPTER 14

"Tell me you are jesting." Devon threw a stiff upper cut to Jordan Holloway's jaw.

Jordan's head snapped back, but he recovered quickly and grinned at his friend. They continued to round each other. The two men were boxing in the ballroom of Jordan's town house. It was a pastime they both enjoyed. Being equally matched, they were challenged by fighting each other.

"I'm afraid I'm entirely serious," Jordan returned, striking out at Devon's right cheek but missing when Devon ducked. "Good form."

"What are the odds up to?" Devon asked next, bobbing.

"Five to four last time I checked. You'll be pleased to know they are in your favor."

Devon's eyebrow shot up. "Barely. How exactly did anyone find out about my challenge to Lily?"

Jordan shrugged and flashed an innocent grin. "I may have mentioned it. It's been bloody dull around here for months. This is just the sort of sport this Season needed. The rake versus the ice queen. It's perfect. Don't worry, old chap, I bet on you."

Devon pulled his roundabout. His fist fell to his side. "How am I to explain to Lily she is the subject of a bet at Brooks's?"

Jordan cracked a smile. "Not just a bet, a scandalous bet. A bet that you will seduce the author of *Secrets of a Wedding Night* before the house party at the Atkinsons' estate."

"The entire thing is ridiculous."

Jordan struck at Devon again. This time his fist met his friend's face. Devon stumbled back, but quickly recovered. "Are you jesting?" Jordan asked. "I thought you'd be delighted. If you win, you stand to gain a considerable amount of money, and you'll be shaming Lady Merrill at the same time. You'll have a much easier time convincing her to write a retraction if you succeed."

Rubbing his newly injured jaw, Devon stepped out of the area they'd designated for their match. He grabbed up a towel he'd left on a nearby chair and wiped his face. Jordan followed, his brow wrinkled.

Devon flexed his bruised knuckles. "I don't relish the whole town being in my bloody business. Not to mention, what Lily will do when she finds out. Seduction is a delicate art. If she discovers there's a bet in the works, she's bound to take it amiss, don't you think?"

Jordan rolled his eyes and grabbed up his own towel. "Who gives a damn? That woman has brought you nothing but grief. This will be the perfect revenge."

Devon considered it all for a moment. He would probably win the bet. He was counting on it actually. But not for money. Never for money. The thought didn't sit well with him.

"If you win the money from the bet, you won't have to play in the tournament in the Rookery," Jordan said.

"Money has nothing to do with my playing in the tournament. There's more to it than that," Devon countered.

When Jordan flashed him a questioning look, he added, "The ring."

"You've got more money than the prince. Why don't you just buy another ring?"

Devon shook his head. "Ashbourne, you'll never understand. You've got no respect for titles or bloodlines."

Jordan wiped his towel across his forehead and tossed it over his shoulder. "I've got no respect for outdated rules, and baubles that aren't worth the trouble. But if it's so important to you, fine. Play in the tournament *and* win the bet. If you bet on yourself you'll be twice as wealthy."

Devon set his jaw and stretched his arms above his head, loosening his sore muscles. "You don't understand. I don't want Lily to—"

Jordan snapped the towel to the floor. "Good God, man. What is there to understand? The woman made a fool of you five years ago. She married an old man and tossed you over. You said yourself she only cares about money. Once she learns you're rich, no doubt she'll show you interest again. And won't it be sweet when you can toss *her* over this time?"

Devon scrubbed a hand through his wet hair. Lily was coming over tonight. He could have this seduction business over with. Take his revenge. "The thought has crossed my mind a time or two," he admitted.

"That's the spirit!" Jordan clapped Devon on the shoulder. "The woman doesn't stand a chance. I've no doubt you'll find the perfect opportunity to win that bet."

Devon draped the towel around his neck and tugged hard on both ends. A twinge of guilt shot through him. He shook it off and clenched his jaw. Jordan was right. This was his chance to teach Lily a lesson. He would take it.

# CHAPTER 15

Lily looked up at the façade of the marquis' town house and gulped. The gracious four-story building sat on Upper Brook Street near the park, a beautiful black-lacquered door with a gold number nine fastened to it.

She pressed her gloved hand to her belly to still the butterflies. She still wasn't entirely sure how Devon had managed to convince her to come to dinner. The kissing, the intimacy, the spider rescue, they'd all been too much for her. And anyway, wasn't she acting like such a prude? It's not as if a dinner translated into a night of unbridled passion in each other's arms. Though the thought did steal her breath away if she were being completely honest.

And it made no sense!

Men were to be avoided, carefully watched, kept at arm's length. But the truth was, when Devon touched her, kissed her, all she could think about was being close to him.

Why exactly had she thought this was a good idea? Staring up at Devon's beautiful home, she was convinced it was not. She turned away, about to take the first step back to the rented coach, when the butler opened the door.

"Lady Merrill?"

She turned around slowly, biting her lip. "Yes."

"Lord Colton has been expecting you."

Lily nodded, swallowed the lump in her throat, and allowed the butler to usher her into the grand foyer. He took her cloak and Lily couldn't help but think the formal man would never fall asleep on the job the way poor Evans did.

She scanned the dark cherries and mahoganies of the foyer. Her gaze came to rest on the luxurious carpets, the delicate French wallpaper, and the shiny silver candlesticks. An immaculate home. An elegant home. How was it that Colton could afford such fine things? Nothing seemed to be worn or shabby here. The man obviously lived on an outlandish amount of credit no doubt given to him by idiotic merchants who were eager to be linked to his illustrious name.

The candles were made of real beeswax, and they were long tapers, not the inexpensive bits she often sported around her own home. The furniture was all smartly polished and not a bit of the wallpaper was peeling as far as she could see. And she looked. Closely.

She narrowed her eyes. Was it possible Colton wasn't the spendthrift and wastrel she thought he was? Was it possible he had money after all? She shook her head. No. Gamblers and drinkers were all the same. They didn't stop until they hurt everyone around them, until they spent everything they had, exhausted their credit, and ended up with nothing. No doubt, Devon's day of reckoning was drawing near.

Lily was escorted into a lovely salon decorated in hues of blue. The butler offered her a drink. She hesitated a moment before declining. This night, of all nights, might just call for a bit of spirits. But no, she would not allow Colton to drag her down into his den of iniquity. Not entirely, at least.

She'd waited only a few minutes before the doors

opened and Colton strolled in. Looking relaxed, handsome, and dangerous all at once. He bent over her proffered hand. "Welcome, Lily," he said in a voice that made her tremble.

"Thank you for the invitation, my lord."

"You are most welcome." He poured himself a glass of wine. "Are you sure you won't have a drink?"

She shook her head at the wine glass he offered.

Devon swirled the liquid in his glass and took a sip. "I must admit I half expected you to cry off at the last minute. You've already surprised me." He winked at her.

"I may be frightened of spiders, my lord, but I am not such a coward as that."

"I shall give you much more credit next time."

The air was chilly. Lily shook a little. Devon moved closer, and this time, she shivered for an entirely different reason.

She gave him a saucy smile. One she had perfected of late. "What makes you think there will be a next time?"

Devon took Lily's hand and led her out to the terrace where a lovely candlelit meal was prepared. There was a table replete with a round, white tablecloth, fine china, wine glasses, silver cutlery, and tiny sparkling candles everywhere. She slid into the midnight-blue velvet upholstered chair he pulled out for her, and took a shaky sip from her water glass, wishing for the first time in her entire life that it was wine.

The evening was cool and clear, a perfect night for a romantic dinner in the garden. She sighed. Of course it was perfect. Colton was a master of seduction.

While the first course was served by two dapper-looking, matched footmen in full livery, Devon poured himself more wine.

"So, tell me," he began. "Why don't you drink?"

She shrugged. "I have my reasons."

"And those reasons are?"

"My own."

"Surely the woman who has the nerve to write *Secrets of a Wedding Night* cannot be so religious as to refuse a glass of wine."

Lily shook her head. "Religion has nothing to do with it. And I've never admitted to writing *Secrets of a Wedding Night*."

He smiled. "Why the intense dislike for alcohol then?"

Lily stared him straight in the eye. "If you must know, my father drank far too much. He couldn't stop. He made many bad decisions. As a result, I've always detested the stuff."

"Ah, then we have that in common," Devon replied. "Drunken fathers, that is. However, I've managed to persevere and develop a fondness for spirits myself."

Lily took a bite of sautéed apples. "Unfortunately, your fondness for spirits is well known." Drat. Had the regret in her voice been obvious?

Devon was quiet for a few moments, eyeing her in a way that made her insides quake with anticipation. "Who was that man leaving your house this morning when I arrived?"

*Confound it!* The apples slipped down her throat, nearly choking her. She took a long drink of water.

"What man?" she finally asked in her most nonchalant voice.

"The man you escorted out the side door. I saw him leaving from the front window."

She batted her eyelashes at him. "Why, Colton, I never took you for the jealous sort."

His eyes became slants, examining her. "I'm never jealous. I'm merely asking a question."

She took another sip of water. What would Devon say

if she told him the truth? "You probably wouldn't believe me."

He speared a bit of stuffed guinea hen with his fork. "Try me. I might surprise you."

She wiped her mouth with her napkin, her decision made. "Very well. What if I told you . . . ?" She leaned closer and dropped her voice to a whisper. "The man you saw was a creditor." She kept her eyes trained on his face. Was it her imagination or did it fall? No, his face gave no hint of his feelings.

Lily waited. Devon's fork would clatter to his plate any second now.

His eyes remained narrowed on her. "Everyone in the *ton* knows Merrill left a great fortune. The odds are much higher the man was a suitor, not a creditor."

Devon hadn't surprised her at all. Should she be relieved or depressed?

Merrill left a great fortune to be sure, but none of it had come to her. His nephew inherited the bulk of the estate. And while the terms of her marriage contract stipulated that she should receive a sizable dower, her former husband's nephew gave her a stipend of no more than ten pounds per annum. There was little she could do about it. Without a nobleman to back her in the courts, she had very little recourse, and she would die of shame before admitting her sad plight to Medford.

Of course the new earl realized she couldn't possibly live on the small amount he'd given her. He'd told her on more than one occasion that she was young and comely enough to remarry and that's what she should do. It was only due to the new earl's good graces that she'd been allowed to remain in the town house in London as long as she had. The earl much preferred the countryside, thank goodness. But he'd written letters of late intimating that he and his wife might be coming to town soon. It was only a matter of time before Lily and her ragtag little household were put out on the streets.

Lily kept her gaze trained on her plate. She'd tried to tell Devon the truth. What more could she do? "This meal is delightful," she said in an attempt to lighten the mood. "It's nice to take a break from planning Annie's debut."

"Ah, yes," Devon replied. "How are the plans coming?"

"I've already presented her at court to the queen and the princesses. All that's left is her ball. It's all arranged for tomorrow night. Medford has seen to everything."

"Yes, as to that, I can scarcely believe he invited me."

Lily's head snapped up. "Medford invited you?"

"I was surprised as well."

Lily turned her attention back to her plate. "I hate to disappoint you, but his secretary saw to the guest list, I assume he doesn't even know."

"Ah, and here I was hoping *you'd* asked him to invite me."

She shook her head and smiled at him. "The entire *ton* is invited, Devon. I want my sister's debut to be a smashing success. Annie has been looking forward to this for a very long time."

"I've no doubt she has, the little imp."

She glanced at him. "Will you be there?" She cursed herself for asking the question.

He shrugged and gave her a wicked grin. "If the whole *ton* will be there, how could I miss it?"

She sighed, and did her best to ignore the surge of happiness that welled in her chest at the news that he planned to attend. "Annie is overly excited about tomorrow night. And I fear I will be forced to beat the young men away from her afterward."

Devon poured himself more wine from the decanter.

"She doesn't share your concerns about marriage, I gather?"

"Not a bit."

"I hate to ask the obvious, but haven't you sat her down in front of your . . ." He cleared his throat. "The pamphlet?"

She gave him a sly look. "No, she hasn't read that particular bit of writing yet."

"High time?"

"You don't think I've offered?" Lily mumbled. "The worst part is, she's already half in love—or so she thinks—with Arthur Eggleston."

Devon inclined his head. "Perhaps you're learning you cannot stop biology, Lily."

"I just want to make Annie understand that marriage isn't all it's purported to be."

He searched her face. "You know what I think?"

"No. What?" She eyed him cautiously, sitting forward in her chair, and folding her hands together.

"I think you don't drink because you're very used to being in control. And you don't like it one bit when you're not. The pamphlet, your ice queen persona, and now trying to keep your sister from growing up. It's more about you than her."

Lily flinched as if he'd struck her. She opened her mouth to issue the denial that sprang to her lips, but promptly snapped it shut again. The truth was, the man was perceptive. Too perceptive. And she didn't like it one bit.

She waited a few moments before she spoke. "Is there anything so very noteworthy about being out of control?"

He took a long drink from his wine glass. "Yes, in fact. I highly recommend it. You must try it sometime and find out."

Lily braced her elbows on the table. If they were passing

out opinions, she intended to have her say. "You know what *I* think?" She batted her eyelashes at him.

"Please. Enlighten me."

"You take perverse pleasure in your reputation as a gambler and a drinker. You're looking to take the easy way in life, and instead of being responsible, you plan to marry a rich woman to solve your problems."

Devon stiffened. He drained his glass before meeting her eyes. "Your opinion of me is that low?"

She inclined her head. "You forget. I've known you for five years."

His voice was even. "No. You knew me five years ago."

"Do you deny that you drink? Do you deny that you gamble? Do you deny that you were betrothed to Miss Templeton and she is quite wealthy?"

He cracked a grin but it held no humor. "I'm drinking at present. I was gambling two nights ago, and Miss Templeton's dowry was positively indecent."

Lily shrugged, trying to dispel a vague feeling of guilt for being so direct. She shouldn't be judging him so. The man had never pretended to be anything other than what he was. Well, not recently at least. She'd do well to remember at all times how infinitely unsuitable he was. He'd tossed away one thousand pounds on a game of chance as if it meant nothing. She shouldn't have been so accusatory, however. It was his money, his affair. But still, he had started it with his detestable comment about how controlling she was.

"Let's just agree that we are both quite opposite, you and I. We will not try to persuade each other to see things differently. Do we have a truce?"

Devon traced the pattern of a figure eight on the tablecloth. He nodded. "Truce."

For the remainder of the meal, they managed to keep

the discussion focused on lighthearted topics and pleasant banter mostly involving Bandit's antics as the newest member of Lily's household. After the last course was served and the plates cleared away, Devon rose and offered Lily his arm. "I want to show you something inside," he said, covering her hand with his. A tingle shot up Lily's spine.

They entered the house again and walked through the polished wooden hallways to the man staircase. Devon began to mount the stairs. Lily stopped, pulling back, she narrowed her eyes on him.

"Where exactly are you going?" She snatched her arm away.

He cracked a smile and the boyish charm of it made butterflies scatter in Lily's stomach.

"It's just upstairs at the end of the hallway. It's a painting. You'll like it."

Still, she hesitated, biting her lip. "Is your bedchamber up there?"

Another small smile. "It is."

"Near the painting?"

He grabbed up her hand again, rubbing her knuckles with his thumb. "Honestly, Lily, if that's what you're worried about, I'll have the servants bring the painting down to us." He called out and within moments two footmen appeared in the foyer. Devon issued instructions for them to bring the painting downstairs, but Lily's hand on his sleeve stopped him.

"No, no, it's fine. I'll go up and see it," she said softly, somewhat embarrassed by the display. "It would be silly to have them bring it all the way down here." Besides, she was somewhat curious to see what a notorious rake's bedchamber looked like.

Devon nodded once and, with a simple hand gesture, promptly dispatched both footmen.

"This way," he said, taking her hand again and leading her upstairs.

At the landing, they turned to the right and walked along a long row of polished wooden doors.

Devon guided her along. They stopped at the end of the hallway in front of a large portrait of a gorgeous, regal-looking woman. Her dark hair and eyes and perfect nose marked her as Devon's ancestor.

"My great-grandmother," he said, gesturing toward the portrait.

"She is beautiful," Lily breathed, staring up at the painting in awe, wondering if anyone would ever paint such a masterpiece with her as the subject one day. No, she decided. She would not be the grand lady of a grand house, and even if she was, she was not half as lovely as the woman whose kind chocolate-colored eyes looked down at her now.

"I thought you'd like it," Devon said, "because of the dogs."

Lily stepped back and looked again. She blinked. This time, she saw them. There were dogs in the picture. Four of them, by her count. One hid under the lady's feet, partially obscured by her skirt. One lay in the corner, soundly asleep. One nestled on the back of the settee just over the lady's shoulder, and the fourth was peering out of the side of the picture as if he'd been barely captured for all eternity, paying a fleeting visit.

"Oh, how adorable. How wonderful!" Lily exclaimed, taking in the expression on each animal's face. "Your grandmother loved dogs."

"Yes." Devon smiled. "I suppose I can credit her with my sudden desire to save Bandit last night."

Lily touched his sleeve. "You're a nice man, Devon. Only an ogre would allow a puppy to fend for itself on the streets of London."

He shrugged. "I don't know how nice I am, but I'm no ogre. I suppose my grandmother would like to know that much, at least."

"I believe people who are kind to animals show their true natures. And the reverse is also true."

"My grandmother had a brooch resembling one of these dogs," he said. "I still have it."

"A brooch?"

"Yes, made out of diamonds, if I remember correctly. It was a gift from my grandfather."

"I should love to see it," Lily said.

Devon's hands had fallen away from her and were shoved in his pockets. "It's in the bedchamber," he admitted with a charming grin. "I'd be happy to show it to you if you'd like. I'll even promise to keep my hands in my pockets the entire time."

She laughed. "If you do that, how will you retrieve the brooch?"

"Hmm. I hadn't thought that far ahead. Very well. I'll keep my hands in my pockets until I retrieve the brooch, then I'll put them right back. I promise. Or I can bring it—"

"Is this your bedchamber?" Lily pushed open the door to her immediate left. Somehow she knew instinctively she had the correct door.

"Yes," he answered softly, following her inside.

His bedchamber was astonishing. That was the only word that came to mind. It must have taken up the entire back half of the house. There was a sitting area with books and a large fireplace with a portrait of Devon as a young boy with an older man who looked just like him. "My father," he said at Lily's questioning stare.

The bed itself was covered in midnight-blue satin and fluffy, down pillows. Raised on a dais, it took up the back half of the large room. Good heavens. Devon could give her a few tips on living a life well beyond one's means. She was in need of such lessons of late, was she not?

Lily stopped about three paces in front of the bed, staring at it. She couldn't help but wonder what sort of pleasures other women had there in Devon's arms. That thought made her melancholy, but the fact that she was here with him now made her shiver.

Devon disappeared into an antechamber. Lily strode over to the bedside table where a letter sat, half folded. She picked it up. "Progress Report for Master Justin," the heading stated. Who was Master Justin?

Devon made a noise in the antechamber and Lily dropped the paper. She shouldn't have looked at it. Couldn't even decide exactly why she had. She bit her lip; the urge to ask Devon who Justin was nearly overwhelmed her, but then he'd know she'd been looking at his correspondence. And it was none of her affair, of course.

Devon shuffled around for a few moments longer before he reappeared and joined her next to the bed. He held the diamond brooch in the shape of the dog in his left hand.

"Here it is." He slid it into Lily's palm.

She eyed the delicate piece of jewelry with reverence, turning it over carefully, examining the gold filigree with her fingertip. "Ah, it's lovely. Your grandfather had fine taste."

"I always thought it impractical," Devon admitted. "But by all accounts my great-grandfather loved my great-grandmother to distraction. I'm not surprised he commissioned such a piece."

"I'm sure she treasured it." Lily handed the brooch back to him and nearly jumped at the spark that ignited along her nerves at the touch of his hand.

Devon's gaze slid from the bed, where he couldn't help but imagine doing all sorts of things to the beautiful woman standing next to him. Lily's jasmine-scented hair was driving him insane and she was so sweet and pretty tonight. He ached for her. It had been a long time—too long—since he'd been with a woman. But Lily standing here, in his bedchamber, this close, torturously close, to his bed was making him feel every single day of his self-imposed celibacy. He swallowed hard.

Something about her trusting him, her coming into his bedchamber. He couldn't betray her trust and seduce her. Not like this. Not tonight. He had to get her out of here. And quickly.

"I'll meet you in the hallway," he said. "Let me just put this away." He disappeared into the antechamber again.

When Devon emerged from the other room, he headed toward the bedchamber door. He stopped short, his mouth going immediately dry. Lily sat on his bed, her skirts spread around her, her comely ankles showing, and her slippers kicked to the rug underneath.

He cleared his throat but didn't dare speak.

"Surprised?" she asked.

"I might use that word." He took two steps toward her, then stopped.

"Do not tell me I've rendered you speechless, my lord," she said with a throaty laugh that made Devon's groin tighten.

"It is rare, I admit." He took one more step. "Lily, I don't think—"

"Nor should you," she breathed. "This is not a night for thinking. What's the trouble, Devon? Don't you want to kiss me?"

"Lily, I—"

"It was gentlemanly of you to offer to meet me in the hallway. Truly, it was. But entirely unnecessary. It occurs to me that I'm alone with you in your bedchamber and such an opportunity will not likely present itself again any time soon."

"But, Lily—"

She put up a hand to stop him again. "I'm destined to live a spinsterlike existence. We cannot actually make love tonight, Devon. I'm not that brave, but I can kiss you again. Let you kiss me, and spend a night—of sorts—here in this bed."

The lady made sense. This time, Devon didn't stop. He wanted to make love to her, of course, and the thought of doing anything less drove him mad. But having some of Lily was better than none of her. He would *not* cross the line with her, even if it killed him.

He moved over to the edge of the bed where he sat, turned, and pulled her into his arms. He let his mouth capture hers. He stopped briefly to shuck his boots from his feet, then he moved back to her. Without letting his mouth leave hers, he pushed her back onto the bed, pulling her up to the pillows and lying atop her. The sweet weight of pressing against her made him groan. Her answering moan, with her fingers trailing through his hair, made him insane.

"Lily, are you sure?" he whispered.

"Just to be clear," she said through kisses, smiling against his mouth. "We're only kissing. You haven't seduced me yet."

Devon smiled. He had her now. He'd make her feel like she'd shot through the clouds.

And he knew exactly how to do it.

The room was dark save for a few candles. One twinkled atop the mantelpiece, one sat on the bedside table, and another blinked in the sitting area. There was enough light to see Lily's beautiful countenance. He had to move slowly. He couldn't risk scaring her away.

Devon moved behind her and deftly unfastened the

row of tiny buttons at the back of her gown. He unlaced her stays quickly, never so glad he was an expert at undressing a woman.

"This is going to be fun, isn't it, Devon?" Lily asked in a shy, but decidedly excited, voice.

She turned her head toward him.

Devon nodded. "Absolutely."

Her dress was down to her waist in short order and her stays were wholly removed. Lily bit her lip. He'd always liked it when she did that. Endearing.

"I expected to feel embarrassed being seen half-nude by a man, but all I feel is warmth," she whispered.

Devon blinked. What did she mean by that? She'd been married. She'd obviously seen a half-nude man before. But now was not the time for interrogation.

He quickly unwrapped his cravat with one hand, and ripped open his shirt. He pressed his chest against her breasts, making him ache. He reached down and cupped one of them and she moaned.

"God, Lily, you are beautiful." He kissed her swollen lips again. "So perfect." He touched his forehead to hers.

She wrapped her arms around his broad shoulders and kissed him with every bit of herself. "So are you," she whispered against his mouth, fitting her breast more closely into his hand and placing her own atop his to keep his hand there. "Don't stop," she murmured. And then with a slight smile. "Yet."

Devon drew a deep breath and shuddered. Lily didn't seem frightened. Why didn't she seem frightened? Given the probable contents of her blasted pamphlet, he expected she might be half quaking with fear when a man kissed her. Instead, she melted against him like marzipan left in the sun.

The ungodly perfection of Lily's tight, full round breast in his hand made his cock throb. He pressed himself against her leg and bit his lip to keep from crying out. "You have no idea what you're doing to me."

He kissed her soft lips again and let his mouth trail to her earlobe. He sucked and bit. He groaned again when she squirmed and moved against him, her hand brushing the tip of his cock. More sweet ecstasy. He let his mouth trail to her neck where he suckled and nibbled. More welcome squirms.

His lips moved to the valley between her breasts. He cupped both of them in his hands and squeezed lightly. He rubbed his thumbs against her nipples and she bit her lip. One of his hands moved up to pull the pins from her hair and the tide swept over her shoulders in dark falls. She sat up slightly and shook it out. And Devon reveled in the sweet scent of it around him. His one hand continued to tease her nipple. He found the other one with his mouth and sucked.

Lily's head fell back on the pillow and she clamped her legs together hard, moaning. He wouldn't let his mouth leave her no matter how much she squirmed. She held his dark head to her breast, allowing him to do anything and everything he wanted with it. Was she silently begging him not to stop?

Just when he hoped she couldn't stand any more, he moved his lips to her other breast and sucked there. He bit softly, scraping his teeth against the sensitive center. This time, her legs fell apart, and he moved to lie atop her. She welcomed him, pulling him tightly against her.

He suckled her breast and moved his hand up to her lips. She took his thumb into her mouth and sucked. Devon groaned. The weight between his legs was getting heavier and harder to control with every movement Lily made. Her gorgeous body writhing beneath him was unholy torture. When she took his thumb into her sweet, small mouth, he nearly lost control, imagining her doing the same thing but with another appendage entirely.

His kisses slackened on her breasts and he gave them each one last peck, moving back up to her mouth and kissing her fiercely. Her dark hair fell against the pillow. He ran his fingers through it. "You've no idea how long I've wanted to touch you like this, Lily."

"Five years?" she breathed against his mouth.

"God, yes."

"Me too."

He kissed her again. Lily was suddenly sad, thinking their time together was coming to an end. He'd done things to her breasts she'd never imagined possible, but they could go no further.

He kissed her eyelids and her forehead, and just when she thought he was going to stop and help her get dressed, his hand moved slowly down her body, past her rib cage and stomach, coming to rest between her legs.

Her heart stopped. Time stopped. She couldn't breathe. Never in her life had she imagined such a thing.

"Devon, I—"

"Shh," he whispered against her lips. "I won't hurt you, Lily. Please."

It was the "please" that was her undoing. She'd never seen Devon Morgan so humble. He was usually so controlled, but now he was humbling himself. Asking her to let him touch her, and somehow she knew he would go no further than she allowed. And if what he'd done to her breasts was any indication, she was about to be amazed again. God only knew what that man was about to do to her. Only one thing mattered. She desperately wanted to find out.

She couldn't make her lips form the word "yes," so she

merely nodded, then buried her face in the side of the pillow, too dazed to do anything else.

Devon shimmied her dress from her hips and it swooshed to a heap on the floor. Lily shivered at the feel of his warm hands on her overheated skin. He pulled the coverlet up over them in deference to her modesty. Lily appreciated that. No doubt she was blushing all the way down *there*.

When her drawers came away from her ankles, she sucked in a deep breath. Then, Devon was touching her. His fingers plied against the wet, hot skin between her legs, his fingers working a magic Lily felt certain would send her straight to hell, but at the moment she didn't care. One finger entered her, so slowly. The sweetness of it made her cry out. And then he moved within her, slowly, carefully, making her ache and want things she didn't even know existed. She twisted her hips beneath him. She whispered his name.

He pulled his finger away. Then he started circling her with his fingertip, in a place so sensitive, so perfect, she wanted to cry. His wet, sure finger made her hips writhe. Her hands tangled under the blanket in his dark hair. She wanted to pull him up, to kiss him, but she also didn't want to interrupt. Wherever this was going, it was a place she desperately wanted to be.

She put the back of one hand to her lip and bit, trying to keep from crying out. And then, time ceased to exist. Devon moved down her body. His hot, perfect mouth replaced his fingers. His tongue circled her now and his large hands held her hips, holding her up against his lips, forcing her into contact with him, giving her something she didn't know until today that she'd always wanted . . . no, needed.

"Oh, God," she sobbed against the pillow. She pulled it

over her face, still twisting helplessly beneath his mouth. He licked her, in perfect laps, kissed her in deep, wet swashes, and rubbed his rough tongue on a spot that made her beg.

"Devon, please," was all she could utter, her limp fingers squeezing the sides of the pillow with as much strength as she could muster. "Please." And while he didn't answer, she knew he was going to give her exactly what she was asking for.

His licks became more insistent, perfectly timed, torturous, and Lily squirmed, hitching her breath as she climbed a precipice of feelings she'd never dreamt possible. It was a journey to the top of a place she never wanted to leave. And when Devon paired his insistent tongue with his finger sliding into her one more time, she reached the pinnacle, crying out against the pillow. She uttered his name on a sob that lingered, while the tentacles of pleasure wrapped around her insides and brought her floating down on a cloud of sharp breaths from heaven.

She lay there for several seconds, enjoying the aftermath, the sharp little pings that zipped through her body, causing her to shudder. Her arms wrapped around Devon's shoulders. He'd pulled himself away from her, but remained hugging her hips, allowing her to enjoy the final moments of her climax. No words were spoken. None were necessary.

Finally, he pulled himself up and Lily gave him a smile.

"I don't know what to say to you," she whispered.

"Did I frighten you?"

She smiled. "No, no. There was absolutely nothing frightening about that."

But it was a lie.

Whatever had just happened, she was not going to be the same. And that thought scared her more than she could say. But that's not what Devon had meant, and there was still the one secret of her wedding night she would never tell him.

They lay in each other's arms a while longer until Devon told her he'd fetch her a cup of water. She didn't need water. He was leaving to give her privacy to get dressed. Lily appreciated that. She leaned back into the pillows and smiled and sighed. Good heavens. The man was perfect in *all* things involving seduction.

Devon let the door to his bedchamber close behind him and only then did he release his pent-up breath. Good God, what had just happened? He'd pleasured Lily, he knew, but he'd nearly made a mess of himself too, and that hadn't happened since he was a lad.

God, he'd wanted her. And he could have had her. He knew it. Just a few whispered words and assurances. She would have been his for the taking. Nothing he'd done in his life had been more difficult than to stop.

But he couldn't do it. Just couldn't.

She didn't know about the bet at the club. He couldn't make love to her without telling her about that blasted bet. It would be unfair.

Lily didn't know about a lot of things, actually. Like Justin.

Devon's first duty was to Justin. And while Devon had felt some spark of a dormant emotion while he'd been touching Lily, he needed a woman who loved him and trusted him, who would help him raise his son. Lily was squared off against him as his opponent now. And of course there was the little matter of what had happened between them five years ago. How could he forget? No, Devon had no right to feel anything for Lily. Anything at all.

What exactly did he feel, anyway? He'd had his chance

to shame her. She'd been willing and pliant in his arms. He could easily have left her unfulfilled. Sent her away wanting more. She'd be out of his life for good if he'd done that. So why hadn't he?

Damn it. He couldn't answer that question.

Instead of summoning a servant, Devon made his way to the kitchens to fetch the glass of water. He wanted to give her enough time to get dressed. He wanted to give himself enough time to think.

When he finally returned, she was standing next to the bed, looking heartbreakingly beautiful. She'd put her hair back up, but it had a sort of tousled quality that made him hard all over again. She'd replaced her clothing, but she stood with her gown hanging open in the back, waiting for him to help her with her stays and all of the buttons. She motioned behind her and he quickly crossed the thick carpet. He handed her the water. She sipped it hesitantly, while Devon laced her up and buttoned the gown. He breathed in her smell too, and closed his eyes, thankful she couldn't see his reaction.

Devon waited until he'd finished with her buttons before he spoke. He bowed his head behind her. She had to know about the bet and she would hear it from him. "Lily, there's something I must tell you."

Lily sucked in her breath. She turned quickly and put her fingertip to his lips. "No, no more. It doesn't matter. Please just take me home."

He opened his mouth to try again, but the look in her eyes stopped him. It looked like . . . pain.

Damn it.

Instead, he nodded.

Devon accompanied her home. They rode together in silence while Lily traced raindrops on the coach's windowpane. She closed her eyes, imagining that if she hadn't stopped him, Devon would have said everything she'd ever wanted to hear. Instead, she was sure he would say something painful. Too painful. Something about five years ago and the reasons why he'd never come back for her. What did any of it matter anymore?

Marriage was out of the question. Of course, Colton would be a perfect person to marry, *if* he had a shilling to his name, *if* she could trust him, *if* she had an intention of ever marrying again. But he did not. And she could not and did not. He was a gambler, as his father had been. And it made her heart ache to know it. He'd told her once, years ago when they were courting, he would never be a gambler like his father. And yet, Devon was exactly that. Obviously the years they'd been apart had changed him irrevocably, completely. It made her sad and made her want to scream too.

Yes, Devon Morgan was completely inappropriate for a score of reasons.

But why, oh why, did her traitorous heart have to want him so?

# CHAPTER 16

Medford's town house was perfectly decorated. Candles glistened in the chandeliers, the refreshment tables overflowed with decanters of wine and bowls of punch. Young ladies and their chaperones mingled against one wall, the pastel colors of their ball gowns heralding their debuts.

And Annie was there among them, finally experiencing her long-awaited come-out.

Her dark hair was pulled up in a bun atop her head. Stray curls fell softly at her cheeks. Her best white dress, the one that Lily had painstakingly sewn for her, accentuated her trim figure. Annie looked stunning and Lily was proud. Exceedingly so.

Annie twirled around, an enormous smile gracing her beautiful face.

There was nothing this moment could use, if not their mother. Oh, Lily had little use for their father. The man had always been domineering. Money and spirits were the only things important to him. He'd demanded Lily marry the Earl of Merrill, and like a good daughter, she had. But their mother had always been kind and happy with the girls, understanding. Their mother may have been ruled by her husband's whims and devastated by his constant gambling, but she loved her daughters. And when their father was taken from them four years ago after a particularly long, harsh winter when he'd come down with a nasty cough, it had been sad, but even more distressing was their mother's coming down with lung fever within days of their father's passing and being gone only weeks later herself.

Lily sighed. If she'd learned one thing in her twenty-two years, it was that life just refused to be fair. And so be it. She would always rely upon herself and never count on fate to be kind to her.

She glanced over at a beaming Annie.

*Annie. So innocent, so hopeful.*

Yes, Annie might not know what sort of trouble she could encounter at a debut ball, but at least she could have this one night of magical fantasy.

Lily's own debut had been that way too, and she wished that for her little sister. Five years ago, Lily had stood on the sidelines of the Wilmingtons' ball and waited for her own debut, the butterflies in her stomach taking flight. It had been like a dream, that night, and she would never forget it. Like a heroine in a romantic novel, the first man she'd laid eyes on had been the hero of her story.

Devon Morgan.

Young, dashing, and oh, so handsome, he'd come out of nowhere and claimed her hand for the first dance. Initially, she'd been convinced her friends had put him up to it, for certainly such a charming bachelor would not be interested in her. And he was the only son of a marquis, no less. He'd twirled her in his arms as if he'd invented the steps and Lily had been hesitant to pinch herself, frightened she would awake from a too perfect dream.

But that had been five years ago.

Things were very different now. She hadn't allowed herself to dwell too long on what had happened between them at Devon's town house last night. It had been a pleasant interlude, to be sure, but their involvement with each other must end there. Surely, Devon realized it too. Surely, he'd give up his intention to seduce her and just quietly go about his business of finding a new fiancée. There were plenty of other rich young ladies to marry. Surely, he could find one who wasn't scared off by the pamphlet. The man was a marquis, for heaven's sake.

"There's Mr. Eggleston," Annie squealed into Lily's ear, shaking her from her thoughts. "Doesn't he look positively dashing?"

Annie's best friend, Frances, was there beside her, wearing a pastel pink ball gown and dutifully squealing with glee also over the thought of Eggleston asking Annie to dance. "No doubt you two will be engaged by month's end," Frances said, her blond curls bobbing against her temples.

"I do hope so," Annie replied with a nervous laugh.

"You don't happen to know if Lord Ashbourne will be here tonight, do you?" Frances asked, a sly smile on her face.

Annie frowned. "Lord Ashbourne? Why, he's older than . . . Lily."

Lily laughed. "Yes, and I'm positively ancient."

Frances sighed. "Who cares how old he is? He's positively gorgeous. Those silver eyes, that chestnut-brown hair, those wide, square shoulders." She shivered. "Oh, I know he would never look twice at me, of course, but it doesn't keep me from wanting to catch a glimpse of him whenever possible." She winked at the sisters.

Lily shook her head, and the two younger girls trailed off giggling together.

Lily scanned the crowded ballroom. She'd seen Medford only briefly when they'd first arrived. She'd barely had a chance to thank him again for his kindness before he was called off to perform a multitude of hostlike duties. She hadn't seen him since.

Her gaze fell on Mr. Eggleston. He stood across the room, his eyes fixed upon Annie who was still off laughing in the corner with Frances. Her sister's laughter made her smile.

She searched the crowd again before she realized she'd been looking for Devon. He wasn't there. She sighed. Perhaps after last night, he'd decided not to come after all. He and Medford were hardly friends. It would stand to reason that Devon might skip this particular event.

She did her best to shake off the odd feeling of melancholy the thought gave her. It was just as well if Devon weren't here. Hadn't she just been thinking moments earlier they should go their separate ways? It made no sense to contradict herself now.

The music began moments later and, with it, the dancing. Lily searched the floor, expecting to see Annie and Arthur Eggleston there together. Frances flew past in the arms of a handsome young buck. But Annie was not there. Instead, a brief perusal of the room revealed Eggleston standing on the sidelines seemingly in a deep conversation with another young man.

Lily swung around to find her sister. Perhaps another young man had caught Annie's fancy or persuaded her to dance. Lily located her sister standing only a few yards away and she hurried over to her.

"I cannot imagine why he does not come," Annie said, her cheeks growing pale. She bit her lower lip.

A twinge of anger shot through Lily on her sister's behalf. How dare Eggleston lead Annie to believe he would ask her to dance and then completely ignore her for the first one?

She glanced about and realized that most of the ballroom was watching Annie. To be left on the sidelines at the first dance at one's debut was unimaginable.

A slow simmer began in Lily's chest. She clenched her fists and glared at Arthur Eggleston.

Annie did her best to maintain a brave façade. She wandered over to the refreshment table and drank punch and laughed with a few of the other wallflower girls and their chaperones. She appeared gay and happy, but Lily knew better.

The strains of the first song came to an end and the dancers returned to the sidelines. Annie returned to Lily's side.

Lily noticed Eggleston making his way out of the ballroom. "Of all the nerve." Lily did her best to keep her voice low, but Annie swung around to look.

"What is it?" Annie's eyes were wide and panic-stricken.

Lily expelled her breath. "Nothing, dear. Nothing. It doesn't matter."

"It's Mr. Eggleston, isn't it?" Annie glanced around the ballroom and caught sight of him. The heartbreak on her face crushed Lily.

"He's leaving," Annie whispered, touching her white glove to her lips.

Lily squeezed her sister's hand. "Please, darling, think nothing of it. You're sure to have a dozen new suitors. Don't give Mr. Eggleston a second thought."

Annie blinked back tears. Lily could see them, unshed, in her younger sister's eyes and the pain ripped at her own heart. She had half a mind to follow that young man outside and take a switch to him.

The strains of a waltz were beginning and Lily glanced around, stricken. She would make this right. Couples were pairing off all around her and still Annie stood there as if frozen to her spot; no young swain came her way. Unthinkable. Annie was the most beautiful girl in the ballroom. It was utterly ridiculous that not one young man asked her to dance.

"Don't worry, darling," Lily whispered to Annie. "Viscount Medford is here. He'll dance with you."

The unshed tears in Annie's eyes hurt more than any tantrum could. "No, no, Lily, please don't ask him to," she whispered brokenly. "I couldn't bear it."

Annie turned away. She slowly made her way to the wall and took a seat in one of the chairs that lined it. Lily watched her go, torn between the urge to hug and comfort her sister and the urge to chase Arthur Eggleston down and rip his beating heart from his cowardly little chest.

Medford. She must find Medford. Her eyes scanned the crowded ballroom, but Lord Medford was nowhere to be seen. Blast it. He was busy playing host. He could be any number of places. Outside seeing to the traffic, in the kitchens seeing to the concessions, or dealing with any number of items that come up when one hosts a ball. There was no time to track him down.

She turned back toward Annie. Comfort. She must offer comfort.

She'd barely made her way back to her sister's side when a deep voice sounded from behind them both.

"Excuse me, Miss Andrews, but would you do me the great honor of allowing me this dance?"

Lily spun around. Her heart leaped in her chest. Her hand flew to her throat.

There he was.

Her knight in shining armor.

*Their* knight in shining armor.

Devon Morgan stood there, looking tall, dark, and even

more handsome than usual. He bowed at the waist to Annie and offered his long, lean hand.

Annie blushed from ear to ear and gave him the most beautiful smile Lily had ever seen. Lily smiled herself, her heart warming as she watched her sister put her hand in Devon's larger one and allowed him to lead her to the dance floor.

The smile Annie bestowed on Devon could not have painted him any greater a hero. "I never thought I'd say this," Lily whispered to herself, "but thank God for Devon Morgan."

She watched them dance, admiring the way in which her sister matched him pace for pace. Colton was a famously good dancer, and the fact that Annie was a match for him spoke to her sister's skill. Lily's chest swelled with pride.

Moments later, Medford appeared at Lily's side. "What's wrong?"

"There you are," Lily replied, not taking her eyes from Devon and Annie.

"Do you require my assistance?"

"No. No. Everything is fine. Annie's dancing with Colton." She nodded toward the couple.

Medford's hazel eyes flickered toward the dance floor. "So I see. I thought that lad Eggleston would be dancing with her."

"So did I. And he best pray I do not find him before my sister does. I swear I will never know why Eggleston didn't ask her to dance. Annie was so sure he would."

Medford expelled his breath. "I think I know why. Though I confess I'm hesitant to tell you."

Her gaze flew to his. She clutched at his coat sleeve. "Why? You must tell me, why?"

Medford cleared his throat uncomfortably. He lowered

his voice and glanced about. "There's been a rumor that Annie doesn't have a dowry. I heard it myself in mixed company. Not exactly the type of thing one needs when one is making one's debut."

Lily set her shoulders and lifted her chin. "So that's why Eggleston didn't ask her to dance, is it?"

There was no telling who would have started such a rumor, but because it was entirely true, Lily couldn't exactly deny it. She'd always counted on Annie's dowryless state to save her poor sister from some loveless, awful marriage, but Lily hadn't expected word to travel so quickly before Annie's debut and ruin her sister's most coveted night.

"I see Colton hasn't heard the rumor," Medford sneered. "That blackguard would go anywhere he smelled the scent of money. Even to your sister. Just proves what a reprehensible rake he is."

"He's dancing with Annie when Annie needed a partner," Lily replied softly. "I find myself in Lord Colton's debt right now."

Medford eyed her askance. He straightened his cravat and cleared his throat. "Yes. Well. You should know there's a rumor floating around tonight about Colton too."

Lily nodded absently. "Really."

"Yes. I've yet to hear the details, but I intend to find out. Now, if you'll excuse me." Medford bowed to her and blended back into the crowd. Lily let him go, barely noticing his departure. Instead, she watched Annie dance with a smile on her face.

The strains of the waltz soon came to an end, and Devon guided Annie back toward Lily. Annie stared up at him like a lovelorn puppy and giggled as he deposited her next to Lily.

"Thank you for the dance, Miss Andrews," he said, bowing to her again. He bent over the hand she extended.

"No, thank *you,* Lord Colton," Annie said, with a curtsy. "I do not know *what* I would have done without you. You quite came to my rescue."

Lily curtsied to Devon too. "Yes, thank you, my lord. My sister and I both are greatly appreciative."

"The pleasure was entirely mine, I assure you." He bowed over Lily's hand and a current of fire ran up her arm. She longed to take him into one of the salons and kiss him until neither one of them could breathe. She snapped her fan open.

Annie placed a hand on Devon's sleeve and looked up at him with her big, brown eyes. "Oh, and I almost forgot. Thank you very much for rescuing Bandit too. I'm sure if she could speak, she'd be most grateful."

Devon smiled at that.

Annie drifted into the crowd where a line of young men quickly gathered around her skirts as the third dance of the evening began. Arthur Eggleston pushed past the other swains and elbowed his way up to Annie.

"Annie—Miss Andrews—you promised me a dance, do you remember?"

Annie looked for a minute as if she might deliver the crushing set-down the lad so obviously deserved, but to Lily's chagrin, Annie turned and offered her hand to him. "Yes, Mr. Eggleston. I remember." She allowed him to escort her to the floor.

"I cannot believe it," Lily said to Devon, resisting the urge to stamp her foot in frustration. "That young man completely abandoned her and now she's dancing with him."

Devon slid his hands into his pockets. "Don't think too harshly of young Mr. Eggleston. Sometimes these swains don't recognize the prettiest and best of the lot without someone a bit older and more experienced, say, pointing her out to him."

Devon's eyes devoured Lily, making her feel warm all over.

She scanned the dance floor for Annie one more time. "Oh, she does look happy, doesn't she?"

Devon nodded. "That she does. And I can remember only one other young lady with such beauty and grace." He smiled at her. "Now, may I interest *you* in a dance?"

A warm blush spread across Lily's cheeks. "Careful," she whispered. "You're wasting your considerable talents trying to charm me."

He grinned at her. "Dance with me then, and put me out of my misery."

Lily agreed. They danced. And, for a time, she was catapulted back to the splendor and excitement of her own debut. When there had been only Devon. Yes, she must have danced with the Earl of Merrill that evening too, though she didn't remember it. But her dances with Devon, especially the one alone with him in the garden, were etched in her brain never to be erased.

Feeling suddenly reckless, Lily glanced up at him and said, "Don't feel too bad about your failure to seduce me, Colton. You're not the first to have tried and failed."

His smile lit up the room. He leaned down and his warm breath whispered in her ear. "Failure? I'd hardly call it a failure given what we did last night."

A rush of excitement flashed through Lily's insides. The man had a point. A delicious point. She closed her eyes and let Devon sweep her around and around. The dancing wiped out everything else in her mind. She'd have this moment to remember forever during the long, cold nights of her future.

Lily spent the remainder of the evening overseeing the many requests for Annie's dances and ensuring her sister rested properly and received enough refreshment in between her multiple trips to the dance floor. It was quite a chore, being a chaperone. No doubt her mother had had her hands full at Lily's debut. But she couldn't have wished a more perfect night for Annie. It had been a smashing success, thanks to Devon Morgan. Lily couldn't help but smile at that thought. The man continued to surprise her. Well, she just might surprise him.

Suddenly, the idea of allowing him to completely seduce her didn't seem so dangerous after all. Ooh, perhaps she'd seduce *him*! She shivered at that thought. Well, perhaps that was a bit too much, but she would be sure to thank him. That much was certain. Just *how* she thanked him remained to be seen.

Long after midnight when all the dances had been danced and all the refreshments had been removed, Lily led her sister to the foyer where they waited for a footman to bring them their cloaks. She'd thanked Medford's butler prettily and even winked back at Devon Morgan when he raised his glass in a silent salute to her sister's success. Lily tried to ignore the gaggle of women who flitted about him, but relished the fact that the two of them had their own secret.

The butler ushered Lily and Annie outside and they made their way to Medford's coach. He'd put the conveyance at their disposal for the evening. Just as they were about to enter the vehicle, Lord Medford himself jogged up.

"Medford, there you are. I wondered where you'd got off to. I looked for you to say good-bye and to thank you again." Lily allowed her sister to enter the coach ahead of her.

Medford was nearly out of breath. "I found out the details of the rumor about Colton, Lily." He pressed a letter into her hand. "I insist you read this at your earliest convenience. I'll call on you tomorrow."

A frown formed between Lily's brows. She'd forgotten

Medford had even mentioned a rumor about Devon and now he was delivering her a letter about the matter? How odd.

"Very well. Thank you," she stammered. She pushed the paper into her coat pocket and allowed the coachman to help her into the carriage.

"What was that about?" Annie asked, reclining against the seat cushions. "Oh, I'm all but exhausted."

Lily glanced out the window to see Medford making his way back into the house. "Not sure, really. Now tell me, darling, what was your very favorite part of the evening?"

# CHAPTER 17

Lily saw Annie tucked in comfortably before she retreated to her own bedchamber.

"Thank you, Lily," Annie had whispered, a smile still playing on her lips. "It was a wonderful evening, thanks to you and Lord Medford and of course, Lord Colton. Thank you for everything."

Lily smoothed her sister's hair and leaned down and kissed her forehead. "I'm glad it made you happy, Annie, truly I am. Mama would have been so proud." She watched her sister drift into a peaceful slumber before she backed out of the room quietly, closing the door behind her.

It was true she had not necessarily wanted Annie to have a debut, but now that she'd had it and it had been a smashing success, Lily smiled to herself, humming a strain of one of the waltzes she'd heard earlier. She made her way into her bedchamber, then her dressing room. God only knew what the future would hold for the two of them, but tonight, Annie would sleep soundly with dreams of her debut floating through her head. As it should be.

Lily stretched and stared out the darkened window. Her thoughts turned to Devon Morgan. Her thoughts tended to do that of late. She smiled to herself. He'd certainly surprised her. She bit her knuckle to keep from a full-blown grin. Regardless of what had happened between them years ago, Devon was a gentleman. And she would never, never be able to repay him for his kindness to Annie tonight. She'd forever be in his debt. Lily sighed. It really was too bad that Colton was completely unsuitable. But oh my, he was handsome, his broad shoulders, his dark hair, his irresistible smile, his deep, dark eyes. And the way he'd looked at her tonight. Why, it nearly singed her eyelashes to think of it.

Lily pulled off her cloak and hung it on a peg on a wall. She was about to call for Mary to help her with her stays when she spotted the bit of parchment sticking from her cloak pocket. The letter from Viscount Medford.

She pulled it out and hastily unfolded it.

*My Dear Lady Merrill,*
*I regret to inform you I have learned about a bet at Brooks's. The bet, placed by the Marquis of Colton, involves you, yourself. The bet is entitled How to Seduce the Woman who Wrote SECRETS OF A WEDDING NIGHT. I further regret to inform you the odds are in favor of Colton.*

*I am your servant and shall call on you at your first convenience tomorrow to discuss how you would like me to handle this distressing news. My apologies for being the bearer of what is sure to be such unwelcome information.*

*Yours,*
*L. Medford*

Lily reread the words quickly. They didn't make sense at first. Question after question popped into her mind like ghastly fireworks. There was a bet? At the club's? Between herself and Colton? And she didn't know about it? How was that possible?

Colton had turned his seduction plot into a moneymaking venture? Lily cupped her hand over her mouth, afraid she would retch. Oh, God. He was still the same awful gambler he'd always been. His seduction plan had always been in place. And that's all it had been to him. A bet. He had no feelings, didn't truly care about her at all. She bit the back of her hand.

Oh, God, it was mortifying. She'd let him do things to her, such intimate things, when it was all about money. All he'd planned to do was lure her into bed, and fool that she was, she'd nearly allowed it! She shuddered. She'd been so close to succumbing to him, had even contemplated seducing him! She doubled over, disbelief and disgust roiling through her.

Oh, that cad had fooled her, but damn it, she would not, would *not* be the laughingstock all over again. She crumpled the letter in her fist and threw it to the floor.

Lily clenched her fists. She had been right about Devon Morgan after all. And she'd never let another man hurt her again. If it was the very last thing she did, she'd find a way to ensure Colton never saw a farthing of that money and she'd make him hurt as much as he'd hurt her.

When Evans ushered Viscount Medford into the white salon the next morning, Lily sat with a ramrod-straight back and a pinched smile on her face. There was no more tea. Even the reused leaves had run out. She sipped a medley of hot water and a bit of lemon that Mary had been given by a neighbor's cook. Leopold was curled in a ball in the corner. Bandit lay at her feet.

"Good morning, Medford," she called in a jovial voice.

Medford hurried forward and bent over her hands

before taking a seat in the chair next to her. "I came as soon as I could. Did you read my letter?"

"I read it," she answered serenely, proud of herself for how calm she managed to remain. "And as you have guessed, I found it most distressing."

"Tell me, what can I do?" He straightened his already-straight cravat.

Lily set her cup aside before pinning Medford with her most serious stare. "I would like you to tell me the details. When exactly is this bet supposed to be carried out? What are the time frames, et cetera?"

Medford's brows furrowed. "Why? What does any of that matter, Lily? It's a completely inappropriate bet. I should call the blackguard out. I am fully prepared to defend your honor."

Lily slid her hand across the space between them and rested it on Medford's sleeve. "You know you cannot do that without revealing my identity. Humor me, Medford, please. What of the details?"

Medford took a deep breath. "There was mention of the Atkinsons' house party."

Lily nodded. The affair was a grand tradition of the Season. "Yes," she prodded. "Go on."

"This is most inappropriate to be discussing with you, Lily."

She refrained from reminding him that he had brought it up. "Come now. What's inappropriate between the two conspirators who brought London *Secrets of a Wedding Night*?"

Medford smiled. "You have a point. Very well. The bet was for him to, ahem, seduce you by the end of the house party next weekend. One may only presume he expects both of you to be there."

Lily nodded. "Yes, and what was the bet for exactly?

How much money does Colton stand to win?" She plucked a piece of parchment and a quill from the table next to her and held the writing instrument poised to capture the figure.

"I hate to say." Medford turned his head away.

"Please," she cajoled. "I must know."

Medford scrunched his forehead, clearly not immune to her pleading. "Very well." He sighed heavily. "Two hundred pounds, once all of the bets have been totaled. Something close to it."

Lily sat up straight and blinked, the quill and parchment forgotten in her hands. "Two hundred pounds! What are the odds?" She discarded the quill and paper.

"Five to four, at present."

"In Colton's favor?"

Medford looked appropriately chagrined. "I'm afraid so. Unfortunately, it seems the entire male population of the *ton* has got in on this particular bet. It's quite out of control. Disgusting if you ask me."

Lily thought for a moment, dragging her tapered fingernail across her chin.

"Medford," she said slyly. "I have decided what I shall write the next pamphlet about."

Medford shook his head. "What does your next pamphlet have to do with Colton's bet?"

Lily smiled. "Ah, but that is the very best part. My next pamphlet shall be entitled *Secrets of a Seduction: How to Deny a Rake*. It shall be an unwitting woman's guide to knowing how to spot a rake's telltale signs and avoid falling for his lies. Yet another public service. And that's why I shall be attending the Atkinsons' house party."

Medford opened his mouth as if he would argue with her, but quickly snapped it shut. A slow smile spread across his lips. "Lily, are you certain?"

Lily smiled. "Yes. I will make money and Colton will lose money. It's perfect!"

Medford shouted with laughter. "You know, my lady, I think you just might be right."

# CHAPTER 18

The next morning, Lily sat perusing the mail at her little writing desk in the breakfast room. In addition to the usual bills, two pieces of mail had arrived in the post. The first was the invitation to the Atkinsons' house party. The second was a letter addressed to her from the . . . Earl of Merrill.

Lily let her teacup full of hot water clatter to the saucer. She ripped open the letter, holding her breath. Her eyes hurriedly scanned the page. Her stomach dropped. Her late husband's nephew, the current earl, was coming to London for the Season. He and his new wife intended to reclaim his town house and expected Lily to vacate the property within the sennight.

Lily squeezed her eyes shut. She'd known it was only a matter of time before she received this letter, but why did it have to come now of all times? She had nowhere else to go.

She shook her head and plucked her quill from its inkwell. First, she wrote back to Lady Atkinson. Yes, she and her younger sister, Annie, would not miss the event. They would both be honored to attend the house party. The second letter was to her cousin Althea in Northumberland. If her cousin wouldn't take them in, they'd be on the streets in a matter of days. Lily shuddered at the thought.

She finished the letters, tossed a bit of sand over the ink, and dribbled wax on the parchment. She summoned Evans and asked him to be sure to get both letters into the very next post. Then, she relaxed back in her chair and took up her cup again.

Everything would work out. Wouldn't it? If Cousin Althea agreed to take them in, Lily and Annie could leave for Northumberland straight from the house party. In the meantime, Lily would ask Medford if Evans and the two dogs could stay at one of his many properties temporarily. Once they were all safely ensconced in Northumberland, Lily would write her new pamphlet from her cousin's house and send it to Medford via the post. Yes, it would all be fine.

Annie walked past the doorway just then, and Lily called to her. Her sister ducked her head into the room. "Yes?"

"Annie, ask Mary to help you pack your things. We'll be attending the Atkinsons' house party," Lily informed her.

Annie rushed into the room, a huge smile on her face. "You're not jesting, are you, Lily?"

Lily laughed. "No. No, of course not."

Annie twirled around in a circle. "Mr. Eggleston intends to be at the Atkinsons'," she relayed, a glowing smile on her face.

Lily nodded. "That's fine and good, dear, but this is strictly business."

Annie rolled her eyes. "I don't know what you're talking about." She wandered back out of the room, humming to herself and surely daydreaming of Arthur Eggleston.

A twinge of guilt flashed through Lily. She would eventually need to tell Annie of her plans to go to Northumberland. Poor Annie wouldn't like it. Not one bit.

The night before they were to leave for the house party, Medford insisted upon escorting Lily to the theater. She spent the entire ride mentally counting the money she would make with her new pamphlet. If she earned enough, perhaps, someday, she and Annie might rent a little house in the country, where the prices weren't so exorbitant. Their little family might have a fine, if not extravagant, life.

"After the house party and this ridiculous bet have been taken care of, there is something you and I must discuss," Medford told her as he handed her out of the coach on the steps of the theater.

Medford sounded serious. Lily bit her lip. She didn't like it when Medford sounded serious. "There will be plenty of time for things like that, Medford," she replied with a laugh, attempting to lighten the mood.

His eyes met hers. "I've asked you several times to call me 'James.' "

Lily nodded slowly. She couldn't call him "James," for the same reason she couldn't call Annie, "Anne." These people, these important people in her life, couldn't change from who she needed them to be. She'd had enough change in her life. "Thank you again," she said. "For allowing Evans and the pups to stay at your property. I feel so awful asking for such a favor, but—"

Medford tucked her hand into his arm. "Don't mention it. You know I'd help you in any way I can."

"You must take their room and board out of my earnings from the next pamphlet. I insist upon it."

Medford shook his head. "That is completely unnecessary, I—"

Lily gave him a warning look. "Please, Medford. You must promise me."

Medford sighed, still shaking his head. "Very well. I refuse to argue with you."

Lily eyed him carefully. She suspected he would claim she'd made more than she really had. She knew she had only to ask and Medford would allow her to stay in London under his care as well. But it would be inappropriate to use him so poorly. He'd already done so much for her.

Medford led Lily to his private box near the front of the stage. Ah, if only she felt a tiny spark for Medford. One bit of love or even lust. Medford was the best sort of fellow. What was wrong with her that she wasn't madly in love with him? Not that he was madly in love with her. But no matter, they would remain friends. And business partners. Yes. She would thank Medford prettily once she made the money from the second pamphlet. And she would relish watching Colton's dreams sour, just as he had soured hers five years ago. The dreams she'd only begun to allow herself to dream again recently, he dashed those too. Which made it that much worse.

Before the performance began, Lily excused herself to visit the ladies' retiring room. She hastily made her way to the little room off the foyer where she pinched the pink back into her cheeks and dabbed her forehead with her handkerchief. She waited there for several minutes, breathing evenly, hoping to calm the swirling worries in her head and prepare herself to enjoy a night of entertainment as best she could.

Soon, the music started, and Lily made her way back toward her seat. As she hurried through the lobby, she did not see the man in the shadows leaning casually against the wall with his ankles crossed until it was too late. She nearly tripped over his feet. "Pardon me," she began. She looked up into the apologetic face of none other than Devon Morgan.

"The fault is entirely mine," he said in his usual confident, deep voice and Lily longed to grind her slipper into his instep.

"Yes, it is." She continued past him.

He gripped her shoulder and softly spun her around. "I'm surprised to see you here."

"Don't speak to me," she snapped.

His brows furrowed. "I said I was sorry, Lily. Surely you didn't think I meant to cause your fall."

"Sorry is not good enough for what you've done." She jerked away from his touch. "And do not call me 'Lily.'"

A deep frown wrinkled his forehead. "The last time I saw you, *Countess,* you were thanking me for helping your sister at her debut. Now this?"

Lily scrunched her face into a scowl. She glanced over both shoulders to make sure they would not be overheard. Thankfully, the lobby was nearly empty.

She pushed Devon back into the corner, poking her finger against his chest the entire way. Her voice was an angry whisper. "Two days ago, I didn't know you had a detestable bet about me at your club. Two days ago, I didn't realize you were using me as a pawn in another one of your reprehensible games. Two days ago, I didn't know you were planning to make money off me."

Devon's face went pale. He reached for her. "Lily, listen to me. You've got it all wrong—"

Lily backed away. "Do I? Then tell me. Do you or do you not have a bet regarding whether or not you can seduce me?" She hissed the last words, glancing over her shoulder again.

He swallowed. "There is a bet, yes . . . but it's not as if—"

Lily's voice simmered. Her words came through clenched teeth. "If I were a man, I would strike you right now. I would call you out."

Devon put his hands up in a conciliatory gesture. "Lily, you must believe me. I was not the one who placed that bet and I did not—"

She turned on him, her eyes flashing. "But you'd surely profit from it if you won, wouldn't you? I knew you were low, Colton, but if I had any idea that you would stoop to this, why I . . . I cannot even fathom how far you've fallen." Her voice dropped to an angry whisper and she swallowed, unwelcome tears filling her eyes. "If I had had any idea when you showed up at my front door that afternoon and threatened to seduce me, that you were planning to make money from the prospect, I would have got my husband's pistol and shot you with it, then and there."

She turned on her heel and stalked away.

Devon reached her in two long strides. He swung her around to face him again. "Damn it, Lily. Will you listen to me? I never intended to profit from it. You must believe me."

She clenched her hands into fists at her sides. "Believe you? A liar? A gambler? A man who prizes money above all else? What sort of fool do you take me for?" She narrowed her eyes at him. "I thought we were playing before, you and I, and I allowed myself to be lulled by you, but now I recognize what you really are. I will not make the same mistake twice."

Devon reached for her, but she flung off his hands.

"You've made an enemy, my lord, a more powerful enemy than you can guess. And let this be a warning to you. The game is on, between you and me. I will see you at the house party. May the best person win."

Devon watched her go, a sick feeling in his gut. Bloody

hell. He'd really done it this time, hadn't he? And the worst part was he had spent the last two days painfully aware he didn't give a damn about that stupid threat to seduce her, revenge, the blasted bet, or anything else. He'd never wanted her to find out about it at all, let alone like this. In fact, he wanted nothing more than that idiotic bet to be forgotten. It sounded as if she'd never forgive him. He couldn't blame her if she didn't.

*Damn it.* Five years later, he was falling for the same quirky brunette again. The thought did not console him, but it was true, nonetheless. And now she hated him because of a bet he'd never placed to begin with. Devon clenched his fist until his knuckles cracked. By God, Jordan Holloway had better watch himself. The next time he saw his erstwhile friend, they'd be boxing again, but not for sport.

He watched Lily's retreating form until she disappeared into the darkness. She was squaring off against him, as an opponent. Not something he relished in the least. *Bloody hell.* How could he convince her that regardless of the blasted bet, he had no intention of seducing her to profit from it?

He needed to think of something, quickly. A bet at the club was not something one could simply cancel.

Devon took a deep breath. He'd decided to travel to Colton House to visit Justin again on the way, but then he and Lily would both be at the house party over the weekend. He must find a way for them both to win.

# CHAPTER 19

"Lord knows, I would claim to be the author of *Secrets of a Wedding Night* if it meant I'd end up in Colton's bed." Lady Eversly giggled to a group of friends who stood talking outside the Atkinsons' library.

Lily kept walking. It was the first day of the house party and the entire guest list was abuzz with the rumor of Colton's planned seduction of the author of the pamphlet.

She wanted to scream. It made it only mildly better that not everyone knew or suspected she was the lady in question. But what made her most angry was that the majority of the comments harkened to what Lady Eversly had just said. All the women were dreaming about it. Wanting to be her, if you could believe such nonsense!

Lily slipped up the staircase and back into her room. She shut the door behind her and leaned against it. How would she ever manage to survive this house party? She opened her eyes and spied her sister, reclining on the bed, reading a book.

Annie snapped the book shut and jumped up. "Oh, Lily, there you are. I spent the morning in a drawing room, sewing with the other young ladies, and you'll never guess what I heard."

Lily tried to manage a smile. "What was it?"

Annie arched her brows. "Seems the talk about the pamphlet has gained the attention of one Miss Amelia Templeton."

Lily snapped open her eyes. "Miss Templeton? What did she have to say?"

"She said she wondered if the author wrote *Secrets of a Wedding Night* with the sole purpose of stealing her affianced from her."

Lily paced back and forth across the floor, biting at her fingernail. "No one stole anyone's fiancé. It's ludicrous. Wasn't she the one who cried off? Does this mean she wants Colton back?"

Annie shrugged. "I'm not sure what it means, but I must admit there were a great many in the company who agreed with Miss Templeton."

Lily stopped pacing and faced her sister with her mouth open. "And what did you say? Did you defend me in any way?"

Annie smiled serenely. "How could I? I couldn't very well reveal your identity. You'd never forgive me."

Lily resumed her pacing. "No, but you might have defended the author," she sniffed. "Instead, you just sat there, silently, while they maligned me?"

"No, of course not," Annie replied, tracing her finger around the edge of her book. "I told them I thought the author was a frigid shrew who had nothing better to do than frighten poor unmarrieds, and Lord Colton shouldn't waste his time or skill on her."

"Annie, you did not!" Lily shrieked.

"No." Annie giggled. "I merely said I'd never read *Secrets of a Wedding Night* and never intended to." She nodded resolutely. "Which is every bit true."

Lily wrung her hands. "Why does Miss Templeton even care? That little fool cannot truly be thinking of renewing her engagement to Colton."

Annie nodded. "I'm afraid it's very likely. Her mother was already saying how she hoped Lord Colton would ask Miss Templeton to dance at the ball tonight and they might renew their affiliation with one another."

"Why, it's utter madness."

"I'm sorry to tell you, Lily, but the general conjecture among the ladies is that whatever the secrets may be in Colton's bedchamber, they would like to find out."

Lily clapped her hand against her cheek and stared at her sister with wide eyes. "Annie Andrews! I cannot believe I am hearing such rubbish come from your mouth. You should be thankful you're too old for me to wash it out with soap."

Annie tossed a hand in the air, completely unrepentant. "I'm not a child anymore, Lily, and you yourself wanted me to read that awful, scary pamphlet. I mean, I do have some idea what happens in private between a man and a woman. The Marquis of Colton is gorgeous. I've been pining over him myself ever since he danced with me at my debut."

Annie hopped off the bed and dreamily swept around the room, her skirts in her hand as if she were dancing to some imaginary waltz, no doubt with the Marquis of Colton.

Lily plunked her hands on her hips. "You should be taking a nap before the ball tonight, and I must go back downstairs and sit with the matrons and do needlework while they fawn over that scoundrel Colton."

"If you say so, but I don't feel the least bit tired." Annie shrugged and gestured to her book. "And if this Hannah More doesn't put me to sleep, I don't know what will."

Lily took a deep breath to steel herself and slipped out

of the room and back down the staircase. She quietly reentered the salon she'd left minutes earlier. Apparently, Lady Eversly had put an end to her gossip in the hallway, because that lady was sitting in the middle of a group of ladies, laughing.

*Oh, please let the discussion of Colton be done.*

"What about you, Lady Merrill?" Lady Eversly asked as Lily made her way back to her seat. "Who do *you* think wrote *Secrets of a Wedding Night*?"

Lily gulped. "Are we still talking about that silly bit of writing? Why, I thought that was old news." She laughed, hopefully enough to seem like she truly found it amusing.

"Perhaps Lady Merrill wrote the pamphlet." Lady Mountebank peered out from behind her needlework. "That is the rumor, you know."

Lily's hands went clammy. She searched her mind for something witty and light to rejoin with, but found nothing.

"Yes, well, we all know it had to have been one of us marrieds. A woman with enough experience to know what she was writing about," Lady Eversly offered. "And you fit the description, my dear Lady Merrill."

"Oh, think what you're saying," Lady Harris said. The woman was an elderly widow herself. "Poor Lady Merrill is a widow. Her husband died soon after their marriage. I'm sure she would not dream of maligning Merrill's good name with such drivel."

Lady Eversly laughed. "Yes, well, I've read *Secrets of a Wedding Night*, and it's nowhere near the truth if you're with a real man."

Lily gulped.

"There's another reason Lady Merrill couldn't possibly have written it," Lady Weston added. Lady Weston was a voluptuous redhead who was married to a man twice her age.

"What's that, Emma?" Lady Eversly asked, looking a bit too interested.

"Why, everyone knows Lady Merrill was rumored to be consorting with Lord Colton before her marriage to Merrill . . . and if that man had anything to do with her education," Lady Weston giggled, "I know firsthand she wouldn't have written anything so condemning about the act."

The women's voices erupted into a chorus of giggles and shrill laughs. Lily was temporarily glad she was saved from the recriminations and further questions as to whether she had actually authored the pamphlet, but she was struck by two very different emotions. First, she didn't relish her name being linked to Devon Morgan's. Had people assumed they'd been intimate all these years? If so, how had she not known about it? And secondly, Lady Weston was very obviously implying that she herself had been "educated" by Lord Colton. And that thought made Lily both miserable and very jealous.

It surprised her, to be sure, to find herself jealous over Devon, but the fact remained. Had Devon taken Lady Weston to bed? If so, and Lady Weston thought the pamphlet was a jest, that must mean Devon was particularly, ahem, skilled in that area. Something Lily already knew from a bit of personal experience. The thought of Devon touching Emma Weston the way he'd touched her made her positively green.

Devon's words from the first afternoon he'd arrived at her town house came back to haunt her. *"I intend to prove to you that your bloody pamphlet is wrong. I intend to show you how a real man pleasures a woman. I intend to seduce you, Countess."*

Lily went hot and cold. She fanned herself rapidly and stood up. "I must rest before the ball tonight." She hastily made her way from the room. Thankfully, the other women were still in gales over the earlier speculation and no one appeared to notice her departure.

She made her way up to her bedchamber. The room was dark and quiet. Annie was sleeping soundly in the adjoining room. Apparently, the Hannah More had done its work.

Lily slid between the cool sheets and expelled her breath. She hugged the pillow closely, closed her eyes, and tried to eradicate the memory of Devon's kisses from her traitorous mind. But all she could recall was his hands on her, his lips on her throat, his tongue brushing hotly against hers.

Oh, God . . . she had been wrong all these years. A wedding night wasn't as awful as she'd imagined it would be with the Earl of Merrill.

Her mind retraced to Devon. She remembered what it had been like five years ago to kiss him. The barest memory of actually looking forward to her wedding night came back to her. If it had been him—damn it, as it should have been—things might have been completely different. If it had been him—as it should have been—her life might be entirely different right now.

She thought of Devon with his dark good looks and all the nice things he'd done for her. He made her stomach leap when he entered a room. Surely a night with him would be exactly as Lady Eversly had described it. Nothing but pleasurable. If he made her feel the way he made her feel when he kissed her—and when he'd done those other things to her—she was certain to enjoy herself.

Lily tossed the sheets from her legs. Oh, whom was she fooling? She couldn't nap right now. No, she'd go down to the stables and find a mount to ride. Perhaps that would serve to tire her out.

Careful not to wake Annie, she enlisted Mary to help her into her chocolate-brown riding habit. Once she was properly attired, she made her way to the stables.

"Ah, Lady Merrill, there you are!"

Lily winced and slowly turned around. Lady Eversly pranced about on a filly.

"You've come to ride?" the lady asked. "I'm just about to be off. Do come with me, dear Lady Merrill."

Lily mustered the best smile she could. She had little choice but to join the woman. With the help of one of the grooms, she mounted a mare, and followed Lady Eversly from the stables.

"I know just the path to take," Lady Eversly said. "The Atkinsons have such a lovely estate."

"Let's go," Lily replied, already feeling better with the wind in her face. She'd think about her lack of money, her confrontation with Devon, and her future in Northumberland later. For now, all she wanted to do was to ride and ride and ride.

"You must call me 'Catherine,'" Lady Eversly called to her.

Lily nodded. "You must call me 'Lily.'"

Catherine maneuvered her horse next to Lily's. They sauntered at a slow pace. "You left the sewing party quite abruptly earlier." She leaned closer. "Do tell me, just between the two of us, did you write *Secrets of a Wedding Night*?"

"As much as I'd like to," Lily replied, "I cannot claim credit for it."

Catherine gave her a conspiratorial grin. "You know, that's just what I told the other ladies this afternoon. Everyone knows you're so proper you don't even drink champagne. You couldn't possibly have written *Secrets of a Wedding Night*." But there was a gleam in her eyes that told Lily she was still very much under suspicion.

Catherine clucked to her horse and took off at a brisk pace. Lily squeezed the reins until her fingers ached, her eyes narrowed on Lady Eversly's back. Finally, she reluctantly followed.

Soon they came to a fork in the road. "Follow me," Lady Eversly exclaimed, and both women galloped side-saddle into a narrow copse of trees. "I know a shortcut across the pasture," she called.

They came to a break in the trees moments later and Lily squinted, making out two figures in the middle of the pasture. A small group of men encircled the figures. Voices were raised, bottles were being passed around, and bets were being placed.

"You can take him, Colton! My money's squarely on you!" one man called.

Lily's head snapped up. Colton was there. But what was he doing? She couldn't tell exactly.

"Well, well, well. What have we stumbled upon here?" Lady Eversly shook the reins and kicked the side of her mount. "Let's have a closer look, shall we?"

Lily tried to call out to Catherine and say no, but the lady was already halfway across the pasture. *Confound it!* She would have to follow. Lily trailed Lady Eversly, still squinting to make out exactly what Colton was up to.

"Hit him with another right, Ashbourne," another male voice sounded as the women drew closer. "Don't let me go home with my pocket lighter."

When they galloped close enough, it was obvious. Lord Colton and Lord Ashbourne were engaged in a boxing match.

Without their shirts.

Lily gulped.

The two men circled each other in a patch of trampled grass while the small group of other men shouted along the sidelines.

Lily raised her voice. "I really don't think we should—"

Lady Eversly quickly turned back to face her. "Don't take this the wrong way, Lady Merrill, but I suggest you do a lot less thinking and a lot more enjoying yourself."

"But it's completely improper to—"

"All the very best things are completely improper. That, you can count on." Lady Eversly winked at her and then set off in a gallop that Lily quickly replicated.

Lily's gaze swung back to the men. She swallowed and raised her chin. Lady Eversly was entirely right. It might not be proper to be galloping full pelt toward an obviously male pastime, but the thrill in her belly told Lily she wanted to get a closer look.

A much closer look.

They trotted within twenty paces of the gathering before one of the men looked up and noticed them.

"Why, Lady E, you know you shouldn't be here," the man said with a wry smile on his face that made Lily think he was very glad indeed to see Catherine.

"If it's proper enough for you, Ellerbee, it's proper enough for me," Catherine shot back.

Ellerbee smiled a wide smile full of perfectly white teeth. "You are very right, E," he said with a laugh.

Most of the other men were still engaged in the sport and barely glanced over when Lady Eversly and Lily cantered up.

"My friend Lady Merrill," Lady Eversly said to Ellerbee.

Out of the corner of her eye, Lily saw Devon's head whip to attention. He stopped the match.

"It's a pleasure to meet you," Ellerbee said to Lily, doffing his hat. "Any friend of Lady E's is a friend of mine."

Lily nodded and returned the greeting, but her every nerve was completely attuned to Devon and his awareness of her presence.

Lord Ashbourne had looked up when the match stopped and he glanced over his bare shoulder at Lily, obviously wondering what had so caught his opponent's attention. He spat a mouthful of blood.

"What do we have here?" he asked, wiping sweat from his forehead.

"Exactly what I was saying to my friend Lady Merrill just now," Lady Eversly called to Lord Ashbourne.

"Do you intend to remain atop that horse or will you get down and watch?" Lord Ashbourne called back.

Lily had never been much for propriety, but even for her, the discussion between Lady Eversly and Lord Ashbourne seemed overly familiar. The casualness with which Lady Eversly addressed the men was entirely inappropriate. Lily shouldn't be here. She wanted to gallop away and not look back.

That is, until she allowed her eyes to rivet to Devon's bare, muscled, sweaty chest.

# CHAPTER 20

Devon wiped sweat from his brow and Lily noted with a funny feeling between her legs that his hair was mussed and his chest was perfect. The sheen of sweat that glistened over him made her imagine all sorts of things, specifically, his rock-hard body glistening above her, his muscles rippling as he hovered over her in bed.

A rush of heat burned her cheeks. She drew a deep breath.

Lady Eversly glanced back and forth between Lily and Devon. "Looking good, Colton," she said in a voice that Lily found *entirely* too friendly. "Which one of you handsome men should I bet on?"

Devon nodded toward the manor house. "Don't you think Eversly would wonder where his money's gone?"

"Not," Lady Eversly shot back, "if I win. Tell me, Ashbourne, which one of you is in more of a fighting mood today?"

"He is," Lord Ashbourne said, cocking his head toward Devon. "But unless I mistake my guess, the bloke is about to forfeit this particular match."

"I'm not forfeiting anything," Devon growled at his friend.

Lady Eversly laughed. "You cannot blame him, Ashbourne. Everyone knows the rumor that he's here for the weekend to seduce the writer of *Secrets of a Wedding Night* and it's entirely possible that that particular lady is sitting atop a horse in front of him right now."

Neither Devon nor Lily uttered a word. Their eyes met. Lily's face burned with shame. She wished the earth would open up and swallow her.

Thankfully, Jordan Holloway broke the silence. "Don't tell me you're the author, Catherine," he said, putting his hand over his heart in a mock sign of pain. "And here I'd always had such a good opinion of Eversly."

"Hardly," Lady Eversly snorted. "I've never been much for writing, but if you're doling out lessons sometime, Ashbourne, do pay me a visit."

Lily barely heard her companion's scandalous words. Just then, Devon seemed to snap himself out of the trance he was in.

"The bet was completely overblown," he said. "There's no such thing as far as I'm concerned. In fact, that's what I'm trying to tell Ashbourne here."

"Pity," Lady Eversly said with a catlike smile pinned to her face. "Because from what I can tell from my friend's reaction to seeing you with your shirt off, you were just about to win."

Jordan cleared his throat. "Yes, well—"

Lady Eversly cut him off. "Tell me, Lady Merrill, who do *you* think will win the bet?"

Lily eyed the group. Time stood still. She wanted to wipe the smug look from Catherine's beautiful face.

Lily was tired. Tired of being preconceived by everyone. Devon, Annie, and now a complete stranger. She was predictable. She didn't drink. She couldn't possibly be the author of *Secrets of a Wedding Night*.

Lily clenched her teeth. Her gaze slid to Devon. He was

gorgeous. There was no denying it. And all the women in the *ton* clearly wanted him.

Well, she wanted him too.

The idea that had begun forming in her mind ever since she'd encountered him at the theater took a full-formed shape.

Now she was sure of it.

Devon Morgan owed her a wedding night.

An unforgettable one.

She'd never be married again. She might as well discover what it felt like to spend a night of unbridled passion in the arms of a handsome man who knew exactly what he was doing. Revenge had nothing to do with it. She could enjoy the pleasures in Colton's bed and still take her revenge. In fact, it just might be the perfect way to exact it.

*Secrets of a Clandestine Night.* That's what she would write. And *that* pamphlet would sell, blast it!

Lily spurred her mount into action, turning in a tight circle.

"No reply, Lady Merrill?" Lady Eversly called out.

"My money's on Colton," Lily tossed over her shoulder. Then she touched the horse's flank with her riding crop, starting her into a fine gallop toward the stables.

Lily grinned. *Ah, the looks of shock they all must have plastered to their faces.*

# CHAPTER 21

Lily entered the ballroom wearing her lavender gown. The one that made her eyes glow like amethysts. She'd brought it with her to the Atkinsons' house party and she'd spent a considerable amount of time late this afternoon removing some of the baubles and lace that marked it as a garment that had been in fashion five years ago. She added a bit of understated edging that made it look like the height of fashion now. And for a bit of added fun, she'd spent the rest of the afternoon retracing the pattern of the neckline to ensure it was lower cut than ever before. The result was a mix of daring and dangerous, one that was sure to attract attention.

Annie was at her side in the white gown Lily had sewn for her. Together, they entered the room, dark hair swept up, curls framing their faces. Annie with the air of innocence about her, and Lily, no doubt, the jaded air of someone who'd seen too much.

Lily promptly made her way toward a hovering footman who provided her with a long-stemmed glass of champagne. She was not Lady Merrill, proper widow anymore. She was Lily, the future author of *Secrets of a Clandestine Night.* And she would begin with a drink . . . or three.

Annie reached for a glass of champagne. Lily gently pushed Annie's hand away and pointed in the direction of the punch bowl. Annie scowled at her.

Raising her glass to her lips, Lily took a sip of champagne. Sweet and ticklish. Ah, champagne was lovely, really. She should have been drinking it long before now.

"Be careful," Annie warned, leaving Lily's side. "That dress can be nothing but trouble for you, dear sister."

"Don't be impertinent," Lily replied.

Annie shrugged, and Lily watched approvingly as her sister went off in search of a glass of that innocuous liquid, punch.

"You are as beautiful as I've ever seen you." The male voice sounded behind Lily's ear and for a moment Lily held her breath, hoping it was Devon. But she turned, instead, to see Lord Medford at her side. Medford was dressed in his dark-blue best, his brown hair clipped close, his eyes brightly shining. He was handsome to be sure, but he lacked Devon's dark dangerousness.

"Thank you," she responded in kind, curtsying to him.

Medford's eyes devoured the cleavage that spilled so generously from her gown.

Lily smiled at that. Good. The dress would work after all. Though at the moment it appeared to be working on the wrong man. She quickly downed half the glass of champagne before searching about for the footman again. Oh, any footman with champagne would do.

Her eyes scanned the ballroom and quickly alighted on Miss Templeton. The young woman stood against the far wall, a tall, blond, willowy thing with far too many curls bouncing about her head. "She looks positively insane," Lily muttered under her breath, downing the second half of her glass.

"Who looks insane?" Medford easily removed two

more champagne glasses from a footman's silver tray and handed one to Lily. "I see you're drinking now."

Lily exchanged her empty glass for the full one and shrugged. "What do you think he sees in her?" She tipped the newest glass to her lips.

"Who?" Medford's eyes narrowed on Lily's face. "How many glasses of champagne have you had?"

"Oh, not enough, I assure you." She placed one hand at her elbow and dangled her glass from her gloved fingers. Tapping her silver slipper on the floor, she glared at Miss Templeton.

"What do I think who sees in whom?" Medford asked, taking a sip from his own glass.

"That dreadful Templeton girl. What do you think Colton could possibly see in her? He's old enough to be her father."

"That's a stretch," Medford said with a laugh.

"Well, uncle then," Lily amended, scrunching up her nose.

"She's lovely and she's quite wealthy," he replied, before quickly amending. "If you like young, blond sorts of girls, which I assuredly do not."

"Wealthy, ah yes, that's it, isn't it?" Lily shot the last of the second glass of champagne down her throat.

"Perhaps it's best to change the subject. May I have this dance, my lady?" Medford asked.

Lily turned around to tell Medford she didn't feel like dancing.

And that's when she saw him.

Standing only a few paces away, his back against a column, his dark eyes boring holes into her.

Devon.

She caught her breath. Time stood still. He stalked toward her, his eyes never leaving hers, and she said a little prayer of thanks for her daring décolletage. He had a cut on the side of his lip, a result, no doubt, of his earlier fight with Lord Ashbourne.

She wanted to float over to him. No, she wanted him to stalk over to her. She wanted him to take her into his arms and demand the next dance. Suddenly, she did feel like dancing after all.

Someone tapped her on the shoulder. "Lady Merrill, I have something to say to you."

Lily jumped and turned around at the small voice that sounded like nothing so much as an angry mouse. That curly-headed Miss Templeton was there, tapping her tiny foot on the parquet and eyeing Lily as if she wanted to slap her.

"Why, Miss Templeton. I haven't seen you in an age."

A shadow fell across Lily's shoulders. Devon had drawn near.

"You've been avoiding me, no doubt, after serving to ruin my life," Miss Templeton squeaked.

Lily gave her her famous innocent look. "Ruined your life? Whatever could you possibly mean?"

"You know exactly what I mean." Miss Templeton's sky-blue eyes were narrowed. Why, the girl might peck Lily to death if she allowed her to get close enough.

"No, I don't actually," she replied in a tight voice. This little bird needed to fly away. "Miss Templeton, allow me to warn you. You couldn't possibly have chosen a worse evening to have this conversation with me. I have every intention of drinking far too much for far too long and I'm entirely sure you won't like anything I have to say to you. Now, I suggest you go take some smelling salts or whatever damsels in distress do when they're overcome with their emotions. And while you're at it, you might see to your hair." Lily glanced up at the curly configuration atop the younger girl's head and frowned disapprovingly.

Miss Templeton shook so hard Lily feared her curls might fall off. Her milk-white hands curled into fists. "Oh! You! Do you deny you sent me your detestable pamphlet?"

Lily glanced at Devon from the corner of her eye. "Pamphlet?"

Miss Templeton's voice dropped to a whisper. "*Secrets of a Wedding Night.* I received a personal copy. It was delivered to my home a few weeks ago. Do you deny you sent it?"

Where was that confounded footman with another glass of champagne? "Now, Miss Templeton, I've heard it said no one knows for sure who wrote *Secrets of a Wedding Night,* but believe me when I tell you, anyone who sent you a copy must have had only your very best interests at heart."

"Is that so?" More birdlike foot tapping.

"Oh, I'm sure of it. And besides, I hardly see how it ruined your life. That's a bit dramatic, dear, isn't it?" Lily finished on a conspiratorial whisper.

Miss Templeton pointed a petulant finger at Devon, who remained just a few paces away, watching the interaction with an interested smile on his face. So like him.

Medford stood beside them glancing back and forth between the two women as if he might be called upon to break up a physical altercation.

"I was engaged to the marquis," Miss Templeton peeped. "And now I am not."

Lily shrugged and took another long sip of champagne. "I hardly see how a pamphlet ended your engagement."

"It frightened me horribly. I was scared witless."

Lily rolled her eyes. "Did the pamphlet cry off for you, then?"

Miss Templeton's pursed her tiny lips. "I cried off, but only because of that hideous pamphlet."

Miss Templeton's mother, obviously alerted to her daughter's outburst by some caring partygoer, hurried over and grabbed the blond thing by the hand.

"Amelia, dear," she cried. "You are making a *scene*."

Miss Templeton allowed dainty tears to slip from her eyes. "I don't care, Mother. Lady Merrill has ruined my entire life."

"There, there, dear. You need to lie down."

"Yes. Go lie down," Lily said in her fake-sweet voice. "Far, far away." With that she downed the rest of the glass.

Thankfully, Mrs. Templeton pulled the incoherent young woman away before a larger scene ensued, but not before tossing Lily a decidedly unpleasant look. Lily breathed a sigh of relief as she watched them go, but an unexpected twinge of guilt shot through her. She bit her lip.

"I'd clap if I could." Devon's deep voice sounded from behind her.

Lily jumped. She hadn't forgotten he was there exactly, but she hadn't expected him to speak first either.

Medford stepped in between them. "Colton," he said, his voice a disapproving growl.

"Medford," Colton replied, nodding to the viscount, his eyes narrowed.

Medford turned to face Lily. "Do you want me to make him go?"

Lily shook her head. "I appreciate it, Lord Medford, truly I do. But I'll handle him."

Medford eyed Devon again, clearly reluctant to leave. Lily put her hand on the viscount's sleeve. "Please, trust me. I'll be all right."

Medford nodded tersely. "I'll see you tomorrow morning. Then, we'll talk." He turned on his heel and stalked off without a backward glance.

Lily watched him go before she whirled around to face

Devon. They eyed each other carefully. "So, you said you'd clap. Why is that?"

He took two steps forward. His black, polished boots clicked against the parquet. "For that performance, of course. You didn't lie to Miss Templeton, did you? Well done, actually. Quite well done."

Lily suppressed her smile. "I don't know what you mean." She glanced around. Thankfully, the other guests had returned to their dancing, drinking, and conversations. They were no longer staring at her.

"Oh, yes you do, though you'll never admit it. I must say, I underestimated you myself. I always had my suspicions that you'd written the pamphlet, but I never imagined that you'd actually been the one to send a copy to Miss Templeton personally."

Lily's cheeks flamed. Blast it. Unfortunate, him overhearing all of that. She raised her chin. "If someone sent the pamphlet to Miss Templeton, it wasn't—"

Devon raised his hand. "Please. Don't ruin your streak of not telling a lie. I couldn't stand it. Let us both pretend it is a mystery how Miss Templeton came to be in possession of the literature."

Lily snapped her mouth closed. Devon held out his hand to her.

"I see you're drinking tonight . . . and wearing the type of gown I've never seen you in before, I might add. Though I must admit I cannot help but admire it."

"Thank you," she murmured.

"Dance with me," he commanded. "Don't let that beautiful gown go to waste. I cannot take my eyes off it."

His gaze dipped to her décolletage and Lily's heart beat double time.

Lily didn't answer. She merely put her hand in his and allowed him to lead her to the dancing.

Devon escorted her to the floor. He bowed to her first, then took her hand, letting his other hand rest on her waist. Lily narrowed her eyes like a cat's and watched him. This was a game, tonight, between the two of them. A game with the highest stakes.

"The cut on your lip looks bad."

Devon smiled. "Jordan's got a hell of a left hook. But you should see him."

"So who won?"

He shrugged. "It was more of a draw. But let's just say we worked out our . . . issues."

Lily let that go.

"I thought you didn't drink," he said.

"Watching me, Colton?" she asked. The smell of his fine cologne made her knees weak.

"Always." His deep, smooth voice sent chills through her insides.

"I thought you preferred to wear gray," he said next.

"Wrong again," she countered. "I do like to surprise you once in a while, you know?"

He raised a brow. "I thought you were angry with me."

"Who says I'm not?"

Devon let his eyes devour Lily's décolletage. The woman looked like a dream. Her tiny waist encased in shimmering satin, her ample breasts pushed up for his eyes to feast upon, her white, creamy skin bared to his appreciative gaze. He shuddered. Could she feel how much he wanted her right now? Had always wanted her? "Why didn't you dance with Medford? Do I mistake my guess or had he asked you before I arrived?"

Lily's eyes met and sparked with his. "Why didn't you dance with Miss Templeton?"

"You sneer that name in the same manner I once pronounced your title," he said with a laugh.

"You're evading my question. Miss Templeton is obviously more than eager to renew your betrothal."

His eyes slid across her skin, devouring her. "What is it you told me once? Ah, yes, souls in Hades want a drink of water."

Lily gave him a brilliant smile.

"It's not surprising," Devon said, his teeth tugging at his lower lip.

"What? Miss Templeton's desire to renew your betrothal? Ah, still arrogant, I see." Lily twirled around him, her skirts caressing his legs.

"No." He laughed again. "I only meant that I was right."

"Right about what?"

He pulled her close. His cheek brushed her temple. "Come out onto the balcony with me," he whispered into her ear.

"I thought you'd never ask," she whispered back.

With a sly smile, Devon pulled Lily along behind him. He grabbed two champagne glasses from the nearest footman on the way out. Devon pushed open the French doors with his back. They fell shut behind the two of them. He turned to face Lily, handing her one of the glasses. She eagerly took it and drank. Thankfully, they were alone with the night. No other partygoers were on that particular area of the balcony just then.

"No doubt we're the scandal of the ballroom," she said, laughing and peering through the windows. She twirled around in a circle. "What with you pulling me out of there like that, God knows what they're saying about us now."

Devon chuckled and sipped from his own glass of champagne. "We were already the talk of the ballroom. Or hadn't you noticed?"

Lily laughed out loud at that. Laughed and drank more champagne. She felt quite reckless and quite wonderful of a sudden. "Tell me. What were you right about?" She twirled around again as Annie was wont to do.

Devon grinned and the moonlight glistened off his white teeth. He winked at her. "The secret to catching a woman is to make her think she is chasing you. Seems to hold true in Miss Templeton's case at least."

Lily's heart fell a bit, but the champagne was making her deliciously carefree. "You admit you want Miss Templeton to chase you?" She advanced on him, hoping her décolletage was still working the magic it was meant to.

"I admit no such thing." His free hand went around Lily's waist. She drank more champagne. "The one woman I've been trying to catch is only just now in my arms."

Lily couldn't help it. She closed her eyes and nearly melted against him. Oh, fine, she should have been offended. She should have been shocked, outraged, or any other number of overused terms that sprang to mind, but instead she was . . . pleased. Yes, that was it. Nothing but pleased. She turned around in his arms. He enfolded her into his embrace. If anyone were to walk onto the balcony at that moment, she would be entirely ruined of course. Perhaps it was the moonlight, or the champagne, or the man, but she . . . Did. Not. Care.

She craned her neck and looked up at him. "You're only trying to catch me so you can turn me in like a voucher."

He winced. "Now, that stings." He ran his fingers up the sides of her arms to the dip in her bodice, his forefinger edging along the trim that framed her neckline. The heat of his fingers drew fevered patterns on her skin. "And it's entirely untrue."

She turned in his embrace, wrapped her arms around his neck, and breathed her champagne-scented breath against his neck. "You deny trying to seduce me then?"

Devon pulled her against his rock-hard body. "Never."

"Why were you fighting Lord Ashbourne?"

Devon cleared his throat. "Because Ashbourne was responsible for that damned bet at the club."

Lily narrowed her eyes at him. "Really?"

"Yes, really. I told you it wasn't me."

Her face softened. "You fought your friend over me?"

"Yes. He damn well deserved it."

"Are you still angry with him?"

"No, we've moved past it. Besides, he should be in the ballroom right now, dancing with your sister, as part of his amends."

Lily giggled. She let her arms drop from Devon's shoulders and moved over to the French doors where she glanced into the ballroom. There they were, Annie and Jordan Holloway, dancing. The two actually cut a striking figure together. "Well, it seems Lord Ashbourne has managed to distract her from Arthur Eggleston for five minutes. Even with that black eye of his. Most impressive."

"A very well-deserved black eye," Devon said. "Ashbourne's apologized for the damage he's done, but I told him it remains to be seen if you've forgiven me."

Lily turned back to face him, a sly smile on her lips. "Very well. I've forgiven you. Is that what you want to hear?"

"Is it true?"

She nodded, biting her lip. "Everything's changed."

"What does that mean?"

"Perhaps I am the master of seduction after all," she breathed.

He moved toward her and reached out, his finger tracing her jawline. "Is that so? What do you know about seduction?"

She pulled out of his reach and turned in a circle. Around and around. "Seduction? Let me think." She tapped a finger to her forehead. "Let's see. There are nice men, shy men, mysterious men, and all-out lovers."

He reached for her again, but she eluded him. "What are you talking about?"

Lily laughed. She set her empty glass on the balustrade. "Everyone knows. Everyone knows about seduction. Everyone but *me*."

His voice was a husky, interested whisper. "What do you mean, Lily?"

She advanced on him, with half-hooded eyes. "Perhaps the tables have turned. Perhaps I'm not waiting for you to seduce me anymore. Perhaps I'm planning on seducing *you* now."

He looked at her as if he feared she'd lost her mind. "Lily, you don't know what you're saying."

Lily didn't answer. Instead, she stepped forward again, wrapped her arms around his neck, and pulled his mouth down barely a breath from hers. She would make sure she sounded serious. Very serious. "Yes. I. Do."

His eyes flared. "When did you come to this conclusion?"

She smiled a cunning smile and silently asked herself the same question. Was it the champagne or the moonlight?

"I came to this conclusion when I saw you with your shirt off."

What had got into Lily? The last time he'd talked to her alone, she was hurling accusations at him at the theater, then her strange behavior this afternoon at the boxing match, and now she was telling him she meant to seduce him. It was enough to confuse the hell out of him.

He watched her, advancing toward him, looking like a siren who'd just emerged from the sea. His mind traced back to a night five years ago, another ball, another balcony, with the same beautiful young woman.

Lily's debut. Devon had come that night because his

father had forced him to. Back when he gave a damn what his father wanted. It had all been a farce, really. Devon might have had an illustrious title, but it was well-known even then among the *ton* that the Colton coffers were completely empty. A title without a fortune might be appealing to an heiress or those who smelled of shop, but a gently reared English girl from a good family would much prefer a title *and* a fortune if given the choice. True, he'd had a variety of flirtations, and an indecent number of offers to spend the night in the beds of Society's most beautiful married women, but the young ladies' parents and chaperones made it their business to keep their sheltered little innocents away from him. A destitute marquis was no one's first choice.

He'd been there that night, halfheartedly attempting to talk Ashbourne out of his obsession with a blond named Georgiana, and counting the moments before he could leave and go to his club, when Lily had sauntered past.

He'd looked twice. Something he rarely did. He'd nearly groaned when he realized her white gown and hovering mother marked her as an innocent. But he'd been unable to resist and had asked her to dance, ignoring the scowl on her mother's face. And he hadn't regretted asking her to dance.

Lily had been just as engaging as she was beautiful, something else he hadn't expected. He'd danced with her twice, unable to help himself, but then he'd left her alone. A third dance with him would do nothing for her reputation and he could not have such an innocent. Even if he had lost his mind and proposed marriage, her mother would have had none of it, the look of disapproval on that woman's face had been evident.

Later that night, he'd been smoking a cheroot out in the garden when a musical voice behind him made him turn. "No more dancing for you this evening, Lord Colton?"

He'd immediately stomped out the cheroot and turned

to face her, a wide smile on his face. "I'm afraid not, Miss Andrews."

A slight frown had marred the porcelain skin of her forehead. "I'm very sorry to hear that."

"I assure you, you'll have no trouble finding other gentlemen to dance with."

She'd nodded matter-of-factly, and Devon had smothered his smile. There was something so straightforward about the girl. Not vain. Just confident and unpretentious. And beautiful.

She sighed. "I'm afraid none of them are such lovely dancers as you."

He'd laughed. "Ah, my mother would be pleased to hear it. She forced me to take dancing lessons for an indecent period of time. Seems her diligence has been rewarded."

Lily laughed then and the tinkling sound filled Devon's mind. He never wanted to be out of her company.

"Being that you're such a lovely dancer, won't you come back in and dance with me once more, my lord?"

Devon couldn't help but smile. "Where is your mother?"

Her eyes widened. "Inside. Why?"

"She doesn't know you're out here, does she?"

A sly smile flashed across her lovely face. She shook her head. "No."

Devon took a deep breath. This wouldn't be pleasant, but it was necessary. He couldn't allow an uninformed innocent to continue her flirtation with him. Damn it, he detested his father for forcing him to attend such events. "The fact is, Miss Andrews, your mother wouldn't want you out here with me."

"Oh, come now. It's not *that* scandalous, being alone with a gentleman on a balcony."

"With me, it is."

Her brow furrowed again. "Why? Have you done something horrendous, Lord Colton?" She smiled at him, a smile he wanted to remember forever.

He nodded. "Yes."

Her smile disappeared, replaced by a look of curiosity. "What?"

He shrugged. "As far as the *ton* is concerned, I've done the most horrible thing there is."

She shook her head. "I don't understand. You're the heir to the Marquis of Colton, are you not?"

He placed a hand on the stone statue next to him. "Yes."

"Then what could you possibly have done to fall out of favor with Society?"

He laughed. "You don't know much about Society, do you?"

She looked confused and he regretted that. "No," she admitted. "I've only just had my debut."

Devon winced. "I'm sorry to inform you, Miss Andrews, that I am poor. Not just poor, destitute. My father and I live on credit and little else. That is the sin for which Society can never forgive me."

Surprisingly, Lily's face had blossomed into a wide smile. "Is that all? I thought you'd done something truly horrific like got a divorce or made an indecent overture to Princess Charlotte."

He swallowed his laugh. The girl was irreverent. He liked that about her. He liked it very much. "You're not horrified?"

She shook her head. "Not a bit. Money's never meant anything to me."

His smile had been ironic. "I can assure you, your mother feels quite differently."

Lily shrugged. "My mother doesn't believe in love."

Love. The word had caught him unawares. It had tugged at his conscience and his heart. "Love?"

"Yes, when I fall in love it won't have anything whatsoever to do with money," she'd assured him. "Character is much more important than money can ever be."

She'd said the words so easily and Devon knew without a doubt she meant them. He'd been drawn to her before, her beauty, her laughter, her spark. But here was a real gem, a gorgeous young woman without the preconceived notions of her snobbish family. Without the drilled-in beliefs of the *ton* in her brain. A true original.

She'd smiled at him, an impish smile, and Devon hadn't been able to keep from smiling back.

"So?" she asked. "Won't you dance with me?"

And they had danced again, there in the gardens, to the strains of a waltz drifting through the French doors. And that's when Devon had fallen in love with her. She was everything he'd ever hoped for and never believed he could find.

Yes, she'd made him believe again. Believe in everything including . . . love. That is, until he'd received her note.

But that had all been five years ago. An age. And now, here she was, talking about seducing him. He shook his head.

"Lily, for the love of God, what are you talking about?" His voice shook with desire.

"Oh, I'll get to that in a moment, my lord," Lily said, draining the rest of Devon's champagne glass before abandoning it on the side of the stone balcony. "First, there is another secret I have to tell."

She turned to him, her eyes flashing, and advanced on him again.

He swallowed. "What's that?"

"Scared, are you?"

"I have no idea what you'll say from one minute to the next tonight."

"Good. You need to be kept guessing. Miss Templeton would never keep you guessing."

"Now you're speaking in riddles."

"It's time for some honesty." Lily slid her hand down his chest. "Between you and me."

Devon leaned back against the balcony, resting his elbows on it. Hmm. With that look in her eye, it might be best to give her some space. "Perfect. I'm more than ready for honesty."

Lily swung around, her back to the French doors. "Are you quite sure you're ready for the truth, Lord Colton?"

"Absolutely." His dark eyes searched her face.

Her voice lowered. Her breathing hitched. "I was in love with you five years ago. I was in love with you, madly, idiotically in love with you, and my heart was broken when you took off for the countryside. In fact"—she stumbled slightly, her slipper catching on one of the stones—"you'll never believe it."

Devon reached for her to ensure she didn't fall. He searched her face, watching her carefully, alertly. His eyes were wide, his breathing heavy. "Lily, what are you talking about?"

"I had packed my bags to elope with you. That's what kind of a fool I was!" She laughed a loud clap of a laugh, but it was entirely without humor.

She pushed his hands away and turned again, another stumble. Her eyes flashed with a violet violence that frightened him. God, she was inebriated. So inebriated that she was reinventing the past. They both knew she'd sent him a letter that night, telling him she'd decided to marry Merrill. Devon reached for her again, but she pulled away.

"Leave me be," she commanded.

He stepped back.

She laughed, a sultry laugh, shaking off all seriousness and reverie. She advanced on him again, this time with fire in her eyes. "I've decided you owe me a wedding night, my lord. And I intend to have it. I'll see you in your bedchamber upstairs," she whispered against his mouth. "In one hour."

# CHAPTER 22

Lily slipped back through the French doors that led into the ballroom. She nearly stumbled over Annie, who was standing there with a surprised look on her face. Lily smiled broadly and looped her arm through her sister's.

"What are you doing here?" she asked in a conspiratorial whisper.

"Looking for you," Annie replied, an inscrutable expression on her face.

"I was just outside getting some air."

Annie glanced through the French doors and replied with eyebrows raised, "So I see."

"Go back and dance. Have fun! Enjoy yourself."

Annie's eyes nearly popped from her skull. "Now I *know* you're sick or something. You're not my sister."

"Whatever do you mean?" Lily asked, smothering a laugh.

"What's wrong with you?" Annie glanced at her, looking nothing if not suspicious. "You don't sound like yourself."

"Nothing is wrong with me. I'm merely enjoying myself. And this wonderful, wonderful champagne." Lily plucked another glass from the tray of a passing footman. "And this marvelous party."

"Lily Andrews. You are foxed!"

Lily swallowed her giggle at her sister's use of her maiden name and took a sip of champagne. "Shh. It's a secret."

Annie's eyes were as round as the bottom of the champagne flute. "I cannot believe I've lived to see the day *you'd* overindulge in alcohol."

Lily glanced around to make sure they weren't being overheard and pulled her sister into a corner. They hid behind a potted palm. "Annie, look. We may be leaving for Northumberland tomorrow. This is our last night to have fun. Real fun. Now go out and dance with Jordan Holloway or your young Mr. Egglethorpe or whatever his name is. Enjoy yourself."

Annie clutched at Lily's hand, real fear in her eyes. "Northumberland?"

"Yes. Yes. I was going to tell you all about it on the way. But the fact is we're destitute and I've asked Cousin Althea to take us in."

"Destitute? What are you talking about?" Annie braced her hand against the wall, her eyes wide.

The haze surrounding Lily's brain lifted momentarily. Oh, dear, she shouldn't have brought this up to Annie tonight. Especially when she hadn't even heard back from their cousin yet. Blasted champagne. Lily did so want her sister to enjoy her last night of Society.

She lowered her voice. "We have no choice, Annie. You must know we've been struggling for some time now. It's more and more difficult for me to pay the bills. The new earl has written that he intends to take over the house. We have no choice."

Annie's face wore a mask of panic. "You were just going to cart me off to Northumberland without telling me? Without giving me a chance to say good-bye to my friends . . . or Arthur?"

A warning bell sounded in Lily's brain at her sister's use of Mr. Eggleston's Christian name. "Keep your voice down," Lily insisted, patting Annie's hand. "You can post letters from Northumberland. Annie, listen, this isn't my first choice either. But there's nothing else for us to do. Once I sell a second pamphlet, perhaps—"

"I suppose you're right, Lily. I should go enjoy myself. For one last night." Blinking back tears, Annie pulled her hand from Lily's grasp and stalked away.

Lily winced. Guilt clawed at her. The last thing she wanted was to hurt Annie, disappoint her. But it was time for Annie to grow up. Her sister wanted to be treated like an adult, well, she'd just have to accept adult information, adult responsibility. And the fact was they had no money. No place to go.

She watched Annie's retreating figure until she saw her dancing with Eggleston, a smile on her face. That was the spirit.

Lily sighed. She'd handled that episode poorly. She knew it. The champagne was to blame. She would make it up to Annie in the morning. Explain everything more clearly. Tonight, she had a new pamphlet to research.

Lily glanced back out the French doors. Colton was gone. Had he reentered the house through another set of doors? Or was he hiding from her? Well, she'd thrown down the gauntlet. Now she must be brave enough to see it picked up.

She must play out this little drama, whether it proved to be comedy or tragedy. She hurried upstairs to ask Mary to help her remove her stays. She knew from experience that Devon Morgan was quite adept at such things, but it would still be preferable to wear more easily accessible clothing if a seduction was her intention.

She rushed into the bedchamber and called for Mary. The maid popped her head out from the adjoining room.

"Mary, quickly, I must put on my night rail."

Mary scurried out. "What? Why, me lady?"

Hmm. Lily hadn't quite thought that far.

"If I told you, you would not believe me," Lily replied. There was one good thing about having a maid who could not remember anything. Mary would not judge her for her indiscretion in the morning. She wouldn't remember.

Mary helped Lily shed her lavender gown and stays and soon Lily was wearing her filmy white night rail. She pulled on her robe. "Thank you very much." She hugged Mary quickly and sneaked to the door. Lily examined the darkened hallway carefully. She must wait for the right moment to make her flight.

She already knew exactly where Devon's bedchamber was.

# CHAPTER 23

Lily paused outside of Devon's room, her entire body quaking. What if he wasn't inside? What if he'd locked the door? Rejected her again? She took a deep breath. She couldn't risk standing in the hall in her night rail, wringing her hands and biting her lip. This was the path she had chosen and she would follow it.

She placed a shaking hand on the cold brass knob, turned, and pushed.

Unlocked, thank heavens.

Expelling her breath, she pressed the door open and swung inside, her night rail swishing about her ankles. She closed the door and leaned back against it, closing her eyes. Her heart raced at what was surely a nearly fatal speed.

Lily opened her eyes again and blinked rapidly. Only a few candles burned intermittently about. One on the mantelpiece, one on the far wall near the window, and one next to the . . . bed.

She straightened her shoulders. Devon stood beside the bed. The look on his face told her he'd made his choice. He wanted her. He still wore his black trousers and white shirt, but he'd removed his boots. He walked barefoot toward her. His cravat was gone too, and his stark white shirt was open at the neck to reveal a tanned, muscular expanse with a shadow of dark chest hair.

Lily squeezed her hands to keep them from shaking. Oh, my, the man was handsome. In that moment, she no longer cared about the bet or the money or even her nerves. All that mattered at the moment was the six feet two inches of pure lust-inducing male headed toward her, the dark eyes boring into her as if they could read her thoughts, the dark hair her fingertips ached to touch.

"You're two minutes late," he drawled, a sensual smile on his face.

He took her hand gently and led her to the bed. Lily walked with him on legs that felt like water.

"You're sure about this, Lily?" he whispered against her hair, his strong arms enveloping her.

She nodded, once.

"Please tell me you're not thinking of the bet right now."

She turned her head to the side and pressed it against his hard chest. "I'm not."

Devon's shoulders relaxed a bit. "Good. You know I never would have made that bet myself and I don't give a damn about it."

Another nod.

"If you're uncomfortable at all, or frightened, say the word and we'll stop."

One more nod.

Then Devon smiled at her, and the sensual curve of his lips banished all doubt from Lily's mind. All she could think about was where his lips had been the last time they were alone together in a bedchamber. Her face heated.

And Devon made it so easy for her with his soft words of love and his lazy caresses. There was no fear here, none at all, just anticipation, sitting like a knot in her belly, spreading its spirals into her arms and legs and making her shiver.

"You're beautiful, Lily," Devon whispered against her mouth, and then he held her away from him, pulling her to the side and obviously enjoying the sight of her shadowy body beneath the flimsy night rail.

"So beautiful," he whispered. He seemed to know she'd feel more at ease if he allowed her to keep her gown on. He tugged her hand and pulled her to the bed. He turned around and pulled his shirt off over his head using both hands.

His shoulders flexed, his arms flexed, his whole back was rigid and muscled and . . . perfect. She couldn't stand it. Oh, she wanted to see more. The candlelight glinted off his smooth skin and Lily bit her lip.

It was lust. That's what it was. Pure, unadulterated lust. And it was . . . powerful. Magical.

"We'll go slowly," he whispered. "Very slowly."

Lily agreed. Only she wanted him to go slowly for another reason. Not because she was frightened, but because she was fascinated.

"Mmm-hmm," she answered with a measured nod. "Devon, may I have a drink?"

A half-smile played around his sensual lips. "I'm not sure you need more to drink."

"Just one glass. You have one too."

"Very well." He crossed the thick carpet with his perfect bare feet and pulled a wine bottle from the top of the sideboard. He plucked up two clean wine glasses and crossed back over to her. His eyes stared into her soul. Their dark brown depths mesmerized her. Her heart skipped a beat. The fluttering in her chest unnerved her. But in such a good way.

"Do you do this for all the ladies who come to your bedchamber?" Lily asked.

"I'm only interested in one lady in my bedchamber," he whispered. "And you must allow that you did notify me of your intent to pay me a visit this evening. What sort of host would I be, were I not prepared?"

"You have a point," Lily replied through dry lips.

The fire in the hearth across the room crackled. The spicy scent of burning logs filled the room. Lily watched with wide eyes as Devon removed the cork from the bottle. He poured two glasses of rich, red wine and handed one to her.

Lily closed her eyes and sucked down the sweet liquid. It tasted delicious. Its fortifying strength was just what she needed. The champagne from earlier was already wearing off. Wine was a delight, but she knew without a doubt, she wanted to make love to Devon and it had nothing to do with wine. She took another sip and crossed back over to the bed with Devon.

He reached to take the glass from her hand and she hesitated, tipping it back and swallowing its entire contents before handing it to him. He raised a brow and she gave him a sheepish grin.

"More?" he asked.

She shook her head. "Not yet."

Devon tossed his own wine into the back of his throat and set his empty glass on the bedside table next to Lily's. Then he took her hand and pulled her onto the bed. He still wore his breeches. She still wore her night rail.

The smooth glide of the sheets against her back made Lily relax. She looked up to see Devon hovering over her, his dark, slightly curly hair mussed, the most sensuous smile she'd ever seen on his firmly molded lips. But there was something else there, in his eyes. Something indefinable. Something that told her he was looking out for her, caring for her, wanting to make this special. She felt it with every touch of his hand, every whisper in her ear.

They lay on their sides together on the bed. Devon kissed her mouth first. So gently, she could almost cry. His lips touched hers and they were firm and wonderful. They probed her mouth, asking how much she was willing to give. Lily wrapped her arms around his broad, square shoulders and pulled him close.

Devon groaned when she fitted her body against the length of his.

His hand moved down to play with her breast through her gown. He cupped her fullness and rubbed his thumb back and forth across her nipple, driving her insane. She fitted herself closer to him to force him to touch more of her, and it was her turn to groan softly when he lightly squeezed, then pinched her.

His palm worked against her nipple, rubbing it, never letting go, and Lily wanted more, more, more. She pressed her mouth against his and let her tongue probe his lips. His tongue met hers and then went further, moving into her mouth and ravaging her, making her his. And in that moment, Lily knew without a doubt this was what she wanted. What she'd always wanted. The past didn't matter. The future didn't matter. All that mattered was this enigmatic, handsome man whom she'd loved as long as she could remember making love to her tonight. And it would be wonderful.

Devon's hand moved lower, pulling up her night rail. So slowly. Lily knew he was making sure he didn't scare her. And she appreciated it so much. His hand dipped down to her knee and he barely raised the fabric above it. His fingers rubbed her knee, staking their claim, telling her without words he would make sure she was all right with each and every touch before he went any further. She shuddered. He was being so gentle. So very gentle.

Devon's hand moved around to the back of her leg and lightly caressed her there. A shiver went up her spine. Who knew a simple touch could feel so wicked?

He played with the hem of her night rail and it drove Lily mad. She wanted to drag it up herself. She wanted to move his hand up her thigh. Put it between her legs exactly where she wanted it.

If he was going to torture her like this, she needed another drink. She turned toward the bedside table and grabbed the bottle of wine Devon had placed there. She hoisted it to her lips and let the liquid pour into the back of her throat. Then she gave him a playful look over the bottle's rim.

Devon arched a brow. "Thirsty?"

"Want some?" Lily countered.

"By all means. If we're going all bacchanal tonight, let's just drink straight from the bottle."

The wine helped, but still Lily trembled. What if Devon found out her secret? Oh, God, he would find out her secret. There was no help for it. Perhaps if he became drunk enough, he wouldn't notice. Perhaps if she became drunk enough, she wouldn't care. Yes, more wine was the answer.

"Here." She pushed the bottle into his hand.

Devon hefted it to his mouth and took a long drink. Lily watched his throat flex, his Adam's apple bob as he swallowed. She wanted to throw herself on his chest and lick him all over. A drop of wine made its way down his cheek. She took full advantage. She pushed herself forward and licked it from his jaw, but she wasn't quick enough. It streaked down his neck and onto his chest.

*Thank you, God.*

Her lips trailed lower, tracing the path of the red wine along his neck. She breathed him in. He smelled like spice and skin and just . . . man. *Oh, God.* The tip of her tongue traced along the collarbone in his strong, thick neck. He sucked in his breath.

*Excellent.*

She pulled the bottle from his fingers, and tipped it toward the indentation in his neck just above his collarbone, letting a bit of wine splash into the spot. Devon gasped. His dark eyes widened.

"What are you doing?" he asked in a husky voice that made her wet.

"Trust me," she whispered, and bent down to lick the wine out of the little cup she'd made in his body.

"Lily, I don't think—"

"Shh." This time she spilled the wine down his chest and he gasped louder. She set the bottle back on the table. She smiled. "This little mess will take a bit of cleanup."

"You just gave me the most enchanting look I think I've ever seen," Devon said before Lily bent her head to lick the wine off his muscled chest. Luckily, some of it had spilled down his abdomen. She gladly followed it, lapping up the red streaks with her tongue. And it tasted good. Sweet and wonderful. She was a bit surprised by her boldness, but that was the beauty of wine. She wasn't about to let this moment, this night, pass without enjoying it. This was her second wedding night, after all. So, no wedding had taken place. It didn't matter. She would have the night she'd always dreamed of and this time with the man she'd always dreamed of.

Lily's tongue tracked its way down Devon's pectoral muscles and lightly skimmed his nipples. His head snapped to attention when her teeth grazed there. He sucked in his breath again. He must have liked that. Was it possible he enjoyed her mouth on his nipples as much as she did? Devon made a move to pull her underneath him, but she shimmied her hips away from his reach.

"Why are you torturing me?" His eyes were hooded, full of lust.

A streak of pride swelled in Lily's chest.

"I intend to enjoy myself," she replied. "And right now, I am. Very much so."

Devon groaned. "What if I told you you're killing me? Besides, I'm supposed to be making it good for you, Lily."

Hearing her name on his lips made her press her legs together in abject lust. She pushed a tapered fingertip to his lips. "Shut up. I'm trying to seduce you."

"Oh, God, you already have," he groaned again. And then he had no more words when she bent her head back down to his abdomen. The muscles there stood out in sharp relief, all six of them. Lily shuddered. The man was perfect. His body looked as if Michelangelo had sculpted it. And here she was licking it. *What* a pleasure.

Her mouth dipped to his navel and she sucked up the wine that had gathered there. She continued her descent and moved even lower until she was confronted with the buttons on his breeches. A thin path of hair trailed below his pants. She so wanted to see where it led. Her hands found the buttons and she greedily unfastened them. His hands found hers and he gently pushed her back onto the bed.

"No. You. Don't," he said in a voice that sent reverberations through her body.

He was on top of her now, pushing against her most private place. Lily groaned. She wanted to pull off his pants even more now. But she knew, Devon had allowed her her fun. Now he was taking control.

*Oh. God. Yes.*

His mouth ravaged hers again. "You taste so good," he whispered. "Like wine."

Her hands pushed through the dark locks of his hair to cradle his face against hers. To keep him there and not let him go. "I can't taste nearly as good as you do," she whispered through kiss-swollen lips.

His fingers threaded through hers and he pressed her hands back onto the mattress. He had her now. Straddling her, pinning her down, holding her where he wanted her and pressing himself against her. "I love wine," he breathed.

Devon's dark head bent as he pushed his face between her breasts, beneath her night rail. When his lips slid to her nipple, she gasped again. His mouth was there, sucking, driving her mad. She grasped his head to her, never wanting him to stop.

Devon moved to her other breast and sucked there too, lightly biting her nipple and making her close her eyes. Savoring the ripples of pleasure that washed through her.

He raised himself over her on his forearms. "Lily, you're so beautiful. You're perfect."

This time, he slowly pulled her night rail up past her knee. Lily wanted to die of pleasure. His large, warm hand was on the outside of her thigh. She wanted to sob.

"Touch me, Devon. Please," she whispered against his mouth.

"You're not frightened, are you?"

She could have cried. Of course she wasn't frightened, but it was thoughtful of him to be worried about her. She'd just have to show him how all right she was. Her hand wandered down to find his. She pulled it up and placed it between her legs. She was naked. Naked, wet, hot, and wanting him.

Devon groaned. His fingers moved through her slickness and one single finger slipped inside of her. Lily groaned. He moved in her, back and forth. She clutched his shoulders, burying her face against his neck. "Oh, God, Devon."

His eyes were closed, his teeth clenched as if he were in a fierce battle to control himself. He pulled his finger out, so slowly, too slowly. Lily's hips bucked. She wanted more.

His finger found the spot between her legs, then. The one that made her sob and want nothing more than for him to touch her and never stop. He pushed in tiny, perfect circles, around and around. Lily's head moved fitfully against the pillow.

She bit her lip. Whatever he was doing, she never wanted him to stop.

Her thighs clenched, sweat pooled between her breasts. She tried to move her hips to be closer, closer to him. Her eyes fluttered open. Devon was braced above her, an intense look on his face. He was staring into her soul.

But he kept his finger moving in perfect little circles until Lily's breath hitched in her throat. She gasped in fitful spurts. Her hands clutched at his shoulders.

"Please, Devon, please."

"God, Lily, yes. Come for me, come for me, love."

And she did. She shattered and broke into a thousand tiny pieces, crying out and burying her face in his neck, still breathing heavily and sobbing. She pulled at his hips.

Yes, she'd just found release, but she wanted more. Needed more. She had to feel him inside of her. Had to be his. They must do this tonight. It was her dream.

Devon pulled away from her then and she sobbed, "No."

He turned back to look at her and traced his thumb over her cheek. "Lily, we don't have to do this."

She pulled him back down on top of her with all her strength. "Yes. We do. Devon, make me yours."

Trembling, Devon let out a shaky breath. He seemed relieved to hear those words and pulled his hips away only momentarily while he fumbled with the buttons on his breeches. He pulled them off quickly and Lily glanced down to see his perfect, lean yet muscled body. He was

Michelangelo's David. In the flesh. And what lovely flesh it was.

He moved back over her then, and braced himself above her. Lily had the vision of his soft, intense brown eyes before she felt his heat probing at her, moving against her thighs, searching. And then he pushed inside of her.

Lily jerked at the pain. She twisted her head to the side, pressing her cheek against the pillow beneath her. Did the look on her face betray her secret? Would Devon know? He didn't move. She dared a glance up at him. In the flickering candlelight, she watched his face. But what was he feeling? Anger? Surprise? *Oh, God, please don't let him be angry.*

"Lily," he whispered.

She put her palms to both his cheeks. "Devon, will you do something for me?"

"Anything," he breathed, kissing her forehead.

"Don't stop. Make love to me."

He pressed his forehead to hers and groaned. "I can do that."

He kissed her hands, her cheeks, and then he closed his eyes and began to move. The world had stopped turning. The brief flicker of pain was gone now, replaced only with the heat and strength of him. The perfection of his body moving inside of her. And she wrapped her arms around his broad shoulders and let the intense joy of the moment overwhelm her. There was no pain or sadness. It was perfect, just the way she'd always envisioned it. And she knew this was right. No matter what happened tomorrow. Or the next day. No matter if she spent the rest of her days in Northumberland, she would always have this night. And it would be perfect.

Just like this.

Devon shuddered and stroked inside of her, building a feeling again. She wanted to cry out against his neck. But instead she kissed him. His ear, his mouth, his shoulder, anything, everything she could reach.

Devon groaned again and buried his mouth in hers. He pushed into her again and again, sweat pooling on his back, his teeth tightly clenched. She shattered again, into another thousand pieces, just before Devon groaned and shuddered, then fell against her. His breath came in unsteady gasps and he kissed her temple. Hard.

He rolled off her, relieving her of his weight, but he kept the back of her hand pressed to his heart. "Lily, that was . . . incredible."

Incredible. She let the word roll around in her brain. Yes, it had been incredible. But was that something Devon said to all the women he took to bed? Was it always incredible? Oh, she refused to think about it. Not tonight. Besides, the wine was finally catching up with her, making her sleepy. She rolled up into a ball, cuddled next to him.

"You know this means you'll win that blasted bet," Lily whispered just before she fell asleep.

He squeezed her hand. His voice shook when he answered. "Lily, I can honestly say I'm not thinking one single thought about that damned bet at the moment."

He wrapped his arms around her. Her eyes drooped shut and she sighed.

Ah, what did any of it matter anymore? All that mattered was the peace in her heart, her satisfied body, and the fact that she could pretend all of this was real, at least for another few hours.

Devon watched her sleep. He nudged a dark curl from her cheek and traced his finger along her smooth forehead. God, but she was beautiful.

The words she'd thrown at him on the veranda reverberated in his mind. *"I was in love with you five years ago. Madly, idiotically in love, and my heart was broken when you took off for the countryside."* What the hell had she been talking about? And did she mean it? Had she truly been in love with him five years ago?

He shifted his weight from his elbow and leaned back against the headboard. He pulled the wine bottle from between the crumpled sheets and grinned. Good God, what they'd done with that wine bottle. Just thinking about it made him hard all over again. He couldn't remember the last time he'd enjoyed a glass . . . well, wine, quite so well. He pushed the empty bottle onto the nightstand.

"Lily," he groaned, rubbing his hands over his face then resting his bent arm atop his head. "How the hell were you a virgin?"

Devon expelled his pent-up breath. Guilt tore through his chest like a physical force. That moment. That one moment when he'd realized it. It was as if time had stood still. It had been awful and wonderful simultaneously.

Thank God she'd asked him not to stop. Yes, he was the veriest blackguard for it, but by that point, the legions of hell probably couldn't have stopped him.

He stared absently into the flickering candlelight. The room smelled like lilies. Just like her perfume. He glanced down at her. Her soft hand rested on the pillow next to her wine-stained lips. What the hell was he supposed to do now? What could he do? It was not as if he'd ruined her. The lady was a widow, for Christ's sake. The proverbial ship had sailed. But why? Why was she a virgin? And how?

Devon closed his eyes and breathed in her intoxicating scent. There would be time to ask her these things tomorrow. Time to ask her all of these things and to decide what to do. But tonight, tonight he would sleep in the shadow of her beauty, in the comfort of her arms.

He rolled over and slipped an arm over her waist and pulled her close. Her little breaths came out in rapid pants, indicating she was still asleep "I have a secret to tell you, Lily," he whispered to her sleeping form. "Not that it matters now . . . but I was in love with you too five years ago. Madly, idiotically in love with you."

# CHAPTER 24

Sneaking back into her own bedchamber proved less difficult than Lily imagined. She did so while Devon was still asleep. His tousled dark hair fell across his forehead in a way that made him look positively boyish. She glanced longingly at him as she tossed her wine-stained night rail over her head.

Everything was wine-stained now that she thought on it. Heaven only knew what the Atkinsons' housemaids would think when they saw the mess. Though given Devon's reputation, perhaps they wouldn't be surprised.

She paused by the bedside long enough to trail a tapered fingernail over his cheekbone. There would be time for regrets later. For now, she must return to her own room without being seen.

She cracked open the door and peeked out. No one. She ventured down the hallway and nearly flew across the landing to the other side of the floor where her own bedchamber was. She pounced upon the door to her room and swung inside. No noise came from Annie's adjoining bedchamber. Thank heavens. Lily closed her eyes and said a brief prayer of thanks for her success. She shucked her night rail, tossed on a new one, and climbed into bed.

Her head ached a bit from her overindulgence of wine, but she snuggled beneath the sheets with a smile on her face, remembering Colton's big, strong hands on her body and the twinges and welcome aches that still lingered.

Lily pressed the balls of her hands against her eyes. She couldn't write a pamphlet about what had happened between them last night. She knew that now, but she had finally had her wedding night. The one she was meant to have all along. And my, my, my, hadn't she been wrong about it all? A wedding night, far from being a frightening nightmare, was more like a dream come true with the right "groom." Devon Morgan had said he knew exactly how to please a woman. *Such* an understatement. She blushed just thinking about some of the things he'd done to her. Oh, yes, that wedding night had been worth whatever happened next. And besides, the repercussions could wait until morning. Well, later in the morning in any case.

Lily awoke several hours later to Mary drawing back the curtains in her room.

"What time is it?" Lily asked, rolling over and sitting up against the headboard.

"Eleven o'clock," Mary replied. "Ye've nearly slept away the entire morning."

Lily pulled up the pillow, hiding her smile behind it.

Mary turned to face her. "The letter ye've been waiting for arrived by messenger. Evans 'ad it sent from London."

Lily sat up straight. "Where is it?"

Mary pulled an envelope from her apron pocket and handed it to Lily. "I've been wearing this string 'round me finger all morning so I wouldn't forget ta give it ta ye."

Lily ripped open the letter, holding her breath. She hurriedly scanned the page. She shut her eyes and exhaled, pressing the letter to her chest.

"Oh, Mary, it's good news. Cousin Althea says we all may come. She writes she's expecting an eighth child and having us there to assist her would be lovely. We'll leave for Northumberland today."

Mary clutched her chest. "Oh, me lady. What a relief."

Lily nodded. "That it is. Where's Annie?"

" 'Aven't seen 'er all morning. She must 'ave got up with the rooster. I expect she's down in the drawing room with the rest of the young ladies, sewing."

Lily sighed. No doubt Annie had told Mary exactly where she was going and the poor woman had forgotten again. But sewing was good. It would keep her sister out of trouble.

Mary bustled into the dressing room. "The men have all gone on a hunt and the matrons are in the breakfast room. Or so I think. I cannot recall."

Lily stretched. "Breakfast sounds absolutely lovely," she called. "Help me get my bath, won't you, Mary?"

There was no reason Lily and Annie couldn't enjoy the morning before they left for their cousin's house. After breakfast, she would write Evans and have him and the dogs meet them in Northumberland. She'd have to send along her last bit of money to assist him with their journey. But it would all be all right after all. With a smile on her face, she hopped out of bed.

Lily was finishing a lovely breakfast when Viscount Medford appeared over her shoulder. "Lily, come for a walk with me."

She glanced up at her friend. "Why, Medford, I'm surprised to see you. I thought you'd be out on the hunt with the other men."

"I decided to forgo it," he said, bowing. "I wanted to speak with you." Something about the serious look on his face made Lily uneasy. "Just let me get my shawl," she said, and hurried to her room.

Medford smiled when she met him on the back terrace. He took her hand and led her down the stone steps. They followed a walking path that circled along the Atkinsons' lovely gardens and led out into the meadow.

Lily breathed in the fresh country breeze and the scent of the bobbing daffodils. So different from London's stale, coal-filled air. Medford remained silent until they were a good distance from the house.

"Are you enjoying yourself here, Lily?" he asked, his voice oddly solemn.

Lily gulped. She had been enjoying herself actually. Very much. Last night in particular. But she couldn't even look at Medford and think of that.

"Yes," she said simply. She paid an inordinate amount of attention to the stones along the path, placing her slippered feet on each one's center. "How are you enjoying the house party, Medford?"

Medford stopped and took her hand. He swung her around to face him. "I'm not enjoying it at all."

For an awful moment, Lily thought Medford knew what she'd done last night. She cleared her throat. "Whyever not?" She glanced away from him, averting her eyes.

"I'm worried about you, Lily."

This time she audibly gulped. "Worried? About me? I don't understand."

"Where are you going to live now that you've been ousted from your home? What are you going to do?"

Lily put her hand on his sleeve. "You're so nice to worry for me. And I can't thank you enough for your hospitality to Evans and the dogs and allowing me to borrow your coach. But I've got it all settled now. My cousin Althea is going to take us in. I just received the letter this morning. She lives in Northumberland and—"

Medford's eyes went wide. "Northumberland! You must be joking. Why, it's hours away and freezing cold."

Lily bit her lip. "I must admit it's not my first choice, but . . ."

Medford grabbed her by the shoulders. "Listen to me, Lily. Don't go to Northumberland. Stay in London. Marry me."

Lily sucked in her breath. She hadn't expected this. "Oh, Medford, you're lovely to offer, but you're not in love with me."

He raked a hand through his hair. "What does love have to do with marriage? I could list a score of marriages that have been built on less of a foundation than we have. Look, I know you need money. I have plenty of it. I'll need an heir someday. Say yes, Lily. I swear I'll make you happy."

Lily wrapped her shawl more tightly around her shoulders and put her hand on her heart. Time seemed to stop. Here was this man, this nice man, her friend, asking her to marry him with all sincerity. And it would be so easy to say yes. Medford had money. He was handsome and titled and respectable. She couldn't ask for a better prospect. And there was something else to consider. She had given in to her base instincts last night and made love with Devon. It was certainly possible that she was with child. The thought scared her and thrilled her at the same time.

She looked Medford in the eye and squeezed his hands. But it would be selfish to marry Medford for those reasons. James deserved someone who loved him and was devoted to him.

Truly, there was only one problem with Medford.

He wasn't Devon Morgan.

No, she couldn't accept Medford's proposal. She opened her mouth to tell him so. "I—"

"Me lady! Me lady!" Mary was hurrying toward them down the garden path.

Lily swung around, clutching her shawl to her shoulders. "Yes? What is it?"

Medford squeezed Lily's hand. "We'll continue this discussion later," he said, before turning to face Mary who had stopped a few paces away. The maid was breathing heavily and her face was quite red. "You must come back to the house immediately."

"What is it, Mary? Tell me. Now."

"Oh, me lady, it's Annie. She's missing!"

# CHAPTER 25

Lily blinked at Mary who had just issued such dire news in a near hysterical voice. "No, no, that's not true," Lily insisted, hurrying over to calm the maid. "You said Annie went to the sewing party this morning." She squeezed Mary's cold hands.

Mary shook her head. "No, me lady, she wasn't at the sewing party, I went looking for 'er. Seems no one 'as seen 'er."

Real fear clutched Lily's heart. "She must be in our rooms," she whispered more to herself than anyone else, trying to convince herself it must be so. "I'll find her." Lily grabbed up her skirts and rushed back toward the house, Medford and Mary both on her heels.

When they reached the back porch, Medford called, "I'll look around the rest of the house." He left the two women to go to their rooms alone.

Lily raced through the breakfast room, into the hallway, through the foyer, and up the winding staircase to the second floor. When she reached her bedchamber, breathing heavily, she swung open the door and stopped. Her stomach dropped.

The room was empty. She hurried through the adjoining

bedchamber, her heart in her throat. Also empty. She returned to her room to see Mary come in, panting.

"I just remembered something." The look on the maid's face told Lily what she didn't want to know.

Mary slowly walked to the dresser and picked up a note. It hung limply from the maid's hand.

Lily's voice shook. "Where is she?"

Tears slipped from Mary's eyes. "I'm so sorry, me lady. I must 'ave seen this note this morning and forgotten about it." Mary shook her head and handed the note to Lily. Lily rushed forth to grab it. She quickly unfolded the single sheet of paper and scanned the page. "No, no, no."

*Dear Lily,*
*Please do not hate me. Arthur and I are going to Gretna Green. We are deeply in love. We must be together. I do hope you'll understand . . . someday.*
*With all of my love,*
*Anne*

"Oh, Annie, no!" Lily crushed the letter in her fist. "Gretna Green? What could she be thinking?" Lily paced the carpet. "Think. Think."

"What will we do, me lady?" Mary asked, wringing her hands and watching her mistress walk back and forth across the room as if she were watching a game of battledore and shuttlecock.

Lily bit her knuckle. "Does anyone else know about this letter, Mary?"

"No, of course not. I told no one. Miss Conner came looking for Annie earlier and I told her she was not here. That was all."

Lily closed her eyes tightly. "Good. Good." She rubbed her temples to dispel the tension that had gathered there.

"There's only one way to stop two people already on their way to Gretna."

Mary's eyes were wide. " 'Ow, me lady?"

Lily looked the maid in the eye. "Chase them down before they make it across the Scottish border. Mary, pack our bags. We must leave at once and do *not* tell anyone about this letter. Do you understand?"

Mary nodded vigorously, her eyes wide, her cap bobbing madly on her head. "What are we going ta do, me lady?"

"We're going after her, of course."

"Not without me." A deep male voice sounded from the doorway.

Lily swung around. Devon Morgan stood there, a determined look on his face. Lily ignored the spring of happiness in her chest. He looked so handsome and completely refreshed, no bags under his eyes, or any signs of fatigue. Flashes of what had happened between them last night leaped unbidden into her mind. Her cheeks heated.

Yes, he looked perfect as usual. It made it more difficult to face him after spending last night naked, wrapped in his arms.

Lily rushed forward to close the door behind Devon. She glanced into the hall. Thankfully, no one was there. "What do you know about this?" she whispered.

Mary glanced between the two of them, raised her eyebrows, and scurried off into the other room to pack.

Devon was the picture of calm. "Your sister's taken off for Gretna with Eggleston, hasn't she?"

Lily pressed her back against the door. "Shh. How do you know?"

Devon took two strides forward. He was standing so close Lily could smell the scent of horse leather and cologne. Why did he have to smell so good?

The look in his eye was serious. "I saw Medford downstairs. He told me you were looking for Annie. I saw Annie and Eggleston together last night, whispering. I didn't think much of it. Until now."

Lily turned around to face the door and bit her lip. The fewer people who knew about all of this, the better. The gossip alone would ruin Annie if word got out. "I must go immediately. Please don't tell anyone about this."

Devon grabbed Lily by the shoulders and spun her around. His dark eyes searched her face. "Listen to me. The trip to Gretna is long and harsh, not to mention dangerous. It's no trip for two ladies. Let me go for you."

Lily squeezed her eyes shut. How had this day turned into such a nightmare? But there was no use pretending with Devon. "Please. I don't want anyone to know about this."

"All the more reason to allow me to help you. I promise to retrieve her as inconspicuously as possible. I will circulate the story that Annie left for London this morning because she was not feeling well. I can have my horses put to and I can meet the coach by the side entrance in ten minutes. You and your maid can take the coach you came in, return to London, and await Annie there."

Lily's shoulders slumped. She was supposed to be traveling to Northumberland today, not chasing Annie to Gretna Green. And here was Devon, helping her and making everything so easy. And it would be easy, so simple, to allow him to take charge of everything. She'd been in charge for so long. Too long now.

She leaned her head against the solid door. "And what will people think when you leave so suddenly?"

Devon was already pulling on his gloves. "Before I leave, I'll tell a select few I'm headed back to London."

Lily bit her lip, indecision torturing her. "It's true. I don't know the first thing about traveling to Scotland." Not to mention, she didn't have the funds for such a journey. The small amount of money she did have left was meant for her trip to Northumberland.

Devon covered her hand with his. "Trust me, Lily. Let me do this for you."

The gentle tone of his voice was more than she could stand. She did need help, whether she wanted to admit it or not. She and Mary were hardly equipped to travel after Eggleston and Annie alone, and the sooner someone got under way, the better. For all she knew, they'd been gone all night.

*"Trust me,"* he'd said. Lily squeezed both hands into impotent fists. She trusted no man. Not completely.

"Very well," she replied, "but if I'm to accept your help, there's one thing upon which I must insist."

Devon's hand gripped the doorknob. He glanced back at her. "Name it."

Lily straightened her shoulders and lifted her chin. "I'm coming with you."

# CHAPTER 26

To his credit, Devon Morgan didn't put up a fight. Lily had expected one, of course. A manly dismissal of her request. A dictatorial insistence that his plan was superior. Instead, he merely inclined his head in an oh-so-attractive manner and bowed to Lily. "As you wish."

Relief shot down Lily's spine. That was easier than expected.

In the next instant, Colton's voice became deep and commanding. Mary had pulled the trunks out and was busily tossing all of their clothing inside. "Mary, get back to London immediately. Tell anyone you encounter that Miss Andrews is extremely ill. Answer as few questions as possible."

Mary nodded and toppled the lid of the trunk closed with a resounding thud. "I packed a smaller bag for ye, me lady," she said, pushing a satchel toward Lily.

Devon snatched up Lily's satchel and hoisted it onto his shoulder. "Wait here. I'll order the coach ready."

While Devon was gone, Lily scribbled off a note for their hostess. She wrote that she was returning to London with her sister, who had suddenly taken ill.

True to his word, Devon was back not ten minutes

later. Lily glanced up at him, biting her lip. "If anyone notices that you and Eggleston are also conspicuously missing, Annie's reputation might be ruined forever."

"Don't worry. I intend to tell everyone that Eggleston and I left together."

Devon grabbed Lily's hand and pulled her from the room. They dashed down the back staircase and through a servants' hallway to the side door. "I've ensured as few servants as possible are involved. The fewer people who know about this, the better." Devon tossed the bag into the coach's interior.

"George," he snapped at the coachman. "We're going to Gretna Green."

George's eyes widened, but he didn't say a word. He just nodded, once, and shook out the reins.

Devon helped Lily into the coach. He stuck his head in the door to see her settled.

Lily dropped her head into her hands and laughed ruefully. "Oh, lovely. Now George thinks the two of us are in fast pursuit of a quick Scottish marriage."

Devon flashed a grin. "George will think what I tell him to. Wait here. I'll be back in five minutes." He disappeared back into the house before Lily could say a word.

Devon's harsh rap on Jordan's bedchamber door was answered immediately. Ashbourne stood there with his bags packed and an inquiring look on his face. "Oh, please tell me you haven't come to challenge me to a duel now," he said to Devon with a grin.

Devon brushed past Jordan into the room. "I need you to do something for me."

Jordan ran his fingers through his hair. "What now? I already asked that Andrews chit to dance last night. Deuced difficult, by the by. She flatly refused me at first. Seems she's only got eyes for the Eggleston lad. Must admit it was a bit of a blow to my ego. I never ask eighteen-year-olds to dance and if I do I expect them to say yes." He grinned.

"Yes, well, it's the Andrews girl and the Eggleston lad I've come about."

Jordan raised a brow.

"Seems they've run off to Gretna. I'm leaving now to track them down. I expect they've taken the road through Leicester but I need you to take the other road just in case."

"A trip to Gretna?" Jordan whistled.

"I wouldn't ask if it wasn't important, and after the trouble you caused me with that blasted bet, you owe me."

Jordan nodded once. "I'll leave immediately."

"I assume they won't travel through the night. Given that they probably left early this morning, if we leave now, with our faster horses, we'll most likely catch up to them at the Gray Horse Inn. If you come around and meet us there tomorrow night, we should be able to track them down."

Another nod. "Consider it done. With utter discretion."

Devon turned to leave. He and Jordan might have their differences from time to time but he could count on him completely. That, he never doubted. "See you tomorrow night."

Devon returned to the coach, pulled himself inside, and ordered George to start the journey immediately. Then, he settled into the seat across from Lily.

She watched him intently. "Where did you go?"

"To cover all possibilities."

Lily shook her head at that cryptic answer. "Why do I think I'm going to regret not bringing Mary with us?"

"Mary is needed in London."

Lily sighed. "You know she's not going to remember a word you told her. I didn't want the poor thing to have to endure the treacherous conditions on the road to Gretna or I would have insisted she accompany us."

"It'll be faster with just the two of us. Now, you should get some sleep. It's going to be a very long journey."

Lily glanced away at his obvious implication that she needed the sleep because she hadn't gotten much of it the night before. Her cheeks burned. The memory of their night together was a specter in the carriage with them. Should she be embarrassed? Regretful? No, she was neither of those things.

The truth was, she desperately wanted to repeat it. Memories assaulted her mind. Images. Devon's taut skin, his musky scent, his broad, smooth shoulders under her fingers. Yes, she *should* be embarrassed. Or perhaps ashamed. But she could summon neither emotion. The only thing she felt was a soft, warm glow. God, yes, she wanted to repeat it. One more time. Completely sober. To see if it was as good as she remembered.

Lily shook herself from her indecent thoughts as the coach bounced away from the estate.

She pulled off her riding gloves and tossed them onto the seat next to her. Now that she had time to look at the coach's interior, she realized how fine it was. Deep, forest-green velvet squabs and shining brass fixtures. More credit, no doubt.

She dared a glance at Devon. If they were to ride together in such close quarters the entire way to Gretna, she must find a way to make things less awkward between them. "I cannot sleep. I'm so worried for Annie." She tugged at the strings of her bonnet under her chin, untying them. "What can she have been thinking? It's ludicrous. Madness." Oh, God. It was the same madness she'd had years ago when she'd wanted to run off to Gretna with Devon, only Devon never came.

Devon relaxed back against the seat. He pushed his long legs out and crossed them at the ankles. Was he remembering the two of them five years ago also? Lily quickly turned her face to look out the window.

"When's the last time you saw her?" Devon asked.

Lily pulled the bonnet from her head. "Last night, I suppose. Before I . . . that is . . . before we . . ." Oh, surely she would burst into flames from embarrassment.

Devon cleared his throat. "At the ball?" he offered helpfully.

She patted her mussed hair into place. "Yes."

Devon pulled off his gloves. "Did she say anything? Give you any reason to suspect?"

"No. Nothing." Lily put a finger to her lips. "Though I did tell her we'd be leaving for Northumberland today. Of course, now that plan is ruined."

Devon's brow furrowed. "Northumberland?"

"Yes. We're planning to live with my cousin."

"Why?" He searched her face.

Lily let her head fall back against the seat. She groaned. "Does it matter now? Annie's gone."

Devon's jaw tightened. "Sounds as if she left to escape her fate."

Lily sensed he'd been about to say something else, but changed his mind. He obviously hadn't liked the thought of her going to Northumberland, but thankfully he dropped that subject, perhaps because he sensed she couldn't stand that particular discussion at the moment. All she could worry about now was Annie.

She covered her eyes with her fingertips. "I knew she was upset with me last night, but I . . . I underestimated how much she wanted to stay in London. And all for that awful Eggleston lad."

Devon cracked a smile. "Ah, he's not so bad. Just young. And foolish."

Like she and Devon were, years ago. Lily sighed. "That's a charitable way to put it."

"When was the last time anyone else saw her?"

Lily bit her lip. "With Mary's memory the way it is, Annie might have been gone all night. Why?"

"We need to determine how big of a lead they have on us. If they've been gone since early this morning, they'll probably be to Leicester by now."

Lily closed her eyes. An awful vision flashed in her mind. One of Annie, standing in front of the blacksmith in Gretna Green, exchanging vows with Arthur Eggleston. Ruining her entire life. Lily squeezed her gloves tightly. "Do you think they will stop tonight?"

Devon shrugged. "It depends on how much money they have and what resources they can find along the way. They're both young and inexperienced, however. My guess is they will stop tonight. If they do, we may be able to catch up to them."

Lily's shoulders shook. "But how will we know where they stopped?"

Devon leaned forward and took her icy hand in his warm one. Sparks flew up Lily's arm. She couldn't look him in the eye. Not yet. Not after the night they'd spent together. But he was comforting her. And she so appreciated it.

"Don't worry," Devon said. "There aren't many inns between here and Gretna. I think I can guess where they might stop."

"How do you know so much about the way to Gretna?" As soon as the words left her mouth, she regretted them.

Devon looked off into the distance, a reluctant, humorless smile on his face. "I looked into it, once upon a time."

Lily bowed her head; the lump had returned to her throat. "Gretna is the destination of fools and the very young."

Devon's voice was quiet, a bit ironic. "Or those who are very much in love."

She didn't answer. Instead, she closed her eyes and swallowed. Then she glanced back out the window. "Oh, Devon. What if they don't stop?"

He leaned forward and squeezed her hand. "Get some rest, Lily. It's sure to be a long day."

Devon was right. The journey north to Scotland was both difficult and uncomfortable. At the pace they'd set for themselves, they were forced to stop to change the horses more often than they liked. By nightfall, they hadn't made nearly the progress they meant to.

Lily woke from a short nap and found herself thoroughly entertained by Devon. He kept her laughing with jests and stories from his various exploits. She enjoyed herself, and she knew, without a doubt, he was doing his best to make her feel better and keep her mind off her worry for Annie.

"I think they may be at the Gray Horse Inn," Devon explained after climbing back into the carriage from the last stop. "From what I understand, that is a popular destination." Lily looked through the window of the coach through bleary, sleep-deprived eyes. Stars blinked in the night sky. She stretched.

"How far is that?" Lily croaked.

"A few hours yet. We must travel through the night."

Lily nodded. "Yes. Yes, of course." She made a move to sit up, but Devon shifted across the seat to sit next to her. He gently pulled her head into his lap and stroked her hair. "Shh. Rest."

It was an impropriety, but Lily couldn't help herself. She was tired. Exhausted, actually. It felt so good to rest her head in Devon's warm lap. Besides, after the wine bottle incident, "impropriety" had taken on a new meaning. His fingertips on her temple lulled her to sleep and soon she was dozing. A sweet, blissful slumber.

When Lily woke, much refreshed, it was still dark and the coach was still bumping along. Her head remained in Devon's lap. Suddenly shy, she struggled into an upright position.

"What time is it?" she whispered, wrapping her arms around her middle and curling herself into a ball in the corner. She shivered. Devon had drawn a cozy blanket over her and she pulled it all the way to her chin.

Devon retrieved his silver timepiece from his waistcoat. The one small candle burning in the lantern inside the coach illuminated it for him. "Nearly three o'clock."

Lily yawned. "Are we almost there?"

"It shouldn't be more than half an hour."

Lily let her shoulders relax. She desperately hoped Devon was right and that Annie and Eggleston had stopped at the inn for the night. What would she do if they hadn't? She shivered again. She couldn't think about that now.

"Annie doesn't understand." Lily sighed. "She thinks I'm trying to ruin her life, but I'm trying to save her from ruin. Why are the young so foolish?"

Devon made a steeple with his fingers. "Ah, now that is a question for the ages, is it not? Some would argue they do not know any better. They are ruled by their emotions. Fools rush in, as Pope said."

"If only she would listen to me," Lily moaned. "I would never do anything to hurt her. She must know that."

"You do not want her to marry. And she wants to, correct?"

"Yes, but if she doesn't marry, she'll never have to listen to a man. Be at his whims and mercy. She doesn't understand how awful it is."

"You were only married for a month. Was it so awful then?"

Lily hung her head. "Before that, I had to answer to my father. And all he ever cared about was money. Annie has the opportunity to escape all of that. She's at no one's mercy."

Devon's voice was soft. "No one's but yours. And pardon me for pointing it out, but you seem to be greatly interested in the subject of money yourself."

Lily snapped her mouth shut. Obviously, it was time to change the subject. Devon didn't understand either. Money was nothing to him. But Lily understood the importance of money. Money meant the one thing she'd always longed for. Security.

She pulled the blanket to her nose. "While it's unfortunate you do not agree with my decisions, it's neither here nor there to me. As soon as we find Annie, she and I will go straight to Northumberland. Our cousin has agreed to have us. We must be close. I'll send for our things."

Devon's eyes narrowed on her. "You're really going to Northumberland?"

Lily's heart fluttered. Was that regret she heard in his voice? Did he want her to stay?

"Yes," she answered, holding her breath. "I have no choice. The earl has asked us to leave the town house and we have nowhere else to go."

Devon shrugged and looked out the window. "Why don't you find a man? Get married? Stay in London?"

Pain squeezed Lily's heart. She turned to look out at the darkness. "It's not as if I haven't had offers. Just before I discovered Annie was missing, Medford asked me to marry him." She lifted her chin and glanced back at Devon.

Devon's face went completely blank. A tic appeared in his jaw. "Did he?"

She nodded.

He clenched his fist. "When are the happy nuptials to be?"

Lily let the blanket drop to her lap. "What makes you think I said yes?"

"You'd be a fool not to. Medford is wealthy, titled. Not to mention his disgustingly impeccable reputation."

*"You'd be a fool not to."* That hurt. More than she expected. But she'd be skinned alive before she'd let Devon know it. She crossed her arms over her chest. "When you put it that way, I suppose it was quite an offer."

Devon glanced out the window at the darkness this time. The muscle continued to tic in his jaw. "Are you telling me you said no?"

Lily traced the pattern of the velvet squabs with her fingertip. Her voice was quiet. "I didn't have a chance to answer. We were interrupted by the news that Annie had gone missing."

Devon pressed his lips together until they went white, but said no more on the subject. "There's no time for you to go to Northumberland now. It should only take us a day or two to return to London if we find them tonight. I must get there myself by Saturday evening."

Lily raised a brow. "Another young widow to seduce?" She winced. That sounded harsh, but she couldn't help it after he'd practically told her she'd be an idiot if she didn't marry Medford.

Devon ran a hand through his hair, making it look more tousled and irresistible. Lily glanced away. He didn't answer, but it didn't matter. She was thankful for his help with her sister, but she still had her plan to carry out. She would not be accepting Medford's suit. She would soon be a governess in Northumberland.

"Why do you need to get back to London by Saturday night?"

He scrubbed his hands across his face. "Does it matter?"

"Tell me."

Pushing out his cheek with his tongue, he regarded her down the length of his nose. "Very well, Lily. Since you're full of questions tonight, I have my own question for you." He leaned forward, bracing his elbows on both knees. He stared her straight in the eye. "How the hell were you a virgin until last night?"

# CHAPTER 27

Lily clutched at the window ledge for support.

*He knew.*

Of course he knew. He wasn't a fool. She'd expected him to realize and to wonder. She hadn't expected him to come out and ask her.

She needed time to invent an answer. She cleared her throat. "Wh . . . what do you mean?"

He gave her a skeptical look. "Don't make me repeat the question. You know exactly what I mean."

Lily turned to rest her forehead on the cool glass of the coach's window. She squeezed her eyes shut. "My husband was very old and very . . ." Her voice trailed off. She could feel Devon's eyes on her.

"How were you able to write *Secrets of a Wedding Night* when you were untouched?"

It was obvious that one could not die of embarrassment, for if that were possible Lily was quite sure she'd be gone by now. It was useless to continue to pretend she did not write the pamphlet. Devon knew. He'd known all along.

She kept her eyes squeezed shut. "I . . . I was so frightened on my wedding night, s-shaking. Merrill, tried, well . . . that is . . . we tried." She winced. "Oh, suffice it to say that nothing happened. He couldn't . . . and it was my fault. He said so. He said he'd never had such a problem before." Guilt and shame washed over her. "No doubt he would have tried again, but he died so soon after we wed . . . it just . . . never happened." She opened her eyes again to see Devon searching her face intently. Oh, God, were her cheeks scarlet or burgundy? "So you see, I have quite the experience in repulsing men, first you and then Merrill . . ."

Devon leaned forward and grabbed her hand, squeezing it. "Listen to me, Lily. It wasn't you. Merrill was an old man. It's very common for elderly men to be unable to perform. It had nothing to do with you."

She opened her eyes and dared a glance at him. "Truly?"

"Yes. Quite common from what I understand."

"But he told me it was my fault."

"Also quite common, I'm afraid. No doubt his pride precluded him from admitting to his own physical shortcomings."

Lily expelled her breath. "It's something of a relief actually, to know that." She gave him a half-smile. "Thank you."

Devon squeezed her hand one more time before leaning back. "But how did you get your information for the pamphlet if nothing happened on your wedding night?"

She shrugged. "I'm a writer. I made it up."

Devon's eyes flashed wide. "Made it up?"

Another shrug. "I used my imagination. And bits and pieces of conversations I've heard through the years. Ever since I was widowed, everyone just assumed I knew anyway, so I've heard a great deal on the subject. I simply did nothing to set them straight. What would be the point?"

Silence rested between them.

When he finally spoke, Devon's voice was oddly calm. "Why me? Why last night?"

"Why not?" But her third shrug held more pain than he would ever know.

"I thought the pamphlet described a physical act. I thought it was detailed."

"Have you read it?"

He shook his head. "No. I merely heard it was so awful that young women were crying off over it. I knew that much was true because of Miss Templeton's reaction."

Lily sniffed and smiled barely. "Well, it doesn't take much of an imagination to scare some young women apparently. And I did describe the truth. I merely skipped the details. I explained how frightened I was and how I wanted to die. I explained how awful the entire episode was."

Devon cracked a smile. "Are you honestly telling me you've scared half of the young women in the *ton* with a pamphlet that describes nothing more than nerves and innuendo?"

Lily pushed up her chin. "I couldn't very well come out and tell everyone my marriage wasn't consummated, could I? Even if they didn't know I wrote that pamphlet. And if I'd described the act in detail, the pamphlet would be absolutely indecent. And I am not *that* kind of lady."

Devon laughed now. A full hearty laugh. He threw his head back and shouted with laughter while Lily watched him with ill-concealed ire.

"Good God, Lily, don't ever change. Only you would have the nerve to carry out such a ruse."

She crossed her arms over her chest and stared him down. "It wasn't a ruse."

"No, no, of course not." His laughter finally died down and he looked serious again. "But you didn't answer me. Why me? Why last night?"

Lily looked away. Tears sprang to her eyes. Horrifying tears. She hadn't felt the sting of tears since . . . Devon had come back into her life. She shook her head and turned her face toward the window so he wouldn't see. "Don't make me answer that, Devon," she whispered. "Besides, you never answered *me*. Why do you need to be back in London by Saturday night?"

He took a deep breath. "If you must know, I intend to play in a high-stakes card tournament in the Rookery on Saturday."

"I'll go in first and make inquiries. See if they're here." Devon pulled on his gloves as the carriage clattered to a stop in front of the Gray Horse Inn.

Lily didn't argue with him. Arguing would take energy. Energy she did not have. Instead, she waited until Devon left, slowly counted one hundred, and stealthily followed him. In the coach, she'd been lulled by him, momentarily lulled, by his kindness and care. But his reminder that a card tournament lay in his future was all Lily needed to recall her objections to the man. It was extremely kind of him to assist her in finding her sister, but she wasn't about to surrender control of this operation to a man. Let alone one whose entire future rested on gaming hells.

Lily arrived inside the inn to see Devon bestowing his most charming smile on a young woman who was obviously employed at the establishment. The two laughed as if they'd invented a jest. Lily sauntered up, arms crossed over her chest, and cleared her throat. Loudly.

Devon turned to look at her, a partly surprised look on his face. "Lily, I was just asking this nice young lady if she'd seen a couple."

The girl smiled, revealing crooked teeth. She giggled. "And I told ye, I 'aven't seen anyfing o' the sort."

Devon flashed her his trademark grin. "Think about it a bit longer," he persuaded. "Now do you remember?"

The girl's eyes widened and Lily could have sworn she batted her eyelashes at Devon.

"The couple? Have you seen them?" he asked.

The girl looked abashed for a moment before putting her finger to her cheek, appearing to contemplate the matter. "Why, yes. Now that ye mention it, I do recall seeing a young bloke. Fine-lookin' man, I might add. And 'e with a nice, new young bride." She guffawed. " 'Course in these parts, everybody is already married, ye know?" The maid poked Devon with her elbow and laughed at her own joke. "Nobody's on they way to Gretna, round 'ere. No, sir."

Devon nodded. "Which room are they in?"

The crooked teeth reappeared in her lopsided smile. The girl pointed a finger toward the back of the inn. "First room at the top. Right up them stairs."

"Thank you," Devon said with a wink before he grabbed Lily by the hand and pulled her with him toward the darkened stairwell.

"I told you to stay in the coach," he whispered, glancing back at her.

Lily batted her eyelashes at him. "You didn't actually expect me to listen to you, did you? And by the way, charming the servant girl? A bit predictable, isn't it?"

Devon rolled his eyes. "Come on."

When they reached the top of the stairs, he put a finger to his lips. He motioned for Lily to remain silent. She waited in the shadows beside a wooden table with a rusty, flickering lantern resting atop it.

She took a deep breath. "I hope it's them," she whispered. "Or we're about to rudely interrupt someone."

Devon rapped twice on the door. No answer. They waited in the silence for what felt like minutes before he rapped again. This time a muffled male voice sounded through the door. "Blast it. It's the crack of dawn. Who is it?"

Lily's heart flipped. It was a young man's voice. English. Aristocratic. She held her breath.

"Eggleston?" Devon's voice boomed through the darkness.

Muttering and curses followed, then the door swung open. "Yes? What do you want?"

Devon grabbed the boy by the throat and pushed him back into the room. Lily rushed through the door, hoping against hope she wouldn't find her sister naked in a tangle of bed sheets.

Devon lit a match and a lantern sprang to a soft glow in the corner of the room. Annie sat up in the bed, quite properly dressed in a night rail that covered every bit of her from head to toe. A pallet on the floor strewn with blankets and a pillow clearly indicated where Mr. Eggleston had been sleeping.

Lily let out a deep sigh. "Thank heavens." She raced to the bed, grabbed Annie by the shoulders, and hugged her fiercely. Then, just as quickly, said, "What were you thinking, you little fool?"

Annie hugged Lily back and sobbed.

Eggleston had managed to wrangle himself from Devon's grasp and he stood huddled in the corner, rubbing his throat and eyeing his captor. Devon paced back and forth in front of him like a lion guarding his prey.

Tears streaked down Annie's face. "I'm sorry, Lily. Truly I am."

Lily hugged her sister again, but she wanted to shake her. "Do you know what this escapade could do to your reputation if it ever got out?"

Eggleston cleared his throat. "We know, Lady Merrill, but with all due respect, it's your own fault. If you hadn't threatened Anne with exile, we wouldn't have had to put her reputation at risk."

Devon growled and lunged at the boy, but Lily got there first and slid between the two. She pointed her finger firmly in Eggleston's face.

"How dare you accuse me! You know nothing of Annie's situation. I am her guardian and I am doing the best I can for her. I daresay living in Northumberland is a far sight more respectable than running off to Gretna Green. Besides, I thought you'd heard a rumor that Annie has no dowry. You didn't seem interested at her come-out ball."

Arthur straightened his shoulders and raised his chin. "That was all a misunderstanding. Anne knows that. I don't care if she doesn't have a dowry. Anne wants a family. And so do I. We are in love. We plan to marry with or without your consent, Lady Merrill."

Lily eyed the boy with disdain. "Don't make me regret stopping the marquis from throttling you, Mr. Eggleston."

Devon kept his eyes narrowed on the younger man. "Say the word."

Annie leaped from the bed. "Please, Lily, don't blame Arthur. He was only doing what I asked of him. It was I who wanted to go to Gretna."

Lily paced across the floor. "Well, you're *not* going to Gretna. Lord Colton and I have come to take you home."

"But Lily, I don't want to go home. Home isn't even home any longer. Northumberland isn't our home." Annie burst into tears.

Lily hugged her sister. "Oh, Annie, you must believe I only want the best for you."

"I know you think you do, Lily," Annie sobbed. "I believe that. But just because marriage and family were not what you wanted, doesn't mean it's not what I want. I'm afraid you'll never understand. I had to show you just how important it is to me."

A lump clogged Lily's throat. She hugged her sister more tightly. "Oh, Annie. This was not the way to do it."

Annie pulled back to look at Lily, and Arthur rushed forward to offer a handkerchief. "I know that now," Annie said. "But I didn't think . . . No, I *knew* you wouldn't listen any other way. I had to do it. I am so grateful for you taking care of me, Lily. I will always be. But I must live my own life now."

Lily slumped onto the bed. Mr. Eggleston was right somehow. She had pushed her sister into this. Made Annie desperate enough to flee in the middle of the night without any regard for her reputation. And Annie thought Lily had never wanted a husband and family. She had wanted both of those things once, very much.

Yes, Arthur was right. It *was* Lily's fault. She was the one who had become inebriated and told Annie they would be leaving for Northumberland. She was the one who had made all the decisions and issued the decrees. But she was the elder sister. She was the one with the responsibility. And she'd never imagined Annie would react like this.

Lily straightened her shoulders. She must rectify this awful mess. She swung her cloak off her back and draped it over Annie. "We'll fix everything, Annie. Somehow. But not like this. Come with me, now. We must go."

Annie hung her head and nodded and Lily ushered her sister from the room.

Devon glared at Eggleston. His arms tightly crossed over his chest, he watched the young man through narrowed eyes.

Eggleston cleared his throat. "I'm qu . . . quite sorry, Lord Colton. Please believe, I meant no harm. Anne and I are in love, my lord. We only wished to be together."

Devon afforded him his most withering stare. The lad looked frightened out of his wits.

*Good.*

"On the contrary, Eggleston, you must believe that had you actually caused any harm, we would not be having this highly civilized discussion at the moment."

Eggleston's Adam's apple bobbed rapidly in his throat and the first bead of sweat dripped from his shiny, young forehead. He nodded rapidly. "I understand, m . . . my lord."

"Do you?" Devon shot back. He paced, his hands clasped behind his back. "Do you understand the enormity of what you've done? You might have ruined Miss Andrews's reputation, her future, her life."

Unshed tears shone in Arthur's eyes, but he pushed up his chin. "I never intended to harm her, my lord. I love her."

"Marriage is important, Eggleston. It's hardly something to be entered into lightly, and certainly not the way you attempted to go about it."

A long sigh came from Eggleston's throat. "But Lord Colton, haven't you ever been in love?"

Devon cursed under his breath. "Damn it, lad. Yes. Yes, I have."

Eggleston nodded shakily. "And what did you do, my lord?"

Devon exhaled slowly and shoved his fingers through his hair. "Bloody hell, Eggleston. I had planned to do the same damned thing."

Devon informed Eggleston of their plans and left to allow the younger man to dress himself in private. Devon shut the door to the room and pressed his back against the wall in the hallway. Expelling his breath, he slid down to the floor and sat with his knees up, his wrists resting atop them. For the first time in the last two days, Devon allowed himself to really think.

Life was ironic. He was halfway to Gretna Green with Lily Andrews. *Damn it.* Why couldn't it be five years ago?

He could just keep going. He shook his head. Thoughts like that were purposeless. No, instead he was rescuing Lily's sister, trying to talk an impetuous young lad out of doing the same thing he'd wanted to do once upon a time, and attempting to keep Lily from running off to Northumberland.

Why?

How had he gone from trying to convince that woman to write a retraction to her silly pamphlet, to ending up being seduced by her at the Atkinsons' house party? His intentions of shaming her, rejecting her, leaving her, he'd abandoned them áll the moment he recognized her vulnerability on the balcony at the house party.

She'd turned to him, her lavender gown making her look like a goddess come to life. After telling him she'd been in love with him five years ago, she'd said, *"My heart was broken when you took off for the countryside."*

It didn't make any sense. His father had told him Lily was engaged to Lord Merrill and Devon had written to her, sent a footman out in the middle of the night to reach her. And he'd received his answer. A letter informing him she was, in fact, engaged to the earl, and she must end her flirtation with Devon. Devon had lived with that betrayal all these years.

But Lily had been telling the truth on the balcony. He knew it. She had been waiting for him that night. But how? And why?

He scrubbed his hands across his face. Lily couldn't marry Medford. The man would drive her insane with his constant perfection. *Blast it.* Why should Devon even care if she married him? Medford was the best choice for her. The pillar of Society. Not a rake or a gambler.

Besides, Devon needed a mother for Justin. And Lily didn't even know about the boy. How could he tell her about him and the circumstances surrounding his birth? Damn it. What did it matter? Lily hadn't been for him five years ago and she wasn't for him now.

Fine. Devon had felt something for her last night. A lot of something, and he'd remembered why he felt so much for her years ago. But the fact remained, Lily had jilted him. She didn't want him now any more than she had back then. The night they'd spent together didn't change that.

But, God, last night. It had been unimaginable. Unlike anything he'd experienced before. It had changed him. For good. After last night, how could she sit across from him in the coach the past day, tempting him beyond all that was holy with her pert nose and pretty lips, and tell him she had an offer of marriage from Medford and planned to go to Northumberland?

Devon leaned his head back against the wall. She was running away from life. That was all. She thought she'd be safe, she and her sister, if they escaped town and all men. But if she was so intent on keeping men out of her life, why the hell had she climbed into his bed last night? What was she trying to do, drive him mad? If so, she was doing a stellar job.

And what was she playing at, pretending not to take Medford's suit more seriously? A life in Northumberland wasn't right for her. Didn't she recognize that? Devon shook his head. It didn't matter. Whatever Lily chose to do with her life from here on out was her affair. He had a promise to fulfill, a tournament to win, a child to raise. He'd spent enough time with his blasted memories.

Devon hefted himself up, a renewed burst of energy

flowing through his veins. He'd accomplished what he'd set out to do, rescue Lily's sister. Now, he must concentrate on his own priorities, the first being to return to London as quickly as possible.

He took the stairs two at a time and pushed his way through the inn's front door to find Lily and her sister standing next to the carriage. Jordan Holloway stood a few paces away, leaning against a low, stone wall. His legs were crossed at the ankles and he had a decidedly annoyed look on his face.

"Ashbourne, you made it," Devon called out.

"Yes, and I'm deuced unhappy to realize I came in second place. I was so hoping to be the knight in shining armor in this little escapade," he said, the annoyed look replaced with a grin.

Annie gave him a narrowed-eyed glare.

"Thank you for your help, Lord Ashbourne," Lily said. "We expect you will keep this unfortunate incident to yourself, please."

Jordan stood up straight and bowed at the waist. "My pleasure, Lady Merrill. And as far as I'm concerned, there's been no unfortunate incident. This entire journey never happened."

Lily smiled and nodded at him and Annie grudgingly mumbled her thanks.

Jordan bowed to Annie. "Ah, I see you're just as happy to see me today as you were the other night at the house party when I asked you to dance, Miss Andrews." He threw his head back and laughed. "You sisters are not easy to please, I tell you. Not at all."

Annie gave him a tight smile.

Lily turned to Devon. "We're close to Northumberland. We'll hire a coach. We'll go straight there."

"Lily, please!" Annie clutched at Lily's hand.

Devon leaned against the side of the carriage. "You cannot go to Northumberland."

Now, what the devil had made him say that?

Lily's head snapped up to face him. "What are you talking about? Why not?"

Devon inclined his head. If he was going to make this argument, he might as well be convincing. "If you don't return to London, the entire *ton* will flay you alive. The rumors will run rampant. Annie's reputation will be beyond repair."

Lily opened her mouth, most likely to issue a retort, but soon clamped it tight again. She slumped against the side of the conveyance, her brows furrowed. "I don't care about the *ton*."

Devon shook his head. "You don't now, but you will when the rumors follow you to Northumberland. Rumors about *Annie*. She must come back to London to be seen again. Otherwise, God only knows what sort of outlandish stories people will invent."

Annie's face was ashen. She buried her face in Eggleston's handkerchief. "Oh, I cannot bear to think about it."

Lily paced away from the coach. "What is best for Annie?" she whispered, pulling nervously at her own handkerchief.

"Returning to London is what's best for Annie," Devon replied quietly. "You know it is, Lily."

Annie's face brightened. She looked as if she might hug Devon. "I think Lord Colton is absolutely right."

Lily glanced beseechingly at Ashbourne. "I must agree with them," he said.

Lily marched back toward the carriage. "Very well. I refuse to argue with all three of you. We'll go to London. We can stay at Medford's property. But as soon as it is seemly, we'll be leaving for Northumberland. Do you hear me, Annie?"

Annie, obviously pleased with her reprieve, nodded eagerly.

The two ladies waited near the carriage while Devon spoke with the innkeeper, arranging for the horses to be changed out. It was the right thing, for Lily to bring her sister back to town. He might not care about her future any longer, but surely there was no harm in performing one more chivalrous act for Annie. She was a nice young lady. He'd just have to ignore the fact that Lily would be staying with Medford.

Devon made his way back to the coach just as Eggleston reappeared.

Devon eyed the younger man. "We're nearly ready to leave, but first let me make myself clear. It should go without saying, Eggleston, that you will not mention a word of this ill-advised journey to anyone."

Eggleston nodded. "Of course, my lord. Upon my honor."

Devon gave him a skeptical glance. "I intend to circulate the story that you were overheard telling everyone you were headed to Bath for a few days, and when you return, that's exactly what you'll tell people. You went to visit friends, became horribly ill upon your arrival, and spent the last few days in bed where no one visited. No one. That's why you haven't been seen in days. Do I make myself clear?"

"Perfectly," Eggleston replied, bowing at the waist to Devon.

Devon rolled his eyes. "Very good. And if I should ever hear that you've circulated any other story, you shall not be pleased by the visit I intend to pay you."

Eggleston nodded vigorously. "I understand, my lord."

"Or the visit I intend to pay you," Jordan called, a wide grin on his face.

Eggleston tugged at his neckcloth. "Lord Ashbourne, I didn't realize you were here. Yes, yes. You've nothing to worry about from me."

"Excellent." Devon pulled on his gloves. "Let's go."

"If you won't be needing my services any longer," Jordan said. "I'll just slip back to London the way I came and do my part in damage control."

Devon nodded to his friend. "Yes, see you back in town, Ashbourne. You have my thanks."

Jordan tipped his hat and grinned at Annie and Lily. "Nice to see you again, Miss Andrews, Lady Merrill." And then he was gone, in a cloud of dust kicked up by his mount.

Eggleston made to enter the coach, but Devon raised his arm, blocking him. "You're riding in the other carriage." He nodded to a space across the courtyard where Eggleston's own carriage waited.

Annie opened her mouth to protest, but Devon cut her off. "Eggleston must arrive from a different direction and cannot be seen with us."

Lily nodded, sighed, and climbed into the coach, pulling Annie with her.

"Now go, Eggleston." Devon gestured to the coach. Arthur, apparently in fear for his continued safety should he disobey Devon, hurried off toward his own coach.

Arthur started to turn back around to say something to Annie, but the collective looks of reproach from both Lily and Devon must have made him change his mind. Instead, he bowed to the three of them and said simply, "Good day."

Annie pressed her handkerchief to her lips.

Lily pulled on her own gloves. "Annie, it's time to leave."

Annie wiped her wet eyes, dabbed at her cheeks, and blew into the handkerchief. "I will miss him so."

Lily rolled her eyes. "I'm sure you will."

Devon climbed into the carriage with the sisters. He relaxed back in the seat across from them and stretched out his legs.

"Ready?" Devon knocked on the door between the coachman and the carriage and the coach jolted into motion.

The first half of the day, they traveled in silence. The two sisters dozed intermittently. Lily tried to catch Devon sleeping, but it was as if the man weren't human. He seemed completely awake and relaxed at all times. Meanwhile, she felt as if she'd been through the wash and back again.

The journey to London was a bit slower than the full pelt trip to stop Annie from ruining her life. Devon kept the two sisters laughing with his stories about the *ton,* his time on the Continent, and his foibles as a child.

Finally, they stopped at an inn for a midday meal. Arthur sat with them, and Lily gasped when she glanced over and saw Annie and Arthur holding hands.

"Stop that," she insisted, pulling Annie closer to her.

Annie gave Lily a defiant glare before glumly plucking her hand from Arthur's grasp.

"It's not fair that Arthur should have to ride back alone," Annie insisted.

Lily swallowed a bite of crusty bread. "I disagree. I think it's more than fair after what he's done."

"Don't look at me like that," Annie said to Lily.

Lily shrugged. "I don't know what you mean."

Annie glared at her. "Yes you do. You've been giving me that I'm-so-disappointed-in-you look all morning."

Lily tossed her bread back on the plate. "I *am* disappointed in you. You have very little idea what you've done. We can only hope the *ton* will believe the story that you weren't feeling well after the party. God knows if one loose-lipped servant says something, your reputation will be shredded beyond repair."

Annie poked halfheartedly at her stew. "But you can hardly blame me, Lily. I did what I thought I had to do. I followed my heart and I will never regret that. Besides, where do you think I got the idea?"

Lily sucked in her breath. She turned to face her sister head-on. "What do you mean?"

Arthur Eggleston cleared his throat and made a show of helping himself to his meal, not speaking. Devon's face was curiously blank.

Annie looked away, her lips tightly drawn.

"Annie," Lily said under her breath in a warning tone. "Answer me."

Annie pushed her food around in the bowl, her eyes downcast. "I heard what you said at the ball. To Lord Colton."

Lily's face burned. "What exactly did you hear?"

Annie still wouldn't look at her. "I heard you tell Lord Colton you'd waited for him, you'd planned to elope with him. You'd planned to go to Gretna yourself."

Lily let out her breath in a rush. Fortunately, there were no other patrons in the inn today to overhear them. "We did *not* go to Gretna."

Annie slapped her palm on the table. "But you were planning on it. You meant to go. Admit it!"

"Thank God, Lord Colton didn't come for me that day," Lily breathed. But even as she said the words, unexpected tears clogged the back of her throat. She glanced away, snapping her mouth shut. "You shouldn't have been eavesdropping," she whispered.

Annie stood and dropped her bread to her plate. "You

don't understand, Lily. You never do! It doesn't matter that it didn't happen. What matters is that you tried. You wanted to. It was in your heart, just like mine, and believe me, I hadn't believed until then that you had a heart! All you want is to control everything and everyone around you."

Lily closed her eyes and took a deep breath. "Annie, can't you understand? I want to keep you from making the same mistakes I did. I'm older, wiser. I know better now and I want you to have the benefit of my experience. All I've ever done is what I think is best for you."

Annie turned away. "I'll be waiting in the coach," she said quietly before turning and making her way toward the inn's front door.

"I'll escort you outside, Miss Andrews," Arthur said, taking a final bite, wiping his mouth, and hurrying after Annie.

Her elbow braced on the table, Lily dropped her forehead into her palm. A mixture of surprise and dread knotted in her belly. Devon had heard the entire embarrassing episode. Not to mention Arthur Eggleston. Yes, Devon had heard it before, the first time she'd told him, but she'd been mercifully in her cups that night. Right now she was completely sober. Too sober. Much too sober.

She turned to look at him. He shook his head and gave her a soft smile. He bit his lip with his perfect white teeth.

"She has a point," he said with a sideways smile that made Lily's heart skip a beat.

"Don't you think I know that?" Lily replied, wishing herself anywhere else. "I never would have said all of that if I thought Annie had been listening."

"Nor if you'd been completely sober," Devon added.

She couldn't help her answering smile. "That too," she admitted.

"Believe me. I know how you're feeling, Lily."

She turned to face him. "What do you think I'm feeling?"

"Guilt. You're feeling guilt because you may have been part of the reason Annie ran away. If her reputation is destroyed, you'll blame yourself."

*How did that confounded man know so much?*

She expelled her breath. "You're right." It felt good to admit it, to not fight with him anymore.

Devon put his hand on her shoulder and pulled her back against his chest and Lily allowed it. It had been so long, so long since she'd had someone to lean on. And leaning on Devon felt so right.

"I'm responsible for her, Devon. Completely responsible," she whispered. She rubbed her cheek against the soft fabric of his shirt.

"Believe me, I understand."

It was on the tip of her tongue to ask him how he understood. How could he? Devon squeezed her shoulders then and she shook it off. The moment was gone. She pulled away from him and made a show of smoothing her skirts.

"We should get back to the coach," he said. "God knows, your sister may have talked George into taking her to London by now."

Lily shook herself and nodded. "Yes, we should go."

Devon settled the bill with the proprietor and put his hand on the small of Lily's back to escort her from the inn.

She glanced at the coins Devon had tossed on the wooden table. "I shouldn't let you pay for all of this," she said, biting her lip.

"Nonsense. What sort of a gentleman would I be if I allowed you to pay?"

Lily nodded wanly. She could not pay even if he were inclined to "allow" her. Gentleman or no, she didn't have a shilling to her name. "Well, thank you, just the same. I do appreciate it, Devon."

He pushed open the front door and allowed her to precede him into the courtyard.

Lily glanced up at him, almost as if she saw him for the very first time. The midday sun glinted off his black hair and the smile on his face made him look positively boyish. It was true when they'd started this journey, Lily hadn't been entirely sure she could trust him. But now she realized Devon had helped her, truly helped her when she needed help. Unlike any man except Medford.

Oh, Medford! She'd forgotten to tell him they'd left. And that after he'd proposed marriage to her. Oh, God, would he hate her? She hoped not. She'd just have to explain after this nightmare was over.

She glanced up at Devon again. Yes, Medford was a good man, there was no question, but the man standing beside her now was Devon Morgan. Like Medford, she could trust him.

But unlike Medford, Devon made her feel things, deep things she didn't want to examine.

She shook her head and followed Devon into courtyard. A cloud of dust had been kicked up by one of their carriages.

Lily glanced around the square, her heart in her throat. George called out to them. "Milord, Mr. Eggleston's coach just took off."

# CHAPTER 28

Devon made his way toward his coach with ground-devouring strides. "I can see that, George. Why did it leave?"

George pushed his hat back on his head. "Those two said you'd be right behind and not ta worry."

Devon cursed under his breath. He turned to help Lily into the coach.

"And you just let them leave?" Lily cried.

The coachman shrugged, a puzzled look on his face. "Aren't ye all traveling together, my lady?"

Lily opened her mouth to retort, but Devon put a hand on her arm and shook his head. "It's better not to let the servants know too much," he whispered. "Annie and Eggleston can't have gone far. They're headed straight south. Even they wouldn't be foolish enough to try to go to Gretna again."

There was no choice at the present but to get in Devon's coach and follow them, so Lily allowed Devon to help her up. The two of them settled into the coach. Lily rubbed her temples. Devon was right. No doubt Annie had merely wanted a few more stolen hours with Arthur Eggleston.

"When did my sweet little Annie become so defiant?" she sighed.

"I suspect it was around the time you began telling her what she could and could not do."

Lily scowled at him. "We must catch up with them and get Annie back."

Devon rubbed the back of his neck. "I agree we should catch up to them and keep an eye on them, but what harm does it do to let them enjoy each other's company a bit longer?"

Lily let her jaw drop. "What sort of a chaperone would I be if I allowed such a thing?"

"A realistic one."

Devon knocked on the door that separated the coachman from the interior. "George, catch up to the other coach. Keep them in your sights. If they change direction, let me know immediately."

"Yes, my lord," came George's reply.

Lily rubbed her hand across her face and groaned. "Oh, I suppose you're right. It's not as if they can be making passionate love inside a coach for heaven's sake. It's much too cramped in here." She smiled, but her face heated at the same time. "We're getting Annie back at our very next stop, however."

"A wise decision, Madame Chaperone," Devon replied with a grin.

Lily settled back and rubbed her hand against the velvety squabs. A prick on her thumb made her wince. "Oh, blast it," she said, staring at her hand.

"What is it?"

"I must have got a splinter from the table at the inn." She squeezed her thumb and brought it closer to her nose, examining it. "I can't get it out."

Devon moved across the seats to sit next to her. His strong thigh slid along hers, rubbing against her gown. Lily gulped. She should have come up with this splinter story long before now. Not that it was a lie. The confounded thing was blatantly stuck in her thumb.

"Let me see," Devon insisted, grabbing her hand and examining it closely.

"It's deep," she told him.

"I can see that." He squeezed her thumb between his two forefingers. "Seems it's a stubborn one. It's not budging."

Lily pulled her hand away. "Perhaps I can suck it out." She promptly stuck the offending appendage into her mouth.

"Here. Don't do that." Devon gently took her thumb and guided it to his mouth.

The heat of his tongue and lips made Lily grasp for the wall. Suddenly, the air was thick and hot in the coach. Devon's mouth on her skin was her only thought.

"No, don't," she whispered, but she couldn't seem to bring herself to pull her thumb away.

Devon, looking a bit chagrined, pulled her thumb from his mouth and examined it again. He drew a small knife from his boot, and before Lily had a chance to gasp, he popped the splinter from her thumb using the blunt edge.

"It's out," he announced. He held out his palm, displaying the tiny stick.

"Th-thank you," Lily whispered, shaken.

Devon disposed of the splinter out the window while Lily made a show of rearranging her skirts. She assumed Devon would move back to his own seat at any moment. She hesitantly looked up at him when he didn't appear to be leaving. He seemed completely relaxed and content where he was.

"What shall we talk about?" Lily asked, still fussing with her skirts. She was so aware of Devon's body close to hers she could barely breathe.

His eyes captured hers. "Who says we need to talk?"

Their eyes met. Locked.

She leaned into him and one of his arms came around to pull her close. His other hand moved up her thigh. His mouth claimed hers, a hot brand.

Lily ripped at his cravat with greedy fingers while he pushed up her skirts. He turned her sideways on the cushions of the coach and leaned over her. They both fumbled with the buttons on his breeches. Devon's strong hand moved up the outside of her thigh and pushed up her shift.

Lily couldn't breathe. Didn't want to breathe. His mouth shaped hers, played with her, taunted her, his tongue moving insistently inside. She pushed her hands into his dark hair, holding his face to hers.

"Devon," she cried out. "Please."

"Oh, God, Lily. I've wanted you ever since you came to my room."

"I want you too," she breathed against his ear, wrapping her fingers through his hair.

Devon positioned himself and slid inside her hot, welcoming sheath.

He groaned, pulling back and pushing inside her again, making them both crazy. Lily cried out again and again until he moved his finger down to play with her sensitive core and then she ceased to think at all.

He rubbed her in little circles, pausing only to move inside her and Lily's head moved back and forth on the cushions fitfully. "Please, Devon . . . I want . . ."

"I know what you want," he breathed against her cheek. "Take it, Lily."

He moved his finger still, over and over in perfectly timed little circles and Lily finally cried out, her hips arching against his hand. Then Devon pushed into her, again and again, sweat beading on his brow. Groaning, kissing her. "Oh, God, Lily I can't wait," he whispered.

She smiled against his lips and kissed him fiercely. "Don't wait."

Devon grabbed her hips and thrust into her once more. He exploded this time, a harsh groan ripped from his chest. His breathing came in spurts and he breathed her name one last time.

He flipped over, taking her with him then. She lay on top of him and they both rested there, breathing heavily on the cushions of the coach.

Lily finally mustered the strength to speak. "What just happened?"

He kissed her forehead. "Magic."

She smiled at that. "I had no intention of doing that again." That was a lie.

"Do you regret it?" His thumb traced her ear.

"No," she admitted, rubbing her cheek against his bared chest.

"Good."

A few minutes later, Lily sat up slowly and moved to the corner of the seat to straighten her garments. She smoothed her hair, smiling to herself. She was tempted to hum. Despite the awful traveling conditions, she suddenly felt simply wonderful.

Yes, it was true she hadn't exactly meant to do that with Devon Morgan today, but oh, that man made her feel good. She couldn't seem to keep her hands off him. There was no harm in it, was there? Soon she'd be off to Northumberland and a chaste, boring life. She might as well enjoy herself a bit.

"Well, that was . . . fun," she sighed.

Devon was righting his own garments and smiled back at her. "That's one way to put it."

Suddenly, Lily jerked up her head, her heart in her throat.

"What is it, Lily?" he asked, his brows drawing together.

"We must catch up with the other coach immediately!" she cried. She lunged for the door that separated them from the coachman and rapped on it sharply. "George. George. Catch up with the coach and stop them. Now!"

"Yes, m'lady," George replied, clucking to the horses. They took off at a gallop and Lily fell back into Devon's lap.

Devon wrapped an arm around her waist and whispered in her ear. "What's all that about? Why the hurry?"

"I just remembered what I said about Annie and Eggleston not possibly being able to make passionate love inside a carriage."

Devon's deep laughter rumbled against the velvety interior. Then he stopped, his Adam's apple bobbing rapidly as he swallowed. He lurched across the seat and rapped loudly on the coachman's door. "Faster, man, faster!"

# CHAPTER 29

The rumors started subtly like most rumors do. Lily had been back in London for only two days when she noticed more whispers as she and Annie walked in the park, more fans snapped in front of faces as she left various establishments about town. The talk about her being the author of *Secrets of a Wedding Night* had been nothing compared to this dustup.

The house party was over and all the guests had returned to town. Apparently, they'd wasted no time in engaging in gossip over the weekend's activities.

The sennight could not pass quickly enough.

Lily scribbled off a letter to Cousin Althea informing her that she and Annie would be arriving a bit later than expected. She hadn't had a chance to speak with Medford yet, but he'd written, telling her she and her company were more than welcome to stay in the town house he'd provided for Evans as long as they needed. Lily was thankful for the reprieve. The next time she saw Medford, they'd have to discuss his marriage proposal. Every time she thought about it, a knot formed in her stomach.

"No matter about the gossip," Lily said to Annie as they walked along Bond Street one afternoon, pretending to shop. "As long as the rumors aren't about you, I don't mind in the least."

"They seem rather nasty." Annie turned to look at a woman giving them a decidedly unpleasant stare. "What do you think they're saying?"

Lily bit her lip. She knew exactly what they were saying. Everyone wanted to know whether she or Devon had won the blasted bet. The truth was, they'd both won, but as long as they remained silent on the subject, no one would know.

And she did trust Devon not to tell.

He might be a gambler, but he'd promised he wouldn't profit from the bet, and she believed him.

She took Annie by the hand and led her down the street, her own head held high. "Like I said, it doesn't matter."

Lily stood in the corner at the Donningfords' ball wondering how long the interested stares and whispers would last. She wore a beautiful golden ball gown, one she'd recently sewn using material from an older gown. She'd planned to wear it to one of Annie's debut evenings. Now she felt as if she were a glowing beacon in the ballroom, drawing all eyes to her. She'd made up her mind to find Annie and leave, when a footman approached bearing a folded note on a silver tray.

She hurriedly opened it and glanced at its contents.

*Meet me in the rose salon—D*

Lily quickly flipped the note closed. She bit her lip. What was Devon doing here and why would he want to meet her in the salon? When they'd arrived back in London, they'd agreed they should stay away from each other for the remainder of her time there. What did he want with her? Another rendezvous? Butterflies scattered in her stomach. *Hmm.* It was tempting. She couldn't allow another tryst, of course, but somehow she also couldn't resist going to see what he wanted.

She moved about the ballroom slowly, aware of the many pairs of eyes that watched her. When a particularly loud thud—caused by one of the orchestra members tipping over his chair—drew everyone's attention to the front of the room, Lily made her move. She quietly slipped out the doors and into the hallway. A few passersby nodded to her. She simply smiled and kept walking. She made her way down the staircase to the front of the house. When she reached the door to the rose salon, she paused and took a deep breath. She smoothed her hair, yanked off her gloves, pinched pink into her cheeks, and slipped into the salon with a bright smile on her face.

Devon was there, leaning against the mantelpiece, the picture of relaxation. Oh, my, the man looked good. As usual. Perhaps a rendezvous wasn't such a bad idea after all.

She struggled to keep the nonchalance in her voice. "Devon, whatever are you doing here? And what are you thinking, asking to meet me like this?"

"We need to talk." He moved to greet her and bowed over her hand. "You look ravishing, by the way."

Lily tamped down her involuntary response to his compliment and raised her brow. "What is it? Why have you summoned me?" She tried to return his smile.

"I hate to be the bearer of bad news, Lily, but I thought you should know. There are rumors—"

She waved her hand in the air. "Yes, yes. I know all about the rumors. It's nothing really. Didn't you expect everyone to wonder which of us won the bet?"

Devon shook his head. "No, Lily. We've got a much larger problem."

Lily looked at him askance. "What could be a bigger scandal than you making a lurid bet about me." She laughed.

"We both agreed how we would handle it. I haven't said a word, have you?" A twinge of apprehension unfolded in her belly. Had Devon said something after all?

"Of course not," he assured her.

She let her shoulders relax. "Then we're perfectly fine." She turned toward the door. She needed to leave. Now. Before she threw herself into his arms and begged him to make love to her again. The settee looked positively inviting.

"Damn it, Lily, will you listen to me?" His voice contained a serious note that made apprehension unfurl in her belly.

She paused, her hand on the doorknob, and looked back at him. "What? What is it?"

"The rumor," Devon said, his dark eyes boring into hers, "isn't about the bet. The rumor is that *you and I* eloped to Gretna Green."

# CHAPTER 30

"How did this happen?" Lily sat down hard on the edge of the settee and glared at the tips of her slippers as if the dainty footwear were responsible for her current troubles.

Devon paced back and forth across the rug in front of her. He scrubbed his hand through his hair. "One of the coachmen must have said something. They can be bought for a few quid. But believe me, if I find out it was George, I'll have his neck."

Lily pressed her fingers to her temples. Her mind raced. "No, no, it's fine. We'll simply deny it."

"It won't be that easy." Devon continued his pacing.

She fluttered her hand in the air, a smile on her face. "Yes it is. You know how gossip goes. A few days and this will all blow over." She stood and shook out her skirts. "Now, I'm returning to the ballroom. Lord knows they are all probably wondering where I went. If they find out I've been in here with you, it'll make it that much worse." Straightening her shoulders and taking a deep breath, she stepped toward the door.

Devon met her there and put his hand on her shoulder. The calm look on his face, the trace of pity, made her breathing quicken. "Lily, if you deny it, if you say it wasn't us, it will only serve to put Annie in a more questionable light. Your sister's reputation is at risk."

"No," she whispered, shaking her head. "No. We can deny it, I tell you." She slipped through the door and left before Devon had a chance to say another word.

Lily moved back into the hallway and up the grand staircase. Thankfully, no one was about. What had Devon been thinking, summoning her to a darkened salon to be alone with him when rumors were already swirling about the two of them? Good heavens. It would only serve to make it all worse.

She paused outside of the ballroom doors, smoothed her skirts and breathed deeply. She must not look flustered. She must remain calm, as if she'd only left briefly to use the convenience.

She slipped through the doors back into the party and gulped when she realized how many eyes were upon her. Lady Eversly was the first to approach her. "There you are, my dear Lady Merrill. I've been looking for you all evening."

"Lovely to see you, Lady Eversly," Lily replied. "We must talk later." She tried to slip past the woman, but Lady Eversly stopped her with a hand on Lily's capped sleeve.

Lady Eversly gave her a sly smile. "You must tell me dear, is it true?" Her voice was a salacious whisper.

Lily blinked at her. "Is what true?"

Lady Eversly's catlike blue eyes widened. "Why, that you've married that rogue Colton? The entire town is agog with the news that the two of you have eloped."

Lily sucked in her breath. Leave it to Catherine to ask such a question. And she'd drawn a crowd, a crowd who stood in a semicircle around Lily. Apparently, enough of the partygoers had imbibed to the point where they weren't satisfied with watching her, now they were actually asking questions. Horrifying questions.

Lily cleared her throat and glanced at the onlookers. "Who told you that, Lady Eversly?" she asked, scrambling to invent an answer that would not cast aspersions onto Annie. But there was no help for it. Lily couldn't allow the *ton* to believe she and Devon had actually eloped.

Lady Eversly leaned closer. "I have my sources, my dear Lady Merrill, don't ever doubt it. The rumor is that Colton's coach left the house party headed north to Gretna. You and your sister left around that same time, did you not?"

Lily swallowed, and attempted to laugh. "Why in the world would two adults run off to Gretna? It's not as if we require anyone's permission."

Lady Eversly's voice was a salacious whisper. "Why, I can think of a score of reasons. Uncontrollable passion"—she winked at Lily—"immediately comes to me. Couldn't wait for the banns, eh? Now, is it true or isn't it?"

Lily opened her mouth to issue the denial lodged on the tip of her tongue.

The doors behind her opened. Devon chose that particular moment to reenter the ballroom. *Perfect! He couldn't have waited five more blasted minutes?* Lily squeezed her eyes shut. When she reopened them, the look of knowing curiosity on Lady Eversly's face was unmistakable.

"Oh, I see you two *do* have your secrets," Eversly whispered a bit too loudly. "I daresay if you didn't already have your scandal broth over that pamphlet"—her voice dipped on the last word—"you'd be quite the outcast, but between you and Colton, this is no doubt going to make you more popular than ever."

"No, no, no." Lily shook her head and backed away from the woman. "You're mistaken."

"Is it true or not?" Eversly followed Lily eagerly. "Do tell."

Lily backed up until she hit a wall, a wall that turned

out to be Devon's chest. She craned her neck to look up at him and gulped.

"Is what true?" Devon asked, flashing his perfect smile at Catherine.

Obviously Catherine wasn't immune to his dark good looks either. The hint of a blush stained her cheeks. "Did the two of you elope to Gretna Green?"

Devon arched a brow. He bent his head a bit. "It's true," he said, wrapping an arm around Lily's waist. "The countess is a countess no more. She's the Marchioness of Colton now."

# CHAPTER 31

Devon ushered Lily through the blur that followed. The smiles, the exclamations, the best wishes. All of it. He planted his hand firmly on the small of her back and escorted her through the throng of well-wishers. He ensured one of the matrons would escort Annie home when she was ready, and then he hurried Lily out to his coach.

The sooner they left the ball, the better.

Once they were safely ensconced in the carriage, Lily dropped her head in her hands. "What. Just. Happened?"

Devon relaxed against the seat and regarded her with a smile on his face. He shrugged. "I did the only thing I could."

"Claim we're married?" Lily's voice held an hysterical edge.

He grinned. "I notice you didn't deny it."

"You're much too calm," she whimpered, leaning forward and burying her face in her hands again. This time she rested them against her knees.

"I don't know what you mean," he answered.

She glanced up at him. "You're sitting there, smiling at me as if you are truly a besotted bridegroom and I am your bride."

He shrugged again. "Why not?"

Lily sat up again and shook her head frantically. "No, no, no. This is madness. This cannot be happening."

Devon leaned forward. He placed a hand on her shoulder. "Listen to me, Lily. It's not such an awful idea. You'd realize that, if you'd calm down and think about it reasonably."

"Reasonably?" she echoed. "There's nothing the least bit reasonable about this."

Devon squeezed her shoulder. "Think about it. The word is out that my coach traveled to Gretna. Thank God, they all think it was you and I. If we deny it, the obvious conclusion will be that it was Annie. Do you want that?"

Lily sucked in her breath. "No, no. Of course not."

"The two of us marrying isn't completely insane."

"How can you even try to make sense of this lunacy? It's ludicrous, that's what it is." She slumped back against the seat, her arms hugging her middle.

"I take that personally," he said with a laugh.

"You should."

Devon sat back against the seat. "It's the only way to save your sister's reputation."

Lily looked up at him with a heartbreakingly vulnerable look on her face. "Why? Why would you want to marry me?"

"I have to marry sometime, don't I?" Devon said. "And you do happen to be the reason my hand is free at the moment."

"And one woman is as good as another?" Lily shook her head.

Devon regarded her. He couldn't keep the smile from his face. It was true that when this had all begun, he'd been intent on revenge, but so much had happened between them over the last days, he couldn't even recall now why he'd been so hell-bent on it in the first place. And for some reason he'd been unable to let her go to Northumberland. The thought of her marrying Medford filled him with anger, an anger born of jealousy. He'd told Lily once that he was never jealous. But over the last few days he realized it wasn't true. No, he couldn't let her marry Medford. Couldn't live with it if it happened. And if she would just see reason, she'd realize this wasn't such a bad idea after all. This way, she and Annie could stay in London, and Annie's reputation would be saved. Lily must see that.

When the coach pulled to a stop in front of the town house where she was staying, Devon escorted Lily to her door. She let herself inside and turned to face him. Devon leaned in and kissed her cheek.

"Don't worry about a thing," he said. "I'll make all the arrangements. No one will know. We'll keep the wedding secret, no servants. Everyone will think we were married in Scotland."

Lily placed her hand on his sleeve. "Devon, I need time." She drew a deep breath. "A day. I'll give you my answer tomorrow night."

She climbed the stairs to her bedchamber, her feet feeling like leaden weights. She didn't bother summoning Mary. Lily needed to be alone . . . to think. She wrapped herself in her night rail and robe and paced the worn carpet in her bedchamber.

She was torn. It would serve Devon right to marry her and discover she was poor. On the other hand, she couldn't very well let him shackle himself to her for eternity not knowing she was destitute. Even if it would save her sister's reputation.

At least Lily knew if she married him, their future in the bedchamber wouldn't be awful. That part was downright tempting actually.

She shook her head. There was more to consider. What about Annie's future? As much as Lily might be willing to marry Devon regardless of his own lack of money, the fact was, they would be forced to live on his inconsistent gambling winnings. She shuddered. She couldn't do *that* to her sister. But the alternative was allowing Annie to face the scandal of an elopement.

Lily pulled her robe tighter around her middle and stared out the window into the darkness. She shivered. What would she do? What could she do?

Lily waited in Lord Medford's well-appointed drawing room, her stomach in knots. She owed him an explanation. A thousand explanations.

She hadn't slept last night. Or today either. No doubt the circles under her eyes were proof of that. She'd spent the entire evening tossing in bed, trying to come to a decision that made the most sense for everyone. She'd spent the day pacing the floor of her borrowed bedchamber, weighing the possibilities. Now, it was late at night and it was time for her decisions.

The door opened and Lily sucked in her breath. Lord Medford strode in, his familiar countenance so welcome. Lily expelled her breath.

Medford's face was tight. "To what do I owe the pleasure, Lady Merrill? Or should I call you the Marchioness of Colton now?"

Lily winced. He'd heard the rumors. Of course he'd heard the rumors. And beneath his devil-may-care façade, she sensed Medford's anger.

Lily stood and hurried over to him. "I came to explain."

"My lady." He bowed and offered her a seat again. Lily's heart tugged. He was being so kind. Kind and civilized. Just like Medford.

She reluctantly sat down. Turning her face up to him, she bit her lip. "I am not married."

His shoulders relaxed a bit. "Engaged?"

Lily shook her head. "No. But Colton did ask me."

"And what did you tell him?" She could tell Medford was holding his breath.

She smoothed her skirts. "That's why I'm here. I must answer to my first offer of marriage before I answer to the second."

Medford squared his shoulders. "And your answer, to me, is . . . no?"

She stared at her hands folded in her lap so serenely, completely belying her inner turmoil. "I'm sorry, James. So sorry." A lump formed in her throat.

His voice was soft. "That's the first time you ever called me 'James.' Did you know that?"

She intertwined her fingers and squeezed. "Please believe I never would have purposely hurt you. But we don't love each other. You know that. I've taken advantage of your friendship too much already. I couldn't allow you to shackle yourself to me for all eternity."

Medford shook his head. "You don't owe me an explanation, Countess." He paused. "Or shall it be Marchioness?" A wry half-smile appeared on his lips.

Lily winced again. "I do owe you an explanation. I should have answered your proposal that day at the house party."

"You're entertaining Colton's proposal, aren't you?"

"It's complicated. I cannot explain it to you because . . ." She bit her lip. "I don't understand it myself."

Medford's handsome face was a cold mask.

"There's something else." Lily shut her eyes briefly. "James, I . . . I cannot write the second pamphlet."

The skin around his eyes crinkled. He reached out and

squeezed her hand. "I know, Lily. I knew that the moment I'd heard the rumor that you'd married him."

She hung her head. "I'm sorry."

Medford stood and paced away from her, his arms folded behind his back. "I'm worried for you, Lily. You don't know him as you think you do. There are rumors about him. Ugly rumors."

She swallowed. "I know. He's a gambler. I've known that for years."

Medford turned to face her, an intent look in his eye. "He's playing in a tournament tonight. A large, illegal tournament in the Rookery. No decent gentleman would engage in such a game. His opponent is a fellow named Gilbert Winfrey. The man is known as the Lord of the Underworld. Colton's rubbing elbows with the vermin of the streets. This is the man you're considering marrying."

Lily wrapped her arms around her middle. She spoke slowly. "I knew he was playing in a tournament. The rest does not surprise me."

Medford shoved a hand through his normally perfect hair. "That is the type of life you wish for yourself? The type of husband you would choose over me?" A muscle ticked in his jaw.

"James, please," she whispered, covering her face with her hands.

Medford took a deep breath. "My apologies for upsetting you, Lily. It's just that . . ." He took a deep breath. "There is something else."

A stab of fear streaked through her chest. She looked up at him. "What is it?"

His voice dropped to a harsh whisper. "They say Colton is harboring his by-blow at his country estate. A five-year-old boy named Justin."

Lily clutched at the arm of her chair. A by-blow? A *five-year-old* by-blow? Her chest was in a vise. "No. That cannot be true. Who told you such a thing?" But the name Justin conjured a memory. Master Justin, from the letter she'd glimpsed in Devon's room.

Medford dropped his hands to his sides. He moved to where she sat and knelt beside her, his eyes searching her face. "The rumors have been rampant since your supposed elopement. All anyone can talk about is you and Colton." He sneered the last word. "Lily, I'm afraid for you. If you were to marry him, you may be a widow again sooner than you think. They say Gilbert Winfrey is favored to win, but the man never plays fair. If Devon wins, he may end up on the wrong side of a knife. Don't marry him, Lily."

Lily shuddered. She couldn't utter any words. None of them would make it past her dry lips. The gambling was awful enough, but now she must fear for Devon's life? What other secrets was he hiding from her? She might not really want to know, but she had to find out.

She squeezed Medford's hand. "I must go, James. Thank you for everything. You're a dear friend."

# CHAPTER 32

Lily arrived at Devon's town house a quarter of an hour later. She leaped down the carriage steps and hurried into the house. Taking a deep breath, she dashed up the stairs to Devon's bedchamber and flung open the door.

Devon was still there. He hadn't left for his tournament yet. She closed her eyes briefly and let out her pent-up breath. He was safe. For now.

She moved into the room, watching him. He was putting the finishing touches on his cravat. He inclined his head toward her when she appeared behind him in the looking glass.

He gave her a sly grin. "Made your decision and couldn't wait to tell me?"

Lily approached him slowly with her arms folded tightly across her chest. "Who is Justin?"

Devon pulled the cravat tight and turned to her, his face blank. "Where did you hear that name?"

Her voice shook. "Lord Medford told me. Justin is your by-blow, isn't he? From five years ago? That's why you left me."

Devon's nostrils flared. "I do not particularly care for that term. Justin is my *son*."

"He's the reason you left?"

He nodded. Once.

"And his mother?" She squeezed her middle so tightly it hurt.

"My former mistress."

She closed her eyes, willing herself to ask the questions she didn't want to know the answers to. "Did you love her?"

"No. But I love Justin more than my own life."

She tossed her hands in the air. "What else aren't you telling me, Devon?"

He turned to face her head-on. He took two steps toward her, reached out, and ran his hands up and down her arms. "I can understand you're upset, Lily, and I will tell you everything you want to know, but it must wait."

Lily shook her head. "I've waited long enough."

Devon squeezed her arms softly and looked her in the eye. "You must trust me, just for tonight. I promise I will explain everything tomorrow."

Lily pulled away from him. She paced the floor, her arms crossed over her middle again. "You're going? To that tournament of scoundrels? Really?"

"Did Medford tell you that too?" he scoffed. "Yes. I must go."

Lily swallowed. Medford's words flashed across her brain. *"If you were to marry him, you may be a widow again sooner than you think. He may end up on the wrong side of a knife."*

She turned to Devon, her voice trembling, knowing their entire future would be decided in the next moment. "Devon, I cannot marry you unless you promise never to gamble again. Promise me you won't play in the tournament tonight."

Devon expelled his breath. Moving over to her, he reached out and traced his thumb along her cheekbone.

"Lily," he whispered softly. "That is the one promise I cannot make."

She squeezed her eyes shut. Oh, God, she couldn't bear it. She loved him. She did. And she couldn't stand the thought of something happening to him . . . but she also couldn't bear marrying him and then losing him. No. She couldn't love this man and keep her heart constantly in peril.

She nodded toward the door. "Go if you must," she whispered brokenly. "But I won't be here when you return. I'm going to Northumberland."

Devon's voice was even, measured, but fire sparked in his dark eyes. "Things are not what they seem. You must trust me."

Tears threatened to spill down her cheeks, but she fought them back. "I cannot." Her voice cracked.

A tic leaped in Devon's jaw. "After everything that's happened, why won't you trust me?"

Lily hugged her arms around herself, squeezing her nails into her flesh. Hard. "You've kept your son a secret from me all this time. What other secrets do you have, Devon? I cannot be the wife of a penniless gambler."

He stiffened and moved behind her. His harsh whisper fell on her neck and made her want him and made her hate herself for wanting him. His voice was flat. "Money is that important to you? Then it seems we both must do what we both must do."

Thank God her back was toward him so he wouldn't see the tears welling in her eyes.

She had lived her entire life controlled by men. She couldn't do it anymore. She must take charge of her own destiny and if that meant living apart from him, so be it.

No. Money wasn't the only thing that mattered in the world, but without it how could they feed themselves? How could they keep Annie safe? Devon's credit would run out eventually. Lily had spent her childhood worried about her parents' fortunes amid her own father's gambling debts. How could Devon ever understand how much it frightened her to be at the whim of an addiction?

She squeezed her arms around her middle and tried to keep her voice from shaking. "Good-bye, Devon."

Devon moved past her toward the door and Lily waited until she could no longer hear the clip of his boots on the stairs before she slumped to the floor. She could not, would *not,* allow a man to play havoc with her emotions again. If she married Devon, she would be giving him the keys to her heart with no guarantees. She had to leave. She must go.

For a moment last night, when Devon had asked her to marry him, she'd thought she'd had what she'd always wanted. Now she knew she had nothing at all.

# CHAPTER 33

Devon stared out the window into the darkness as the carriage rattled closer to the Rookery. Jordan Holloway sat across from him. Whatever temporary lunacy had overtaken Devon when he'd thought he could marry Lily was over now. Thank God.

Lily had issued him an ultimatum. Ultimatums had never sat well with him. Defeating Winfrey, regaining his signet ring, those were two things he'd promised his father and he would not break that promise. If he did, he'd be just like his bloody father.

Yes, he could have explained everything to Lily, told her why he had to go, but she'd immediately thought the worst of him. She didn't trust him. And trust was something he demanded in a partner.

So be it. She could have her perfect Medford.

Devon pounded his fist against the side of the coach.

"Can't wait to get at Winfrey, eh?" Jordan asked.

His friend's words shook Devon from his thoughts. His reply came through clenched teeth. "I'm ready to get this bloody well over with, that's what I am." He pulled on his gloves.

Jordan nodded. "I'm glad I'll be there with you. There's sure to be trouble. How did your father manage all those years without Winfrey harming him?"

Devon's laugh was humorless. "Quite simple. My father never won. As long as he was giving Winfrey money and not taking it, he was quite safe. It's the same reason I've been safe up to now."

"But your father expected *you* to win eventually. He must have known he'd be placing you in danger if you challenged Winfrey and beat him."

A humorless smile this time. "Make no mistake. My father never put people ahead of money a day in his life."

When the coach pulled to a stop in front of a rotting storefront in the Rookery, Devon stretched his legs and took another deep breath.

"Ready?" Jordan asked.

"As I expect to be," Devon replied.

"My eyes will be open. Don't worry." Jordan pulled on his cloak.

They descended the steps of the coach and treaded over refuse in the muddy, wet street to make their way to the front of the establishment. Raucous music spilled forth from the creaky, haphazard door. Street urchins ran up to them and tugged on their coats.

"Please, guv'na, please. Can ye spare a shillin'?" one small boy begged.

Devon glanced down at the children and swallowed. They were all scraggly and unkempt. Not to mention they looked half-starved. He considered their plights. The children of the dead or unwanted. One was a small boy with dark hair. He looked to be no more than Justin's age. Devon swallowed again. It was only blind luck that Justin had been parented by someone who took him in, gave him an education, actually claimed him. Some of these children were no doubt the products of affairs with mistresses, as Justin was. Devon pulled a handful of coins from his pocket and tossed a pound to each small hand.

Beside him, Jordan shook his head. "You're only encouraging them." But Devon noted with a wry smile that Jordan had pulled money from his own cloak and tossed it to the children, even as he continued to shake his head.

The two men continued past the urchins and pushed their way through the door that barely clung to its frame, supported only by rusty hinges. The smell that hit him overwhelmed Devon. He pressed the back of his hand to his nose. Rotting food lay scattered on the floor, drunken men urinated in the corners, and the stench of unwashed bodies surrounded him.

"Quaint," Jordan said, stepping over a pile of refuse as they advanced toward the large table in the dark, dank back of the place. A gnarly assortment of ne'er-do-wells already inhabited most of the rickety chairs surrounding the table. Gilbert Winfrey sat at the head of the table, a grimy king surveying his dirty kingdom.

Devon winced. How had his father been able to stand this? Abide this company? Be a part of this? Not only was gambling a disgusting habit that ruined lives and families, it also made false friends out of the most unlikely of compatriots. It just proved what a sickness his father had, the complete addiction to gambling that had taken over his life and ripped everything from him, including his own son.

"Ah, Colton, there ye are," Winfrey said. He swept out his hand and offered Devon a seat at the opposite end of the table. Devon watched the men with narrowed eyes. There was the usual group of suspects, a stomach-turning assortment of men who had also allowed the game to rob them of everything. It was tragic, really. Heart-wrenching. But these men were doing this to themselves, and had no one else to blame. Devon thought of their wives and children at home, the people depending on these men who would be forever disappointed.

His thoughts turned to Lily. She *thought* she would be one of them if they had married. She had so little faith in him, she refused to wait and listen to his explanation. She'd jilted him again.

Devon sat at the table and Jordan took a seat several paces behind him along the wall with the other spectators.

"I believe we're all here now," Winfrey announced. "Let the gaming commence." He smiled his crooked-tooth smile. "The first bet be fifty pounds." He tossed a voucher on the table.

"The game is faro, laddies," Winfrey said to the table as a whole, "and McGee 'ere is the banker. We're all o' us punters tonight. Including 'is 'igh-and-mighty lor'ship 'ere."

Devon ignored the jibe and watched as the cards were shuffled by a questionable-looking man with an even more questionable moustache. Devon eyed McGee carefully. Then his gaze slid to the cards. Dirty and torn, they looked like they'd been plucked from the trash heap.

Devon raised a brow. "Isn't it customary to use a new pack?"

"It's me lucky pack," Winfrey sneered.

Devon narrowed his eyes. "Lucky? Or stacked? If that banker's box is rigged, I'll know it."

Winfrey spat on the ground. "Careful, yer lordship, ye don't want ta end up wit a knife in yer belly for calling me a cheat."

Devon returned his cold gaze. "Then. Don't. Cheat."

"Would ye prefer another banker, yer lordship?" His ratlike eyes narrowed.

"Yes." Devon looked him straight in the eye. "I would."

Winfrey nodded and spat again. "Yer the banker now, Monty."

A hulking man lumbered up and took over. He gathered up the filthy stack and shuffled the cards again.

Devon watched the deal carefully. His years of gaming had taught him much and he knew when he was being cheated, when the sleight of a hand pulled a card from the bottom of the pack. Whether Winfrey would risk cheating on the first deal or whether he planned to lull his victims into a sense of security, Devon didn't know, but the cards in the banker's pack appeared to have been shuffled fairly. This time, at least.

"Care fer a drink, yer lordship?" Winfrey asked, eyeing Devon carefully.

"No," Devon clipped. "Something tells me keeping my wits about me will be most important tonight."

Winfrey growled again but nodded to a servant to bring drinks to the entire table. Soon, ale mugs were plopped in front of each player. Devon ignored his.

"'Ave a pint, Lord Ashbourne?" Winfrey called to Jordan.

"No, thank you," Jordan replied coolly. "Nothing could entice me to partake of anything served in this establishment. As charming as it is, my health is of great concern to me."

Winfrey grunted at Jordan's response and turned back to the game. He tossed some checks on the table. The other men eyed them carefully and placed their bets.

"My checks," Devon said, tossing his on the table.

The banker moved the spade layouts on the board. The players each placed their stakes. Winfrey placed fifty pounds' worth of checks on the king at the top of the layout.

The pack was placed faceup in the dealer's box.

"Ah, and first we burn off the soda," Winfrey said, pulling the first card off the top of the pack and discarding it. It revealed the next card, the jack of hearts. The banker's card.

"The losing card," Winfrey announced, pointing to the banker's box.

Monty placed it on the right side of the banker's card. Then he placed the next card, the player's card, the four of spades, on the left. "The winning card," Winfrey called.

Devon watched the man sitting to Monty's right. He was the case keeper and would ensure the banker wasn't palming the cards. But Devon had no such issue. His mind kept the numbers inside in perfect order, and for every two played, he would know what was left, what was still in play.

And he would win.

Five hours later, Devon eyed Winfrey across the sooty, smoke-filled room. All of the other men had long since lost every shilling they'd come with. Devon himself had lost thousands. The only two players still in the game were Devon and Winfrey. Devon's glance slid across the table to Winfrey's hand. A garnet and gold ring blinked at him through the smoke-filled room.

It was time to end this.

"One more hand," Devon said calmly. "Give me one more hand to attempt to win back my money."

Winfrey smirked at him. "Just like a bloody Colton. Don't even know when ye's been bested. Ye've only got ten quid left, ain't ye?"

Devon nodded. Once. "One more hand."

Winfrey shrugged. "Ah, why not? It'll be me pleasure takin' that last ten from ye, yer lordship." He tossed a ten-pound note on the table. "There ye go, Colton. I'm bettin' all ye got." He laughed.

Devon slowly shook his head back and forth. "So, you are worried about me after all, are you, Winfrey?"

Winfrey sat up straight. "What do ye mean? I ain't never been scared o' a Colton. Yer father would still be payin' me off, if he weren't six feet under right now." He laughed a sickening laugh.

Devon squeezed the tablecloth so tightly his knuckles turned white. "Seems you're scared of *me,* however. Otherwise, you'd bet everything *you've* got."

"Why should I bother? We both know who's walking out o' 'ere a winner." He smirked again, and beside him Monty chuckled.

"Then you shouldn't mind giving me a chance to win back my money. Unless you're scared."

Winfrey's eyes narrowed on him. "I said, I ain't ne'er been scared o' no Colton." Winfrey pushed the entire stack of money forward. "I bet it all."

Five thousand pounds. The entire pot.

Devon nodded. The dealer set the cards out and Devon and Winfrey gathered theirs. Devon eyed his hand. So did Winfrey.

"Well?" Winfrey spat onto the dirty floor next to him. "What say ye, yer lordship?"

Devon played two cards. Winfrey played two. Four more were dealt.

Devon kept the game moving quickly. The faster the play, the greater advantage he would have. Two more cards discarded, two more accepted. Winfrey wiped sweat from his forehead.

Four more discards.

Then two more.

One.

Devon tossed his hand on the table. "I win." He smiled at Winfrey.

Winfrey stared at Devon's hand in disbelief. He blinked repeatedly, muttering a string of expletives that would singe the hair off a drunken lout's ears. Winfrey crumpled his cards in his fist and threw them to the filthy floor. "Blast it. How did ye do it?" He gave the dealer an evil stare. The dealer shrugged and loosened his cravat, looking decidedly nervous.

One of the other men pushed all of Winfrey's money across the table to Devon.

Without saying a word, Devon pulled the money into his satchel and stood to leave.

"It's been a pleasure," Devon said, nodding at Winfrey.

"Blast it all, Colton," Winfrey shouted. "I don't know what dark magic ye just used but ye've got to give me a chance ta win me money back now."

Devon inclined his head toward the man. "My pleasure." He paused. "Do you have ten quid?"

Winfrey growled. "Ye know I don't."

"Very well. Again, my pleasure." Devon turned to leave and Jordan moved to follow him.

"Wait! Wait," Winfrey called. "I've got this." Devon turned and Winfrey pulled the garnet and gold ring from his finger. "I'll use this as me voucher."

Winfrey tossed the ring on the table. It rolled across the pockmarked wood and came to a stop in front of Devon. His eyes sealed to it.

His father's ring. His ring. His family's signet ring. The one Devon had worn as a small boy and dreamed of owning one day. The value of the piece, its gold and garnet, might have been worth five hundred pounds or vastly more, but Devon had never cared about its monetary value. The piece had been a symbol of his ancestry. It was meant to stay in the family, to be treasured and protected and given to . . . his own son one day. Not to be tossed on a dirty wooden table by the likes of Gilbert Winfrey.

"How do I know that trinket is even worth anything?" Devon managed to say evenly.

"Take a look," Winfrey replied. "I won it in a tournament. From yer bloody loser o' a father."

Devon's knuckles cracked.

Half an hour later, Devon stood to leave again. He pulled the entire pot of money back into his satchel. He eyed Winfrey with excruciating distaste.

"We're even now, Winfrey, you and I."

Winfrey's eyes nearly popped from their sockets and his mouth had a fine sheen of froth around it. He spat his words at Devon. " 'Ow the devil do ye think that?"

Devon hefted his bag of winnings to his shoulder. "You cheated when you played my father and everyone knows it. You stacked the cards, had ringers in the game with you. I'd venture to say you've never played an honest hand of cards a day in your life."

All of the other men around the table turned to stare at him with wide, anxious eyes. Winfrey's face turned a mottled shade of purple.

Devon tossed his next words at the crowd. "It cannot be news to all of you that this man is a cheat."

No one answered. They were all suddenly concerned with looking at their torn, dirty boots or examining their filthy fingernails.

There was a sharp scrape of a chair against the floor and Jordan stood up, his cloak billowing behind him. "To hear it said out loud and directly to the man's face is shocking to these fine gents, no doubt," he said. "I'd venture to guess none of them have ever heard anyone take on Master Winfrey this way before."

"What about ye, Colton?" Winfrey sneered. "Do ye deny cheating me tonight? Ye've never won before. And suddenly ye cannot lose?"

"Cheating? Hardly," Devon retorted. "I merely allowed you to win the few times we met before. Make you think you were better than you actually are." He smiled at the blackguard and watched as Winfrey's pockmarked face fell.

"'Ow dare ye!" Winfrey screamed, his face purpling further. "'Ow dare—"

Devon stepped up to him. He spat his words through clenched teeth. "My father was never particularly good with numbers, but I am. You've been playing someone actually worthy of your skill at deception, Winfrey. How does it feel to be bested by a Colton?"

Winfrey frothed at the mouth and looked as if steam might billow from his ears.

Devon chuckled. "Before you say anything you'll regret, I'll be taking *the rest* of my winnings." He grabbed the gold ring from the dirty tabletop, tossed it in the air, and caught it in his palm. He slipped it onto his third finger.

"This is for my father," he hissed to Winfrey. "Your filthy hands will never touch the Colton signet ring again."

Winfrey shook with rage, his fists clenched at his sides.

Jordan moved next to Devon. He bowed from the waist to Winfrey. "Can't say it's been a pleasure." Jordan eyed the crowd and the place. "Your housekeeping skills are sorely lacking. Thankfully, my friend and I won't be returning. Will we, Colton?"

"I have what I came for," Devon said, rubbing his ring with his thumb.

They turned to leave. The floorboards cracked as one of Winfrey's cohorts rushed toward them. Jordan quickly stuck out a booted foot and tripped the man, who fell to a heap on the moldy floor. Jordan stepped on the man's back and ground his boot into his coat before whipping out a pistol and glancing around. "Any other takers?" His voice was casual.

Their hands raised, the other men backed away slowly. Two of them ran from the room.

The giant, bald man in the corner eyed Devon and Jordan with ill-concealed animosity. The giant cracked his knuckles and shuffled restlessly on his massive feet.

Winfrey held up his hand. "Not now, Monty," he said through clenched teeth. "We'll be seeing Lord Colton and Lord Ashbourne again soon." He cracked his own knuckles menacingly. "They can count on it."

Devon and Jordan quickly made their way out of the broken door and into the streets where the urchins still huddled and begged. Devon tossed his small change purse to them to sort out themselves as he and Jordan climbed into the carriage.

The coach took off at a good pace and Devon rapped his knuckles along the cool glass of the window.

"Was it worth it?" Jordan asked, expelling his breath and relaxing against his seat.

"There was only one thing I wanted." Devon held out his hand and stared at the ring. He slipped it off his finger and hefted it in his palm. "Only one thing I ever really wanted. And I've got it."

But even as he said the words, Devon knew they weren't true.

The one thing he ever really wanted had probably just finished packing her bags.

# CHAPTER 34

Lily eyed herself in the looking glass. She still looked tired. The bags under her eyes had not been alleviated by leaving the city. She pinched her cheeks.

It had been a sennight. One week since Lily and Annie had appeared on Cousin Althea's doorstep and she still felt as if her heart had been ripped from her chest.

She sighed. It merely required time. Coming to Northumberland had been the right thing to do. Hadn't it? She bit her lip. The last words Devon had uttered repeated themselves over and over in her mind. *"It seems we both must do what we both must do."*

And that's exactly what she had done. Very well. It was true that Lily was in love with Devon, but the man couldn't give her the one thing that would make her feel secure. His promise to stop gambling. And if he couldn't do such a simple thing as that, she couldn't ever fully love him. Open her heart to him completely.

But she couldn't seem to stop thinking about him either. Him and the entire messy situation. No doubt by now, Devon had told the entire *ton* they were not actually married. She regretted that he would have to deal with the consequences. But it was only fitting. He'd been the one to tell the lie.

So be it. She couldn't live with his secrets and his addictions. He had a son, a child she'd never known about. No, she couldn't live with his secrets. But why was it proving to be so difficult to live without him?

Her cousin's many children were charming and intelligent. She enjoyed spending time with them. She could see herself living a life here among them, watching them grow. But they would never be her own. That wistful thought crept into Lily's mind whenever she had a moment to herself. She would never have her own children. She couldn't stop herself from wondering what Justin was like. Did he have his father's dark hair? His eyes?

Lily shook her head. Turning from the mirror, she grabbed up her bonnet and cloak and hurried from her room and down the staircase.

Annie and the four oldest children were waiting in the foyer.

"Ready for our walk?" Lily asked with her nearly perfected false-happy voice.

At the chorus of nods, Lily led the little group out the front door, across the courtyard, and into the meadow beyond.

The children soon scattered through the field like colorful little bees, and Annie caught up to Lily.

"You're looking worse and worse," Annie said, lifting her skirts to navigate through a particularly high patch of grass.

"That's terribly kind of you." Lily looped her arm through her sister's. She couldn't even bring herself to smile at her own sarcasm.

Annie squeezed Lily's hand. "I would have thought the country air would do wonders for you, but you're so melancholy, one would think you were pining for your lost love or something." Annie cracked a smile.

"I am doing no such thing," Lily shot back too quickly.

"My, my, my. Touchy, are we not? I was only jesting."

Lily watched the children's tiny blond heads bobbing through the willows. She let her own feet drag. "I wonder why *you* seem so happy here," she said to Annie. "Weren't you the one who refused to come to Northumberland no matter what?"

Annie sighed. "Ah, what a difference a few days makes. Arthur wasn't sufficiently coming up to scratch, and I thought his attitude might benefit from my absence for a bit."

Lily's eyes widened. "Well. Dare I say you're becoming more savvy, Miss Anne? You're learning the art of keeping a man waiting."

Annie winked at her. "I've learned from the best, dear sister."

Lily furrowed her brows. "You mentioned a few days. You do realize we'll be here indefinitely, don't you? Cousin Althea has agreed to let us stay."

Annie nodded sagely. "There was another reason I came, Lily. I thought the journey here would be good for you. You were so insistent on leaving London. I thought you'd finally realize what a mistake you were making trying to leave your troubles behind."

Lily stopped walking and turned to face her sister. She let out her breath in a long, weary sigh. "If I was trying to leave my troubles behind, it hasn't worked. It hasn't worked at all."

Annie nodded again. "I know. You are madly in love with Lord Colton, my dear sister, and the two of you will not stay apart for long."

Lily plunked her hands on her hips. "What in heaven's name makes you say such a thing?"

Annie rolled her eyes. "Do you deny you love him?"

Lily bit her lip, dropped her hands to her sides, and began walking slowly again. "No," she whispered.

"There, you see? And it's obvious to anyone who's seen the two of you together that Lord Colton loves you to distraction as well."

Joy leaped in Lily's belly. "How do you know?"

"He simply cannot keep his eyes from you. You have that man twisted completely around your little finger and you don't even know it."

"Annie Andrews! Now I know you have gone mad!"

"I have not. Anyone can see it. You cannot see it because you are too busy trying to punish him for what he did to you five years ago. You're not even interested in the happiness that's right within your grasp now."

Lily bent over and plucked a daisy from the ground. She twirled the white flower around in her fingers. "Punish him?" Her voice drifted away, as she watched the children playing.

"Yes. It's quite frustrating, really. You've received a proposal of marriage from the most perfect man for you, and you don't even realize it."

"He only asked me to marry him because he's under the mistaken impression that I'm wealthy."

Annie tossed her hands in the air. "You cannot honestly believe such a thing? The man is a handsome marquis. He could take his pick of wealthy young ladies. And believe me, there are plenty who would give their eyeteeth to marry him even *after* they read your scary pamphlet."

Lily groaned. "But he's a gambler. He's a rogue. He put himself in danger on a regular basis and he has a son who—"

"So what?" Annie pulled the daisy from her sister's limp fingers and pressed it to her nose.

"So what?" Lily echoed, blinking.

"You heard me. So what?"

"Annie, what are you talking about? You're speaking in riddles and making no sense."

Annie tucked the flower behind her ear. "You've always been so concerned with propriety and rules and responsibility, Lily. But where has it got you? Destitute and unhappy, that's where. You're obsessed with controlling everything, but what has that left you with? A defiant sister and a broken heart. You've tried it your way for quite some time now. May I suggest trying it my way, for once?"

Lily furrowed her brow, her sister's words not forming coherently in her brain yet. "And what exactly is *your* way?"

Annie winked at her. "Why, following your heart, of course. You love Lord Colton desperately and everyone knows it but you. Go to him. Tell him you're sorry. Let him explain. Would you rather have a life filled with the knowledge that you were right, or a life lived with the love of your life? Lily, you'll be fine. But you must learn to let go."

*Let go.* The words echoed through Lily's mind. Tears brimmed in her eyes. Annie was right. Her sister, her little sister whom she'd always found foolish and in need of guidance, was now the one pointing out the obvious and making everything seem so simple. Lily loved Devon. She had always loved him. She didn't want to lose him.

Lily pulled Annie into her arms and hugged her. "Oh, Anne, when did you become so wise?"

Anne smiled a knowing smile. "When you weren't looking, dear sister."

The children had dispersed like so many fireflies across the meadow. Lily clapped her hands. "Children, come quickly. We must get back to the house."

"Why, Cousin Lily?" one of the girls called back from across the field.

"Because your cousin Anne and I must return to London immediately!"

# CHAPTER 35

"The first few days of your rampant drinking spree were amusing, Colton. I might even use the word 'droll,' but it's been a bloody sennight, and I fear I might have to hang you on a drying line to sober you up."

They were sitting at Brooks's, and Jordan rolled his head back and forth against the back of the leather chair where he was propped.

"You're more than welcome to leave, Ashbourne." Devon's voice was clipped.

"No. I intend to see you through this bloody awful drinking binge. I swear I haven't seen you this bad since your father died. In fact, I'd say this time is a sight worse. Your recklessness is a bit refreshing, actually. I'd thought you'd given it up once you became a father."

Devon growled. "Justin is safe. I'd never allow him to see me in such a state."

Jordan nodded. "Now, *that* I would never question."

Devon scrubbed his hands across his face and took another drink. "I finally did it. And this is what happens."

"Did what? What are you mumbling about?"

"Asked her to marry me. Again. Like a bloody fool."

"Well, I won't argue with the fool part, but you might start with finding the woman and telling her—"

Devon slapped his hand on the table. Hard. "I tried to tell her. She didn't want to listen. And now I'm through with explanations." Devon tipped the bottle to his lips. He'd slipped the footman a guinea to hand over the entire thing and now he drained it.

Jordan whistled and then he clapped. "Quite a performance. I haven't seen someone polish off a bottle that quickly since . . . goodness, probably the last time I did it." He smiled wryly.

Devon set the bottle down shakily and wiped his mouth with his sleeve. "Let's go." He stood on unsteady feet and lurched toward the door. "This place bores me. I have better brandy at home. My coat, if you please." He tossed the same footman another guinea.

"Be careful, Colton," Jordan warned, with a snort. "At this rate, you'll be poor again before you know it."

The footman bowed and rushed off to retrieve their cloaks.

Devon and Jordan made their way to the front door of the club and pushed it open, stumbling out onto the steps facing the street front of St. James.

Jordan glanced around the darkened street. "Damn that boy. You should take your coin back. The coach isn't here yet." He turned to summon the footman.

The sound of hooves slapping against the packed dirt of the street penetrated Devon's drunken haze. The night was strangely quiet except for the noise made by the lone rider drawing nearer. The air was chilly. Images blurred in front of Devon's eyes. He tried to focus. He leaned against the balustrade.

The glint of his signet ring drew his attention. He pulled it from his third finger and eyed it carefully. "Were you worth it?" he asked the inanimate object. "Were you?" He squeezed the ring in his fist.

When he let go, his hand slipped and the ring fell to the step in front of him. The pinging sound made his head turn. His stomach roiling, Devon bent to retrieve the ring just as the rider passed by and fired a shot.

At him.

Devon slumped onto the steps. The scene played out in slow motion. The sounds muted, the figures draped in shadows.

Jordan leaped down the steps, ripped his pistol from his coat pocket, and fired a shot at the rider. The rider fell to a heap in the street. Jordan turned, his cloak billowing behind him like a specter come to life. He yelled for help and the sound echoed off the building.

Jordan rushed toward him then, caught him by the shoulders, and hauled him up. Devon's head slumped. Bright color caught his eye. His shirtfront was stained scarlet.

"A doctor! We need a doctor!" Jordan yelled, Devon's blood trailing down his fingers.

# CHAPTER 36

Lily rushed through the front door, nearly toppling the butler. Lifting her skirts, she took the steps two at a time. She barreled through Devon's bedchamber door and came to a stop only when she saw him, resting quietly in bed. His eyes were closed, his dark hair fell over one eye, his chest rose and fell peacefully. He slept. She pushed her hand against her heart, closed her eyes, and released the pent-up breath she'd been carrying around for over a day since she'd received word that Devon was hurt. She'd heard the rumors during a stop in her journey from Northumberland. A traveler from London had been at the same inn with a copy of the *Times* in his hand. Apparently, the entire town was agog with the news that the Marquis of Colton had nearly been murdered.

Upon Lily's entrance, Jordan Holloway stood up from a chair in the shadowy corner of the room. "You've come."

Lily's head jerked to face him. "Of course I've come, you fool. How is he?"

Jordan cracked a smile. "They tell me he will be fine."

Lily rushed forward and took Devon's hand. She

rubbed her fingertips along his knuckles. "Who did this to him?"

"Gilbert Winfrey. But don't worry. I killed the bastard."

Lily pressed her lips together and swallowed hard.

Jordan eyed her. "I didn't think you cared, Lady Merrill. You did leave him, didn't you?"

Lily turned on him, her loose hair swinging over her shoulder. "I only left because, because . . . I was so worried for him. And I was right to be worried, look what's happened."

She squeezed Devon's hand. It was warm. It felt so good. Slightly rough, and oh, so familiar. Grabbing it up, she rubbed the back of his hand against her cheek.

Jordan cracked another smile. "So, you do care, after all?"

"I refuse to dignify that with a response." She kept her eyes trained on Devon's face.

Jordan expelled his breath. "Ah, Lady Merrill, the truth is I've always known you cared about him. I saw the way you used to follow him around like a lovesick schoolgirl when you were seventeen. You adored him then and you adore him now."

Lily's head snapped up. "If you thought that, Lord Ashbourne," she asked, feeling a sudden newfound respect for Devon's closest friend, "why did you doubt that I cared?"

He winked at her. "Because I've never been called a fool by anyone so lovely before."

Lily caught herself smiling back. "Then you are obviously consorting with the wrong ladies."

"Oh, without a doubt." He bowed to her. "Now, I'll leave you alone with him."

"Thank you, Lord Ashbourne," she whispered.

"Please call me 'Jordan.' " He nodded toward Devon on

the bed. "He's doing much better. But don't let him fool you. The bullet went straight through his shoulder. If he hadn't bent over when he did, I'm afraid he wouldn't be with us now."

Lily smiled and squeezed Devon's hand even more tightly. "Thank you for taking care of him, Jordan. And you may call me 'Lily.' "

Jordan nodded once. "By the by," he said with a much lighter tone to his voice. "How's that spirited sister of yours? Did you bring her with you or is she off causing havoc elsewhere in the kingdom?"

Lily smiled at him. "Annie's fine. And I thank you again for your help on the way to Gretna."

"It was my pleasure entirely." Jordan winked at her again before stealing away from the room.

Lily dragged a chair over to the bedside and sat rubbing Devon's hand for what seemed like an hour. Finally, his long, dark lashes fluttered open and he blinked at her a few times.

"Would you like some water?" she offered, hurrying over to the side table to pour him a glass from a pitcher left there.

Devon struggled to sit up. His face was blank. "Why are you here, Lily?"

She rushed back to his side. "No, no. Don't move. You mustn't strain yourself. I spoke with the doctor. He said the less active you are, the faster it will heal."

He grunted. "I'm not about to languish in bed for a fortnight."

"Devon, you were shot. You won't be yourself for a bit. You must rest." She paused for a moment and glanced down at her hands. "I heard Winfrey was killed."

Wincing, Devon relaxed back against the pillows. "Yes. Most unlike him to come at me himself. I was sure he would've sent a lackey to do his dirty work. He must have been consumed with revenge to try to murder me in the middle of St. James. Nearly succeeded too."

Lily shuddered. "Don't say that."

"Well, he did, but he paid for it with his own life. Jordan's a crack shot. Amazing aim, really. It was dark as sin that night." He took a deep breath. His voice was flat. "Lily, why are you really here?"

Lily's hand trembled. She rested it atop his. "I'm sorry, Devon." She struggled to say each word. "I never should have left. I was just so worried—"

Devon pulled his hand from hers. "Stop, please."

"No. I need to say this."

"No. You don't. Why are you really here?"

"Devon, I don't care about the gambling, the money. We can work it out. Justin, everything. When you got hurt, it made it even more clear to me. I love you."

"Lily, damn it, I'm not a gambler and I never was. It was all an act, all—" He stopped, his eyes narrowing on her face. "None of that matters now."

Lily winced at the anger in his voice. "Why?"

"You've never been willing to trust me. You jilted me twice. We were never meant to be together."

Lily's hand flew to her throat. "No," she whispered. "Don't say that. You cannot think that."

His eyes were cold. "Yes. I. Do."

Lily shook her head. "It's not true. Please, Devon. You must give us another chance."

His voice was emotionless. "No."

Lily dug her fingernails into her wrist. "Can't we go back? Start again? Pretend the last five years never happened?"

He stared at the wall. "Impossible."

Lily grabbed up her skirts, squeezing the fabric in her fists. "But it doesn't have to be. You asked me to trust you, Devon. To listen. I'm here now. I'm ready to listen."

Devon turned his head away from her on the pillow. His voice was solemn. "I have nothing more to say."

A weight crushed Lily's chest. She couldn't breathe. She closed her eyes.

Oh, God. She was too late.

# CHAPTER 37

Lily arrived on Lord Medford's doorstep with her sister, two aging servants, and two rambunctious dogs in tow. "I've nowhere else to go," she said, her head hanging low. In a matter of hours, Medford had her entire little ragtag household set up in the town house they'd formerly occupied.

"I do not know how I can ever repay you for your kindness, James," Lily said that afternoon as they sat down to tea. She'd just finished telling him the whole sordid story of her attempt to get Devon back. And her subsequent humiliating failure.

"No need to thank me," Medford replied. "I cannot let one of my most famous authors languish on the streets, can I? Besides, I've no doubt when Colton finally comes to his senses and realizes what he's lost, he'll be indebted to me for the kindness I've shown you."

She forced a smile. "I'd believe many things, James, but that you're doing this as a favor to Devon isn't one of them."

This time Medford laughed. "I'm doing this for you, Lily, and only you, but the truth is, I've found out quite a lot about Colton over the past few days."

She put the back of her hand to her forehead. "I'm not sure I want to hear it. The last time you had news about Devon, it did not go well."

Medford shrugged. "Actually, everything I've discovered this time has made the chap look positively saintly."

Lily raised a brow. "We cannot be talking about Colton."

"I'm afraid we are."

Lily sipped her tea. Ah, cream and sugar. Old friends. She'd missed them. "Well, by all means then, tell me. What have you learned?"

"Well, for one thing, the man is indecently wealthy."

Lily's cup clattered to the saucer. She widened her eyes. "Indecently? Wealthy? How can that be?"

Medford shrugged. "Seems he's been hiding his wealth from the *ton* for several years now. He's made a fortune using his penchant for numbers while gambling and then investing his winnings quite wisely."

"But he famously loses," Lily replied.

"In *St. James,* he famously loses," Medford replied. "On the Continent and elsewhere he does nothing but win. He's made a score of magnificent investments, completely renovated the Colton estates, turned around the entire situation. Seems Colton's made a pastime out of becoming rich without anyone knowing. He never needed to win that bet at White's or Winfrey's tournament, for that matter."

Lily shook her head. "Then why would he play? It makes no sense."

Medford shrugged. "You'll have to ask him that."

"That's unlikely. He won't even speak to me," Lily said wryly.

"There's more," Medford replied.

Lily cocked her head to the side. "What?"

"The man has started a foundation for orphans."

Lily sat up straight in her chair. "Orphans?"

"Just recently. He's put a very large sum of money

aside to help establish a home where unwanted children can live. I suspect it's the five thousand pounds he reportedly won from Winfrey in the tournament."

Lily absently traced the rim of her teacup with her fingertip, her brows knitted together. "My astonishment is beyond measure."

Medford flicked an imaginary bit of lint from his sleeve. "Believe me, I don't relish painting Colton as a saint, especially in your eyes. But it's true."

Lily slapped her palm to her forehead. "Next, you'll tell me the man heals the sick."

"No." Medford laughed. "Not that I know of. But he did do one other thing."

Lily took a sip of tea and leaned toward him. "I'm on tenterhooks."

Medford sighed. "Apparently, Colton's paid off the entire list of your creditors. Believe me, Lily, if I'd have known you were in such straits I'd have done so myself."

Lily pressed her palms to her cheeks in a desperate attempt to stop her heated blush. "Oh, good heavens. How did he know? And more importantly, why would he do such a thing? I thought he hated me."

"Another question for Colton."

Lily sighed. "If he was going about doing all this, why wouldn't he tell me?"

"My guess? He didn't want you to want him for his money. Colton's gone to a great deal of trouble to cultivate his image of being a dissolute gambler, rake, and drinker. And something tells me you were his main reason for that."

"No," Lily replied solemnly. "He doesn't care a whit about me, which, of course, is very unfortunate, considering how desperately I love him." She smiled wryly, propping her elbow on the table and resting her chin in her hand.

Medford covered her free hand with his. "Lily, are you quite sure of your feelings?"

"I'm sure." She nodded slowly. "I cannot help it. Believe me, I would if I could."

Medford nodded. "Very well. I've one last revelation, and you might want to prepare yourself for this one."

Lily gulped. "What else could there possibly be?"

Medford straightened his already straight cravat. "It seems he's never denied your elopement. Colton has not told a soul—that I can find—that the two of you are not, in fact, married."

# CHAPTER 38

Jordan Holloway tossed a handful of playing cards onto the table. "Not even a simple game of whist? Vingt-et-un? Nothing?"

Devon crossed his legs at the ankles. "I told you. I'll never touch another bloody card again."

"This is the club. What else are we to do here if you refuse to play cards? We cannot go shooting in the park until you get that sling off your arm. And Lord knows fisticuffs are out of the question."

Devon rolled his eyes.

"Can I interest you in a bet?" Jordan flashed him a mischievous smile.

"No." Devon's voice was clipped.

"My God, man, you've been absolutely no fun whatsoever since you were shot." Jordan threw his hands in the air. "Just tell Lily you're indecently wealthy and put an end to this madness."

"I have no intention of doing that." Devon snapped open the paper in front of his face.

"Why the devil not?" Jordan ordered another drink from the hovering footman.

"Because," Devon replied, "she doesn't deserve it."

"You're going to give me a mental problem. I cannot keep up with the dialogue. Did I just hear you say she doesn't deserve it?"

Devon let the paper drop. "Precisely."

"And what, pray tell, is that supposed to mean?"

"She didn't give me a chance to explain. She ran off. Telling her I'm wealthy is the exact opposite of what I should do. If she didn't want me for myself, I'm not about to try to lure her with money."

"You cannot honestly believe that."

Devon folded the paper and eyed his friend. "Very well. You tell me. What exactly do you think telling her I'm wealthy would accomplish?"

Jordan rolled his eyes. "Nothing, you dolt. It's simply the truth and since when is that overrated?"

"Lily had to trust me on her own terms. She didn't. I refuse to try to change her mind about me."

Jordan stretched his arms above his head. "Ah, the tragedy of it all. The drama."

This time, Devon rolled his eyes. "There is nothing in the least dramatic about it. It's simply the way it is."

"But the two of you are supposedly married, Colton. Or have you conveniently forgotten that fact?"

"I haven't decided what I will do about that."

"Well, until you do, you're going to have to be in her company sometime. Like tonight at the Stanhopes' for instance."

"I'm not going to the Stanhopes'. I'm going to Colton House to see Justin."

"And then what do you plan to do?"

A shadow loomed beside them and Devon glanced up.

"Ah, the dissolute Lord Colton. I thought I'd find you here." Lord Medford pulled up a chair next to the other two men.

"I thought I smelled perfection and too much starch. Did I invite you to sit, Medford?" Devon sneered.

Medford shook out his sleeve. "No, but I fear I'd be standing all day, should I wait for that invitation."

"You're right." Devon gave him a thin smile. "Very well. Out with it. What do you want?"

"You get right to the point, don't you, Colton? I hate to say it, but I've always liked that about you. Very well. I won't waste your time. Lily is staying at one of my homes."

Devon's fist clenched over the arm of the chair. His knuckles cracked. "And?" he asked through clenched teeth.

Medford arched a brow. "I see you don't like that one bit."

"Get to your point, Medford," Jordan interjected.

Devon narrowed his eyes on the viscount. "I assume she's come running back to you after I turned her away. You're welcome to her, by the way. You two announcing your engagement will spare me the necessity of seeming to cry off."

Medford eyed him with distaste. "How do you intend to do that when the entire *ton* thinks you're already married?"

Devon shrugged. "Naïve of you, Medford. You know anything can be controlled when whispered to the right gossip with the right amount of confidence. I'll laugh it off. Pretend the entire thing was merely a jest."

Medford leaned back in his chair and crossed his legs at the ankles, a mimic of the other two men. "That makes what I've come to tell you even easier."

Devon shifted in his seat. "Really. And what's that?"

"I've come to tell you, Colton, what a fool you are."

Jordan made a move toward Medford, but Devon stopped his friend with a hand on his chest. "I can fight my own fights, Ashbourne. Besides, I'm intrigued. Why does the bastion of Society think I'm a idiot?"

Medford flicked a nonexistent bit of lint from his sleeve. "Not an idiot, a fool. There's quite a difference."

Jordan cleared his throat. "Feel free to tell us why you're here sometime before the Prince Regent is crowned king, Medford."

Medford smiled at them both before settling his gaze on Devon. "You're a fool, Colton, because you had the love of the most perfect woman in the world and you tossed it away. Lily's not with me. She never was. She didn't accept my suit. In fact, she's nursing a broken heart, thanks to you."

Devon narrowed his eyes on Medford, but he didn't say a word.

"She wants you," Medford continued with a sigh. "Though God knows I'll never understand why. She wants you and always has. Lily was ready to marry you even after you refused to stop gambling, even when she believed you were destitute." He laughed a humorless laugh. "I'm richer than the bloody pope, far richer than you could ever be. If Lily were after money, she'd marry me, but she's flatly refused. In fact, she intends to return to her cousin's house and live in poverty. You're a fool, Colton, because you pushed her away."

Devon's chest tightened. Every word Medford said was true. He knew it. He just hadn't realized how much knowing it would hurt. And he wanted to kill Lord Medford for saying it.

Medford stood up, straightened his cravat, and nodded to them. He gave them a tight smile. "Not to worry, Colton. I shall remain at her side until she's over you."

Devon lunged at Medford then, but Jordan got there first, blocking him.

He watched Medford walk away with narrowed eyes and a tic pounding furiously in his jaw.

# CHAPTER 39

Devon wiped Justin's hair from his eyes and pulled up the blanket over the sleeping boy. Devon glanced around the room. A model of a ship rested on a bookshelf in the corner, schoolbooks lay piled on a desk near the window, and a journal full of numbers lay open, a long string of numbers. Justin had obviously been practicing his arithmetic.

Devon still wore a sling on his right arm. With his left, he took a swig from the bottle he was carrying, and made his way over to the desk. Setting the bottle down momentarily, he ran his finger along the row of numbers. Correct. All correct. Justin took after his father, not his grandfather. Thank God.

Devon stretched. Grabbing the bottle again, he crossed the room to look down at Justin.

"My lord?" The whisper broke the silence. Devon turned to see Mrs. Appleby standing in the doorway.

Justin rolled over in his sleep and Devon raised his finger to silence the housekeeper. She nodded and he made his way toward the door, the bottle still dangling from his fingertips. Once they were both in the hallway, Mrs. Appleby shut the door behind them.

"I must say I'm surprised to see you here, milord," she

said. "I thought you wouldn't be back again until Master Justin's birthday. Did you bring your new bride with you?" Her smile was wide.

Devon took another swig from the bottle. "Yes, well, plans have the most unexpected way of changing at times. And no, Lily's not here."

Mrs. Appleby's face fell and she gave him a wary look. She crossed her arms over her chest. "How long have you been drinking, my lord?"

Devon's crack of laughter followed. "Not long enough." Another swig and Devon made his way unerringly down the hallway and then down the grand staircase. Mrs. Appleby dogged him.

"Where are you going, my lord?"

"If you must know, I'm headed straight for the library and the next liquor bottle that awaits me there."

His strides were long, but Mrs. Appleby managed to keep pace. She panted along next to him.

"If you don't mind my saying, my lord, you seem tired. Your eyes are bloodshot and you look as if you haven't slept in days."

Devon groaned. "Feels like weeks, actually, and yes, I do mind your saying." He pushed open the door to the library with his good shoulder, and marched inside. Several candles were already lit. They blinked in the breeze caused by the door sweeping open. Devon made his way directly to the sideboard.

Mrs. Appleby had blushed at his reprimand, but she crossed the carpet toward him with a determined look in her normally soft blue eyes and put her hand over his on top of the stopper on the decanter of brandy.

"It cannot be good for your recovery to be drinking like this," she said.

"Right again. The doctors assure me it is not."

She patted his hand. "Master Devon," she whispered softly, real caring in her voice. "What is it? What's wrong?"

Devon's shoulders slumped and he let his hand fall away from the decanter. "You haven't called me Master Devon since I was in short pants, Mrs. Appleby."

She nodded. "I haven't had to."

He turned his head toward her. "Why must you be so astute?"

The older woman patted his hand again. "It's one of my many duties, my lord, and you know I pride myself on my work. Now, come, sit down, and tell me what is wrong."

Mrs. Appleby crossed over the rug again and placed herself on the chair in the middle of the room. She patted the seat of the cushioned chair next to her and waited for Devon to join her.

Devon expelled his breath and followed his old friend across the room.

"There, now," Mrs. Appleby said when he was settled. "What is it?"

A muscle ticked in his jaw. "It's nothing."

"I see. If I don't miss my guess, that nothing is named Lily, is she not?"

His eyes widened momentarily and then he smiled. "Astute, I tell you."

Mrs. Appleby clasped her hands in front of her. "It's no mystery when I heard you had married, and you show up here, half in the bottle and with your new bride nowhere to be seen."

Devon sighed. "Mrs. Appleby, the truth is . . . I'm not married."

The housekeeper's brow furrowed slightly. "I see. But it seems to me this Lily must be someone very special if you're allowing the rumor of your marriage to continue."

Devon slumped back in the chair and closed his eyes.

"It's more complicated than that. I asked her to marry me, then I sent her away."

"Away? Where?" She blinked.

Devon growled. "She's staying with that fool Medford."

Mrs. Appleby nodded sagely. "Ah, so there's another gentleman involved?"

"I suppose Medford is a gentleman, but it's more complicated than that still. I never told her about Justin or my promise to my father. She was the one I had planned to marry five years ago before all of this . . . Ah, I don't know why I even care."

The housekeeper shook her head. "I do see, my lord. I truly do. And it's high time I told you the truth about some things."

She hefted herself up from her seat, crossed over to the sideboard, and poured two glasses of brandy. Devon watched her with a half-smile on his face. She returned, handed him his glass, and proceeded to down half the amber liquid in her own, before settling back into her seat.

Devon eyed her warily. "Now you're beginning to worry me, Appleby."

She smiled a humorless smile and rested the glass on her belly over her apron. She stared off into the shadowy corner of the room. "I need a drink if I am to tell you this tale. I promised your father I would keep it to myself, but the time has come."

Devon took a hefty swallow of his own drink. "By all means, proceed."

Mrs. Appleby took a deep breath. "You see, I remember that night nearly five years ago now when you came racing back from London at your father's request."

Devon nodded. "Yes, he'd written to me to tell me Justin was here."

"And you came, just like you always did. You were

always such a loyal boy." She smiled at him, before continuing. "'Appleby,' your father said, 'don't you dare breathe a word of what you know to Devon when he gets here.' And Lord knows I've fretted over it these years since."

"What?" Devon sat forward in his chair and eyed her intently. "What did you know?"

"Oh, Master Devon. The truth is, your mistress, Celine, came to your father months before Justin was born. You were out of the country at the time. She told your father she was carrying your child and she needed money."

Devon sucked his breath between his teeth. "Go on."

"Your father turned her away. He said he had no intention of paying for your bastard. Too bad for Celine, she didn't even realize your father had no money. And of course he didn't tell her the truth."

Devon set the drink down on the table next to him. Hard. "If that was the case, how did Justin come to be here and why did my father summon me?"

Mrs. Appleby closed her eyes. A tear leaked from the corner of one of them. "That was the worst part, my lord. Your father wanted nothing to do with Justin. He told Celine she and the baby could live on the streets . . . until the Earl of Merrill paid him a visit."

Devon's head snapped up. "Merrill? Lily's husband?"

Mrs. Appleby nodded. "He wasn't your Lily's husband quite yet. In fact, that's why he came. You see, he was courting Lily at the time. It seems he knew he had competition in you and he didn't like it. Not one bit. He told your father to call you home. To draw you away from London so that you and Lily would be apart."

Devon shook his head. "That makes no sense. Why would Merrill ask my father such a thing? And why would my father agree to it?"

"You don't understand," Mrs. Appleby continued. "Your

father owed the Earl of Merrill money, a great deal of it from what I understand. So your father repaid him with a favor. Merrill wanted you away from Lily and, in return, he forgave your father's debt."

Devon slammed his fist against the tabletop. "Now *that* sounds like my father. But what did Justin have to do with it?"

"Your father spent days trying to think of what would lure you from Lily's side and could think of nothing. Finally, he realized your child was the perfect thing. He would find the baby and make you come home."

"Why did Celine give up Justin?"

Mrs. Appleby closed her eyes. "She didn't. Your father hired a man in London to find them. By the time he learned what had happened to Celine, she had died in childbirth the day before. The other women in the poorhouse where she'd been staying were caring for the baby."

Devon dropped his head into his hands. His voice was a harsh whisper. "My father knew I had a child in this world, but he had no intention of telling me until it suited his purposes. He allowed Celine to die alone. He would have allowed Justin to be raised in the gutter." Devon looked up at Mrs. Appleby. "Unimaginable."

Tears streamed down the housekeeper's wrinkled face. "I know, my lord, I know."

Devon clenched his jaw. "He made me promise. He made me promise him on his deathbed . . . He pretended to care about his grandson. It was all an act."

"Oh, Master Devon, your father always knew you were more full of honor than he ever was. He knew you wouldn't turn the lad out on the streets. He knew you would refuse nothing for your son. It was clear you didn't care about money for yourself, but he'd always wanted you to use your skill with numbers to restore his coffers. And he finally found the perfect plan. He used you, Master Devon."

Devon expelled his breath harshly. "That's why I haven't been able to locate Celine all these years."

Mrs. Appleby nodded. "That was my fault, my lord. I deceived you there too. All the letters you wrote her . . . to try to find her, ensure she was all right. I never sent them. I knew there was no place for them to go. I'm sorry, my lord. I wouldn't blame you if you turn me out without a reference for what I've done. I know it's no excuse, but that's why I didn't tell you for so long. I was worried for my position. I know it was wrong of me." She hung her head. "Very wrong."

Devon stood and paced the room. It turned his stomach to think of how close Justin had come to a life on the streets. Justin, who was as blameless as Devon in his father's game.

Devon turned to face the housekeeper. "You shouldn't have kept such secrets, Mrs. Appleby, but I can understand why you did. My father was not one to cross."

Mrs. Appleby wrung the handkerchief in her hands. "I should have told you after he died, my lord. I just couldn't see what purpose it would serve and I was scared . . . for myself." She pushed the handkerchief to her eyes. "I'll pack my things and leave immediately."

Devon moved over to her and placed a hand on her shaking shoulder. "I could no more turn you out on the streets than I could my own mother."

The housekeeper sobbed harder for a moment. "Thank you, my lord. You are too kind."

Devon let his hand fall back to his side. "Now, who else knows about this, Mrs. Appleby?"

She rapidly shook her head. "No one. No one. I'm sure of it. I was there that day when the baby arrived and never spoke of it with the other servants. Your father wouldn't allow the gossip. Of course, everyone had an opinion, but no one knew for sure."

"See to it that you continue to keep that secret," Devon commanded. "Justin will have a difficult enough life without the details of his birth being known."

"Yes, my lord, of course. Whatever you like." She shook her head. "I'm so, so sorry."

"You've nothing to apologize for, Mrs. Appleby. My father was the sorry one."

"Yes, my lord." She nodded solemnly. "Should I prepare your room, Master Devon? Will you be staying the night?"

Devon pushed his half-empty glass away. He pressed his palm to his forehead, the coolness of the Colton signet ring slid against his temple. He slipped the ring from his finger and stared at it until his eyes were unseeing.

The bloody ring. Jordan had asked him once why he didn't buy another to replace it. If only it had been that simple. No, this ring had been earned with every bit of the man Devon had become over the last five years.

He clenched it in his fist, squeezed it until his palm ached. What had he given up in return for this ring and for the promises he'd made to a man who had no honor?

Lily.

She was exactly who he'd thought she was five years ago. True. Original. She'd had to fight for herself all these years and nothing had been easy. She'd lived through hell. And managed it like only she could, with a strength born of necessity.

He'd loved her five years ago because she'd ignored all the rumors. She'd seen him and only him. He didn't care anymore about the damn letter she'd written. She would have married him if he'd come for her that morning. He knew that. He'd read the truth in her eyes that night on the balcony at the house party.

Yes, Lily had always seen him. And now he saw her. Exactly as she was. Loving, strong, and willful.

Devon closed his eyes and turned his head toward the ceiling. Ironic that he should think himself so very good at games of chance. He'd always been so damned skilled at cards. Cards were like people, predictable, easy to guess. But not Lily. She was completely unpredictable. And he couldn't live without her.

Devon opened his eyes and glared at the ring again. Medford was right. He was a fool. It had taken him five years, but he'd won back the wrong prize.

He turned to face his housekeeper. "No, Mrs. Appleby, I won't be staying tonight. I'm returning to London. I must get to the Stanhopes' ball."

# CHAPTER 40

"You've done nothing but mope around this house for the past fortnight." Anne pointed an accusing finger at Lily.

"I have not been moping." Lily petted Leo, who lay curled in a ball on the bed next to her.

"Yes you have." Mary's voice floated out of the adjoining dressing room.

The maid poked her head out of the door and Lily stuck out her tongue at her. Bandit, who had taken an especial liking to Mary, stuck her head out too.

"Very well. What, exactly, do the two of you think I should do about it?" Lily asked.

Anne laughed and clapped her hands. "Oh, I'm so glad you asked. We've been thinking about it, you see, Mary and I, and we have an idea."

Lily glanced warily between the two. "I don't like the sound of that one bit."

"No, of course you don't, but leave everything to us."

Lily picked up Leo and cuddled him like a baby. The dog licked her on the nose. "What do you plan to do?"

Anne glanced at Mary and back to Lily again and giggled. "Well . . . we think you should seduce Lord Colton."

Lily's mouth dropped open. She set Leo back on the bed. "Seduce Lor . . ."

Anne nodded, her dark curls bobbing. "Yes, Lord Colton promised to seduce you once, didn't he? Now it's your turn."

Lily crossed her arms over her chest and eyed her sister warily. "Something tells me you've learned what the word 'seduce' means." She raised her voice. "Mary? Did you tell her?"

An innocent whistling sound floated from the dressing room. "Um . . . I don't seem to recall."

Anne lightly shrugged. "Do you like the idea or not? The Stanhopes' ball is tonight and Lord Colton is sure to be in attendance. It seems you have two choices. You can sit here and mope, or you can get yourself together and get your husband back."

"He's not my husband."

Anne crossed her arms over her chest. "Not yet."

Lily contemplated the matter for a moment. She hopped off the bed and marched over to thc looking glass. She eyed her reflection. She pulled a handkerchief from her bodice, wiped at her tired eyes and blew her nose in a most indelicate manner. Then she straightened her shoulders.

Anne was right. This was it.

It wasn't a game. She loved Devon, blast it, loved him and wanted to marry him. And while her first marriage might have been a sham, her second would be a success no matter what she had to do to make it so.

She pinched color back into her cheeks and smiled, already feeling better. She wasn't one to give up. She wasn't one to lose. It didn't matter what had happened five years ago. What mattered was what she'd found in Devon's arms recently. Devon had told her he wasn't a gambler. She believed him. He loved her. She knew he did, as surely as she knew she loved him. And she would prove it. To both of them.

Lily stood up straight and pushed a wayward curl behind her ear. She was beautiful, wasn't she? Or so people told her. And Devon wanted her. Or at least he had. Yes, there was one way to get him back that couldn't fail. Devon might have been the one to seduce her the first time and he'd plied his skill like a master. Well, this time she would be the one plying her skill.

She would get him back.

Lily would go to the Stanhopes' ball and seduce Devon Morgan.

She spun around quickly, her skirts pooling at her ankles. "Quickly, Mary, help me dress. I'm wearing the lavender ball gown. Devon loves that gown."

"But me lady, that one is cut so low, I need to remake it for you."

"Precisely," Lily replied with a gleam in her eye, "why I want to wear it."

Mary blushed but nodded and turned back to the dressing room to retrieve the scandalous garment.

Anne gave her an impish grin. "Does this mean you've agreed?"

Lily floated over to her dressing table and pulled out a pot of rouge, a pot she'd never used before. "Yes. I intend to have a great deal of fun tonight. I *intend* to seduce my future husband."

# CHAPTER 41

"I swear I don't know why I allow you to involve me in these sordid things," Lord Medford whispered in Lily's ear hours later as he escorted her into the gleaming ballroom at the Stanhopes' town house.

"Because," Lily replied, "we are friends."

He smiled down at her and sighed. "Don't pretend for one moment that you didn't ask me to escort you tonight because you want to make Colton jealous."

Lily snapped her mouth closed, her smile immediately fading. But then it spread slowly, completely, across her face. "Maddeningly so. I want him to be so jealous, he cannot see straight."

Medford laughed. "Happy to help. Few things give me more pleasure than making Colton angry." He tucked her hand under his arm and led her farther into the room.

Lily glanced about. All eyes were upon them. She swallowed. Hard.

"Not to worry," Medford whispered. "If Colton doesn't have a conniption at the sight of you in that dress"—he allowed his eyes to dip appreciatively to her generous décolletage—"I'll make sure I finish him off with my complete adoration of you."

Lily gave him a sidewise glance and smiled sweetly. "Precisely what I had in mind."

"Ah, and here's the bloke now." Medford nodded toward a dark figure ahead of them.

Lily's head snapped up to look. Yes, there he was. She pressed her gloved hand against her belly. She hadn't expected to be quite this anxious. Her gaze followed him.

Devon moved across the ballroom. Despite the sling he wore over one arm, he looked devastatingly handsome in his perfectly tailored black evening attire. He stopped by a column only a few paces away and rested his good shoulder against it. Lily watched him. Her stomach twisted in knots as beautiful ladies approached him like lovely moths attracted to a gorgeous flame.

He was engaged in flirtatious discussion with a buxom, red-haired lady who laughed at everything he said and touched his arm entirely too often. When the redhead turned, Lily recognized her.

Lady Weston.

Medford cleared his throat in what seemed suspiciously like an attempt to cover up his laughter. "Ahem, seems Colton had the jealousy idea first."

Lily gritted her teeth. "Dance with me, Medford," she said, not taking her eyes from Devon and Emma, Lady Weston. "Dance with me until my head spins off."

She pushed her chin in the air and threw herself into Lord Medford's arms. They danced. And the entire time, Lily ensured her brightest, most radiant smile was plastered on her face. And she carefully ensured that she never, ever glanced Devon's way.

Devon leaned against a pillar, surveying the crowd. He'd been searching for a way to get Lily alone all evening, but that nuisance, Medford, never left her side.

And it was driving him insane.

Devon's gaze flicked across the ballroom. Lily stood in a group of people in the corner, smiling and laughing. If she touched Medford's sleeve one more time, Devon would just have to snap the viscount's neck.

Devon growled under his breath. He shoved his one good hand into his pocket and narrowed his eyes on her. She was wearing that lavender gown, the one with the décolletage he couldn't ignore. That was it. He'd tried it the polite way long enough, now was the time for action.

He stalked over to the group, his resolve strengthening with each pace. He grabbed Lily around the waist with his good arm, hoisted her up, and easily tossed her over his uninjured shoulder.

Lily gasped. "Devon! What are you doing?"

He didn't reply. He merely turned on his heel.

Medford stepped in front of them. Devon narrowed his eyes on the viscount. "I've been fantasizing about ripping you limb from limb all bloody evening, Medford. Don't give me an excuse."

Ignoring the looks of shock on the faces of the other guests, Devon pushed past the other man, Lily pummeling his back, and stalked out of the ballroom. He didn't stop until he'd kicked open the wooden doors to the Stanhopes' library. He took two strides into the room and tossed Lily unceremoniously on the settee before quickly turning back toward the doors and locking them.

When Devon faced her again, Lily's eyes were shooting violet sparks at him. She scrambled up from the settee. Her breath came in violent puffs, her lovely breasts rose and fell in her daring décolletage with each inhalation. Her entire body shook.

Moving carefully behind a group of delicate antique chairs, she put distance between the two of them. She glared at him. "Just what do you think you're doing?"

The doorknob rattled. "Lily, Lily? Are you all right?"

Medford's voice was full of concern. He pounded against the wood. The doors shook.

A muscle ticked in Devon's jaw. "Tell him to go away. Tell him, or by God, I'll kill him. I swear it."

Lily's chest still heaved. God only knew what had got into Devon. She knew he wouldn't hurt her or Lord Medford either, but there was no sense antagonizing him when he was being like this. "I'm fine, James," she called, doing her best to make her voice sound confident.

Devon's nostrils flared. He crossed his arms over his chest. "James?"

"Are you sure, Lily?" Medford's voice penetrated the heavy doors. "Just say the word and I'll break down the doors. I'll—"

Lily raised her voice, hoping she could continue to sound calm. "No, James, really. I am fine. Please, just give us a few minutes."

Silence for a few moments and then, "As you wish." The fading sound of Medford's boots clipping against the marble floors signaled his retreat.

Lily nodded toward the doors. "Have you any idea what sort of scandal you've caused?"

Devon's eyes never left hers. "It'll blow over eventually. Besides, they think we're married. As far as they know we're having a *domestic* dispute."

Lily pressed a hand to her chest, willing her heartbeat to slow to normal. "Fine then, Lord Colton, what is it you wanted to *talk* about?"

"I don't want to talk." He stalked across the room toward her, shoving the chairs out of his path.

Lily sucked in her breath, backing away from him. "That's surprising. You seem to have been doing a lot of it with Lady Weston tonight." Her voice shook.

Her back hit the far wall, stopping her, and Devon

advanced. He stood in front of her, looming over her, pinioning her into the corner, his good arm braced against the wall on the side of her face. His brandy-laced breath was hot on her neck. "You cannot believe I've been lusting after Lady Weston when I've had you in my peripheral vision all night like a goddess come down from the heavens."

His mouth swooped down to capture her lips and Lily ceased to think. His mouth claimed hers, ravaged hers. His lips forced hers apart and his tongue entered her with force and longing. Lily clung to his neck and kissed him back.

When Devon finally lifted his head, Lily was still breathing heavily. "Are you purposely trying to drive me mad?" she asked. "One minute you hate me, the next you kiss me."

His crack of laughter bounced off the wooden bookshelves that lined the walls. "Hate you? Hardly. Damn it, Lily, I've spent the last fortnight trying to, but I can't."

"Isn't *that* romantic?" She turned her head away and took a step to move past him, fluttering her hand in the air.

Devon grabbed her wrist. "Don't."

Lily stopped, her heart pounding furiously in her chest. "What?"

"When you wave your hand in the air like that, you're trying to be flippant. But I know it means you care more than you can say."

She swallowed. They were so close she could make out the dark irises of his eyes. "Why haven't you told anyone we're not married?"

"Because I want it to be true."

Lily snapped her head to the side. Tears sprang to her eyes. Tears. Real tears. They slid, unbidden, unwanted, down her cheeks. She clenched her fists at her sides and willed them away. "Devon, don't—"

His voice was calm. "Why do you hate *me*?"

She wiped away the tears with her fingertips. She turned to him then, and the vulnerability in his eyes nearly sent her to her knees. "I don't." She shook her head. "I never did. I was so sure you would hurt me again."

Devon pulled a handkerchief from his coat pocket and pressed it gently into her hand. "I never meant to hurt you the first time. But you chose to marry Lord Merrill."

Lily pressed the white cloth to her cheeks. Her voice shook. "I only agreed to marry the earl after I received your letter that morning, telling me you had changed your mind and must marry a girl with a larger dowry."

Devon clenched his jaw. He searched her face. "I never wrote a letter. I received one from you."

"I never wrote a letter," Lily breathed. "I—" Lily doubled over, understanding finally dawning. She squeezed the handkerchief. "Oh, God. It was my mother. I know it. I always wondered how she came to me so swiftly that morning. It was as if she knew I was waiting. She was so quick to tell me I'd been wrong about you, to comfort me, to suggest I marry Lord Merrill."

Devon clenched his fist so tightly his knuckles cracked. "And my father wouldn't have been above such a thing as forging a note from me either. I left you that night because my father drew me away."

Lily put her hand to her throat. "I feel ill," she whispered.

Devon rested a hand on her shoulder. "We've blamed each other all these years, when our parents were at fault."

Lily stepped away from him, her arms tightly crossed over her chest. "But that wasn't the only thing separating us." She breathed in deeply and turned back to face him. "Devon, why did you gamble again if you detested it? Why couldn't you stop when I asked you to?"

He scrubbed his hands through his hair. "You have to understand, Lily. I made a promise to a dying man—my dying father, no less—that I would reclaim the signet ring."

Lily reached out and touched Devon's hand. "Why hadn't I ever heard of Justin before?"

Devon expelled his breath. "The story we circulated in town was that Justin was my half brother. My father's second wife had died roughly around the same time Justin was born. It had been during the winter and we simply told everyone she'd died in childbirth. Most of the servants didn't even know any better. Only Mrs. Appleby, my father's housekeeper, and a few others knew the truth."

Lily sucked in her breath. "I'm sorry, Devon. Truly sorry. For everything."

Devon pulled her into his embrace. Lily rested her head against his chest. His lips grazed the top of her head. Tears slipped down her cheeks and Devon tipped up her chin with his finger and thumb to look into her eyes.

"Why are you crying, my love?"

"I want you to know why it was so difficult for me to trust you. I was so scared for you. My father was always gambling and I never felt safe. It wasn't about money. It was never about money. It was about security. I never cared that you were penniless."

"I understand," Devon replied. "But why the tears still, darling?" He kissed them away one by one.

"Because you said we can never go back. Too much has happened."

He kissed her forehead. "It's true. We can never go back."

Lily's heart stopped. She knew it. It was still too late.

Devon pulled her down next to him into the nearby window seat. Her brows furrowed. He tilted her face up to look at him.

"We can never go back, Lily," he repeated, "but we can go forward, together, and build something better, something stronger than the past. I've lost you, twice. Once because of our parents' schemes and again due to my own pride and foolishness. I cannot lose you again. I won't lose you again."

He kissed her lips. So softly, so sweetly. Lily wanted to cry harder. She'd been so sure she'd never feel his touch again.

Devon tugged her back against him and cradled her in his arms. "There's something else I must tell you, Lily." There was a smile in his voice. "I know you've had your heart set on being married to a poor bloke who has no means of income other than his spotty gambling winnings, but the truth is . . . I'm quite wealthy."

She grinned against his chest. "Medford told me," she admitted. "But you should have."

Devon raised his brows. "When did Medford tell you?"

"A few days ago. He also told me you'd paid off all my creditors." She glanced at her hands. "When did you discover I was poor?"

"When I saw Mr. Hogsmeade leaving your house that day I came with Bandit. I recognized him from the many visits he'd paid to my father over the years. After that, I looked into it and discovered how many creditors you had."

Lily sighed. "It's been a struggle for a very long time. But I still don't understand. Why do you want everyone to think you're destitute?"

He shrugged. "You quickly learn who your true friends are in such a situation."

Lily nodded. "Including me?"

"Oh, God, Lily. The reason I became rich, the reason I worked so damned hard at it, was for you. I believed you'd refused my suit because of my lack of money and it drove me mad. Yes, I did it for Justin and my father, but I also did it for you. I won the Colton signet ring back. But what I almost gave up for that damned ring. The blasted promise I made to my unworthy father was more important to me than what we could have had. I pushed you away to protect myself. I realize that now. I expected the worst of you. Instead, I showed you the worst of myself." He hung his head. "I'm sorry, Lily."

Tears flowed down Lily's cheeks. She smiled through them. "I love you, Devon. I always have."

Devon wrapped his good arm around her. "I love you, too, Lily. I've loved you since we danced in the gardens at your debut ball. I'm sorry for the last five years, how difficult your life has been."

"It's not your fault, Devon." She squeezed his hand.

"No, but I'm partially to blame." He fell to his knees on the floor next to the window seat. He clasped her hand. "Lily, I love you, and I'll never let you forget it. I'm asking for the third time, the last time. Will you marry me?"

She smiled through her tears. "Yes, Lord Colton. For the third time, the last time, I will marry you."

# EPILOGUE

"We could not have chosen a more perfect day for a wedding." Devon winked at his new wife as they strode arm in arm around the grounds of Colton House. They'd spent the whole day celebrating with their friends and family and had just finished a late dinner on the lawn. The smell of summer jasmine floated through the summer air. Stars twinkled in the sky above.

"Without a doubt." Lily smiled and squeezed Devon's arm. Justin ran across their path, a puppy nipping at his heels. He waved happily at them.

Lily laughed and waved back. "Justin is such a wonderful boy and he loves the new puppy you gave him for a birthday present."

Devon tucked her hand closer into his arm and escorted her toward a walking path. "No doubt you'll have the whole ragtag group of dogs out here before long."

Jordan Holloway caught up to them, a crooked smile on his face as he gave them a jaunty salute. "Congratulations, Lord and Lady Colton." He shook his head. "I must say you two took your time getting together, even after all of my machinations."

"Machinations?" Lily furrowed her brows.

Devon crossed his arms over his chest. "What are you talking about, Ashbourne? Do you mean to imply you attempted to matchmake?"

"Attempted?" Jordan slapped gloves against his thigh. "I did everything short of abducting Lily and tossing her into your bed."

Devon shook his head. "I seem to recall you gave me a speech about how Lily had tossed me over and it was time to take my revenge."

Jordan flashed them both a grin. "Perfect. Wasn't it? Starting the rumors and the bet at the club was only the first part of my plan. So dedicated, I was even willing to take a beating for it."

Devon put his hands on his hips. "Now I know you've gone mad. You've been staunchly against marriage for years."

"A fact I cannot deny," Jordan answered. "But you were so determined to get yourself leg-shackled, I couldn't very well allow you to do so with the wrong lady. Could I?"

Lily laughed. "What was the second half of your ploy then, Jordan?"

"Why, getting this bloke to realize he couldn't live without you, my dear. And it worked, perfectly if I do say so myself."

Devon rolled his eyes. "Don't let us keep you, Ashbourne. I hear Lord Hawkins is working up the nerve to propose soon. Perhaps you should save him from that dreadful institution."

Jordan's grin widened. "Perhaps I should." He tipped his hat to them and headed off across the lawn.

Lily snuggled against Devon and he wrapped an arm around her. "Devon, look, Anne appears to be having a wonderful time, doesn't she?" Lily pointed across the lawn to where her sister was dancing along with a merry group of partygoers. She sighed. "Oh, I do hope Anne finds the kind of love we have. Mr. Eggleston's not remotely right for her, of course, but I'm waiting for Anne to realize that in her own time."

Devon squeezed her shoulders. "She's a strong young woman, much like her sister. I'm sure she'll make the right decision." He stopped and turned Lily to face him. "Now, Lady Colton, I have a question to ask you."

Her eyes widened at his sudden seriousness. "Yes, Lord Colton?"

He arched a brow. "Admit it. You sent that copy of *Secrets of a Wedding Night* straight to Miss Templeton, didn't you?"

Lily worried her bottom lip with her teeth. "Well, the truth is . . . I, ah . . . had a copy personally delivered to Miss Templeton."

Instead of the anger she'd expected, Devon shouted with laughter, his eyes sparkling with amusement.

"As I suspected," he replied. "But, why did you do it?"

Lily ducked her head against his chest. "I read your engagement announcement in the *Times*. I couldn't let you get married. Not when I loved you so desperately . . . and especially not to a ninny like Amelia Templeton. Good heavens. She would have bored you silly."

Devon gave her a tender kiss. "Thank you for sending her a copy."

Lily cleared her throat. "I didn't just send it to her, Devon. I wrote it for her."

Devon's eyes widened. "Are you jesting?"

"Not at all," Lily admitted with a catlike smile on her face.

Devon laughed and pressed his lips into her hair. "Ah, my darling, don't ever change." He drew back. "Since you made a confession, I suppose I've one to make as well."

Lily glanced up at him. "Yes?"

"I was the one who started the rumors about us eloping to Gretna Green."

Her jaw dropped. "Devon Marcus Sandridge Colton. How dare you?" But her smile belied the tone of her words.

"What? Aren't you happy with the outcome?"

She shoved one hand against his broad shoulder. "Of course, but I cannot believe you would have the audacity—"

He quirked his lips. "Can't you?"

She shook her head. "You're right. I should have assumed it was you from the start."

"You cannot blame me, can you, love?"

Lily snuggled back into his arms. "No, I'm glad you did."

Devon reached into his inside coat pocket and pulled out something. "And now for the true reason I took you for a walk this evening. This is for you, my love." He held it out to her.

Lily gingerly took the leather-bound case from Devon's hand. "What is it?"

He grinned at her. "Open it."

She cracked the lid and squealed. Lying on a bed of dark blue velvet was a little diamond brooch in the shape of a—she blinked—raccoon.

"It's Bandit," Lily said, tears filling her eyes.

"Seems I'm just as big a fool in love as my grandfather was."

Lily reached up and wrapped her arms around his neck. "I love you so." Kissing his cheek, she sighed. "I've found such happiness with you, Devon. I suppose I've done a grave injustice to the young women of the *ton* by writing *Secrets of a Wedding Night*. But don't worry. I shall do the right thing." She nodded. "I shall write a retraction posthaste."

Devon kissed her fiercely. “That reminds me. As it is officially our wedding night, there are some more *secrets* I want to show you.”

He kissed her neck and Lily closed her eyes, shuddering. “Mmm. That, my love, is an entirely different pamphlet.”

Read on for an excerpt from
Valerie Bowman's next book

# Secrets of a Runaway Bride

Coming soon from St. Martin's Paperbacks

***London, Late September, 1816***

Annie Andrews was halfway up the side of her neighbor Arthur Eggleston's town house—scaling an oh-so-convenient and strong ivy vine—when the telltale clip-clop of horse's hooves stopped her. She squeezed her eyes shut. Oh, this was *not* good.

Despite the fact that she was in the alley at the back of the house and it was dark as pitch, she'd just been discovered. She knew it.

*Please let it be a servant.*

But even as she wished it, she knew it wasn't true. A servant in the alley on horseback? No.

And the odds of it being Aunt Clarissa were decidedly low as well. Annie had ensured that that lady had been well into her cups and asleep before she'd even attempted tonight's little escapade. Besides, Aunt Clarissa was horribly frightened of horses.

Annie bit her lip. Then she slowly turned her head.

She gulped.

It was worse than a servant. Much worse.

"Lost?" The arrogant male voice pierced the cool night air.

Jordan Holloway, the Earl of Ashbourne, swung his leg over his saddle and dismounted.

Oh, drat. There was absolutely no plausible way to explain this. Annie lifted her chin in an attempt to retain her dignity. As much as one could when one was clinging precariously to a vine.

The moon peeked from behind the clouds, casting a bit of its glow upon the scene as Lord Ashbourne strode up the steps and stood regarding her, his arms crossed over his chest. He leaned back against the stone balustrade, crossed his booted feet negligently at the ankles, and watched her with a mocking look on his oh-so-handsome—too handsome if you asked her—face. The man was easily two inches over six feet tall, possessed wide shoulders, narrow hips, a straight nose, dark slashes for brows, dark, ruffled hair, and the most unusual knowing gray eyes.

"If it isn't the runaway bride." He grinned. "What are you up to this time, Miss Andrews?"

Annie gritted her teeth. She hated it when Lord Ashbourne called her by that ridiculous name. The Runaway Bride. Hrmph. As the closest friend of her new brother-in-law, Lord Ashbourne had just so happened to have been involved in coming after her after an unfortunate incident in which she'd run away to Gretna Green with Arthur last spring. But that had been months ago and things were different now. Ahem, present circumstances notwithstanding. And it was so like Lord Ashbourne to mock her while she wasn't in a position to kick him or at the very least give him a condemning glare. It was exceedingly difficult to conjure condemnation while perched on a plant.

Her palms sweaty, Annie tightened her hold on the vine and summoned what indignation she could muster. "I don't see how it's any of your business." But even as she said the words, she knew how ludicrous they were.

"No, no. Really. *This* I must hear. Before I assist you in removing yourself from this ridiculous . . . situation," he drawled. "I insist you tell me why, exactly, you're doing this."

Annie blew an errant leaf away from her mouth. "I don't require your help, Lord Ashbourne. I'm quite capable—" She glanced down. It was at least a five-foot drop to the porch below. She'd just have to jump. She tugged away from the vine, but discovered, to her dismay, that the hem of her gown was seriously snagged upon the brambles.

Lord Ashbourne shook his head. "Seriously, Miss Andrews, why?"

She expelled her breath, still trying to retain a modicum of dignity. Oh, very well. Some explanation was obviously in order. "It's not as bad as it looks. I merely wanted to get Arthur's attention. I planned to toss a rock at his window and—"

"A note sent round to his door would not suffice?" Lord Ashbourne's mocking tone did not waver.

Annie clenched her jaw. Why, oh, why was she always at her very worst when Lord Ashbourne appeared? It was quite a phenomenon, actually.

"And Aunt Clarissa?" Lord Ashbourne continued. "She's asleep, is she not? After imbibing a good bit of port?"

Annie bit her lip. "Sherry." As companions went, Aunt Clarissa was a great deal of fun, but an apt chaperone, she was not. The woman was overly fond of spirits, in a variety of forms.

"As I suspected. Very well, there's no help for it." Lord Ashbourne uncrossed his ankles and took a step toward her, lifting his arms to pluck her from the vine like a foolish little grape.

Just then, the back door opened. A ray of candlelight splashed across the porch. Annie's eyes flashed wide. Pure terror pounded in her chest.

She held her breath. Who had discovered her? Please don't let it be—

Lord Ashbourne didn't wait. He quickly grabbed her by the waist and pulled her down. She gave a small yelp before tumbling into his arms and sliding down the front of him, her body pressed to his.

And that's how Annie came to be completely tangled in Lord Ashbourne's arms when Arthur Eggleston, the man Annie loved, the man Annie intended to marry, strode onto his back stoop.

Jordan's first instinct was to set Miss Andrews's delicate form on the porch and break their contact.

She was a nineteen-year-old troublemaker with a penchant for putting her reputation at risk. The little baggage had proven nothing but trouble since her sister, Lily, and his closest friend, Devon, had left for the Continent on their honeymoon trip. They'd both begged Jordan to keep an eye on the chit. Miss Andrews, it seemed, required more than one chaperone, especially since their closest female relative and only suitable companion, Devon's eccentric aunt Clarissa, was overly fond of the bottle.

Jordan had spent the past sennight following Miss Andrews around and ensuring she was not making a fool of herself in her dogged pursuit of that sop, Arthur Eggleston. But it seemed the closer Jordan watched her, the more outrageous her antics became, culminating in this particularly egregious bit of madness here this evening.

She was about five foot four, with a mass of wide brown curls, an impertinent nose, warm dark eyes, and a penchant for trouble. Spitfire was the word that readily came to mind. And while Jordan was mentally counting the days until Lily and Devon returned to properly see to the girl themselves, he had to admit to a sort of reluctant admiration for Annie. Things were never dull when Miss Andrews was involved. That much he would allow.

At the moment, her lithe body pressed against his was making him feel things he shouldn't, however. He needed to disentangle her from his arms. Immediately.

Eggleston cleared his throat and sanity returned to Jordan's mind with a vengeance. He quickly plucked Miss Andrews's arms from around his neck and let her slide down the length of him until she was standing on the porch next to him, a chagrined look on her pretty face.

Arms crossed over his chest, Eggleston glanced between them, a mildly outraged expression on his face. "Miss Andrews, Lord Ashbourne. What is the meaning of this?"

Annie backed away from Jordan quickly, her breath coming in short pants. She snatched her arms behind her back and didn't meet his eyes. "Arthur. We were just . . ." Annie bit her lip. That was her tell. Jordan had played enough hands of cards to learn a person's giveaway and the last week spent in Miss Andrews's company had informed him that when she was up to no good, she nibbled her pink lips with her perfect white teeth. It was a bit endearing, actually. And extremely convenient for him.

She glanced away. Her other tell. "That is to say . . . I'd come over to . . ." She stopped, words obviously failing her.

"Anne," Eggleston said, giving her a stern stare. "For your sake and the sake of your reputation, I shall pretend I didn't see this."

Jordan fought the urge to roll his eyes. First of all, this was the same man who'd nearly destroyed Annie's reputation last spring. His concern now was a bit too little too late for Jordan's taste. Secondly, if Annie had been Jordan's potential fiancée and he'd just caught her in the arms of another man, he'd be pounding the bloke into a pulp about now. But this dolt obviously wasn't jealous enough even to take a swing at him. Probably better for Eggleston's sake, of course, but leave it to Arthur Eggleston to be little more than inquisitive.

Annie swallowed. "Yes. Arthur. Quite right. It won't happen again."

"I'm glad to hear it. Now, may I escort you home?" Eggleston asked Annie, giving Jordan a once-over.

"No need. I was just about to escort her myself, Eggleston," Jordan replied with a smirk.

Annie nodded. "Yes, I'll be quite fine."

"Very well," Eggleston continued, looking down his nose at the both of them. "Then I shall call upon you tomorrow, Anne, for our usual afternoon ride in the park."

Annie bit her lip. "Yes. I should like that very much."

"Good evening." Arthur turned on his heel, reentered the house, and shut the door with a resounding thud.

The whoosh of air from the door tousled Annie's curls. She plunked her hands on her hips and glared at the door, completely ignoring Jordan. "He didn't seem a bit jealous, did he? Next time I shall just have to kiss you."